Hall Gardner

Year of the Horseshoe Bat—In Exile
Or the Legend of JV

Hall Gardner

Year of the Horseshoe Bat—In Exile

Or the Legend of JV

Edition Noëma

Bibliografische Information der Deutschen Nationalbibliothek
Die Deutsche Nationalbibliothek verzeichnet diese Publikation in der Deutschen Nationalbibliografie; detaillierte bibliografische Daten sind im Internet über http://dnb.d-nb.de abrufbar.

Bibliographic information published by the Deutsche Nationalbibliothek
Die Deutsche Nationalbibliothek lists this publication in the Deutsche Nationalbibliografie; detailed bibliographic data are available in the Internet at http://dnb.d-nb.de.

ISBN-13: 978-3-8382-1906-6
Edition Noëma

Printed in the EU

"If a single homicide is considered a crime, but a multiple homicide involved in attacking another country can be considered a good and legal action, then how can we possibly call that a reasonable distinction between good and evil?"

—Mo Zi (ca. 479-381 B.C.)

"Money is not words and companies don't even have free speech. So when they invoke this right they are trying to make our democracy plutocracy."

—Barbie

"End of the World
End of Month
Same Struggle!!!"

—French Protest Slogan

"Citizens, if the storm breaks out, we will have to act as soon as possible to stop the crimes of our leaders. If there is still something we can do, if there is still time, we will double our efforts to prevent catastrophe..."

—Jean Jaures, July 25, 1914

Chapters

General Introduction

by Hall Gardner

I.

Year of the Horseshoe Bat—in Exile paints a dark satire of governance and society in the United States, France and China during the COVID-19 (Horseshoe Bat) pandemic written from the first-person viewpoint of Chia Paoyu—the Chinese dissident who was forced into exile after playing a significant role in helping to organize the student-led protests on Tiananmen Square in April-June 1989—as depicted in the prequel, ***Year of the Earth Serpent Changing Colors***.

As one of its primary themes, this second novel seeks to explore how the rapid (in historical terms) rise of the Chinese Red Dragon onto the world stage, as a power *for itself*, has begun to impact global, regional, national, local, and inter-personal relations—given the geo-pornographic reality that Beijing has begun to forge a new Eurasian Axis with Moscow, Tehran and Pyongyang, among other states—in the effort to counter the global hegemony of the American Balding Eagle and its Oceania Allies.

In becoming a power *for itself*—in terms borrowed from the French philosopher and former Maoist, Jean Paul Sartre—the Red Dragon is no longer being exploited by other major powers as was the case during the historical period that the Chinese Communist Party has called the "Hundred Years of Humiliation" from the mid-19th century Opium Wars to the victory of Mao in 1949.

A major theme of the novel is to illustrate how rival, and seemingly uncontrollable, global forces—as symbolized by the 12 Riders of the Posse Comitatus—can drag both societies and individuals unwillingly into systemic conflicts that transcend their daily lives whether they like it or not. When alliances and wars call for pledging allegiance to the flag, it is risky, if not impossible, to resist…

II.

Look at the bizarre way in which power and political ideologies have been transforming in the post-Cold War period. It is certain that *Homo Geopoliticus et Economica* is once again entering into perversely dangerous times. There are so many self-proclaimed Tsars, Duces, Caudillos, Mini-Führers, Vozhds, Conducătors, Guides, Mullahs, Maréchals, Marszałeks, Monarchs, Kleptocrats, Presidents for Life and Prime Ministers for Multiple Terms, who are raising their hydra heads much as they once did in the 1920s and 1930s.

Many of these individuals claim that they, as Fearless Leaders, know the best way to make a better society—that is, if only the executive branch can put the parliament and the population under its direct control—in the effort to break and eliminate any form of resistance....

Look how ideologies are rapidly transmogrifying. Look how former Soviet "Gulag" KGB officials have so suddenly metamorphosed from arch-Communist atheists into militantly Orthodox Russian FSB nationalists under a Tsarist Leader Maximum.... Look how Sade-damn "Abu Ghraib" Hussein's Iraqi Ba'ath Socialists and their secret service Mukhabarat have so militantly, and over just a few years, become flag waving "Islamic State" execution fanatics.

And look how the Iraqi Abu Ghraib prison space itself has been expropriated from the post- "Sade-damn" regime by the "Boys of the Company"—to practice the "democratically" approved humanitarian use of "enhanced interrogation techniques". Look how Chinese Maoists and their Red Guards, who once vandalized the cemeteries of Confucius, the poet, Li Bai, among many others, have not-so-gradually rebranded themselves by planting Confucian "soft power" propaganda institutes across the globe under the guidance of Xi Jinping Thought.

Perhaps even more hypocritically bizarre are the American Democrats who pretend all is well with the "rules-based international order"—even if the military expansion of the Balding Eagle and NATO's White Compass Rose, the war on drugs, the global war on terrorism, and multiple US-led military interventions (endorsed by Democrats and Republicans alike)—and the LIES associated with those Wars after only pretenses of diplomatic engagement to resolve those conflicts—have wreaked havoc in country after country and are now threatening the prospect of major power war. Aging Cold Warriors are just itching to get their first chance for global military action since "World War II" ...

For their part, American Republicans can be diagnosed as "bipolar." On the one hand, the Republicans—some of whom believe in the most preposterous conspiracy theories—have denounced Black Lives Matter, Antifa and other domestic home-grown American protest movements as being inspired by "Maoism." On the other hand, the Republican's Fearless Leader, former President Donald Trump—whose Chimera (or really his fake Social Media image, not his "real" person) plays a role in this book as Donald "Secret

Agent Orange *Jee-Zus!!!"* Drumpf[1]—has strongly praised Mao's totalitarian legacy by flattering Xi "Winnie the Pooh" Jinping when he became China's "president-for-life."

In this fictional story, Chia Pao-yu is outraged to hear an American President extoll the virtues of China's "President-for-Life" and his totalitarian powers—that Chia had thought was a vital element of the American DNA to oppose and that he himself had risked his own neck to oppose by helping to organize the pro-Democracy and anti-corruption movement in China in April-June 1989. Drumpf's praise for "Winnie" leads Chia to suffer even more profoundly from depression, self-doubts, and impotence.

Chia Pao-yu simply cannot understand why so many people of differing societies and cultures—now including the Land of the Free—appear willing to submit themselves to dangerous self-serving dictatorships that will rule arbitrarily according to their Benevolent Big Brother whims, folies and pursuit of personal profits—and not in accord with the general interest of the country and the world… Such Fearless Leaders call themselves "Champions of the Forgotten Man"—but will easily turn against their former friends and popular supporters in the effort to sustain their power when it suits their interests…

---

[1] The "Orange Jesus" is a moniker that one of Trump's Republican sycophants called him when he said "the things we do for the Orange Jesus" when asked by Trump to sign electoral vote objection sheets for each of the states that Trump (falsely) claimed had falsified votes in the 2020 presidential election. Drumpf is said to be the real last name of Trump's forbears.

And much as Chia Pao-yu himself had predicted the rise of "new authoritarianism" in China in 1989 just prior to the Tiananmen Square repression, Chia now sees that the Land of the Free is being confronted with the real possibility of dictatorship. It is incredible how the public media personality of Secret Agent Orange *Jee-Zus!!?* appears to mimic that of Berzelius "Buzz" Windrip in Sinclair Lewis's *It Can't Happen Here* (1935). In that novel, Windrip takes over the American presidency backed by armed Minute Men militias—much like Il Duce Benito Mussolini took over Italy in 1922 after his March on Rome…

In Chia's view, President Drumpf's call in June 2020, with Bible in hand, for a military crackdown[2] on peaceful American protestors, whom Drumpf had dubbed "Maoists," "Wokeists" and "Anarchists," among other monikers, had ironically raised almost exactly the same quandary with respect to the relationship between the Executive Branch and the Pentagon as had been the case when then Chinese leader, Deng "Little Bottle" Xiaoping, had called upon the People's Liberation Army (PLA) to crack down on the

---

[2] Drumpf's actions were in technical violation of the 1878 Posse Comitatus Act that was passed when white supremacists had returned to power in both southern states and Congress after the Reconstruction. The Act was intended to prevent the intervention of northern Federal troops in the affairs of southern states. See Joseph Nunn, https://www.brennancenter.org/our-work/research-reports/posse-comitatus-act-explained Then, as now, Trump's actions raise questions as to who should have the power to "enforce the peace"? The Federal government? The State? The Locality? Ironically, Trump was claiming the autocratic right of the Federal government to crack down, while his supporters advocate States' rights. The 12 Riders of the Posse Comitatus becomes a theme of this novel… and possibly the next!

Chinese democracy movement on June 4, 1989 in a very violent action that challenged the very beliefs and values of the Communist Party and the PLA itself.

The parallel between Drumpf and Deng appeared plausible in Chia's mind—even if Drumpf's orders to crack down on protests against the police killing of George Floyd, in addition to Drumpf's own corrupt, militarist, autocratic, plutocratic, and anti-ecological domestic and foreign policies, were ultimately not implemented by American G.I. Joe's—as Drumpf had threatened. Much like the Chinese military, the U.S. military did not want to be dragged into domestic politics, but were not called into action.

The parallel becomes even more pertinent just a few months later, on January 6, 2021, when President Drumpf's violent "March on the Capitol" shook the very foundations of American democracy and its claims that Congressional compromise is the best way to make reforms—even if it is true that the complex American system of "checks and (un)balances" does not always permit significant reforms that would better benefit the American people and the world—very easily to implement.

After flying from France to the U.S. for the first time to participate in a "Future of China" conference in Washington, D.C. in June 2020, Chia is able to witness two highly polarized democratic societies experiencing multiple crises. These crises involve major social protests, coupled with the rise of rightwing political factions that attempt to scapegoat immigrants and minorities—in a situation in which finances and public resources are increasingly being siphoned off into the gluttonous mouths of plutocratic elites. Chia now realizes that both democracies, France and the United

States, are in a deep crisis. Even the movie character, "Barbie," is concerned that "our democracy" risks becoming a "plutocracy."

As Chia soon realizes, the multiple crises facing Democracy are not just national—but global. Contrary to the hopes raised by the international "End of History"[3] democratic peace argument, whose critique was a major of theme of ***Year of the Earth Serpent Changing Colors,*** *Homo Geopoliticus et Economica* is now entering a geo-pornographic situation somewhat like that of the interwar crisis between 1918 and 1939... but with major differences…

Will the democratic "checks and balances" of both American and French/European governance be able to prevent the very real possibility of dictatorship? Will Democracies be able to prevent major power war through a mix of the threat and use of force—plus, most urgently, engaged diplomacy aimed at conflict resolution?

III.

Another significant issue for this novel is that the totalitarian nature of Beijing's political and economic system has increasingly begun to inter-penetrate the predominant (yet dysfunctional) American "democratic" system, its economy, and its culture. Until the early 21st century, it was America that represented the "shining city on the hill" and that inspired Europeans and much of the world. The Chinese themselves called America the "land of rice"—despite the

---

3 See my critique of the End of History argument, https://www.meer.com/en/46316-the-vengeance-of-history; Hall Gardner, *Crimea, Historical Analogy and the Vengeance of History* (Palgrave 2015).

initially poor reception and treatment of Chinese and other immigrants.

During the Year of the Horseshoe Bat lockdown, the depressing reality that the American Dream is rapidly fading leads Chia Pao-yu to reflect and comment on Chinese/Asian impact on French/European and American culture, religion, arts, literature, and values—with a focus on European impressionists, as well as American pop artists and Beat poets. Chia also reflects upon how the testing of China's A-Bomb had led him to become a political dissident.

Even the ostensibly children's movie *Barbie*—whose anti-patriarchal critique sails way over the heads of children and of most adults as well—has been accused of pro-Chinese propaganda. This is because of the way a simplistic map of the South China Sea was shown in the movie that appeared to legitimize Beijing's claims to much of the region. The fact that a child's movie could provoke such geo-pornographic tensions leads Chia Pao-yu to question: Are America, Europe, China, and the world moving toward a new humanized planet where Ken's and Barbie's can live in mutual respect? Or toward a martial world where multicultural versions of Ken's "action figure" rival, "G.I. Joe," reign?

It is that latter martial world that pits the "Arsenal of Democracy" and its Christian *Jee-Zus!!! Freak* America First True Believers in alliance with the anti-Red China "Blue Team,"[4] plus Rabbi Dr. Geyer's anti-Palestinian, anti-

---

[4] The Congressional Blue Team swears that the Chi-Com "Red Tide," if not stopped at Taiwan, will soon spread across the Silk Road through Eurasia, the Middle East, and Africa, up through

Iranian, messianic movement[5] against the Chinese Red Dragon and Russian Double-Headed Eagle and their allies.

And it is a dark revelation for Chia Pao-yu to later learn that the American, British, and French secret services had all worked with Chinese Triads and other nefarious groups to exfiltrate him and other leaders of the democracy movement out of the land of the Red Dragon in June 1989.

IV.

This story is an exercise in *empathy*—or what the poet John Keats called "negative capability"—the ability to wear the eyes of others and see how the other sees the world. Then again, the ability to wear someone else's eyes raises the question of how much one sees of the other's point of view. How much is a figment of one's own imagination in the dialectical interaction between one's own perceptions and one's interpretation of those perceptions and how those individuals who are then perceived and interpreted? How much is the character and how much is the author?

The challenge is even greater when the character is not of one's one nationality, race, religion, culture, or sexual

---

the Balkans and into the Greek Achilles Heel of Europe and across the Pacific to Latin America and Mexico—which Beijing would use as a base to "subvert" North America through the free trade pact between Mexico, Canada, and the U.S.

[5] In his novel, *Old-New Land*, by the founder of Zionism, Theodore Herzl, Rabbi Dr. Geyer (which means 'vulture' in German) was the leader of a messianic political party who opposed Herzl's vision that Arabs should be equal to Jews in Herzl's proposed "co-operatist" and "mutualist" society in the Holy Lands.

preference—in this case, the celibate Chia Pao-yu possesses nightmare fears of being forced at knife point to become a "eunuch" as punishment for his leadership in the April-June 1989 Tiananmen Square protests—if he does not confess to the "crime" of "disloyalty." Is it feasible to depict a character not like oneself? Is it possible to speak for those from another civilization? To speak for those who fear to speak?

The French novelist and diplomat André Malraux wrote *Man's Fate* through Chinese eyes and without even having stepped foot for very long in China itself. His work may have been clouded with an Orientalist understanding of the Chinese and of the Chinese revolution, but the moral dilemmas confronted by his characters are universal. While Malraux's novel dealt with characters engaged in the violent struggles of China's Revolution, this novel, ***Year of the Horseshoe Bat—in Exile***, examines the essentially nonviolent protests taking place in France and America, as well as in China—before and after the Horseshoe Bat pandemic.

After having risked his neck in protesting against the Red Dragon on Tiananmen Square in April-June 1989, Chia Pao-yu once again dares to challenge the Chinese regime in nonviolent protest when he goes to Hong Kong under his French pseudonym, Jean Valjaur. And after the totalitarian Red Dragon sucks up Hong Kong's not-so-fragrant waters after 1997 sip by sip, he opposes Beijing's ongoing threats to pressure Taiwan's Black Bear into submission.

Even in the realization that it is becoming increasingly difficult to tell "Truth" to Power in the age of mass surveillance, media manipulation, and "Deep Fakes" of Artificial Intelligence (AI), Chia Pao-yu also protests against the *unfulfilled* promises of French social democracy and American neo-liberal democracy—after he has lived in Paris long enough to (more or less) understand French politics and after he visits the still hegemonic Balding Eagle.

V.

Chia Pao-yu's democratic idealism is confronted with numerous questions: Given their cultural-linguistic differences and the present negative state of their inter-relationship as "mental aliens" (in the expression of Jack London), is it at all possible for America and China to reconcile their very different concepts of "human rights," "freedom of speech and protest," and "democratization"? What happens when "freedom of speech" becomes "freedom of action"? And how much and what kind of "action" and "protest" is deemed legitimate and appropriate by these political elites of very different political cultures?

Given the very different, yet nevertheless comparable, nature of "democratic" America and "totalitarian" China—is it at all possible on the domestic level for both the Red Dragon and Balding Eagle to engage in significant reforms that would seek to reduce the glaring inequities in wealth of both societies, while concurrently seeking to interact more closely with the environment in developing systems of sustainable development? Is it possible for both countries (and others) to establish more direct systems of democracy and power sharing in both political and economic spheres of governance?

And, on the international level, given the escalation of greater violence throughout the world after German unification, Soviet collapse, and NATO enlargement, can Washington, Moscow, and Beijing reach compromises without capitulation? Is it possible to engage in diplomacy to prevent a direct major power war between NATO's

White Compass Rose and the Russian Two-Headed Eagle over the muddy Ukrainian *rasputitsa*, while likewise preventing confrontation between the Red Dragon and Taiwanese Black Bear that could drag the Balding Eagle and many other countries into the fray?

Will the "Global War on Terrorism" and the new 21st century "Crimean War" over the Black Sea and Holy Lands continue to escalate and expand??? Will the boots of war trounce the hopes of Ken's and Barbie's throughout the world for global peace?

Or will saner voices prevail? Can the Balding Eagle, Lady Europe, the Red Dragon, and the Russian Double Headed Eagle, eventually reach out for some form of geopolitical compromise despite their divergent concerns of power, interests, influence, as well norms and values? It it possible for these rival amoral/immoral Dragon Chimera to act in their true national and international interests—and thereby work to establish a new local, national, regional, global, and cosmic equilibrium—a new ***Tai Ping Dao***—a major theme of the prequel, ***Year of the Earth Serpent Changing Colors***?

These are the immediate, not easily answered, questions that plague Chia Pao-yu—as he finds himself unwillingly caught up in the midst of geo-pornographic struggles between the American-led Oceania Alliance and the China-Russia-led Eurasian Axis of the new Golden Hordes....

—Hall Gardner

Paris, March 19, 2024

Guest Editor's Preface

by Mark King Hayford

Chia Pao-yu, who became Jean Valjaur, has been resurrected—against all expectations! But where is he now?

I was honored to have known Pao-yu, when he was a young PhD student at Beijing University in the field of American/Western Culture and Civilization. It was he, above all my other assistants, who had helped me to better understand China when I was then reporting on current events for *NewsBlitz!!!* Magazine.

Naïve as I was at the time, however, I had no idea that our in-depth discussions, which would soon blossom into a true friendship, could make him a suspected spy in the eyes of the Chinese leadership… I can swear he never told me any top secrets or anything worth passing to the Boys of the Company. He did absolutely nothing wrong.

And yet about a week or so after the June 4, 1989 Tiananmen Square crackdown, he suddenly disappeared without a trace. While I had already been expelled from the country because of the "critical" articles I had written that allegedly used Chia's "top secret" sources, I was unable to track him down through my remaining Chinese contacts.

And as I later learned—contrary to the rumors that were purposely spread by those who exfiltrated him from the country—Chia Pao-yu was not tortured and executed (as the prequel to this novel, ***Year of the Earth Serpent***

Changing Colors, led the reader and myself to believe). Instead, he was able to escape to Paris where he re-appeared under a pseudonym, Jean Valjaur, or JV for short.

He never contacted me until 30 or so years later—just before it was too late to help him. Once in France, he started out waiting tables before finding a "real" job as a glorified secretary and researcher at the Foundation for Human Values Forever—an American non-profit foundation, with its HQ in Paris. The HVF Foundation was managed by a presumed heiress and charismatic feminist, named Bereft LaPlante, who was advised by two conflicting personalities, the international human rights lawyer, Aidan Russell, and the business manager, Gaspard G. Prophita.

After having survived the AIDS/HIV scare in China, as I did too with great trepidation and anxiety, Pao-yu then had to survive the COVID 19 Horseshoe Bat pandemic in Paris. In the years before the Horseshoe Bat pandemic, Pao-yü had participated in the "We Are All Charlie" and the "Yellow Vest" protests and witnessed Notre Dame in flames. The Foundation for Human Values Forever then funded Chia's voyage to Hong Kong to observe the protests taking place there—protests that unfortunately came to horrible end somewhat like the Tiananmen Square repression in June 1989. And Chia would later witness the refugee crisis on the Franco-Italian border.

Likewise funded by The HVF Foundation to participate in the conference, "Future of China," he flew to Washington, D.C. just at the onset of the Horseshoe Bat crackdown, where he, by accident, witnessed a pro-Trump rally before the White House—just after attending a lecture by Dr I.C.N Jabber, the neo-Con, neo-Martian, anti-China expert that had once spoken in Beijing. Pao-u's visit to Washington, D.C. corresponded with the major protests that took place after George "I Can't Breathe" Floyd was murdered by overzealous police incompetence in May 2020.

Chia Pao-yu's changing colors can be contrasted with those of Galvin. For his part, Mr. Mylex H. Galvin, a "Wokeist" before his time, had only begun to break free of Maoist ideology in the process of witnessing the rise of the Chinese democracy movement in April-June 1989—as depicted in the prequel to this novel.

By contrast, Chia Pao-yu somewhat similarly becomes disillusioned with both French-style social democracy and American-style neo-liberal democracy, without becoming totally cynical, and continues to oppose Benevolent Big Brother Benefactor totalitarianism. As portrayed in this novel, Pao-yu begins to urge the implementation of a more decentralized participatory democracy that would permit greater participation and power sharing in both political and economic spheres of governance...

Once the dust settles after the Horseshoe Bat pandemic, Chia finds himself unwittingly caught up in an unexpected battle between two non-governmental organizations: between the "non-profit" Foundation for Human Values Forever of LaPlante, who unscrupulously enriches herself in the name of the struggle for human rights and democratic principles, and the "for-profit" Society for the Exploration of Cosmic Consciousness that, with tremendous financial and AI technological resources, seems to suddenly appear from nowhere as it takes a "novel" approach to "human values" and "democratic" governance....

I am proud to present to readers Chia-Pao-yu's memoirs, plus excerpts from his *Planetary Manifesto*, that he forwarded to me just prior to his second sudden and unfortunate disappearance in August 2023… Although my eyes have begun to fade, I have tried my best to annotate/ anecdote his essay on his life and thought where I believe to be appropriate.

Chia is truly a Chinese Jean Jaures—the French political leader, who warned, just prior to being assassinated in July 1914, of the horrific wars to come…

We must continue to demand to know Chia Pao-yu's whereabouts—and if he is still alive, demand his release!!!!

—Mark King Hayford

London, February 28, 2024

I.

Escape from Being: The Memoirs of Chia Pao-Yu

Escape from Beijing

They must have just started to investigate me a few weeks before the Tiananmen Square repression. Someone from inside the *Zhongnanhai* sent me a photo in which I was talking to the journalist, Mark King Hayford inside his apartment just a few days before the crackdown. When the PLA started to fire real bullets at peaceful protesters on June 4, 1989, I got the message. It was time to escape, somewhere, anywhere. I will never know who it was I should thank.

Even inside even the most repressive states there are sometimes a few individuals with a heart and a soul. In today's world those who leak secrets can be real heroes, but it is often at great risk—with no rewards. And they usually get their pants very wet—if not deep in crap. They need to go at great lengths to make certain that they will not be caught leaking even the most innocuous material. There is simply too much top-secret info to be kept secret! Most of which is pure porn!

ooo

I immediately contacted some of my friends in the anti-corruption pro-Democracy movement, which, before they knew it, was becoming an underground resistance. It was on June 14, 1989, [just] after the Beijing Municipal Public Security Bureau ordered the arrest of Chinese student activists on June 13, more than a week after the June 4 crackdown on Tiananmen Square and throughout the country, that a strange man with a shaved head and brown-green eyes contacted me. He whispered the secret code, "the yellow fowl flies free."

The man, with intense eyes that always seemed to look straightforward and never seemed to blink, returned an hour later to shave my head, and dress me in the three-piece orange robes of a Buddhist monk, a *kāṣāya*, that was said to originate in ancient India and named after a saffron dye. It was worn by Siddhartha Gautama's followers. He gave me a small suitcase to carry with a candle, some lotus flowers and three incense sticks. On the inside was a secret compartment with money and a false passport.

The democratic resistance had created myths about me becoming a Tiananmen Square martyr to cover my escape. Contrary to those fabricated legends, I never sold or gave away my jade pendant that I still wear... Nor did I did I become one of the many devotees of the Buddha, the awakened one—although Buddhists had helped me to flee. Nor did anyone open my stomach, and put my kidneys, heart, and eyes on sale... Nor did they shatter my teeth with an electric cattle prod...

I then took a series of the coal-fired choo-choo trains with a group of real monks, often changing routes. It was a long voyage and I said nothing to the others. I did nothing but read and re-read *Dream of the Red Chamber*. It was the only book I was able to take with me in a black cloth sack that I hung on my back. As it was not at all an approved Buddhist text, it potentially made me suspect! And, as I realized much later... it could have made the monks travelling with me suspect as well...

I also learned that several leaders of the Democracy movement—who had likewise been highly involved in organizing the protest movement—had also taken various routes to the south. They too had to change places to sleep every evening. A good number were unfortunately captured. Who knows what has happened to them since!

Now, as the Benevolent Red Emperor governs all, and as the Chinese population is generally, but not always, subservient, always living in fear of their own shadows and of anything the government might deem is "criminal," it is almost impossible to hide for too long in the countryside—as once did Mao, then the "red bandit"—as did many ancient outlaws of the marsh…

Eyes are everywhere in China…. And Beijing's sophisticated systems of cameras and mass surveillance, linked with 5-G and Artificial Intelligence (AI), are now moving beyond the country…

ooo

My last pleasure was to savor a *yim guk gai* chicken encased in pure salt to prevent the flavors from escaping. It was a culinary treasure that I was able to purchase from a vendor when we stopped at a station in the South close to Guangdong. It would be the last decent meal I would have in mainland China before reaching Hong Kong. At that point, however, it was evident that my disguise as a monk in orange *kāṣāya* would no longer provide cover. As the real monks left the train in their quiet, self-effacing manner, I was whisked by truck to a factory safe house.

There I was given a wig to cover the fact that my hair was growing back and sticking straight up. The place, full of large boxes and containers of different kinds, with who knows what goods, perhaps contraband, packed inside, was cold and filthy. I hid in the dark during the day and even at night—trying not to cough. The air stunk of a horrid mix of coal dust and the oil refinery nearby. I still remember the flames burning like funeral pillars high into the sky for no apparent reason—releasing their toxins into human and planetary lungs.

As I knew no one, and as no one knew me, I knew I could be sacrificed to the Chinese State Security Agency if there were any problems. No one could trust anyone. Anyone could be bought off or could give info to the Chinese authorities about my presence—if they or their families were threatened. Anyone might squeal if they thought they could obtain a decent-sized reward for their "patriotic" service.

It was perhaps a week or so later that about ten of us were hoarded onto a small speedboat. As the boat picked up speed, I puked on a few of my own comrades—who will probably never forgive me, after we were stowed away in a tight cabin and jumped over bouncy waves in the Shekou industrial zone—that was home to the oil giants for energy exploration in the South China Sea. At long last, we landed next to the largest coal fired power station in Hong Kong, the Tuen Mun's Castle Peak Power Station.

It seemed to take forever to get there—in the region that was all part of the great 21st Century Maritime Silk Road. That is the global infrastructure project that would boost the overseas trading and military power of the Chinese Dragon—as its Red, Brown, and Black skin shimmered like a Leviathan through the dark waters—in its rivalry with the Red, White and Blue American Balding Eagle that still rules the skies and waves…

Who could believe that the Red Dragon—the country where I grew up and still love—in which only a few big wig Party members with dark blue Maoist collars and berets drove Red Flag limos through the streets of Beijing teeming with throngs of two wheelers—would, in just a few years after I was forced into exile, become inundated with bumper to bumper auto traffic way before most people could imagine it!!!

○○○

It was within the territorial confines of this not-so-"fragrant" Hong Kong harbor that we were given our freedom after being separated into different spaces. Or really, not yet free—that is, we had no freedom yet—as we still could not make our presence known. They housed me at the Nai Chung camp in Sai Kung along with several other activists after we were subdivided into different groups.

There were initially five of us in my group before we were broken up for security reasons. As a joke, we gave ourselves code names of classic poets. I had the honor of being named "Qu Yuan," after the poet, the author of the *Cosmic Questions*. Qu Yuan was a leading diplomat of the Kingdom of Chu who had opposed the forced unification of China by the Chu's devious rival, Ying Zheng, the King of the Qin dynasty.[1] As powerless and impotent as I felt, however, it was difficult for me to accept the honor of bearing the moniker of the great poet and diplomat, Qu Yuan…

○○○

After our escape to Hong Kong, we hoped that we would be lucky enough to be sent to some foreign land—that is, if the leadership would be willing to vouch for us and support us. Several activists and intellectuals were sent off to the land of the Balding Eagle's Red, White, and Blue flag. Although it was not my first choice, I was among the few to go to the land of the French Marianne with her *bonnet phrygien* (Phrygian cap) et *son bleu, blanc, rouge Drapeau (her blue, white, red flag)*—but only after what turned out to be an eight year wait…

Eight years of trepidation! Eight years of reading and rereading the same Chinese classic! Eight years of reading trashed magazines and newspapers! Eight years of playing the same card games! Eight of playing the Game of Go (*wei chi*) over and over again. Eight years of not having anything to say! Eight years of eating bowls of fatty pork and rice! Eight years of recurrent nightmares! Eight years of repeatedly seeing my head pushed into a toilet bowl whirlpool of sardine-like fish with red eyes and human faces! Eight years of fearing horrific electric shock torture in the Chinese *Diyu* (Earth Prison)! Eight years of waiting for the swat team in flak jackets and handcuffs to burst through the doors! Eight sickly years of wanting to forget those eight years!

Hounded by the chortling of Dragon Chimera, the Surgeon straps me to the ice-cold operating table in a clean white room alit by flickering of candles. I acquiesce without resistance. As he approaches, holding his curved blade in the air, he unexpectedly demands, "Are you ready to confess?" …

ooo

No one could imagine that we would have to wait for so long. Most of us hoped that if we escaped to a free society for just a few years we could then return to China to help build a new society on democratic grounds. No one expected the Communist gerontocracy to remain in power for forever. Their brains had already started to jell—unable to remember even basic trivia! We were certain significant social and political change would be just around the corner! We believed that the Chinese people would support us! We truly believed we would be granted amnesty once the Chinese people realized our cause was just and patriotic!

And now it is more than 30 years later! There is nothing but collective amnesia as to what happened on Tiananmen Square on June 4, 1989 and later throughout the country—as many as 10,000 civilians were reportedly killed on Tiananmen Square alone.[2] And who knows how many more were sent to the countryside, or to *laogai* prisons, or who were simply "disappeared"…

The paranoid leadership, frightened by its own warts and shadows, protected by millions of plexiglass warriors and clandestine Black Rat finks, has continued to insist that whatever had taken place on "6/4" or "8964" was a non-event or a fairy tale—or "fake news" in current jargon. Nothing about what did "not" happen must be mentioned on the T.V., or in the newspapers, books or on the internet and not-always-so-Social Media. Much like the efforts of the ancient Legalists to erase the past of the Warring States after Qin Shi Huang took power, the goal of Communist authorities has likewise been to erase any popular memory of the violent repression that took place on that historic square of Tiananmen before the Gate of Heavenly Peace.

ooo

Despite the government's repeated efforts, however, there is absolutely no way the authorities could perform lobotomies on the brains of all the Chinese people—or somehow alter their thinking processes and memories. In their resistance, Chinese dissidents and internet activists have ingeniously sought to code their Social Media messages about Tiananmen Square in more than 200 ways.

On the one hand, the danger was that citizen journalists who tried to criticize President for life, Xi "Winnie the Pooh" Jinping, in coded messages—in the hope to break through the Great Firewall which the Party's "Ministry of Truth" has built on the internet—could be tracked down and sanctioned—or suddenly disappear. On the other hand, given the fact that the Ministry of Truth cannot sufficiently censor such discussion, the Fearless Leadership has also sought to sugarcoat the "memory" of Tiananmen Square in a *trompe-lie*—in a façade within a greater political façade—in the effort to both repress and co-opt dissent…

In such a way, the Fearless Leadership has invented new narratives about the June 4, 1989 repression that downplay the social and political and moral significance of what had really transpired.

ooo

After being helped to flee from China, I must admit the fact that I was much luckier than most of the 32.5 million other refugees around the world—not to overlook the even greater numbers of internally displaced persons—estimated at 53.2 million!

To escape poverty, war, oppression, famine, fire, drought, floods… many of these refugees have had to cross deserts or flee upon metal Rafts of the Medusa only to reside in no man's lands… to (un)live in camps with unsanitary conditions and limited rations behind barbed wire… to (un)live in a place where there seems to be no hope for escape… no hope for asylum… and where the climate is becoming more and more inhospitable.

More and more people from around the world—men and increasingly single women with children—have been trying to find a better life—some more lucky than others, others not so lucky at all… There are so few countries—democratic or totalitarian—that fully provide the necessary basic human needs of their citizens…

And it is despicable to see how xenophobic opposition to migrants and foreigners is being used to build the power base of domestic political leaders. In the effort to achieve or sustain their power and privilege, many Fearless Leaderships have begun to play the upon the domestic population's fears of foreigners to advance their careers. In many ways, these elites fear that their position of power and privilege might somehow be endangered—that is, if they would dare try to help the poor and needy, and particularly if they would give them any real voice in governance. Once homeless… a human is no longer considered "human" …

There is no way that Fearless Leaders would even share the crumbs that trickle down to the poor and needy and thereby let themselves be accused of wasting funds, of assisting "terrorists," of providing money to immigrants and others "who don't deserve it," of assisting mere animals… insects… microbes… Instead of working out viable solutions that deal rationally with migrants and the homeless, such xenophobic Fearless Leaders seek virucidal ways to eradicate those, who they claim, would contaminate or "poison the blood of the nation."[3]

Despite their denials, these Fearless Leaders cry out in the same vulgar language, *limpieza de sangre,* of the re-conquistadors in the late 15th century—at the time of the expulsion of Jews and Moslems from Queen Isabel's Spain—exactly when Columbus began his (failed) overseas quest for Cathay in 1492. Despite their denials, they use the same language of the Society of Righteous and Harmonious Fists—a xenophobic group that violently accused Christian missionaries and foreigners of "tainting" Chinese civilization at the very end of the 19th century. Claiming to "know nothing," these so-called "Leaders" reiterate the fascist clichés of Hitler of the 1920s and 1930s.

From the standpoint of such Fearless Leaders, it was far better to spend money on border walls and weaponry… It was far better to point fingers at presumed enemies at home and abroad—and expel or eliminate foreigners and aliens—even if those foreigners and aliens worked in jobs that no one else wanted and contributed to the society and economy…[4] Migrants, homeless, foreigners are no longer considered respected members of *Homo Sapiens*—which ironically means "wise man" in Latin.

Year of the Fire Ox

I was one of the lucky ones, one of the few who did not drown after capsizing in an overcrowded boat on the way to Lampedusa. I was one of the few who did not plunge into the depths on the former slave route from Gorée Island, now, tragically, a World Heritage site, to Cape Verde, where the bones of captured Africans, forced to walk the plank, bleach the shoals…

Nor was I eaten alive by sharks in stormy waters from France across the English Channel. Neither did I freeze to death in a refrigerator truck on a cargo ferry from Belgium, nor dehydrate in the Libyan Great Sand Sea. Nor did I fry like a greasy hamburger, but without food or water, in Arizona's Sonoran Desert. Nor was I bitten by a poisonous snake or murdered by smugglers for a few dollars in the Darien Gap of Panama in the desperate effort to make it to the Tex-Mex border…

For this, I am truly grateful…

ooo

In my case, I still had to survive in horrid conditions in constant fear that one of many Black Rats would squeal on us for a few Yuan. And after eight rotten years of waiting came the time when we could wait no longer—for it was the year 1997, the Year of the Fire Ox. We had to leave Hong Kong then—or else Beijing authorities were certain to smoke us out.

For 1997 was the treacherous year that Perfidious Albion had agreed with Yellow Dragon, the ancient Monarchy, to give up Hong Kong after the warships of John Bull-dog had decimated my country in the mid-19th century, simply for the right to sell and smoke Opium. I can hardly tell you how much the Chinese people suffered after British East India Co. had forced those drugs down our throats—just when our Monarch was struggling to stop drug addiction.

That was a time when the British Monarch, Queen Victoria—perhaps too worried about Anarchist assassination attempts (the "terrorists" of that era)—or perhaps hoping the East India Co would continue to amass massive profits—had either ignored the plea of the Emperor Daoguang, whose own son had died of an overdose, to put an end to the Opium trade—or else had never read his message? Perhaps the Queen's advisors had hidden the Emperor's letter, sent by the Viceroy Lin Zexu? The latter was then forced into exile for his failure to prevent that war that so devastated China and its people....

After all these years, after those despicable 19th Century Arrow/Opium wars, the Communist Leadership had naturally refused to recognize the "unfair and unequal treaties" under which the "new territories" of Hong Kong Island and Kowloon had been ceded "temporarily" for 99 years to the British roast beef eating Perfidious Albion. Yet then, in 1997, because of the 1984 Sino-British Joint Declaration, it was finally time for *all* of Hong Kong's sovereignty to be transferred to the Communist regime—against the wishes of the Hong Kong people who had no say in the matter!

Under the British Bulldog, Hong Kong, as the Crown Colony's "fragrant harbor," at least had a semblance of freedom and autonomy. Under the Chinese Red Dragon, Hong Kong, would have no longer possess even the scent of such a free fragrance. As far back as 1989, I could foresee the grim possibility that Beijing would renege on its promises of "one country two systems". I knew the Party would stop at nothing at safeguarding its power and preventing its own downfall. Someone had to help us—or we were doomed!

ooo

We had no idea whether someone would ultimately come to our rescue. We could easily be abandoned for political expediency. The states involved could deny their involvement. And if anyone would be discovered by Beijing to have anything at all to do with what was called, "Operation Yellowbird"—with the color "yellow," color of the ancient Monarchy, unfortunately chosen as a part of the secret code—they could disappear or suffer some other ill fate…

Nevertheless, as the transfer of Hong Kong to the Red Dragon became imminent, secret last-minute diplomatic efforts were frantically taken to save our souls before Beijing took over the islands and began to root out its enemies and dissidents.

I was lucky—very lucky indeed.

ooo

That was way back in 1997—in the Year of the Fire Ox. That was after I had survived eight miserable years in Hong Kong on international handouts that humanitarian groups had provided. At long last, I was finally, and hastily, flown out of there on yet another false passport with the promise of political asylum. I was sent out along with a couple dozen other brave Chinese dissidents now banished from China—all forced into exile despite their love for China. All were pressed out of the country like squeezing a lemon—just for daring to speak out peacefully for the need for deep social, political, and anti-corruption reforms.

And even in democratic France, the *Land of Liberty, Egality, Fraternity*—and even under a new name—I would still need to remain in hiding…

ooo

At long last, the French put me in this tiny, yet overly heated, apartment. It was a space, a cubicle with a bed and desk, which was not much different than my former dorm at Beijing University where I had been working on my PhD on American/ Western Intellectual History, Literature, and the Arts, with a focus on the cultural movements of the 1960s and 1970s. As the room was on the back corner of the apartment complex, I could see an obstructed view of the Seine. Through the trees, I could barely see the barges, péniches, tourist and police boats as they sailed or sped up and down far from the Eiffel Tower, *la Dame de Fer.*

ooo

Although the apartment was tiny, with only a hot plate for a stove, and no air conditioning, there was the unexpected relief that I did not need to share it with anyone else—as would have been the case at Beijing University. The French even provided a small monthly stipend and a work permit. And all my French language classes were paid for. All at taxpayer expense. That included a charming personal assistant who picked me up at the CDG airport and directed me through customs. She took me to my new lodging.

A head taller than me, thin like a black swan, soft brown skin, her luxuriant black hair glistened when she unpretentiously told me that she was studying international law at the elite École des Hautes Études de Droit. She assisted me for a few months and helped me get through the process of translating and signing my *contrat d'intégration républicaine* (contract of integration with the French Republic). As her name was Dihya Meghighda, I guessed she was French

Moroccan, but I never asked. I was too shy to say anything in her sensual presence.

It was Dihya who proposed my alias—Jean Valjaur or JV for short. I thought the name had a nice ring… unlike most Western names in Chinese or Chinese who adopt English names so that Ling becomes Lynn or Zhao becomes John. Why can't people just keep their own names! But then again, if your name is Wang or Ding or Dong or Chien (dog in French), you could become the brunt of cruel jokes in western cultures.

In my case I came to like my adopted French name—a synthesis of Jean Jaures and Jean Valjean. Jaures was the French Socialist leader who was assassinated just before World War I for demanding that French revanchists engage in peace negotiations with the Imperial German Eagle after Berlin had seized Alsace Lorraine way back in 1871.

It was Jaures who warned, just before his assassination in July 1914, against the Great War that would then provoke another great war…

"Citizens, if the storm breaks out, we will have to act as soon as possible to stop the crimes of our leaders. If there is still something we can do, if there is still time, we will double our efforts to prevent catastrophe..."

Valjean was the protagonist of Victor Hugo's masterpiece, *Les Misérables*—who sought to redeem himself after serving a long prison sentence for the minor crime of stealing bread to feed his sister's starving children and for then escaping from prison…

ooo

"Like you escape from China," Dihya said gently, with an air of real concern, "This why I think of this name... Jean Valjaur...or JV..."

"Fortunately, I had escaped before I obtained a prison sentence," I replied... "but I am definitely in need of redemption, of amnesty—for I did no wrong. Unlike Jean Valjean, I was not even accused of something like theft!"

ooo

As kind and beautiful as she was, however, there was something about her that unfortunately reminded me of Mo Li, the former "girlfriend" of that Wokeist before his time, that "Maoist" Gao/Galvin. Everyone but G/G knew that Mo Li worked for the Party, and it was probably she who reported on me. And my paranoia from living in a police state had no limits: As Dihya was working for the French government, I became suspicious...

I thus thought it best to keep my distance—even if nothing would have happened between us anyway. I had always dreamed of being a poet admired and loved by women like my namesake "Chia Pao-yu" in the great novel, *Dream of the Red Chamber*. But I became too heavily involved in politics to fully engage myself in creative writing... And I had no time, nor really any interest, in women at all... I was married to the impossible cause of transforming China for the better... And I vowed I would remain loyally married to that Cause...

Dihya soon disappeared from my life after helping me find a meaningless job waiting tables at a typical French restaurant specializing in crepes—almost like every other miserable migrant seeking work from all over the planet—

except for the fact that I was one of the fortunate few who was able to obtain working papers and social security.

Nonetheless, given my new circumstances, I had no choice but to pursue something practical. And even if the bureaucratic phobias of French academia would have accepted my previous PhD work, I could not afford to continue my studies. What could I do? There was no way I could become, like Leon "Loves Frida" Trotsky or James "Porno" Joyce, a language teacher, a teacher of Chinese, at the Berlips School for Foreign Languages, for example. How Mylex H. Galvin managed to teach pidgin English as a foreign language in China, repeating phrases, spelling out words, singing songs, was beyond me.

In no way could I risk working in a Chinese restaurant.... Someone might recognize me... And with a French name I might be considered even more suspicious since I did not speak a word of French. I had to say I was adopted. And there was no way I could even reach out to my friends and family in China. As I now stood in total solitude, I soon realized my whole life had become a whole tangled quilt of woolen, moth embedded, LIES—very easy to unravel!!!

ooo

It was thus the French—and not to the Americans as I had hoped and expected—to whom I am forever indebted for my exfiltration. At first, I was sure the Americans would take me in. After all, I had been studying American/ Western Intellectual History, Literature, Arts, and Culture at Beijing University. Then again, my focus on the so-called Counterculture of 1960s and 1970s was perhaps problematic. Even if I were critical of the Beat Generation, those were the years of the Vietnam War that U.S. officials perhaps wanted to ignore or even forget—the years when Beijing's backing for Hanoi prevented the Balding Eagle from landing ground forces onto the territory of the North Vietnamese Water Buffalo—and when Beijing's support for revolutionary movements around the world included the Black Panthers… After all, it was China—and not the American anti-war activists—who prevented the Pentagon from winning its Napalm Agent Orange war by protecting Hanoi—in a "war" that the Balding Eagle never considered a "war."

ooo

My dilemma: Having no knowledge of the language is considered a great fault for the French who are forever asserting their cultural and linguistic "exceptionalism." Even though they boast of nuclear autonomy and "multipolarity" in global relations and argue for the need for a stronger Europe more independent of NATO's White Compass Rose, they often denounce "multiculturalism" and "communitarianism" in their domestic affairs—i.e., those people who do not speak French! *Vive la francophonie*!

In essence, for this state and society that claimed a linguistic and cultural "exceptionalism" against the rest of the world, the terms "multiculturalism" and "communitarianism" were truly dirty words. In 1972, Paris had actually prohibited the collection of data on race, ethnicity and religious belief by means of national censuses. The French simply don't want to admit that there are any social and ethnic or linguistic differences—even if they once, in the words of the writer, Anatole France, proclaimed "*Vive la difference!*"

The problem is that many French xenophobes ridicule and protest against immigrants from other cultures and languages and religions. And they even tend to look down upon people from Brittany or Corsica or the Basque region or Franco-Germans in Alsace Lorraine—where the border had been contested for centuries. Conflicts over the latter region had sparked the 1870-71 Franco-Prussian war—and eventually helped to spark what were called "World Wars I and II"—even if those conflicts were not really the very first "global" wars. Alfred Dreyfus—unjustly imprisoned for allegedly spying for Berlin before World War I—was both Jewish and Alsatian. Which made him more suspect?

And even though the predominantly white Atheist/Catholic post-French Revolution society may be able to accept some degrees of religious multiculturalism, accepting both Protestants and Jews, for example, the French are at a total loss as to how to deal with their burgeoning Moslem populations and other immigrants… even if the family origins of these "non-French" populations generally stem from France's own colonies…

Given the social pressure to see the world through French eyes, I too, over the years, would become a Chinese-born frog slowly boiled and flavored with parsley and garlic butter.

ooo

I understood very well that helping me flee from China was an action taken at great risk to the French Marianne's relations with Beijing. And it was only years later that I learned that one of the French diplomats responsible for helping to organize Operation Yellow Bird had said… "There was a cry of distress, and there was no way we could uphold our beliefs and not respond…" I then learned that French President François "Dieu" (God) Mitterrand had asserted at the time, "A regime that shoots at its own youth has no future."

It was a strong and risky statement in support of the Chinese democracy movement. Yet can one honestly say that Beijing's days are counted, that the regime really has "no future"—as "Dieu" once asserted as a reason to help people like me escape the clutches of the Red Dragon?

There remain warrants out for the arrest of many like me… There appears to be no hope for reconciliation, no hope for amnesty…

"We are All Charlie!!!"

Thousands of protesters massed upon the Place de Bastille. One man with a backpack jumped up onto *La colonne de Juillet.* He climbed all the way up to the gilded globe, where stands Augustin's star-crowned nude *Génie de la Liberté* (the "Spirit of Freedom")—who flies as fleet-footed as does Giambologna's *Mercury* who brandishes the torch of civilization and the remains of his broken chains.

He unfurled his banner… "We are all Charlie!!!"

In the demonstration against the *Charlie Hebdo* massacre, huge demonstrations took place through France and in major cities throughout the world. The entire staff and interns of LaPlante's *Foundation for Human Values Forever* raced out to the streets and onto the crowded Place de la Bastille—along with tens of thousands of people.

It had been Dihya who had suggested that I might be able to find some extra part-time work with the non-profit group, *Foundation for Human Values Forever…* She had whispered that it was HVF Foundation that helped me escape China in working with the French government…

ooo

It was on January 7, 2015, that two fanatical Islamicists in black hoods and masks armed with Kalashnikov assault rifles murdered in a blaze of fifty bullets the editorial staff of the *Charlie Hebdo* magazine. The two were able to force their way into the building, after making one of the artists push the door code at gunpoint and invade the office space. There they massacred 12 people without pity. The Islamicists had years before accused the magazine of blasphemy and threatened its editors after the journal had published a series of perverse portraits of the Prophet of Islam.

At first, one eyewitness had thought it was a Special Force operation, with the good guys shooting the bad guys. Another thought the shots were firecracker celebrations of the Chinese New Year. Incredible!

Also incredible was seeing Mark King Hayford discuss the attacks on Arab Gulf Media station, *Al-Jazzhisteria*—as he was no longer working at the American magazine, *NewsBlitz!!!* Yet I was still afraid to contact him for fear of exposing my new identity.

ooo

The attacks were a great national tragedy and trauma for France. And they were truly an international tragedy—given the reality that the U.S.-led global war on terrorism (GWOT)—that had been given a blank check by the United Nations (UN) North Pole Olive Tree Wreath and by the American Congress—had fallen into the obvious trap set by the Al-Qaida leader Bin "Kill Anyone but Me" Laden.

The Land of the Free fell face first into the quicksand by first invading Afghanistan in 2001 and then Iraq in 2003—as if either of those governments and their societies were responsible for the horrors of the September 11, 2001 attacks on the World Trade Center and Pentagon that had transformed passenger aircraft into weapons of vengeance.

In effect, Washington, as the HVF Foundation's human rights lawyer, Aiden Russell, repeatedly pointed out, had completely failed to engage in real diplomacy: "In their crusade to defeat Al Qaeda, the Americans failed to pick up the signals that the Afghan Taliban did not want anything to do with Bin Laden. They did not think through an innovative way to take advantage of that fact in negotiations… And they failed to recognize that Sad-damn "Abu Ghraib" Hussein had no close relationship at all to Al Qaeda—and that Baghdad did not possess nuclear weaponry!"

Washington's blank check to GWOT had worked to spread Ben Laden's hatred and call for revenge against the western crusaders throughout the Arab/Islamic world. And now France was being targeted by the so-called Islamic State (IS), who detested French/ American/ Western decadence and hypocrisy—symbolized by discos, rave parties, and heavy metal bands—while the French and American Allies were concurrently bombing IS fighters in Syria and Iraq.

And as conflict over the Holy Lands has not ameliorated, Islamicist vengeance has not yet ceased… "Revenge is a kind of wild justice" the English philosopher Francis Bacon had once said—but it is not "justice" at all…

ooo

After the September 11, 2001 attacks on the WTC and Pentagon, the French had all claimed, "We are all Americans!" And now, after these horrific Islamist attacks in January 2015, individuals who had never read puerile teenage humor of *Charlie Hebdo*—and who never saw the porno picture of Mohammad in the nude on all fours with a star covering his ass that had enraged militant Islamicists—became Charlie himself: *"Je suis Charlie" "I am Charlie!!!"*

I could only think: 'After the September 11, 2001 attacks, the French had all become Americans—and now, after the 2015 assassinations, they had all become Charlie!'

With the catch phrase ricocheting around the globe by the internet and by twitter, the irony was that very few knew anything about the often-controversial weekly that described itself as anti-racist, secular, feminist, and Anarcho-libertarian. In publishing critical articles and often crude, if not perverted, cartoons and drawings, the editors claimed to "equally" assault Christianity, Judaism, and Islam.

Yet despite its claims of "equal" criticism, not only was *Charlie Hebdo* hated by both Islamicists and the French Far Right,[5] but it was also denounced as being "racist." Depending upon the nature of the issue criticized and perversity of the cartoons, some Christians thought the magazine was "anti-*Jee-Zus!!!,*" while some Jews thought it was "anti-Semitic." Moslems believed it attacked Islam much more often than it did the other major religions—and that its cartoons linked the Prophet Mohammed with acts of terrorism.

"That allegation, however, did not hold up in the French courts who saw the cartoons as attacking both terrorism and Islamicist fundamentalism—and not Islam, nor the Prophet himself—as France, given its revolutionary history—could only defend the right to blasphemy," explained Russell.

ooo

In seemingly contradicting the French legal position, however, Russell then made the critical remark, "as tragic and horrific as the attacks on the editors of *Charlie Hebdo* were, they were nothing in magnitude as compared to the wars and acts of state-supported terrorism committed by major and regional powers in war zones in Afghanistan, Chechnya, Iraq, Syria, Yemen, Sudan, Lebanon, the Palestinian territories, and many other places in the world…

What concerned me was that in his list of states accused of supporting terrorism, or engaging in major acts of repression, or other forms of geo-pornographic activities, Russell seemed to have overlooked China and its allies, like the Myanmar junta. Nor did he mention China's violent treatment of Tibetans and Uighurs put in re-education camps. Nor did he ever say much about Beijing's previous support for the Khmer Rouge. Was it just oversight?

He continued: "It is state leaders of the major and rising powers who have engaged in much more significant and horrific acts of terrorism than have even most active anti-state terrorist movements."

It was already a frightening observation, before he added: "There are more pressing concerns, other than 'terrorism,' that cause even greater death, destruction, disease that need to be addressed… Yet as the State seems to hold itself as primarily responsible for territorial security, it does not fully address issues such as automobile accidents, mass killings, cancer, heart disease, domestic murders and feminicide, among others…."

I did not respond. This politically "incorrect"—or really, politically "explosive"—thought nevertheless struck me profoundly…

Aiden continued: "In reality, most of the latter issues generally cause greater numbers of death in statistical terms, but such issues are not seen as directly challenging the *legitimacy* of government leadership and its goals as much as acts and propaganda of 'terrorism' appear to do… even though those issues should more directly concern state leaderships… 'Terrorists' claim that there are better forms of governance… that is why they are so worrying for governments…"

The Prof/Lawyer had almost won his case in my mind—but it was evident politicians were not responding…

ooo

As I learned more about it, I understood that not everyone thought very highly of *Charlie Hebdo*—even if everyone in their right mind would agree that the publication of mere cartoons, even if considered pure porno by many, did not represent a capital offence deserving execution… No one "normal" would try to assassinate them… that was a job reserved for psycho's and fanatics!!!

Given its vulgar nature, the key problem was that not everyone saw the protests against the vicious attacks on *Charlie Hebdo* as the best means to build universal solidarity. And as time passed, the magazine was seen, rightly or wrongly, by its detractors as not denouncing many acts of state terrorism and state repression. That was the critique that led others to cry in counter-protest, "*Je suis pas Charlie!*" "*'I am not Charlie!*'"

The weekly, for example, was accused of not condemning the French government's use of "emergency powers" (that were implemented after the Islamicist attacks) to isolate and ban protests by other groups that were not Islamicist. A demonstration planned in late November 2015 by environmental activists to protest lack of action by the COP Climate Talks was banned by the French government. 24 members of the group were placed under house arrest.[6]

As Aiden confided, "The environmentalists have a just cause. It is crucial that governments cut subsidies to Big Oil. Yet that issue is not even on the table for discussion at the COP Climate Conference talks. It is despicable!"

As I came from China that was so dependent on cheap polluting coal, it was difficult for me to reply. Other less polluting energy sources seemed more expensive… At least that is how Chinese leaders initially saw it…

Aiden continued: "The Environmentalists are rightly furious: Some 30,000 species are going extinct yearly! The extinction of bees is catastrophic and could end life as we know it! … The Apiarists certainly have something important to say… Green Environmentalists are not like Green Islamicists willing to strap suicide bombs onto their chests—even if they wave the same color flag!!!

ooo

Ironically, it was the violence of the Green Islamicists themselves that initially "saved" *Charlie Hebdo* from probable bankruptcy. The assassination of most of the editorial staff—just after the French authorities had removed the guards previously standing before its offices despite the previous firebombing in 2011 and continuing death threats—unexpectedly brought the *Charlie Hebdo* magazine incredible world-wide attention that it never had had before. In opposing Islamicist fanatics, the Editors had suddenly been transformed into martyrs to the secular cause of free thought and the right to "blasphemy".

As Aiden documented, millions in Euros were raised and readership suddenly jumped from 50 to 60 thousand people to a print run of millions just after the attacks. At that time, 7 million people were almost all Charlie!!!... Readership would, however, drop substantially several years later… The reality: The magazine was not very popular…

ooo

It was these largely unexpected and horrific events—the terror attacks of that year 2015—that had led all those then working at our Foundation, interns, fellows, and directors alike, to bond in unprecedented solidarity. We felt, thought, and acted together. « *Tous pour un, un pour tous* »… *One for all and all for one…* in the Three Musketeer's cheer… After these horrific events we all realized it was crucial to continue our struggle for Human Values Forever!

The day after going to the Bastille "We are all Charlie" protest with LaPlante's staff, I was suddenly offered a full-time job at her Foundation for Human Values Forever. This LaPlante was very hard to figure out… It seemed to be real Solidarity at that time… at that very troubled time!!!

Human Values Forever

I was thus grateful that I was finally entrusted with an "assistant" position (a glorified secretary, researcher, and "go-for"). At least I would no longer need to wait on tables for rude people who only saw me as a slave. Although I was not trained as a secretary, I could at least be helpful as I spoke, read, and wrote English fairly well—even if it was a struggle for me to speak French.

The intellectual spirit of the Foundation was the human rights lawyer, Aiden Russell, PhD, LLD. With longish gray matted hair that looked as if it were an 18th century powdered wig, he was laid back, "cool," as the French now say, in imitating the Americans who generally appear much more relaxed than the still heavy cigarette smoking French population—even if the existential smoking fad was growing out of fashion.

Russell never sported a noose around his neck yet was always dressed in a sports coat and blue jeans. He was truly an expert in international politics and international jurisprudence. Very articulate, always seeming to brood over contemporary human tragedies—that he was convinced were not intractable and could almost always be resolved by diplomacy… He could take on anyone with a rational argument that was almost impossible to undercut… Yet his proposals did not always seem very practical to implement… Realists detested him…

ooo

Then there was Bereft LaPlante's business partner, Gaspard G. Prophita. Almost entirely bald, but with a few thin strands of hair that he used in a vain effort to cover over his shiny beige scalp, he almost always wore a three-piece suit and a noose around his neck. By contrast with Russell, Prophita was cynical, and seemingly could only think about $$$. His argument was not so rational, always emotional, if not biased… Yet because there was a strong logic to his evident prejudice, he too was very difficult to tackle… in that he was faultlessly practical.

What a duo!

ooo

As I soon learned, the main concern for the Foundation of Human Values Forever were the "grant junkies" who always wanted $$$... $$$... and more $$$. With cheesy smiles, and detailed proposals, they would harass Prophita and Russell for a piece of LaPlante's pie—if they could not reach LaPlante herself.

Proposals poured in for health clinics, elementary schools, food distribution, technologies devoted to sustainable development, clothing and food stuffs, drones for environmental surveillance and research. There were also requests to develop advanced AI and blockchain technologies that permit refugee camps and others to obtain interlinked solar panels, wind turbines and piezoelectric floor tile energy for 24 hours daily. And there were even offers to write and distribute comic books dedicated to explaining the refugee crisis for children...

To flatter her, some called their proposed projects, *The LaPlante School* or *The LaPlante Clinic*, or *LaPlante Rescue Center*, among other similar names... The dilemma for the Foundation was to weed out the bad projects and then determine which proposals were truly valid, which were fraudulent, and which might be worthwhile and that truly needed additional support and development...

ooo

Occasionally, there was a visiting scholar on a fellowship who would do research for a month or so at the Foundation. I never got to know any of them very well. They often came to Paris to do their research floated by external funding. They then left almost as soon as I had gotten the chance to meet them.

And then there were numerous faceless, unnamed, unpaid student interns who came and went, some of whom were more interesting than others, and some who may have genuinely absorbed something from their internship.

Sometimes they could do more than just serve coffee or babysit LaPlante's three overweight Dachshunds. The interns often helped to arrange the logistics for the visits of famous human rights speakers and journalists from around the world. And they could talk to these famous people in person—if they were not too shy to do so.

It was unfortunate, however, that some of the interns, even the older ones, would talk so pretentiously with a highly inflated sense of their importance. Holding their noses high in the air, they believed themselves to be among the honored few who had the opportunity to work for this important Foundation.

ooo

And then there was the charismatic feminist, Bereft LaPlante, herself, a star, *une étoile,* of feminist leadership, with her oval face yet broad brow, with her thick make-up and thick red lipstick on her thin pursed lips that revealed her American, not her French, side. She had perfectly permed scarlet curls that surrounded her tiny narrow blue eyes, with pencil-thin eyelashes. Her face was pale and lightly freckled that made one think she was of Scot Irish descent—but that was no proof of origin. She was tall, over six feet, but with thin arms and legs that did not seem very athletic. It seemed certain that she had never suffered physically. Never had she been deprived of her rights, nor exploited in any way. Then again, very few really know anything about a person's possible childhood traumas, the relations with his/her father, mother, sisters, brothers, and those around them.... Those Freudian head shrink concerns...

With the colors of her designer Prima shoes and handbags almost always matching her designer dresses, as well as her finger and toenails, she was a famous Socialite, with roots in both the Land of the Free and in the Land of

Liberty, Equality, Fraternity (and Sorority?) … There was no one quite like her. It was said that she was one of the very few individuals who had devoted their entire fortunes with all their soul and energy to the quest to protect human values and democratic rights anywhere and everywhere, now and forever. She was a legend, a goddess, a guru(ess) and a guiding light. Everyone was at her feet!

An Ex-Soviet Dissident

"We are greatly honored today. The first speaker of our lecture series this year is Georgi Plakhanov."

Dressed in a dark navy dress with horseshoe designs and bleach white shirt, LaPlante introduced the thin, seemingly never eating, ex-Soviet dissident: "He is a brilliant scientist and mathematician who was arrested, along with his so-called accomplices, for advocating free speech in the Soviet Union in the 1960s. Since his release from the Gulag, he has continued his trail blazing work in the United States and Europe in the field of Artificial Intelligence, or AI for short—a long time before its time had come. It is incredible that Moscow did not recognize his exceptional foresight as we do…. Without further ado…"

Plakhanov stood behind the podium with a commanding presence. "After waking me in the middle of the night, they first put me in a dark room like a sauna, but with only freezing water. There they pushed me naked into the slime… Never had I experienced such fear… As I believed then and learned later… that was place where the executions took place…"

The audience felt his fear…

"If they did not execute me then, I assumed that they would send me to the judge for a puppet trial. Instead, they put me in a psychiatric clinic… as if I were schizoid…"

The audience gasped.

"I went on a hunger strike. I believed that there was no way that I should be locked in a lunatic asylum. I wanted to stand trial in a court—even if my chances of appeal were limited. I assume now that that made me look even more crazy!"

"Why were you arrested in the first place?" asked a young student who must not have read his bio or listened to LaPlante.

"Simply for trying to start a free speech society. We considered ourselves "neo-Marxists" or better, "revisionists." We were for peaceful reforms, not violence. We believed it was time to take a stance against the system that Lenin and Stalin had installed by brute force… We wanted to make the government live up to its promises. We did not want to seize power by force. Our manifesto urged the creation of a Union of Intellectual Freedom. We hoped it would appeal to all academic, religious, professional, and military institutions. To our regret, no one at that time was willing to put their lives on the line."[7]

He passed around a translated copy of the manifesto that he helped write in 1962. I could not believe it: The demands were so much like ours in 1989! We too wanted reforms and not violence. We too wanted to end the hegemonic monopoly of the Chinese Communist Party—but not necessarily abolish the Party altogether. We too wanted to boost the democratic power to co-govern the state! The parallels were too similar!

As he spoke, I realized that Mikhail "Prohibition" Gorbachev had tried to implement some of Plakhanov's proposals—as did Boris "Vodka Shot" Yeltsin. Now, however, Vladaspeare Pootin was stomping all previous domestic Russian reforms into the ground one by one by centralizing his power and accumulating $$$megabucks$$$.

ooo

Plakhanov looked around the room, before he stopped and froze in place. In the audience were two goons in long white trench coats (such a stereotype!) who had most likely been sent by the Russian embassy to watch him—even if they probably did not speak English. He seemed to become even more nervous.

"During my imprisonment I refused the offer of the guards of cigarettes and other favors. I knew they could use such means to manipulate me..."

He paused and drank a sip of water. "After years... I finally had a break... I learned that American diplomatic pressures were pressing Moscow to release Soviet dissidents and particularly Jewish refuseniks..."

He looked at the two huge rats in trench coats in the back of the room...

"I thought it out carefully... here was my opportunity... I borrowed a kippah from another prisoner... I put it one and started to pray... Before long, the authorities pulled me out of my cell and placed me on a jet to Tel Aviv. Once in Israel, I was received with great warmth and praise!!!"

Some in the audience began to applaud.

"Everything was going well. That is, until I decided, in all honesty, that I could not continue the masquerade forever. Finally, I told them, 'I am sorry I played this game… I sincerely thank you for saving me from a fate worse than death…. You see I could not think of another way to get out of there… I then pulled off my Hasidic black velvet dome and handed it to the man beside me… For you see, I stuttered, I am not Jewish.'"

Someone in the audience groaned in apparent dismay…

"All of a sudden, their warm faces turned sour and very grim. For days no one came to speak to me at the hostel where they had kindly put me… After waiting for what seemed to be an eternity, I heard a knock at the door. I hesitated to open it as I feared that Israeli officials had decided to expel me… as if my religion was more important than my humanity… With great trepidation, I opened the door…"

"At first, they just stared at me as if I was a criminal. Then, stammering with apologies, they told me that unfortunately I could not remain permanently on the territory the Jewish state. I almost fainted on the spot. I was afraid they were going to send me back to Moscow!"

"And just before I started panic, they said, 'No… no… please Sir, don't worry, we have made other arrangements for you. The International Freedom Foundation has kindly offered to host you so you could settle in Europe or in the U.S. We are very sorry it took this long to reach this solution… We hope you will accept it.'"

"Evidently, I had no other choice... I thanked them for their efforts and said I would welcome the opportunity to stay with the Freedom Foundation."

ooo

It was incredible... Plakhanov had been able to escape Soviet prison by pretending to be Jewish. I had been able to escape China by pretending to be a Buddhist monk! Neither of us were true believers!

At the end of his talk... and staring directly into the eyes of the two brutes sitting in the back row... he forewarned, "As I have been warning for years... A new dictatorship will reveal itself shortly... Gorbachev had warned... Yeltsin had warned... Both warned that NATO enlargement and renewed U.S. containment would provoke a Russian revanchist backlash... For now, Putin puts on a Janus mask... He pretends to play the democratic game since he knows that is what the Americans want to see... But beware! The new dictatorship will soon prove itself to be more insidious than any Russian dictatorship of the past..."

With that, he picked up his coat and quickly ran out of the room without waiting for more questions... The two goons quickly got up to follow him...

I could only think: 'How could such a state—by squashing reforms and repressing the most basic civil liberties and human rights—destroy someone like this who could possibly have become one of its most brilliant scientific minds—and in the new field of AI?'

Women as Collateral Damage

I was able to meet many intellectuals, investigative journalists, and whistleblowers, who had very different experiences, in countries with divergent forms of governance—in addition to the ex-Soviet dissident.

With LaPlante introducing each speaker, I learned that even countries, such as the Balding Eagle and its Oceania Allies—that claimed to be "advanced democracies"—had, in some way, repressed, tortured, jailed, or severely sanctioned journalists and political critics who had spoken out against state leaderships and war crimes. Many told similar and horrific stories of brutal murders of human rights and environmental activists. Many more than I expected. I was stunned. China did not stand alone…

These journalists and whistleblowers spoke out in strong terms about their investigations of torture and human rights violations, of the corruption of democratic processes, of the refusal of state judges to investigate evident war crimes and horrific abuses, of innocent men and women imprisoned. Such war crimes included the tactics of assassination by drone strikes aimed by video game pilots thousands of miles away… And now, I learned, the military Targeting Directorates—inspired by the Gospel of AI's guesstimating foresight ("garbage in, garbage out")—could calculate the extent of "collateral damage" to be caused by drone attacks to the civilian non-combatants. How humane!

The lecture hall at the prestigious *Cercle Trans-Atlantique*, where LaPlante held her lecture series, was packed to a hilt. Founded in 1917, on its walls hung photos of the wartime leaders of that era—John Bull's Lloyd George, the Gallic Cock's Georges Clemenceau, the Balding Eagle's Woody

Wilson—the President who promised to establish a one-term presidency… yet then ran for a second term… the President who engaged American G.I. Joe's in the "War to End All Wars"… after repeatedly promising not to….

ooo

In her introduction, LaPlante explained how Leila Zarwish, a women's rights activist, working for *Equity Now*, "has been examining how crimes against woman—household beatings, harassment in the workplace, date rape, forced surrogate motherhood, as well as feminicide—could all go unpunished due to patriarchal impunity. And as Leila will soon explain, what we are seeing in the news today—the many sex scandals coming out of Hollywood and high levels of government—are only the tip of the iceberg...."

"Yes, Bereft, you are right, only the tip…" replied Zarwish, as she stepped onto the stage. There was a hush. No one expected a woman in a black abaya and head scarf.

"And although I am very glad to visit Paris, I must nevertheless mention the fact that, among the Europeans, France has very high levels of feminicide… Not only that, but there are many issues concerning women in France and Europe in general that must be dealt with ASAP—although I do recognize that the French, to their credit, are way ahead of the Americans on the abortion question."

Zarwish looked deep into eyes of the stunned audience: "Throughout the world, there are many horrific crimes perpetrated by fanatics—but also by 'normal' individuals—against women from all walks of life and cultures and countries—in both the developed and supposedly "developing" world…. At least 200 hundred million women, for example, have been forced to be circumcised… for no other reason except for culturally accepted devotion to tradition…"

The audience gasped....

"I know women whose faces were burned with acid simply because they were wearing short sleeves, or a short dress, or not wearing headscarves... And I met women who suffered death threats accused of atheism and blasphemy. Many were even accused of 'propagandizing' in favor of scientific evolution, or other acts presumed to be against "god"—as if any human being could speak for the latter!"

Zarwish provided more detail... "And now there is a new/old phenomenon. Chinese Triads and mafias of many other nationalities have been seizing young women... Some are sold to Mafias by their own families... Some are refugees from wars... Others have been promised university training, modeling careers, or other jobs. Instead, they find themselves lured like insects into spider webs... then assaulted... gang raped... threatened with death..."

So many women, Zarwish said, were being trapped to work for strip clubs, erotic massage, child porno... Some were forced into marriage or used as surrogate mothers in unhealthy and dangerous conditions... Children and teens, she affirmed, were actually cheaper to handle than drugs as youth were good for years of use and abuse... And if they did become sick, exposed to AIDS or the Horseshoe Bat... "they would be thrown onto the street and swept away like cigarette butts."

Upon hearing this, the audience fell dead silent. As I interpreted her observations, Mafias throughout the world had begun to fabricate a new form of commercially "humanized" Brave New World baby assembly lines. White slaves, as the Alpha class, were able to obtain much more $$$ for Mafias as baby makers—for they were more socially "presentable" than were non-whites—who were considered mere Zetas by the baby market—as last born, last choice.

Zarwish continued to speak defiantly in a clear British accent: "No state or society is innocent of these crimes… And not to be overlooked are the doped-up child warriors, mainly boys, but girls too, who are forced to fight for states, for war lords, for transnational corporations, for Narcos, for Militias, for Mercenaries, in the killing fields of Africa, Asia and Latin America… forced to dig up this or that rare mineral or that… forced to distribute this drug or that… Their only real value is to load more bullets into the bedroom antechambers of machine guns…"

The curly hair of a normally placid LaPlante flushed even redder with rage… Sometimes Bereft seemed to be like a pressure cooker unable to release her steam… but she rarely exploded…always kept her calm…

ooo

As one of the major focuses of the HVF Foundation were crimes against women, LaPlante had invited many feminist groups in France, such as *Ni Putes Ni Soumises*, *Femen*, *#BalanceTonPorc (Me Too)*, to present their perspectives. I had thus heard of the Hollywood "Me Too" sex scandals yet did not know what LaPlante was referring to when she had spoken of scandals at the highest level of government.

It was at the reception that I learned that a very "privileged" few out of some 2 million youth, both male and female, who had been trafficked in the huge sex trade in the U.S. and Europe had been "loaned" to business executives, a few presidents, prime ministers, members of royalty, among other powerful individuals…

As the human rights lawyer Russell explained, a once respectable high finance priest had used his managerial talents to organize a major sex trafficking operation.[8] And as the rumors spread world-wide, it became more than a scandal… It was a crime against humanity that reached the highest elite levels of society. As the affair had touched global power elites—the investigations uncovered very little or were hushed up where possible… As Shakespeare's palace guard put it in *Hamlet*, there is definitely "Something rotten in the democratic states of…."

"So, knowing this, how could a self-righteous Western leadership claim superior values and morality," asserted Russell, "Many human rights critics point their fingers at the so-called 'developing world' where crimes and corruption appear so grossly evident and horrific. Yet the fact of the matter is that many powers of the so-called 'democratic world' were better at hiding their crimes and corruption, both at home and abroad…"

I remember responding, "Yes, that may be true, but what is the real difference between these perverse affairs organized by privateer sex traffickers–and the Chinese Emperors and Empresses who had formally socialized life 'on the other side' of the Forbidden City with its harem and Eunuchs? Even old Mao and his cronies were 'into' village teens in the post-1949 version of the Forbidden City…"

I added: "In fact, I think the ethics of the 'new' Communist man has regressed by several millennia." Aiden looked at me as if he might agree but did not reply. That was generally not the view of western sympathizers of the Chinese Communist Revolution…

ooo

The words of Zarwish struck me deeply: "The most dreadful form of warfare is not government against government, but warfare by governments who betray their own people's trust by turning their weapons against them—and by using rape as one of those weapons. Governments must not only respect each other—but just as importantly, they must respect their own citizens, men and women—as well as the planet's environment."[9]

I too wanted to believe that an alternative "planetization" (as Zarwish had put it) was possible, that it was possible for states and populations to respect each other and to cooperate more closely together and in closer interaction with the natural environment. She was right: The whole world must oppose a mindless globalization run by an "invisible hand" secretly guided by the manipulations of the major powers, transnational corporations, and by Triads and Mafias and Mercenaries with differing kinds and colors of amoral/immoral Dragon Chimeras tattooed to their skin….

ooo

I had been amazed to see how articulate and radical this seemingly religious woman was—as I superficially judged her because of her black dress and scarf. There was, however, not a hint of Islamicism in her talk. What I did notice was that her shoes and classic handbag on the chair beside her were the latest *Adori* fashion… I saw a gold chain around her neck, but her fingers were ringless…

At end of the reception, crying out in an effort to hush the packed room, LaPlante announced that Zarwish had just been nominated for the Nobel Peace Prize. A very impressive woman... Pure Dynamite!

Martyrdom

No one would have believed it at the time, but the attack on *Charlie Hebdo* was just the beginning of more terror to come…

A few months later, on November 13, 2015. LaPlante took all the members of her staff, including the interns, to watch the soccer ball bounce between the shoes of French and German players to the roar of crowd in the French National Sports Stadium *(Stade de France)* in Saint Denis, with the stands divided between rowdy heavy beer drinking fans of the Krauts and drunken *gros rouge qui tache* wine fans of the Frogs.

As it was a game between the French and Germans, it possessed evident historic symbolism—even if it was just a game. As usual, LaPlante's business associate, Gaspard G. Prophita, made snide remarks about the fact that the French and Germans took centuries to make a real and concrete peace.

"I couldn't believe it. But back in the late 1980s, I saw some uniformed German officers eating sauerkraut in an Alsatian café!" Prophita exclaimed, "What a historic event!"

"You think the leaders of that era could have listened to Victor Hugo!" the human rights lawyer, Aiden Russell replied, reciting from memory, "A day will come when you, France—you, Russia—you, Italy—you, England—you, Germany—all of you, nations of the continent, shall, without losing your distinctive qualities and your glorious individuality, be blended into a superior unity, and shall constitute a European fraternity…."

Russell then paused… almost seeming to cry, "Those words were spoken way back in 1849… Look how long it has taken to achieve peace!"

To which Prophita responded, "Oh, yes, Hugo, yes, please tell me when we will all be united!... Oh, yes, Russell… please tell me when the Europeans will cooperate! And with Moscow too! Sure thing!!! You know very well the Europeans will never get their act together…"

Russell looked like he was about to respond… yet Prophita cruised full speed ahead: "The Europeans can't even get their inter-state train schedules running on time, let alone cooperate on building their fighter jets. And it's still the Americans who run the jet set show over the heads of the Europeans!!! And nothing is going to change the Pentagon's military might!"

Russell replied crisply, "As hatred is always artificial, and based on nothing but special interests, it is certain that the peoples of Europe, including Russia, and the whole world, can learn a much faster way to cooperate and very soon! Peace was implemented between France and Germany after a century of war. It can be done elsewhere!"

"Like never!" sneered Prophita.

Everyone in the group, and even those people sitting close to us in the stands, then stared at this man, this Mr. G. G. Prophita, with his MA in Business and Technology, who was always jealous of PhDs like Russell. Prophita was always talking at the top of his lungs—seemingly not afraid to say anything.

"People are smart enough to stand up for themselves… Prophita added, "They don't need your elitist condescension…"

The two stared at each other as if they were about to punch each other out.

ooo

Unexpectedly, with everyone's attention on the soccer game, I sensed that LaPlante had moved very close to me. She was certainly not sitting close to either Prophita or Russell as I had expected. At first, I couldn't tell which of the latter she might prefer, if either—but now it seemed her hand had brushed gently against my thigh. At least I don't think I imagined it—that was just before we all heard an unexpected *BOOM!!!… BOOM!!!… BOOM!!!* … That, briefly, hushed the rowdy spectators' voices.

The game seemed to momentarily move in slow motion like a pilot flying amid thick clouds unable to see where the plane was going—before the referees blew the whistle to start again…

ooo

As we were all intently watching the game, none of us had any idea of what had just happened. Unknown to any of us at the moment, three Islamicists, waving their Black and White flags, had set off their suicide vests just outside the National Sports Stadium *(Stade de France)* in Saint Denis—dynamiting themselves into bloody chunks of raw meat along with a pedestrian…

All we knew was that France had beaten Germany 2 to 0. It was revenge for the German Iron Cross starting two World Wars—not to overlook the series of Franco-German conflicts over Alsace-Lorraine since the Thirty Years War—if not a long time before that. It is incredible how national sports can help soothe over domestic tensions and disputes, particularly on the side that wins… while the politicians on the side that loses need to speak out and make excuses for the loss—if they are not to lose their posts!

ooo

Even after the leaving the stadium, it was not until I returned home in a cab driven by a young man who looked like a long-haired classical musician who listened to Camille Saint-Saëns' *Danse Macabre*—that I learned what happened. I turned on the TV in my cramped apartment to see what horrors had taken place that evening in that very area of Paris—and not at the national stadium alone.

It was only hours later that we learned that President "Flanby" Holyland (but not the German foreign minister) had been quietly escorted out of the stadium so as not to cause a panic… The game continued—but so too did the mass killings by other members of the gang of Islamist White and Black Flag fanatics who randomly machine-gunned people eating on sidewalk tables outside three restaurants before they opted to siege the Bataclan nightclub—as if they were playing a close quarters battle video game in a real wartime…

Or perhaps they were merely imitating any one of the growing numbers of mass shootings in America itself over the past decade—often by white neo-Nazi sympathizers and other wackos??? There is now no need to read or watch crime fiction and mafia stories anymore. Just watching the recent mass shootings in France and in America (and increasingly elsewhere) on the channels of global Media Fourth Estate News was far more entertaining. And very profitable too—for the Yellow Press Media Moguls that is.

ooo

I soon learned that many innocents, including one of Aiden's students at the elite *École des Hautes Études de Droit* had been machine gunned gangster style for no other reason than she was sitting outside at one of the cafés. When I asked Aiden about it, he almost burst out in tears… before holding himself back. For the first time, I saw a hint of emotion ooze out of this seemingly refrigerated intellectual… He attempted to catch his breath…

How horrible! The student was Dihya Meghighda, the beautiful women who helped me to adjust to life in France! She had been waiting for Russell for a late dinner at the restaurant, *La Belle Équipe*—after the soccer game.

As Aiden later related, as if in a process of catharsis, his student, whom he evidently knew outside the classroom, had been named for the poetess Meghighda and for the warrior Dihya who fought against the Arab invasions of North Africa… That was when the Amazigh people forced to submit to Islam. Later they submitted to the French "civilizing mission" under the French propaganda pretext that they were being "liberated" from Arab/Islamic domination…

The Human Rights lawyer explained, "The Amazigh had been considered 'Berbers'… or 'barbarians'—by the Romans."

I added, "Like the Mongols were likewise considered barbarians by the Han Chinese and by Russians and Europeans alike."

"To each his own Barbarian!!!" he replied, and then added, "The Romans considered everyone Barbarians—the Anglo-Saxons, the Swedes, the Celts, the Germans as well as the peoples from the Land of Silk."

It was all a vicious cycle of name-calling that never seemed to end… These militant contemporary "barbarians" had just murdered a beautiful woman whose ancestors had been "Islamicized" centuries before they were "French-fried" in an overly buttered cast iron pan. In killing innocent unarmed people, these cowardly avengers appeared to have invented their own form of "justice" for killing 130 people (90 at Bataclan alone) with 416 people were injured (almost 100 critically), while sacrificing their lives (except for one who chickened out) in the name of martyrdom.

'Such was the brilliant (il)logical "1984" logic of terrorism,' I reflected… 'that may have only achieved something in the empty space of their own heads… Then again, how many fanatic followers would their violent actions attract?'

ooo

There were thousands of Islamist *jihadi* militants and many others suspected of possibly turning toward violence—many, but not all, under the surveillance of the French police. There were also many French nationals who had joined Islamicist movements abroad as foreign fighters. I was now worried that there might be some individuals or groups, whether backed by states, or acting as lone wolves, who might want to attack the Human Values Forever Foundation because of our support for the rights of women and those oppressed…

It was not abstract speculation or paranoia. After the *Charlie Hebdo* attacks, the French National Stadium and the Bataclan, the Nice truck massacre, the beheading of the teacher Samuel Paty—among other murders and acts of violence… It was a time when Christian, Moslem and Jewish cemeteries were all being desecrated by breaking crosses and painting Stars of David and Swastikas on tomb stones—heinous sacrilegious acts committed by who knows what individuals and groups… *Why???*

We feared for the worst… I could feel the pressures, tensions, and fears inside our Foundation... After all, we were highly critical of the "terrorist" actions waged by both states and violent anti-state organizations... And more pertinently, we were one of the major non-profit organizations who were supporting the rights of women, ethnic minorities, and LGBTQI+… in addition to political dissidents, whistle blowers, and militants of different, sometimes rival, causes…

"A"

The *Jihadist* fanatics—who were waging war in the belief that the only way to counter the imperceptible forces of globalization was by acts of martyrdom—were not the only ones moaning…

A few years or so before the Year of the Horseshoe Bat had shut down the French economy, someone had painted a large phosphorescent orange "A" onto the wall of the Italian Embassy. Another "A" was then painted on the top of a black limo with green diplomatic plates... Other French public and EU buildings were "tagged" as well…

It was not really a very artistic professional "tag." Just a few quick strokes of bright colors, orange or red, by someone, probably masked, who wanted to protest and run. Not at all at the level of urban street art worthy of big money speculation like that of the artist, Ernesto Pignon Ernest, or that of Banksy. Nor was it at the level of the *Free Ai Weiwei!!!* street art campaign in Hong Kong after the Chinese artist, Ai Weiwei, had been arrested by Beijing in April 2011.[10]

I saw a few plains-clothed French inspectors of the Police Nationale running around with open shirts in the streets, trying to disguise themselves like hippies with long hair and scraggly beards. In looking for clues, they were stopping random people to ask if they had seen anyone painting cars in the middle of the night.

I ducked down a side road, not wanting to be questioned.

ooo

I soon learned that, in the middle of the previous night, a band of Anarchists, covering their faces with black *cagoules* (hoods), had decided to go on a rampage and spray paint the Italian embassy with giant phosphorescent orange @'s in curlicue designs. There, across the street, on the sidewalk, it read in bright orange, in French, "*Remember Diaz!*"

Diaz? Who is Diaz? I thought the name sounded like the explorer, Bartholomeu Dias, who rounded the Cape of Good Hope—setting the path for Jorge Álvares to be the first European to reach islands near what is now Hong Kong and Guangzhou by sea—hence initiating the trans-Pacific "blue water" globalization that would circumvent trade through the Ottoman Empire and Central Asia.

Yet the name Diaz had nothing to do with globalization—nothing to do with the meeting of East and West—as I had imagined.

ooo

I had no knowledge of the tragic events that had taken place during the massive "alternative globalization" protests in July 2001. The Italian police had beaten the hell out of a number of peaceful protestors who had stayed overnight at the "Armando Diaz" school. They were staying there over night to protest the G-8 summit of the major western industrial powers (France, Germany, Italy, Japan, the United Kingdom, the United States, and Canada, the President of the European Commission, plus a much less developed and instable Russia) in Genoa, Italy.

Ironically, the school had been named for the General who became the Chief of Staff of the Italian army after Italy's defeat at the 1917 Battle of Caporetto. That was the absurd battle where Austrian soldiers urged the Italian soldiers not to attack—for they would be slaughtered like deer meat in *polenta* if they tried to hop up the mountainside into the machine gun fire. The Italians were nevertheless ordered to climb up anyway—into certain death for the glory of the *Patria*… In Wilfred Owen's line, "The old LIE: *Dulce et Decorum est Pro Patria Mori.*"

ooo

As I learned from Aiden, the police raids at the time of the G-8 summit resulted in the arrest of some 93 protesters. Many of the protesters were almost beaten to death in that violent police raid—purportedly because they were believed to be associated with the militant Anarchist group, Black Bloc—a group who had no fear of violently confronting the police head on. At least 61 individuals were seriously injured and taken to hospital. Some of the militants were tortured in a temporary detention facility before being released. To them, the Italian state had become the enemy.

In a trial of the 125 policemen involved, not one was punished for misconduct—due in large part to the fact that torture was not even recognized as a crime in Italy. What a beginning for the new millennium! I had no idea that there were no laws protecting individuals from police brutality in democratic countries like Italy. I did not think it was possible. I assumed all rights were guaranteed by the Italian Constitution and by the European Union. I mean Europe was not China in 1989!

ooo

After learning this I began to realize that the Alfred "Dynamite" Nobel Peace Prize winner Dario Fo was not exaggerating these issues—and then crudely blaming "capitalism" for them. After living in France… after learning what had happened in Italy... I began to see that it was I who was seeing the world through a Red, White, and Blue colored kaleidoscope…

In no way should Dario Fo's play *Accidental Death of an Anarchist* be considered as a clever, entertaining, absorbing, funny, or as a hilarious "furiously funny police satire" as some theatre critics called it—given the despicable events that the play depicts about the "terrorist" acts of the "Boys of the Company" and of Italian government in the 1960s and 1970s… Dario Fo had wanted his play to concern itself with the big geo-pornographic picture that fully revealed the way inter-state global rivalries impacted everyday people…[11]

The police raid on the Diaz school may have taken place some 20 years ago… yet the anger was still steaming as if in a pressure cooker… Carl Sandburg, the Chicago poet, once wrote "the People forget." But there are always a few people who simply do not forget… After what my fellow dissidents and I went through, I know I could never forget....

ooo

Aiden was an expert on the peaceful revolutions then taking place throughout the world at the time. Stroking his beard and smoking his glass Vape, he explained how "alternative globalization" protests had just initiated a series of worldwide protests in the state-capitalist world after the protests in 1988 and 1989 had initially overturned the Communist world in both eastern Europe and the Soviet Union. A few democratic states also came into being in Latin America—but not many in the wider Middle East and Africa—and definitely not in China and Southeast Asia. In China, it seemed to be one party rule 4EVER!

The Seattle Protests against neo-liberal capitalism began in 1999. The "Occupy Wall Street" movement in the so-called "Land of the Free" opposed the planetary rule of the "1%"—while also criticizing the top 20% of each country who most benefitted. These protests were followed by the protests of the World Social Forum. Then, there were almost simultaneous world-wide protest movements in the period 2009 to 2014—even in "democratic" Hong Kong and Bangkok.[12]

It was a great tragedy but almost all of these democratic revolutions were met with a social and political backlash as had been the case in China in 1989—resulting in societal tensions, severe repression and/or horrific wars….

ooo

I was very astonished to learn of a hunger strike in France, against of all things—a major highway. It appeared that French authorities believed the A69 highway (with its erotic numerological signification) in regions of the Toulouse and Occitania was essential for the area's development. The road was expected to reduce travel times and encourage commerce.

Yet the local population did not believe or accept the government's computerized *guestimations.* Militant protesters clashed with police to stop it. The Green activists argued that the project was not only detrimental to the environment, but that it would further harm French agricultural production—making France even more dependent on food imports. And the highway project would not fully develop the region.

I then learned that some of the hunger strikers who opposed the highway were going to engage in a water strike as well—at even greater risk to their health and to their lives!

ooo

It all reminded me of the demonstrations against Three Gorges Dam and the Tiananmen Square protests when Chinese students had risked their lives in a hunger strike. And as Beijing has been building bridges, train tracks, highways, ports, and other infrastructure rapidly throughout China and much of the world, in accord with its global, and financially risky, Belt and Road project, it was incredible to hear that there were major protests against similar ventures in France and other countries.

I had opposed Beijing's efforts to construct, as rapidly as possible, dozens of Chernobyl-like nuclear power plants, like the one in Ukraine that melt down in 1986, spewing radioactive clouds into the air. I also opposed the fact that major industries were permitted to heavily pollute the land and waters with no environmental controls. In some cities—Wuhan, Chengdu, Hangzhu, among many other urban landscapes in China—it is literally impossible to breathe! But so too, I learn, Italy's Milano!!!

That was not development! Just because the Land of the Free and Lady Europa had massively polluted their urban and land space by poisoning the air and the earth to produce energy and to grow crops in larger and larger spaces with vegetables produced in Our Ford assembly lines... Just because they had sent their DDT and other pesticides—that were eventually banned in the U.S. and Europe to other countries with less environmental restrictions—did not mean China should pollute as well! Nor did it mean that China, or any other country, should be permitted to pollute the rest of the world either!!!

ooo

I likewise had opposed Beijing's Three Gorges Dam project—one of the largest dams in the world, 180 meters high—that was intended to stop the Chang Jiang region from being flooded. It was a massive, ecologically destructive project of the Party's massive ego, the Soviet-trained hydro-electric "expert," Premier Li "Yu the Great" Peng.

The very building of the Dam led to the flooding of some 13 cities, 140 towns, 1,352 villages and about 650 factories. The project initially displaced more than 1.2 to 1.4 million people—most without adequate compensation—while it concurrently destroyed hundreds of historical and cultural sites. The dam further harmed the habitats of the Chinese alligator, sturgeon, among other species, while severe flooding, landslides, and waterborne diseases have all contributed to the rapid extinction of the *Baiji*, the Chang Jiang white river dolphin.

For me it was a disaster foreseen… although others still disagree despite many incidents.[13]

ooo

And now in France, I was seeing a similar push to further develop nuclear fission and a general refusal to consider more decentralized and safer forms of energy. And much like the Chinese government, the French government apparently would not even discuss the issue with the protesters—even though the individuals involved were not only protesting, but willing to risk their lives—and even die—to stop a mere highway!

I have no stake in the issue as I am an outsider, an "Alien," and cannot participate in French politics. At the same time, I don't know what is best. These protests raised real questions as to ultimate necessity and purposes of such infrastructure projects, including those of China! Were there other more decentralized and more "humanized" alternatives?

Of Liberty Enlightening....

I would often jog up the *Ile aux Cygnes* to see the moldy green oxidized copper model of what was originally called "Of Liberty Enlightening the World". It was area on a small isle in the Seine where people would do exercises and body building… I was too fearful to meet anyone… It was this mini model of the oxidized copper Statue of Liberty that had accepted me with welcome arms—and not the giant patina version.

It had been the French Marianne who helped raise the funds to give the Statue of Liberty in 1885 as a present to the Americans—who then placed it on what was once called Bedloe Island, close to Ellis Island—that was once the entry point of those immigrating to the Land of the Free from across the Atlantic. An early draft of the statue's design represented Lady Liberty as holding broken shackles in her hand—symbolizing the abolition of slavery. The position of those shackles was then changed to be located at her feet—barely visible except high in the air…

To make it clear that this massive statue did not represent a brazen symbol of imperial might of "conquering limbs astride from land to land," much like the ancient Colossus of Rhodes, Emma Lazarus wrote a poem called the "New Colossus" that praised the statue as representing the "Mother of Exiles." In her view, the statue symbolized the welcoming of all those fleeing tyranny and oppression. In the poem, the young country, the Land of the Free, newly unified after its Civil War, would dazzle all its citizens—including the poor and the pariahs, with the promise of new freedoms—and with the liberating technological promises of electricity, the flaming torch of "imprisoned lightning."

ooo

After a HVF conference on the migrant crisis in North America, Aiden had told me how he had taken the long trip to the Darien Gap in Panama several years before… "That is a 66-mile trek in one of the wildest jungles where migrants seek to pass without maps…where they are threatened by poisonous snakes, floods, as well as smugglers and paramilitaries who steal their food and valuables… If they survive, they continue their trek up through the Central American states to Mexico to the Rio Grande in the effort to find their way to San Diego or the cities of El Paso and Eagle Pass, and then up to Chicago and NYC… the so-called "sanctuary cities."

As he denounced injustice and highly uneven levels of development, jumping from place to place in a *tour du monde*, he confided, "I had told Bereft the task in Central America was too great for us… We could not make the local population see that HVF could do something positive. I thought it was better that we turn our attention to precarious migrant situation in Europe and in North Africa and the Middle East where we could probably obtain greater funding and diplomatic support…"

"Yes, I suppose I could understand that. Not enough resources..."

"It is not just that… Washington has been backing the petty fiefdoms in the region… No one wants to remain… There are no jobs… Most of the pro-American countries in the region are repressive police states… Nicaragua is a dictatorship of another kind, while Venezuela is a corrupt socialist disaster… despite all its oil wealth."

"That is dreadful!"

"Yes, except that I did not tell you the whole story… The shame is that we had to abandon the whole project… The promises we did not keep were so destructive! How disappointed the people were. They would never trust us again… Nor any other NGO (Non-Governmental Organizations) for that matter…"

I saw his face turn sour. He seemed to become depressed, but tried to fight it off, just as he had after the brutal indiscriminate killing of the beautiful Dihya. In continuing his story, Aiden told me that when the Foundation first arrived in the area, the people had been very cold… suspicious… It took a while for them to warm up.

I asked why… "because they thought we were some religious group that wanted to convert them," he replied somberly, "We had to assure them that we were not…religious…"

"I suppose that over time they began to trust you?"

"Not everyone."

"Soon there were more rumors that we were a sect… that we were involved in kidnapping children. Imagine that!"

"After a year… after all the good work we did in providing food, clothing, lodging, some of our staff workers were threatened…. the truck tires were punctured… rocks were thrown at windows… Everything snowballed… the threats against our staff corresponded with a decrease in international donations… And we were not getting local political support… We had to abandon the whole project… We had to abandon the people who most needed us. We were nothing but temporary band-aides!!!

I tried to make a joke… "Now it is we who want to study their religion, not force them to adopt ours… It does not seem like it was your fault…"

"Yes and no. The problem is deeper, much deeper. Without real development assistance and political reforms, hundreds of thousands, if not millions, of people will try to cross over the Tex-Mex border in the next few years…"

He quickly added, snickering, "Montezuma's revenge is not limited to diarrhea."

ooo

It was an area of the world in which I had always held an interest. I had always wondered whether there was any Mongol Chinese influence in the region's history and culture.

With a conch shell hung around his neck, much like I wear my jade pendant, I had always wondered whether Quetzalcóatl—the ancient god of the Teotihuacán civilizations, the feathered serpent that symbolized Venus, the Sun, in addition to the arts and crafts, knowledge and learning, as well as merchants—had any relationship to the Chinese myth of *Zhulong*, the Torch Dragon Chimera? That was the Chimera who possessed a human face and serpent's body and who just by blinking, had created day and night, and who just by breathing, created seasonal winds…

Was there any relationship between these Chinese Chimera myths and Quetzalcóatl? … Or perhaps with a similar Mayan god, Kulkukan? Or was it more like the case between the mythical gods of the Mongols/China and Mexico/Central America and the glowing white candle serpents, painted by surrealist artist Rene Magritte, returning to nature? In other words, no relationship whatsoever?

As I would later discover, the ancient religious myths of the Central and South American region were among those creation myths that were being studied by the mysterious Society for the Exploration of Cosmic Consciousness

(SECC)—for their possible interconnections with other religions and cultures. The SECC also wanted to comprehend their ancient advances in mathematical calculation… and particularly the concept of Zero... It was the SECC that would later… unexpectedly… offer me a job…

ooo

Incredibly, Washington had stuck its busy-body nose into the affairs of so many other countries and regions around the world, yet Mexico and Central America were totally ignored by an indifferent and irresponsible American imperium—even if those countries and peoples were in the Land of the Free's front, not back, yard.

As long as Uncle Sam continued to receive its daily fix of black gold, avocados, frozen taco shells, tequila, marijuana, and as long as the U.S. was able to peddle to the Mexican Jumping Bean subsidized corn, corn syrups, semi-automatics and All-American apple pies, all was fine—all was "Cloud 9"!!! Yet, over time, even the extra supplies of mail-packaged Fentanyl failed to fully dope over the much more than podiatric health problems in the Tex-Mex relationship… There were problems that afflicted weary wetbacks from there and all over the world who clamored thousands of miles to enter the Land of the Free *where you could be what you want to be…*

It was evident that if Uncle Sam—who had once promised to open his arms to the wretched refuse abroad—was not able to handle bunions, bruises, callouses and other health concerns by himself, then neither could the HVF Foundation. I would later read in news coverage in the Media Fourth Estate how some Republican governors of states in Florida and Texas had sent busloads of thousands of Latino refugees to "safe havens" such as NYC and Chicago—

cities controlled by Democrats in the North. The latter had their own problems and could not handle the influx... Not enough food... not enough housing... not enough jobs... not enough $$$...

American society was dragging its feet and polarizing over the migrant issue... And that fact was also becoming an ethical and existential issue for me now living in the no longer so revolutionary French Marianne with her *bonnet phrygien* ... and for others seeking refuge elsewhere...

Aiden Russell's words were prophetic: Yet Montezuma's revenge was not just limited to diarrhea, it also regurgitated the puke that would spew forth from the xenophobic hoof and mouth disease of self-congratulating demagogues in both the Land of the Free and the French Land of Liberty, Egality, Fraternity (and Sorority???) ... and many other countries...

ooo

From the *Ile aux Cygnes*... from the mini-statue "Of Liberty Enlightening the World" ... I would run down the Seine and under the Metro trestle that passes over the Bir-Hakeim Bridge, with its view of *la Dame de Fer* and the Seine, a favorite of young "selfie" takers.

There I would stop and gaze at the bridge's hourly influx of honeymooners, often eastern European brides in white lace with long sooty gray trails side by side Chinese/Asian brides in short red dresses. Rented limos would stop on the bridge for the photographers to take pictures of honeymooners, arm in arm with their black-tux grooms, as they stood straight and tall before the monument, *La France Renaissante.* The statue was initially designed to represent Jeanne d' Arc who, despite the name change, was still pointing her sword at the British Isles of Perfidious Albion...

ooo

I began to reflect. I was lucky the French mini-Statue of Liberty took me in from tyranny and oppression. Yet what would be the fate of Central and Latin Americans and others who were similarly fleeing from oppression abroad? Would the Statue of Liberty welcome them? Would other states take them if they could not return to their homelands? Would America live up to the words engraved upon its (in)famous statue?

I learned that the Land of the Free had turned back boats of Jewish immigrants, and other people persecuted for their race or religion or political beliefs, who were fleeing the rise of Fascism and Communism in Europe and Russia in the later 1930s and early 1940s—on the pretext that some of the immigrants might be Nazi spies. And now the Balding Eagle, in building Tex-Mex walls, had resurgent fears of criminality and terrorism invading.

Would the Americans, like so many of other peoples, finally capitulate to the uniform stomping of leather boots and Kevlar helmets—thereby transforming the Statue of Liberty back into the militarist Colossus of Rhodes? Would the Americans be able to resist the neo-Vulture Timocratic trumpets of war tooted by Fearless Leaders of many political persuasions—both "right" and "left"?

It seemed clear to me that America's formerly hopeful image of tolerance and mutual respect was rapidly fading… if not tarnishing to the point of cracking… No longer did the Land of the Free appear to be holding high a torch guiding bright…

"Keep, ancient lands, your storied pomp!" cries she
With silent lips. "Give me your tired, your poor,
Your huddled masses yearning to breathe free,
The wretched refuse of your teeming shore..."

MKH: No Longer in the News

In Paris one knows the *manif or manifestation* (protest or demonstration) is about to start when all is almost silent under acid gray skies and when fewer and fewer people walk the streets… The traffic comes to a virtual halt. Before long, much like the persistent and penetrating *crachin* (spitty) rain that froths before a larger storm, the protestors suddenly surface from the underground, from the buses and metro, from the back streets and alleyways. They rise to the streets in pent-up rage and frustration… It is at that moment, the vans of police swerve between slow moving traffic, their sirens wailing like accordions—and not at all like the frightening elephant roar and stampede of American police cars as seen on TV with spotlights blinding.

The storm floods the city: With thousands taking to the street… each labor union … each political party… each social organization… each non-governmental organization…. holds their banners and hastily written and indecipherable signs high for differing social and political causes… Some hold Corsican or Basque or Catalan or Palestinian or Kurdish or Cuban or Tibetan flags… Some of these causes are compatible… Others not…

The *manif* is not just a political statement, it is also a social gathering, a party, a song, a dance… a place where groups and individuals encounter each other… It is where some people meet and begin to talk and get know one another… A place where friendships and love affairs can be made or not made…

ooo

We march proudly with our banner, a picture of a blue planet earth with the slogan *Human Values Forever!*

Ecoutez la Colere du Peuple… Liberté…C'est la lutte finale !!!… the marchers sing in rough voices, out of tune, more or less in unison, "It's the final struggle" …

Yet the struggle never seems final and is repeated in differing variations....

ooo

As the *manif* grows in numbers, and the protest continues day after day, it was not uncommon for the garbage bags to pile up bag by bag even higher than the street signs—if the protest is accompanied by a major strike. Sometimes the demonstrators crowd onto the roads and highways to block the traffic. And if the farmers join the cause, to protest their 7 day a week long working hours, their meagre salaries relative to the price of their products set throughout the country by the food distributors, the high costs of taxation and of sustaining environmental norms, and the unfair competition of those international producers who do not meet the tough standards, their tractors buzz over all over the major routes…they dump manure… set tires… trash… hay… on fire… They threaten to block access to Paris and other cities… *I learn there is large number of farmer suicides…*

No one knows what bus or metro to take, and whether this or that bus or metro will even go all the way to the destination that it is supposed to go… And if one can't use the public buses and the metro, then good luck finding a taxi before they go home to evade the chaos… even if they want to continue working… And if one needs to get to work on time in the morning… that's just tough luck…

ooo

Flares flame red… Most of the fires are very far from the *Manif*. On can smell the stench of plastic garbage sacks smoldering. The tires of dicycles and cars and buses and are soon smoking sending ghastly fumes into the air… A white Mercedes is set aflame for no apparent reason other than it is parked in the wrong place at the wrong time… a presumed symbol of inequity under attack….

Navy blue gladiators charge into the crowd… Backed by armed vehicles, machine guns, grenade launchers—weapons used to fight armed insurgents—the police strike protesters with high velocity flash balls… Dogs then harass those who fell to the ground… Eyes, noses, and throats of those without facemasks choke with tear gas…

The Police are met headfirst by Black Bloc Anarchists in bicycle and motorcycle helmets waving pirate and Anarchist flags… One man, who cursed the police to their faces, is beaten to a pulp with Billy clubs (*matraques)* flailing… Joggers and bicyclists run in counter directions. Self-declared journalists run up to take pictures on cell phones… raising police fears that their violent actions may lead to legal charges against them… A few take selfies, smiling, with the clash of police and protesters in the background… Others watch from windows and up upon tree branches… With a very serious air, a blogger reports to her followers...

The French slogans were not exactly like Chinese *Da Zi Bao* or Big Character Posters—but some were much cleverer than others…

Qui Sème La Misère Récolte la Colère !
Who sows misery reaps rage!

Enrichissons les salariés,
Pas les actionnaires !
Enrich the employees,
Not the stock owners!

Travaille, consomme, obéis
Work, Consume, Obey!

Le climat n'attend pas
The climate will not wait!

Fin du Monde
Fin du Mois
Meme Combat!!!
End of the World
End of Month
Same Struggle!!!

ooo

Here, in democratic France, I could not believe the police were fighting face to face with the demonstrators… I watched on the side as the windows of restaurants, businesses and banks were smashed… A tear gas cannister fell about 20 feet from me! It becomes the police—and not the law—who is in charge…

The next day… "But no one died" was the response of the overwhelmed French leadership in justifying their brutal actions in which four people lost their eyes to plastic flash balls… It was just as brilliant a comment as that of China's Fearless Leadership!

The protest poster plays on the words *ça crève les yeux*, meaning "it is so obvious" and the verb *crèver*—meaning to "puncture" or "kill" or "pop" or "burst":

On est en démocratie, ça crève les yeux !
"So we are in a democracy, it is so obvious, your eyes burst!"

ooo

Once the *manif* starts to boil, armored police, *les flics*, are overwhelmed and overworked and spread out all over the city…. Some, not from Paris, don't know where they are and what streets they on… Yet even if they are from Paris they are seen by the demonstrators as Martians. They are spit on, insulted, abused, sometimes rocks and metal bars are thrown at them. It is all because of policies and laws that they are not responsible for, yet must nevertheless uphold regardless how unjust and ridiculous… despite the fact that their presence as guardians of law and order will do nothing to resolve the deeper social and political disputes… disputes that cannot be resolved without diplomacy and decent legislation…

And in upholding idiotic laws the armed police presence can often provoke even more rage on both sides… and when, in their fears and frustration, the police are accused of using undue force… shooting tear gas cannisters into the crowd… spraying tear gas directly into the eyes of those caught up in the protest whether part of it or not… firing flash balls indiscriminatingly… breaking hands, smashing skulls and popping eyes… And yet sometimes, their aim is very discriminate…

ooo

Mark King Hayford (MKH) was once again in the news, now writing from London, but no longer for *NewsBlitz!!!*... I had not remained in contact with MKH after the June 4, 1989 Tiananmen Square crackdown. I was afraid he would be spied upon by Chinese spooks and hackers, and if I had tried to contact him, and let him know I was in Paris, Chinese surveillance—who could watch everything and nothing—would have found me out for sure! Nevertheless, I found I too could spy on him through Social Media.

It was said that MKH lived like a hermit, not talking to anyone, not meeting anyone, ever since he had been expelled from China for simply doing his duty as a journalist, for digging up information that was, in fact, known to a few, but was not "top secret." And as such, Hayford's inquiries proved embarrassing to Chinese authorities. They, like leaders in France, the United States, and anywhere else, did not want the whole world to see their dirty underwear hanging on the line, ready to be picked up by the trashy Yellow Press and scandal sheet editors. As the Chinese elites see it, the mere effort to obtain some form of info becomes an act of espionage—primarily because it was often info that could possibly hurt some careers, even if the culprits deserved it!

In such a way, I had become one of many scapegoats in a country of post-1984 mass surveillance... The root of the problem was that Beijing did not know how to manage the globalization of information—nor how to deal with criticism—whether it was inaccurate or accurate, fake or not fake—except by censorship and repression.

ooo

I later learned from reading his blogs on the internet that MKH had luckily escaped the first commercial

September 11, 2001 flight, hijacked by the Four Riders of the Apocalypse, which took *Homo Geopoliticus et Economica* into hell... He was on his way to the *NewsBlitz!!!* offices in the World Trade Center and, as usual, too late for a rare jet-lagged Tuesday morning meeting. Some individuals are extremely lucky! I don't believe in the *I Ching*, Chinese astrology, or stale Chinese fortune cookies. And neither do I believe that Chinese stone lions nor European gargoyles provide protection for anyone…

I also learned that MKH's formerly famous photographer sidekick, Poncho, quit *NewsBlitz!!!* to go freelance. Poncho became a war photographer and found himself in the Al Rasheed Hotel in Baghdad—where the inhabitants were dodging laser guided "smart bombs" and the Nighthawk Stealth bombers of Desert Storm. Almost decade later, Poncho took the famous shot of the Chinese embassy in Belgrade—after it had been precision bombed by a U.S. Stealth aircraft during "Slick Willie" Clitone's Air Force war "over" Kosovo in 1999.[14] After all that glory, Poncho must have fizzled out—unable to adapt to the new digital and computerized photoshop market. I never saw another photo attributed to him. There was a rumor he had become a photographer for a "war tourism" company… I guess it is better to risk death in some kind of glory…

ooo

Hayford had once been a beacon for journalistic freedom. His editorial critiques in *NewsBlitz!!!* were always devastating—even if always ignored by those in power! Now, having stepped down from his cushy post, he has tens of thousands of followers on Social Media. His articles had denounced injustice in many countries around the world.

Way back in December 1989, for example, when it was disclosed that just after the crackdown on Tiananmen

Square in June, the White House had sent a secret emissary in a dark pinstriped power suit to the *Zhongnanhai* in an effort to kiss and make up, MKH was on top of it. He wrote one of his most famous highly critical editorials, "Stealthy Mission of Capitulation" for *NewsBlitz!!!* Magazine.[15]

Now however, for some reason, his words no longer seemed as strongly pro-American apple pie as they once did when he was living in China. At that time, he was almost always praising the American apple as the most delicious on the planet. (As I know from living in France, *tarte tatin* tastes much better!) Now, however, although he would not fully admit it, America had increasingly become a stale "Host-essages" pie with 25 days of packaged shelf life heavily dosed with 39 ingredients… That was a brand that urban legend declared could survive a nuclear explosion and remain edible…

ooo

Even before the meteoric rise to power of Donald "Secret Agent Orange *Jee-Zus!!!*" Drumpf, MKH was already beginning to have second thoughts about where his once venerated country was heading... after it had been engaged in one overseas military mission after another, all fought for the religion of "democracy"—but that had accomplished virtually nothing except subsidize the arms industry and the Pentagon, plus private transnational construction companies and other suppliers of good and services. Americans may not realize it, but not all the world now dreams about the now blurry "beacon on the hill"—that for many has transmuted into a nightmare! And those who still do believe in the Statue of Liberty are either caught on barbed wire or else are drowning in the Rio Grande!

Did those U.S.-led overseas military interventions serve any purpose other than make chaos even more chaotic?

ooo

I could not believe that MKH was no longer writing for *NewsBlitz!!!* magazine, but was now a freelancer for subscribers on the online platform *UPSTART*—not really wanting to go into retirement… He was writing alongside a coterie of others who had been forced into retirement or who were unable to tote the Party or Corporate lines of the local and national journals, newspapers, and magazines. MKH stood alongside those who wanted to sustain an independent voice—but who were often not even close to his talent…

Yet, much like Poncho, I was not certain if he willingly retired or was phased out. It seemed that the big Media Firm no longer needed him once they entered the digital realm which sought shorter, jazzier, pieces of info with no detailed research evident. The new digital Media of the Fourth Estate wanted writers who were witty and clever, not those with intellectual depth. Nor did they want writers who would significantly challenge the status quo of received ideas. Photographers, writers, and many other employees could be replaced by computers and drones—and most gravely, by Artificial Intelligence (AI), by the "Great Automatic Grammatizator."[16]

And those media outlets that did try to remain independent had a hard time finding funding that could pay their staff… It seemed every firm in every field was reducing itself to a skeletal crew… and concurrently eliminating commercial office space too… forewarning yet another 2008 real estate financial Crash…

ooo

France was now amid weeks of protest. Every Saturday for weeks, supporters of Yellow Vest movement passed out flyers explaining their demands—after French President "Jupiter" Macaroon decided to place an additional tax on gasoline and diesel to pay for his proposed green revolution. As an estimated 9 million French live in precarity, the Yellow Vests—who generally lived outside the big cities and who are doctors, lawyers, professionals, teachers, taxi drivers, and small business men and women, not to overlook small farmers—and who are not only average workers in the construction industry, metros, the trains, the airports—did not believe that the government was doing enough to help them survive.

This was one of Hayford's editorials that I found online:

Popular Protest: China Then, France Now

by Mark King Hayford (www.MKH.com)
December 30, 2018

Almost thirty years ago, I witnessed Chinese students risk their livelihoods and lives in a massive, purely non-violent, popular demonstrations against official corruption and in support of democratic reforms. The protest arose spontaneously in April and lasted until the Communist Party ordered a violent repression on June 4, 1989. Now, in France, I am witnessing a very different form of mass protest that is demanding a more inclusive form of democratic governance. The "gilets jaunes" (Yellow Vests) movement has thus far demonstrated for 20 consecutive Saturdays.

The Yellow Vests demand greater regional political power against French centralization. They seek to mandate term limits for politicians who can be both a mayor of a major town and a senator, for example, while also remaining in office for several terms. The *gilet jaunes* are generally opposed to French membership in NATO.[17]

They are generally divided as to how the EU can be reformed. Some, for example, seek a new EU policy to protect quality agricultural production—so that French farmers are not undercut by producers who firms do not live up to high environmental health norms—and are not ripped off by distributors. Others think countries should break out of the European Union, as did the United Kingdom, and forge their own path.

One slogan of the Yellow Vest movement is "Step I: Macron; Step 2: the World;" may prove dangerously disillusioning… Macron, who is often derogatively referred to as "Jupiter", his lofty head stuck in the Paris smog, did not take the route of severe repression as did Beijing on June 4, 1989—yet his police still use repressive tactics and flash balls that can wound and blind.

Macron has claimed to engage in "dialogue" by initiating a grueling three-month National Debate; yet yellow vest critics have accused him of stalling for time. With few concrete results, Macron has been accused of doing nothing but preach to himself—not listening at all.

ooo

I clicked the article off the computer screen. True, MKH had explained what the movement was all about, yet his writing no longer seemed to have the same global impact that it once did when *NewsBlitz!!!* publicity had given his words more bark than a bite. Now his words on the screen were even more like a tree falling in the wilderness with no one around to hear it. Unlike Chinese journalists, Hayford certainly seemed to be free to say what he believed. Then again, he was not a French journalist working for the national media. And he was no longer an American journalist working for a Media Fourth Estate firm whose profits and CEO salaries were larger than the GDPs of many countries.

After reading the editorial online, I could only think about Li Peng, the Chinese leader who had truly earned the moniker, the "Butcher of Beijing." Li Peng was just one of many examples when (somewhat respected) state leaders metamorphose into state terrorists by repressing his own citizens… instead of engaging in dialogue...[18]

In France, the so-called "dialogue" appeared to be going nowhere despite the so-called Great Debate that sent President "Jupiter" Macaroon to travel to speak to town halls around the country… Then again, it looked like Jupiter ultimately did give in to some of Yellow Vest economic demands after months of protests—but did not accept their key political demands.[19] What a game—that was not always non-violent!

ooo

I searched on my computer for Hayford's next editorial on the Yellow Vests. I felt so obsessed by this man who had seemed so charismatic to me in China. Ironically enough, as convincing as his words were, MKH had never even stepped foot in Paris, or anywhere in France itself as far as I knew. He only observed the protests from afar—from NYC or London.

Then I found this editorial that expressed larger concerns about European unity. It raised more questions than answers.

The Yellow Vests: Spontaneous Protest

by Mark King Hayford (www.MKH.com)
January 30, 2019

The Yellow Vests claim they are apolitical. Yet political parties from both the rightwing and the leftwing have been trying to obtain the support of this now popular social and political movement.

Even before the Yellow Vest movement gained momentum, many Yellow Vests were angered when French President Macron humiliated a rightwing General and forced him to step down after he spoke out against Macron's defense cuts. That just after the July 14, 2017 military parade, which in turn inspired President Donald Trump, who had been invited by Macon to participate, to demand that Washington, D.C. set up a costly military parade—a demand opposed by Washington's mayor.

Given their militant perseverance, there is concern that the protests planned by the Yellow Vests will prove costly and weaken the French economy—if the government does not carry eventually carry out much needed reforms. There is a further danger that Macron's European Federation project will splinter as divisions between the Center, Left and Right augment due to his lack of a coherent and decisive strategy. Europe does not need to become a "fortress" as feared by Americans in the 1980s.

That was before Trump "tweeted" his support for anti-immigrant national populists who foolishly splintered the UK from Europe. A more prosperous Europe will not be obtained by strengthening the sovereignty of individual nation as demanded by the Far Right, but by better coordinating policies of taxation, immigration and defense spending among states

> and regions and by engaging in measures of joint sovereignty…
>
> A weak Europe in which the European states find themselves further splintering into regional secessionist movements will only fall prey to many predators: The Eagles of Russia, Germany, and America. An increasingly assertive Chinese Red Dragon is already picking off Portugal, Greece, Slovakia, and Hungary on the European periphery. Lady Europa needs to link more closely together—or else be splintered like pulled pork.
>
> Two questions remain: Will the Yellow Vest movement be absorbed by the rise of Far-Right nationalist and anti-immigration movements throughout Europe? Or will it align with elements of the Far Left? And could these Right and Left opposition movements undermine both the EU and NATO? Or can the Europeanists build a more unified and democratic Europe by working with the Yellow Vests?

I must agree that France, my adopted country, had to help forge a stronger, more politically integrated Europa.[20] Yet Lady Europa has not yet seemed able to overcome her sense of humiliation and shame, her unease and anxiety, her nightmares of the Nazi and Fascist White Bull who raped her once again… in the struggle to build herself anew…

Notre Dame is Burning!!!

Those were only some of the differing protests and conflicts to strike France—in those years after I had begun to work for LaPlante at the HVF Foundation. Sometime later, in April 2019, I was in my apartment reading when the flames started glowing in the sky at twilight as I looked toward the Seine…

It was not the sight of the flames, but the dense stench that drew me to the window to see what was happening. And it was not long before the arrondissement was swarming with police cars, fire trucks and ambulances. Sparks from the cinders were flying all over and could set anything on fire. In the past, I had heard of several apartments and hotels that had caught on fire, due to faulty gas lines or splayed electrical wiring. This was perhaps the reason the city had begun the rebuild the buildings nearby—a renovation that had driven me crazy during the Horseshoe Bat crackdown.

ooo

I ran down the stairs and soon realized that the Notre Dame Cathedral was on fire. I knew that the structure of the Cathedral had already begun to deteriorate from pollution, rain, and the winds of time over a period of some 800 years. But no one was expecting this…

The 800-degree flames were 10 to 15 meters high. The stained-glass windows melted as the tower fell into a pit of embers. I could see the skeletal structure alit by beams of light that illuminated water pumps that were shooting water from the Seine. There were some 400 firefighters risking intoxication and death.

It was a millennium of history in flames… A treasure chest of art and religious icons… destroyed in a few minutes… It was not just French history and culture that had entered an unexpected holocaust… It was European civilization as a whole!!! Never could the Cathedral and its valuable treasures be rebuilt with the same meaning and way…

ooo

Soon, a thick grey smog hovered over the entire area, and the sky was alit by red sparks like the glowing eyes of giant insects blown up 10,000 times by magnifying glass, hideous faces that scowled, screeched, and then hissed hysterically… As the edifice glowed with the Dragon Chimera flames of red and orange and yellow with winged creatures of ash and flake hovering in mid-air. Even the stone towers were not invincible: Connected by lead lining that could melt in the high heat, they then spumed poisonous particles into the immediate vicinity.

Scowling, the arching backs of these ashen gargoyles the color of lead collided with radioactive *Gonggong* Dragons who had traveled from afar to spy like gas powered Zeppelins upon the historic scene… Victor Hugo's hunchback Quasimodo and the cracked Gargoyles and had failed to protect this crowning achievement…

ooo

I stared into the nothingness of a sky turning green and yellow in twilight and the Seine sparkling like firecrackers when suddenly the mobile phones startled me, ringing out of control. There was a stunned silence. Soon everyone began to SMS back and forth as rapidly as possible. Some people appeared to be weeping. It was not long before someone cried out in desperation, "Notre Dame is Burning."

At the time, the burning of Notre Dame seemed to cause a greater Yellow Press Media reaction than did the Charlie Hebdo assassinations or the November 2015 terror attacks against the Bataclan's heavy metal music scene and a real, and non-fabricated, slaughter of the innocents who were casually eating dinner in outside cafes.

How could I forget Dihya's grace and charm?

Yet now there seemed to be something different, something that seemed to stab the French directly in the heart, literally in the heart of Paris, Notre Dame, at ground zero—not far from the square that Jacque de Molay had been burned at the stake after his Knights of Malta militias had been called by Pope Clement to engage in yet another crusade…

ooo

I went back to my cubicle and turned on the news on my mini-TV. It turned out that President "Jupiter" Macaroon had annulled his speech that was intended to reconcile France after many weeks of yellow vest *gilets jaunes* protests. Instead of talking to stinging yellow jackets who had been protesting weekly, and who were demanding a significant number of reasonable democratic reforms, Jupiter called out, *Notre Dame was Burning!!!*

It was an unexpected and useful diversion!

ooo

That next week, the Foundation held an evening Happy Hour where we managed to talk to each other without looking at our mobile phones. Before I had gotten to know them, I had thought they were buddy-buddy. But the tones of their comments were not very friendly. Something more seemed wrong.

LaPlante opened the conversation: "The original Cathedral had been built upon a hallowed Gallo-Roman temple dedicated to Jupiter... Iconography shattered by Iconoclasts rebuilt by Iconographs! And now shattered again!"

"Truly, they were the two towers of most glorious church of the most glorious Virgin Mary, mother of God, shining like the sun among stars. Now utterly destroyed! Too bad!" scoffed Prophita, the business manager, sarcastically…

"At least it is not a total disaster. The statue of Mother Mary and Jesus were apparently untouched—even with the flames were burning right in front them!" interjected LaPlante.

"Yeah, no different than the miracle of Saint Denis when he walked with his severed head in his hands, blood dripping onto to his tunic, several miles outside of Paris to his abbey and basilica in what is now the Neuf Trois. All the time preaching a sermon on repentance!" once again joked the business associate…

"How could you say that… such sacrilege!!!… I mean I am not Catholic, but still… have some respect…" La Plante admonished…

"I heard a great jazz concert there, I mean in Saint Denis, by the musician… A-ma-heem Mon-wolf," interrupted the Human Rights lawyer. It was clear he wanted to bypass a possible argument by changing the topic.

"How can anyone believe these peasant tales! The Saint Denis story is no different than the shroud of Jesus that dates way past Christ's time! And then there's that grotesque vial of sticky orange blood in Bruges! How can anyone believe such bull lip!" exclaimed the business whizz—once again in a very provocative tone, "Those stories undermine the very religion they are trying to preach."

"Hush!" replied LaPlante, "The crown of thorns was saved! So too the True Cross and Holy Nail!"

LaPlante seemed to be genuinely upset, and perhaps unexpectedly revealing her religious side… even if she had not been brought up as a Catholic… It seemed to me that the general counter-culture movement and watering down of religious belief during the Cold War was causing a backlash against disbelief—even among Liberals, humanitarians, and existential followers of Sartre… At least that was one the themes of my PhD thesis that I would probably never finish… "All But Dissertation" (ABD)… I felt like one of those ancient scholars, a dotted forehead, trying to pass the challenging Imperial Chinese Civil Service exam that very few passed.

"Maybe the Cross and the Holy Grail survived somehow. But not all the gargoyles… In any case they were worthless as they did not protect anything at all!" The business associate paused… "The Islamicists must be rejoicing... There must have been Arabs among the workforce..."

"All religions, including Islam, will question why God would permit one of humanity's finest treasures to be annihilated!!!" asserted Aiden, the human rights man.

"Yeah, tell that to the Taliban who blew up the Buddhas of Bamiyan… And now the Islamicists eliminate the most precious symbol of the Catholic crusaders—Notre Dame…" exclaimed the business associate—even more upset, if not very angry.

Russell piped in, "The Taliban had complained that much needed money was going to maintain the Buddha statues, but not enough funding was permitted to support children who were hungry… Blowing up the Buddhas was an attack against the absurdly defined goals of western grants and development assistance. The issue was this: Why maintain idolatry that brings no benefits when the country is getting bombed anyway!"

LaPlante and Prophita appeared stunned, seeming to think, how could anyone say such a thing—and then seem to rationalize it? …

Suddenly Russell added, "I am not justifying it—but that is what the Taliban claimed. If we can't at least understand them, we will never stop them!"

"For me, it was like watching helpless as the twin towers collapsed in NYC. Yet watching Notre Dame melt was even worse... Unlike the WTC, there appears to be no one to blame... A freak accident!" explained LaPlante.

"Or so they say! You just don't see it. It was mass destruction aimed at the reconquest of France. The Catholic Church, France, and the whole Western world was the target... France is at war!!!" exclaimed Prophita.

ooo

I found the whole conversation spinning out of control. I finally piped in by citing Spinoza: "Those who wish to seek out the cause of miracles and to understand the things of nature as philosophers, and not to stare at them in bewilderment like fools, are soon considered heretical and impious, and proclaimed as such by those whom the mob adores as the interpreters of nature and the gods. For these men know that, once ignorance is put aside, that astonishment would be taken away, which is the only means by which their authority is preserved."

There was a heavy silence... LaPlante seemed to be cooling down and looked at me with a strange smile, as if it was not possible for a non-Westerner to cite a more or less obscure philosopher like Spinoza. The focus of the conservation suddenly changed...

"Now what are they going to do? How will they raise funds to fix it?" questioned the Human Rights expert.

"I heard that they would start a new campaign to raise money… Maybe LVIP, L'Orealis, Totaley Enarchgies and other companies will donate…" replied LaPlante.

"I doubt they will keep their promises," asserted the business associate, "even if the French billionaires raise the 100s of millions of Euros that they claim they will donate, a large percentage can be deducted from their taxes—so it is the French citizens who will really pay for the Notre Dame because there will be less funds for the French treasury…"

LaPlante replied, twisting her nose, with a strange look on her face: "It was just yesterday when we were talking about how the French would not charge people even a few Euros to visit the Cathedral and other churches and public monuments to pay for their upkeep... Now it was up to the wealthy French donors who seek tax breaks to foot the bill for Notre Dame's destruction. Outrageous!"

"Yeah, with more tourists visiting Notre Dame than the Eiffel Tower, you'd think they would charge at the door!" countered her business partner.

"Yeah, it seems the people will donate… Did you see how many were bowing and praying outside the Church? It was a moving ceremony with great emotion and spirituality. A real spirit of solidarity. The Evêché of Notre Dame called for church bells to ring throughout the country!" exclaimed Russell.

"Well, I'm not donating a red cent!" affirmed LaPlante.

There was a weird silence…

ooo

I posed the question, "It seems we have all been avoiding the main question, was it burned to the ground, accidentally? Or on purpose? All seems to be speculation."

"No one knows exactly what the government and the Church might know for sure as to how the fire started," responded Russell.

"They say a hunchback had been seen leaving the rooftop area an hour or so before the flames became manifest…" said LaPlante… trying to make a joke.

"That hunchback must have been a pyromaniac, and not a lover of the *bells… bells… bells…* like Quasimodo!" Russell replied, seemingly mimicking Poe's poem, laughing.

"Where's Esmeralda in your story? Where's the poet, Gringoire? No, this was not a Gypsy… ooops… a Romani plot—but an Islamicist one… The Moslems have not finished waging holy war after the Bataclan attacks… It's another serial killing…" exaggerated the business associate very seriously, if not in sheer rage.

"We can't be certain who did this. No proof yet!" interjected Russell. He then ventured back into the past, "It was not the first time the Cathedral confronted danger. During the French Revolution, Notre Dame was expropriated. The revolutionaries called it the *Maison de Raison* (House of Reason). In it was placed the Goddess of Reason."

"I wished the Church had always remained so reasonable… after all, look at what horrors are being uncovered about the behavior of priesthood pederasts! It is worse than the Festival of Fools of the Middle Ages," interjected Prophita. Once again, he was making a joke that did not seem so politically correct.

"The Church can't seem to investigate its own crimes. The situation is serious. Many innocent boys have been taken advantage of" asserted LaPlante.

"That's why the Festival of Fools should not be considered a joke. It rightly mimics the Catholic Church hierarchy. There is a reason why Quasimodo was chosen as the Pope of Fools!" replied her business associate…

The Human Rights expert replied, "In any case, it's not certain the sexual abuses of children by the Clergy are above the national average. That, of course, is no excuse for old patriarchal clerics in authority to take advantage of their position of power and influence!"

"You can say that so calmly because you are not one of the statistics!!!" asserted Prophita belligerently, repulsed by Russell's Zen attitude. "I mean, what was I supposed to do when the Priest told me that he and the Church were my salvation…"

ooo

It was a dark revelation… It was perhaps the first time Prophita had, more or less, admitted in public what had happened to him when he was mere teen, without stating the details… It was as if everything that had been discussed in LaPlante's Lecture Series was staring us in the face. You could see the anger boiling inside him… It helped explain his cynical attitude… How could anyone respect any authority—particularly religious authority—after experiencing what he had experienced along with all the guilt and shame that went along with it… And the deep feeling that he was somehow responsible—even if he was not at fault…

Out of the blue, Prophita cried out, now staring into the sky, and not at anyone in particular, "*Just go the hell!!!*"

ooo

LaPlante looked at her diamond studded Ricardo Mills watch and abruptly said she had to leave. As it was clear she did not want to deal with personal controversies, particularly among her staff, her departure appeared intended to prevent the conversation from exorcising any more demons lurking deep inside Prophita's haunted soul that could easily clash with the Zen master, Russell—whom I, by this time, considered to be a close friend—much like MKH.

Aiden appeared to be an honest man… unlike the others… even if his sophisticated and critical viewpoint never seemed very practical and was rarely accepted by anyone in a position of power… who often raised questions about the veracity and feasibility of his observations…

ooo

That week the Protesters call out:

Nous sommes aussi les Cathedrals !

On est aussi *les Miserables* !

We are also Cathedrals!

And also, *les Miserables*!

Daily Jackhammer

The jackhammer had finally stopped its daily pounding, every morning, every afternoon. The noise had blasted my eardrums for weeks when I was not permitted to leave my cubicle except for a brief hour period for shopping and exercises. I was being locked inside like a mental patient during the policed COVID 19 pandemic restrictions that came into effect in March 2020 in France. It was all blamed on the Horseshoe Bat—whether that creature was truly guilty of spreading the virus or not!

The pounding began at 08:30, but only after the pickup truck had already jolted me awake at 04:00 each morning—making it impossible to return to sleep. It was not legal to begin work at that time, so early, but that didn't stop the Construction Co. and its crew, who were mainly from eastern Europe, from working…

Judging by the sound of the language, my guess was that many of the workers came from Poland—whose Solidarity movement overthrew the Polish Communist Party way back in 1989. That action led to the downfall of Communist Parties throughout Eastern Europe—and eventually to the collapse of Soviet Communist Party itself by 1991. Not so ironically, it was the very success of the Solidarity movement that had led Deng "little bottle" Xiaoping to repress our Democracy and Freedom movement.

Deng had justified the June 4, 1989, crackdown on our movement—that was seen by him as being backed by the Balding Eagle, the Taiwanese Black Bear and Lady Europa. He hoped to prevent the eventual overthrow the Red Dragon's Communist Party—just as the Solidarity movement had overthrown the Polish Communist Party, or so Deng claimed at the time…

After 1989, these eastern European workers were free from Communist controls and soon free to travel and work abroad… while the Chinese remained in chains…

ooo

The entrails of the massive former apartment building next door were being ripped apart and gutted. A new structure, three new floors, was being added. The pounding never stopped. My tiny apartment shook with the infernal heavy metal intensity of a Psyops campaign from 08:30 in the morning to 17:30 in the afternoon—with an hour break for the workers' lunch.

The slosh of smoky white debris repeatedly ran down the slide like children screaming and shouting at the water park. All the scraps, the dry wall, the wooden frames, the doors, and what looked like fuzzy grey lung-like fibers of asbestos, were being dumped into the great green bin on the side of the building—and just below my cubby hole. That was also the place where the rest of the neighborhood of apartments, office buildings and high rises, secretly dumped their larger pieces of junk into the bin, such as baby carriages and toilet bowls and stained mattresses in the middle of the night—whatever they wanted hauled away at someone else's expense.

Sailing through my open window, the white chalk dust drew cryptic logograms onto my unpolished stone floor. Whatever that dust was attempting to communicate to the human world was neither explicable in English nor Chinese. A computerized Rosetta stone with new advances in AI would need to be invented to figure out the meaning of these intricate designs—if there was any meaning at all to be discovered. As I would later joke: 'That would be quite a job for the Society for the Exploration of Cosmic Consciousness (SECC)'…

ooo

I could not bear the stress. With my sleep constantly disturbed, my recurrent nightmares became more and more vivid, more and more terrifying… *I burst awake into consciousness after believing I was immersed in a toilet bowl whirlpool of sardine-like fish with red eyes and human faces… drowning… A surgeon was approaching my crotch with a scalpel in hand…*

ooo

It was in March 2020 that the French leadership had first announced that all schools and universities across the country would be closed. Then it was announced that all pubs, restaurants, cinemas, and nightclubs would likewise be closed. One day after the first round of the municipal elections, French President "Jupiter" announced the beginning of a lockdown period from 17 March. The parks, swing sets and exercise machines were all fenced off. And even Marie "Madame Deficit" Antoinette's *Temple de l' Amour* was suddenly abandoned by its weekend lovers sneaking kisses.

The Horseshoe Bat restrictions kept me inside all day, except for a brief hour, when I could leave for exercise and other necessities. Each day, I had to fill out, and sign, an *Attestation de Deplacement Derogatoire*. That form had to be printed out and dated with the exact time I left my "home" if one could call it that. I then had to list my address and my reasons for going outside checked in neat boxes.

Can you believe it? Everyone had to explain their motives for leaving their home or apartment, sign and date, day and hour…[21] And if you had no access to a printer, you had to write it out… I had never expected anything like this in a democratic country...

It was just the beginning of the Year of the Horseshoe Bat.

ooo

During the lockdown, Horseshoe Bat restrictions meant that I was only permitted an hour of freedom per day outside my home address. It was unbearable. Most of the day there was nothing to do but roam in circles like a rabid monkey in a tiger cage. Or else swim in circles like goldfish with parasites in a bowl of fungus perfect for cleaning feet. I needed my freedom!

To breathe, to get out of my stuffy cubicle for as long as possible, I had to constantly hide from the police, sneak around corners and into the shadows of back streets. Fortunately, I had an official letter from my boss stating that I was working for her... I could always claim that I was on the way to work... that is, if I did not stray too far from her *péniche* on the Seine...

In sheer loneliness, I even thought of turning myself in and returning to China—even if that meant certain imprisonment, if not worse. It is dubious that Chinese authorities would give me a break unless I became a Black Rat, and turned in others, or in some way admitted guilt...even if I wasn't guilty of anything... There was no way I could return... *It seemed every time I dreamed of my homeland; I had a nightmare of a surgeon holding a knife next to my crotch....*

Then again, it was clear that the fate of many of my fellow country men and women in China was much worse than my fate in France. They were literally locked inside their even more cramped apartments, screaming—with some reported to have jumped from the windows to the concrete below. That was, until thousands and thousands of the average Chinese in the major cities started to riot.

ooo

Each time I felt dizzy, I went into the pharmacy for my free Horseshoe Bat infection test, paid for by the benevolence of French Social Security. Yet those who did the actual testing for the Horseshoe Bat virus, those working for the pharmacy, or those who were often nurses in training, were definitely not so kind and benevolent. They often twirled the cotton swab like a feathered top into my nose, drilling down and down, until I bled, almost blocking my breath. I could not tell if they were just bored, angry, frustrated—or really sadistic!

There were many rumors of people suffering negative reactions… but no proof, no statistics… Those who opposed the vaccines worried that the testing for potential side effects was not a long enough period. And even if Big Pharma vaccinations seemed to work for most people, there were still not-so-Social Media stories of heart failure, illness, fainting. Not all were "fake news" … One of the women in my dorm for artists and intellectuals was sick for weeks after the first shot. Another was sick until near death twice, after taking all three shots plus two boosters. The fruit vendor down the street had taken all three shots and died suddenly just after the third. And I fainted after the third shot.

Without long term testing, the leaderships of all countries were putting their populations at risk… and particularly the children… for the $$$stakes$$$ were huge…. And instead of bringing all the countries into cooperation to fight the pandemic—as should have happened—the response and actions of almost all the governments resulted in the opposite: The countries and their Pharma Companies (big and small) entered into a nasty rivalry.

It was Sinovac/Sinopharm vs Sputnik vs Pfizer-BioNTech vs Moderna vs Novavax vs J&J/Janssen vs Cuban Abdala, and some others that never made the grade. In essence it was a battle between Messenger RNA that gives your cells instructions about how to deal with Covid-19 versus the non-Messenger.

The question was: Could you trust "the Messenger"? Was this new messenger a herald of the gods like Hermes/Mercury that could save humanity from the new pest? Could it provide the survival link between the mortal world and that of the "divine"? Or was it a mercantile trickster and a pickpocket always running away after he used and abused you—with his winged staff of two snakes copulating?

ooo

In the meantime, the developing countries complained about the costs of the Big Pharma vaccines and the latter's refusal to permit reproduction of the vaccine by waiving intellectual property rights—even if much of the research of Big Pharma itself was funded by U.S., European and other government and university sources. Countries like South Africa claimed that they were charged more than most western countries.

With the body bags piling up, and ambulances overloading the hospitals, hospital workers protested in frustration and in despair for lack of beds, equipment, facilities, and vaccines. In some cases, Italian, Spanish and French doctors were using specially adjusted full-faced plastic toy snorkeling masks to protect themselves.

That was truly Chinese-like innovation by necessity!

ooo

While the unsuspecting victims of the Horseshoe Bat virus suffered, and while the first defenders against the virus made do with what little resources they possessed to battle the disease, the wealth of the world's 10 richest men concurrently skyrocketed as did many of the incomes of many billionaires and most of the top 20 percent. At the same time, the working incomes and life expectancy rates of most of the planet plummeted.[22]

Even if they did not become ill, many students of all levels lost more than a year of valuable training that could impact their future education and careers. That could eventually mean more bitterness, more frustration, more anger, more infernal chaos, more acute suffering, more grinding poverty, more indiscriminate acts of terror…

Accompanied by massive public and personal debts, the Year of the Horseshoe Bat meant even greater economic, gender, and racial inequalities within countries and even greater inequalities of wealth and power between countries—inequities to be exacerbated by means of using AI by those same Superrich and All Powerful. And in the coming chaos, effective and foresighted diplomacy would prove even more difficult to achieve—even if it could possibly be envisioned by a few foresighted politicians—as if Platonic philosopher kings and wanna-be Chinese Kong Fuzi (Confucius) public intellectuals actually existed!

The Messenger

I would often go jogging along *le quai de la Mégisserie* toward *la Dame de Fer.* It is there I saw, in the early morning, the *bouquinistes* opening their green treasure chests of souvenirs, classic second-hand books, copies of etchings, and mass-produced hippie-era posters of rock stars. The *bouquinistes* were a relic of French society that would probably soon disappear… Somewhere amid these meaningless tourist items, there were probably some real treasures hidden away in those often-rotting green wooden boxes—artwork and classic books that I was beginning to be able to read in French. It would take me hours to search for those… And I had little money…

ooo

I would jog past Zadkine's epic sculpture of the "Messenger" on the corner of the *Pont des Invalides* and the *Quai d'Orsay*, past the sunrise and sunset glowing domes of the Russian Orthodox Church amid secular Paris on one side of the Seine. I would then turn and run back on the Seine's other side through the *Jardin d' Erevan* and past the statue of Reverend Komitas dedicated to the mass killings of the Armenians on the other side. I could only think how many other people in history had suffered such horrors?

I liked to believe that I was a "messenger" (but not like Hermes/ Mercury) for the multitudes of Chinese who had suffered over the millennium—but who had no statues in remembrance to that suffering… no memorials to their lost souls… Those individuals and peoples who disappeared without a trace…

I vowed I would write my own form of memorial—a history of what really happened in 1989, in the Year of the Earth Serpent—even in knowledge that there was little hope for obtaining a national Chinese readership in the future… forever banned…

ooo

But in stopping there, closer to the Champs-Elysées and looking toward the *Place de la Concorde*, I also wanted to see no such memorial like that *Bouquet of Tulips*. It was something I absolutely loathed—a giant plastic fantastic sculpture depicting a handful of bright, artificially-colored Tulips that had been insincerely planted in the park by benevolent donors for a truly obscene commemorative in the name of those massacred in the terror attacks of 2015. It was an act of (un)worthy artistic $$$speculation$$$ intended to raise the value of the artist's already excessively expensive and overrated artwork for dreamy-eyed know-nothing tourists to worship....

ooo

Just up the street from my apartment was *La Conciergerie*. It was the center of power when the Concierge was appointed by the King to maintain order. At that time, it was *La Conciergerie* who directed the police and that registered and controlled the prisoners. The building itself was where the Palace Parliament, the highest judicial body of the kingdom, ruled over the people in the name of the Monarch. With the advent of the French Revolution, however, the building was transformed from a symbol of the power and influence of the King and the Palace Parliament into a display of the French Revolution's ability to exert absolute penitentiary controls. It was in *La Conciergerie* where Marie-Antoinette, Robespierre and Danton were all imprisoned.

ooo

I could only reflect on the irony of the term *Conciergerie*. It was the Concierge who takes care of all the comings and goings of the inhabitants of an apartment complex in France. And in China—there is also the red-faced version of a Concierge—the Black Rat who overlooks everything. It is the Concierge who will report to the Chinese Media and Mind Control Bureau—if he or she or it sees or hears something suspicious. Then again, I wondered if Concierges were not the same in France as they were in China and elsewhere.

ooo

As the Chinese people were being blamed for spreading the Horseshoe Bat / "Kung Flu" pandemic throughout the world, with the heavy howling of ambulance sirens of utter prejudice and hysteria, I was doubly paranoid that I could be denounced as being a carrier of the virus... And then my real identity could be exposed… I heard stories about Chinese and other Asians who had been beat up for no apparent reason. Nothing like that happened to me; nevertheless, I felt the icy stares upon my shoulders following me as I jogged down the street—as if warning me that I better get out of there. And sometimes, I felt as if I was being followed…

ooo

It was here, amid this open square, where the historical crisis of France begins—way back to the aged lady killer, the "Vert-Galant" (the Green Galant), King Philippe le Bel. Envious that the Knights of the Templar had hidden a colossal fortune that they would not share with him, it was Philippe le Bel who had ordered the Grand Master of the Knights of the Templar, the Crusader militia leader, Jacques de Molay, to be burned at the stake in this very place, on the *Île aux Juifs*—the very place where Jews were once executed in the Middle Ages. Later to be called the *Île des Templiers.*

It was de Molay, accused of heresy, sodomy, and other deviant behavior, who had sought to protect the Christians of Cyprus and Armenia against the Egyptian Mamluks and who still believed that the reconquest of Jerusalem was possible. And now, I must add, it seems the Holy Wars have still not ended—and a new Crusade had begun after the attacks on NYC and the Pentagon on September 11, 2001!

ooo

I am telling you this as I felt much the same anger and rage as did Jacques de Molay when he cursed the French crown and demanded that his executioner to turn his body to face eastward toward the towers of Notre Dame.[23] False accusations of heresy and "obscene" practices were also made against me—allegations that could have led to my imprisonment, if not my execution.

At times, I can hardly contain my anger as the Communist Party had killed or executed many of my friends and colleagues who had peacefully protested on that fatal day, June 4, 1989. None of us had committed any crimes! We wanted reforms, not revolution! And we never advocated violence—even though some provocateurs may have done so during the Tiananmen Square protests. I was not Malraux's character, Chen Ta Erh in *Man's Fate*—who became an assassin and terrorist. We did not organize militias or guerrilla fighters!

After all these years, the Chinese leadership still pretends that the world's condemnation of the Tiananmen Square atrocity does not faze them. Yet if that were so, then why must they try to ban any reference to "6/4" or "8964"? Why must they lie about what really happened that day, June 4, 1989? Why can't they simply give amnesty to those who have been jailed or banned from returning to China?

ooo

Just a jog up from the *Île aux Juifs / Île des Templiers* is the infamous Place de la Concorde, originally named Place Louis XV. That is where a large equestrian statue of the King Louis XV had once been placed at the center, much like that of Henry IV on *Place des Vosges*… After the storming of the Bastille in 1789, the statue of Louis XV was torn apart, and the "Great National Razor" was hoisted in its place on the square renamed, *Place de la Revolution.*

That is where the head of Louis "Monsieur Veto" XVI rolled into a bucket in front of a boisterous crowd in January 1793. Nine months later, Marie Antoinette Josèphe Jeanne de Hapsburg-Lorraine met the same fate. She was called "*l'autrichienne*" meaning, Austrian woman, but implying in intonation, "Austrian bitch," or even, "ostrich bitch". Sometimes she was called Madame Deficit. It was not long after those executions that the French Revolutionaries declared war on her family's "eastern realm"—along with thousands of others who were also guillotined on the *Place de la Revolution*—the advent of one of many Armageddons that did not quite put an end to all of humanity… but certainly helped to reduce the size of the population…

ooo

There were many other unfortunate souls who were executed as the result of whatever allegation or actual crime, by the Sanson father and son team. The father, who had executed Louis, slipped off the scaffold while displaying a bloody head to the crowd and died. The good son then took over the hereditary job, executing Marie.[24] What an honor!

That's just a bit of the gory detail… Yet the real question is this: whose revolution was bloodier and gorier? The French? Or the more recent Chinese? Was it the French revolution where about 30 heads rolled each day—so that between 15,000 and 17,000 were executed by the "great national razor" during the Reign of Terror?[25] Or was it the Red Dragon's Cultural Revolution where millions were said to be killed, directly or indirectly?[26]

ooo

As I studied French history, I realized a better analogy to the Tiananmen Square massacre in June 1989 with respect to French history was the massacre of the Protestant/ Calvinist Huguenots in Paris and throughout the country.[27]

Then again, perhaps an even better analogy is to the Paris Commune. The French Communards had stood up in revolt against both the six-month war with Prussia that had been initiated by Napoleon "Battle of Sedan" the III's bungling diplomacy (in part influenced by his wife, Eugenia) that fell into Bismarck's trap and that resulted in France's swift defeat and punishment: Paris was forced to hand over billions of Francs to Berlin…

It was an insurrection two months long, from March to May 1871… The people of Paris were starving, eating cats, dogs, rats… even animals of the zoo… More than 43,000 Parisians were arrested and held in camps before being released… More than 7,000 were deported… At least 10,000 to 20,000 people were killed in that bloody week (*la semaine sanglot*) … The repression of the Communards—the "time of cherry picking" (*le Temps des Cerises*) by the Thiers government of the Gallic Cock—was swift and cruel…

The number massacred in France then was perhaps close to the numbers killed in Beijing and in the cities throughout China in June 1989 … but who knows the real statistics??? … On June 4, 1989, Beijing had its own the "Wall of the Communards" *(Mur des Fédérés)* … where many were executed. Like us in the Beijing Spring, the French Communards had fought for a more direct democracy…

ooo

Additional parallels were even more disconcerting: The effort of the French to repress democratic Socialist and Anarchist ideologies that had fostered the Commune and to seek revenge on Prussia/Germany for annexing Alsace-Lorraine, helped fuel a social and political pressure cooker that would explode decades later into the 'Armageddon to End all Armageddons' in August-September 1914.

In the view of Paris then: It was "Alsace-Lorraine… say it never… think of it always" … *Revanche!*

ooo

Today there is a similar danger: The ultimate direct and indirect social and political consequences of the June 1989 Tiananmen Square repression could soon (de)generate into demands of the Chinese Red Dragon to force its unification with the Taiwanese Black Bear for the greater "good" of Chinese Spiritual Civilization…

Much like French revanchists had wanted to retake Alsace Lorraine before World War I—and much like the Russian Double-Headed Eagle eyed the Crimean Dolphin after Soviet collapse in 1991 and then seized it from its Ukrainian cousin in 2014—the Red Dragon has likewise continued to claim the Taiwanese Black Bear ever since the Samurai of Japanese *Shuten-douji* had seized the island from the Yellow Dragon in 1895. And now the Red Dragon wants the American Balding Eagle to give up its hegemony over the isle—after the troops of the Kuomintang leader, Chiang Kai-chek, had taken Taiwan in retreating from the battle with Mao's Communists.

In the view of Beijing now: It's "Taiwan… say it a lot… demand it always" … *Revanche!*

Tear Smoke!!!

Tonight, the sun is clouded with the scourge of poisonous Red-Brown-Black clouds.

Once again hundreds of thousands march down the streets. The police charge, teargas cannisters plummet from the skies. The crowd scatters with no way to go but backwards. We block entrances and exits to major pro-government businesses as well as to the offices of the major finance companies and banks—to protest the omnipresent mass surveillance state that is seeking to take control of our lives.

Young activists, faces and noses hidden deep in black scarves, rush forward firing stones from sling shots. Archers shoot flaming arrows against the police who fire tear gas, rubber bullets and pepper spray. Other militants set bottle after bottle of gas-fueled Molotov cocktails aflame and toss them against the police who squeeze the crowd like a vice from all sides. The water cannon knocks to the ground a few daring men who believe they can withstand its blunt force. Helicopters hover above, belching forth blustering winds that intimidate the crowd. The police and military take thousands of pictures of the masked protestors with burning eyes who try not to trample those who have tripped and fallen beneath the raging crowd.

In a policy of violent harassment, police are conducting indiscriminate stop-and-search procedures on everyday shoppers, passersby, and journalists. Many of us, young and old, have been beaten, then arrested. If I am arrested, the Authorities will send me back to the mainland…

WARNING: "TEAR SMOKE"!!!

ooo

This was Hong Kong—not Paris—and not the non-violent protests that took place in Beijing and throughout China in 1989 that I had once participated in. As soon as I could, I had flown from Paris to Hong Kong to stand with the movement. The HVF Foundation had funded my voyage so that I could see what was really happening… My new French passport sailed through customs with flying colors. Nevertheless, I could not, and did not, tell anyone my true identity.

It took decades, but the white sculpture of the Goddess of Tiananmen was finally resurrected. With the birth of the Umbrella movement, hundreds of thousands of people, if not millions throughout the world, arose against both Hong Kong and Beijing authorities in the struggle for direct elections and multiparty democracy.[28]

As was the case in the Beijing Spring of April-June 1989, Hong Kong protesters did not see themselves as foreign agents acting in the interests of Uncle Sam. Nor did they see themselves as acting for rich Taiwanese *Tuhao*. Instead, they were protesting in their own interests for open government, for rule of law, for freedom of press, for freedom of religion, for human dignity, for greater autonomy and free elections of their governing representatives—and for an end to corruption and mass surveillance. Having tasted the possibility of freedom under the City's rule, many in Hong Kong refused to wait patiently for the Chinese New Authoritarian promises of an "evolution" toward democracy to take place sometime in the undefined distant future.

How could anyone trust such New Authoritarian promises after the Red Dragon had begun to pressure Hong

Kong journalists, bookstore owners, and writers who were critical of the Chinese regime? How could anyone trust Beijing after it had arrested just enough protestors, and put a few loud mouths on show trial, while promising the poor cheaper housing—all in the effort to absorb the isthmus like a giant sponge... with the Bank of China overlording all?

In its interpretation of the 2019 Chinese Zodiac, the Year of the Earth Pig, Beijing convinced itself that the people of Hong Kong were getting fatter and more docile—and hence less likely to resist the Red Dragon for very long. Taking Hong Kong was seen as the steppingstone to smothering the Taiwanese Black Bear—by sanctions, economic containment and blockade—or by force if deemed necessary.[29]

Much as I had predicted, Beijing had passed its Anti-Secession Law in 2006 that was primarily aimed at blocking Taiwan's claims to independence—but that implicitly included Hong Kong. The People's Congress later rubber stamped a new National Security Law on June 30, 2020 that banned all "seditious" activities and foreign interference in Hong Kong.[30] China's Fearless Leadership warned, "Anyone who attempts to split any region from China will perish, with their bodies smashed and bones ground to powder."

Beijing was backing off on its promises to sustain a "one country two systems" model of government. Reform was no longer possible. The Red Dragon had decided to take the risk of breaking political, social, and financial ties with the Balding Eagle and Lady Europa. If the Europeans and Americans protested, so what? Russia and other states, in Eurasia, the wider Middle East, Africa, Latin America and much of Asia would not give a damn about its decision to crack down even more severely on Hong Kong....

The not-always-fragrant City was the last line of defense before the battle for Taiwan…

ooo

At Victoria Park, Causeway Bay—normally a fun spot for tennis, football, basketball, handball, volleyball, swimming, jogging, fitness, roller skating, and bowling—hundreds of thousands of people masked themselves against the Horseshoe Bat pandemic and to protect their identities from mass surveillance cameras and Bei Dou space satellites. Covering their faces, they peacefully protested China's refusal to accept universal suffrage for the wind-blown City once controlled by the British Crown.

The fact that many of the demonstrators were willing to risk their livelihoods—and even their lives—should have made it quite clear to the Chinese leadership that they could not hold down popular demands for "Democracy" and "Freedom" forever. And there was no need to adopt American or European "values"—for these demands were part of China's own values and civilization.

We stand by the white Lady Liberty with her helmet, gas mask, goggles and upon Lion Rock. In no way should Hong Kong send those arrested for opposing Beijing's takeover of the isle back to the Chinese Mainland for trial!!!

I vowed I would stay in that windy city for as long as I could…

ooo

In 2019, MKH had written a new editorial published on the UPSTART website just a few weeks before the 70th anniversary celebration of Mao's victory speech on October 1st. Hayford evoked the past to reveal the nature of struggle then taking place in Hong Kong:

Flashback to the Beijing Spring 1989
by Mark King Hayford (www.MKHayford.com)
September 15, 2019

In calling for "power to the people" in the words of the ex-Beatle John Lennon, Hong Kong protestors have written poems, lyrics, epigrams, and graphic designs on post-its and on *Dà Zì Bào* (Big Character Posters).

These *Dà Zì Bào* began to rise spontaneously throughout the windy city of Hong Kong in 2019 after the "umbrella movement" had constructed a "Lennon Wall" in 2014—inspired by the original "Lennon Wall" in Prague constructed after his assassination in 1980.[31]

The pro-Beijing Hong Kong leadership has claimed that the nature of the conflict transformed significantly in late July 2019 after protesters splashed black paint and pelted eggs on the golden-starred red emblem of the Chinese government's Liaison Office in Hong Kong. Using the excuse that the protesters had been challenging the "one country, two systems" principle, Beijing appears ready to act. With some 12,000 police officers, tanks, helicopters, and amphibious vehicles practicing intervention maneuvers deployed in neighboring Shenzhen since August 2019, Beijing Authorities made the overt threat to deploy the People's Liberation Army on the streets of Hong Kong—much as they did on June 4, 1989, on Tiananmen Square.

In seeking to break up the protests, the Communist leadership has been paying White Shirt Triads to beat pro-democracy Hong Kong protestors with sticks and rods. This appears reminiscent of Nationalist Kuomintang leader Chiang Kai-shek when he hired drug-dealing Green Gang Triads to severely repress the Communists and workers in Shanghai and elsewhere in April 1927. Concurrently, pro-government militants threatened to "clean up" some 77 Lennon Walls so they could celebrate the 70th anniversary of the Motherland on October 1st in "peace."

For their part, some pro-Democracy and Freedom demonstrators trampled and burned the People's Republic flag in a major protest at the

Hong Kong airport—that is symbolic of Hong Kong's influential role in globalization. The Hong Kong government then became even much tougher. After all, it was October 1st 2019—the 70th anniversary of the People's Republic. Masked police—some of whom could have been working for Beijing—were ordered to arrest journalists, demonstrators, and the leaders of the protests. Hong Kong authorities also began to threaten the families of those known to be protesting.

The protesters have called for both Chinese and Hong Kong authorities to immediately stop using the term "riots" to describe their movement. Such insulting language had also been used by Beijing in 1989 in comparing the peaceful student-led nation-wide Democracy movement to the Cultural Revolution. Hong Kong *Dà Zì Bào* posters proclaim: "There's no rioters; there's only tyranny."

Prior to the June 4, 1989 nationwide crackdown, Zhao Ziyang, General Secretary of the Communist Party, had considered the option of engaging in discussions with the student leadership. Yet dialogue was the precisely the path eradicated by Chinese leader, Deng Xiao Ping and his Minister, Li Peng.

So too today—the Hong Kong leadership could enter a dialogue with the Umbrella Movement—that is, only if that Leadership will eventually agree to the Five Demands. [32]

ooo

Unfortunately, Hayford was overly optimistic. The Hong Kong leadership, under orders from Beijing, was not willing to compromise. Police began a severe crackdown.

Hands raised, fingers outstretched in a three-fingered salute, it was a struggle for future generations… for democracy, for true autonomy, for freedom of speech and protest, for human rights, for local culture, for protecting Cantonese culture and language, for being able to say what you want freely and responsibly without any negative consequences….

Mimicking the words of the Bee Gees… a singer protested… "*by accepting CCP rule… the Brits… started a joke… which started the whole world crying…*"

It was too much… The protesters, protected by umbrellas the colors of a rainbow, screaming in tears beneath the threat of thundering red-brown-black clouds, cried out,

"Please help us against the CCP!
Today it is us, but maybe tomorrow,
it is you! Stand with Hong Kong!"

We all sang "Glory to Hong Kong" and then marched to the beat of the drums—now that the Fearless Leadership had made it a crime to mock the Chinese national anthem.

"Our tears rain upon our land,
don't you feel the rage in our cries?
Our voices urge you to rise
So freedom shall shine upon us all!"

ooo

I returned to Paris a few days just after the French Horseshoe Bat lockdown in March 2020. It was a strange atmosphere in Paris. With everyone wearing masks, it seemed everyone was suspicious of everyone else. But I guess because I was on a "business trip" for the Foundation, I had no problem re-entering the country.

ooo

A few months later, on the Chinese mainland, demonstrations against Beijing's much stricter Horseshoe Bat crackdown that started in Wuhan in January 2020, and that spread to fifteen other cities, began to escalate. An incredible total of 57 million people soon found themselves literally jailed in their own tiny and cramped apartments! Nothing of this magnitude had happened in Europe or the Land of the Free!

All public transport, including buses, railways, flights, and ferry services had been suspended until further notice! No one was allowed out on Chinese New Year. In some cities, only one person from each household was permitted to go outside for provisions once every two days—except for medical reasons or to work at shops or pharmacies. With the Chinese stock market crashing, the people feared not being able to obtain food and medicine.

The lockdown seemed purposely designed for humans to obtain the same diseases that animals obtain when they are locked in cages! Beijing nevertheless claimed they had supposedly saved between 18,000 and 70,000 people. Yet by December 2020, Chinese authorities just as suddenly lifted most of the restrictions as swiftly as they had imposed them… It took a while, but they realized the lockdown was a dangerous failure that was provoking the masses to riot…

One can question whether the lockdown was really for health reasons or really to repress the possibility of widespread protest as "Winnie" began to centralize his power… Once the Red Dragon starts something it generally goes all the way—but in a clumsy and heavy-handed fashion. And it rarely apologizes for the destruction it causes…

And even though the Fearless Leadership had banned demonstrations due to the Horseshoe Bat outbreak and warned pro-democracy militants not to participate, thousands still came to the June 4, 2020 demonstration on anniversary of the Tiananmen Square repression… Yet not enough to make any major dent in the Red Beast's determination to sustain power…

Voyage to America

It was with a mix of excitement and trepidation that I crossed the Atlantic in June 2020 to step foot for the first time upon the territory of the Land Free and watch my maroon French passport be stamped with a Red, White, and Blue customs stamp—but that turned out to be dull Grey.

I cannot say my flight in a fully packed passenger jet in crowded seats, squished next to a huge sweaty mastodon, who coughed and sneezed constantly, and who could barely fit between the arm rests, was very comfortable. I did not sleep for a moment. I had heard one story where the blubber of a massively overweight man, to be politically correct, had unintentionally suffocated the old lady sitting next to him. I did not think it was possible that it could happen to me... Nevertheless… I forced myself to remain awake…

In the morning upon arrival, the TV screen flicked on: *Attention!!!* What was it??? The Benevolent Big Brother of Homeland Security was speaking to all passengers as we landed at Dulles International Airport!!!

ooo

The name Dulles had been long engraved upon the Chinese Communist Party's political conscience. It was Dulles who envisioned the "containment" policy that most impacted my upbringing and that of my contemporaries, and that had turned Red Dragon and Balding Eagle into bitter rivals. His speech "The Threat of a Red Asia" way back in March 1954, set the stage for the *Dìyù* or warfighting inferno to come: "Under the conditions of today, the imposition on Southeast Asia of the political system of Communist Russia and its Chinese Communist ally, by whatever means, would be a grave threat to the whole free community…."

And now fears of a Sino-Russian alliance were reviving…

ooo

It was John "Containment" Foster Dulles, who had closely linked the Boys of the Company (CIA) and the State Department together, before the 2001 PATRIOT Act had linked all the defense and intelligence agencies even more closely together.

As the first major step toward strengthening indiscriminate mass surveillance, the PATRIOT Act was passed by a vast majority of Congress who had neither the time, nor the intention, to read the entire lengthy document in fine print that, in effect, represented an accumulation of security complaints that had appeared to have originated, at least in part, but not entirely, from the separation of fiefdoms of the Boys of the Company (CIA) and J. Edgar's Bureau (FBI).[33]

And as it was labelled with the contrived anacronym 'PATRIOT,' there was absolutely no way Congress could oppose such all-encompassing legislation that vastly expanded American spying capabilities.[34] Almost all Elected Officials pledged allegiance to the flag and voted (99 to 1 in the Senate and 357 to 66 in the House) in favor of what was a truly rubber stamp exercise in democracy and rule of law—exactly like the Chinese parliament!

Although the Americans gave it no thought whatsoever, the whole PATRIOT Act exercise was a godsend for totalitarian Beijing—who saw the Balding Eagle becoming more and more like the Red Dragon itself!!! If Balding Eagle could spy on its own citizens and the world, so could Beijing! *Same! Same! But different!!!!*

ooo

And as Aiden had explained to me, it would be at the advent of the Vietnam War in the 1960s—when Hanoi was seen as being backed by an Alliance of the Red Bear and Red Dragon—that the Balding Eagle would establish an "innovation ecosystem" called DARPA (Defense Advanced Research Projects Agency). This Agency would help coordinate academic, corporate, governmental partners to work with the Pentagon to bring the world such scientific advances as precision weapons and stealth technology.

DARPA helped develop the Internet, automated voice recognition and language translation, plus miniature Global Positioning System receivers so tiny that they could be embedded in myriad consumer devices in a perfect system of mass surveillance! And most crucially for the future of human-machine relationship, DARPA planted the roots of "engineering alchemy"—for the creation of AI…

President "D-Day" Eisenhower at least initially wanted to call it all the "military-industrial-congressional-university complex"—which is what it was—but the moniker was then shortened to "Military Industrial Complex" so to avoid its totalitarian implications.

ooo

As I walked out of the plane, I saw something bizarre. On the walkway, jacked up above the ground, there were at least a dozen wheelchairs. It was a large plane, but I could not believe there would be so many wounded warriors traveling with me, those who fought in America's many post-Cold War blank check forever wars…

Those were the wars for which "Silver Spoon 2" obtained a blank check from both the Vultures of the U.S. Congress and from the UN Security Council in the effort to fight against "terror"—as if it were possible to eradicate such a volatile emotion. That was after the September 11, 2001 attacks on the World Trade Center and the Pentagon—and whatever was target of the fourth plane: the White House, the Three Mile Island nuclear plant, or the Fort Detrick U.S. Army Futures Command installation that houses the U.S. Bio-Chem defense programs, or most likely the Capitol. No one seems to know for sure…

ooo

I could not believe that there were so many wounded warriors on the plane that could have been injured by what the Pentagon called "improvised exploding devices" (IEDs) on battle fields in Afghanistan, Iraq, Libya, Syria, or elsewhere and that needed wheelchairs… Those were the brave soldiers who did not come home wrapped in a Red, White, and Blue box, but who were proving much more costly and embarrassing for administration after administration.

In the name of the PATRIOT Act, the "Chickenhawks" of the American leadership had transformed these youthful "Ken's" and "Barbie's" into "G.I. Joes" and squandered much of the country's resources and $$$trillions$$$ on wars that bloated the coffers of arms industries and that were not strategically necessary, that were destructive, and much like the Vietnam war, impossible to "win" in any traditional sense… All absolutely futile wars in which no real diplomatic efforts were expended to prevent…

I could envision the agony of these brave souls who may have lost their eyes or hands or feet of faces in wars that now have no meaning… I envisioned the absurd battlefields of Celine's *Journey to the End of Night … the Soldiers fighting for free, the heroes of everyone, mere monkeys that chatter words that suffer, mere minions of King Misery!*[35] I saw the masks of Albert Dupontel's film *Au Revoir Là-haut* that covered the horrific smashed faces, the *gueules cassées*, of the French *poilu,* the bearded ones, who had fought in the trenches of the 'Armageddon to end all Armageddons'… And I know I saw those, in the post-September 11, 2001 era, who had been transmuted into helmeted Kevlar Space Invaders aiming drones in global video wars in fighting for the Balding Eagle …

These Innocents Abroad—who had once believed in GWOT, in the "global war against terrorism"—soon began to see themselves as manipulated and as risking their lives in meaningless wars without end in sight… Then again, as long as G.I. Joe's, volunteers, mercenaries and proxies do the actual war fighting—and not the average Ken's and some Barbie's—no one seemed to care…

ooo

I waited a distance away from the plane's exit doors to see these wounded warriors… even if that meant I would have to wait in a longer line to pass through customs… One after another came out of the aircraft, individuals pushed on wheelchairs by young men and women who looked like airport personnel.

To my astonishment, all except one was perfectly intact, their eyes, arms, legs, faces all appeared without injury.... The one injured had become a bionic man with a high-tech artificial leg and prosthetic hand… His mouth hung open as if in a permanent daze perhaps caused by a roadside blast… One of his eyes stared straight without moving… I could see his scarred face heaving and sneezing… Who knows how much unseen damage the bomb must have caused to his hearing, his brain, his organs…

As for the others, I could not believe my eyes! One was the heavy man who had sat beside me, the man who could barely fit between the arm rests… Most of the others were like him, heavy weight boxers, yet with flab, not a single muscle… Some could hardly hold their necks up… It was not clear if they could really walk… or just wanted to get through the airport as easily as possible…

What I saw were not America's brave wounded warriors, but the civilians wounded in the daily crossfire of unhealthy eating habits and thoroughly processed and reprocessed industrial and frozen foodstuffs… If any of these individuals had fought in any one of the "blank check" wars, it was behind a desk… assuming they were healthy enough to be accepted as volunteer G.I. Joe's…

These were not people who were in some way injured by improvised exploding devices or were physically handicapped, but my fellow human beings who could not walk long distances due to their huge size and weight. It was a terrible dilemma: to lose weight they had to walk and exercise to a greater extent—but could not. Would a gutsy gastrectomy ever go down in price? And what about the miracle weight loss pill and other medicines promised by alchemical AI research and development?

Then again, with more and more Americans taking antipsychotic meds, perhaps these suffering individuals could not help but gain weight? And, as I had also learned from Aiden, those considered "overweight" by society were demanding their rights to become accepted as the "new normal"—even if that "new normal" was, for the most part, artificially induced and could be cured by healthier eating habits and better regulation of the agro-industry (plus its pesticides)! Soon, over half of the adult American population over 20 will look just like one of Fernando Botero's paintings or sculptures—while another portion will be just plain plump and overweight.

And America is not alone. The rest of the world was catching up. It seems TV advertising and fast food go hand in hand, mouth to mouth. And contrary to the French elite image of itself, the reality is that many French also love Mac Do's or Mickey Dee's, or whatever one wants to call the tits of the golden mammary arches that attract so many customers. And with what righteous indignation do even five-year-olds, their eyes glued to dancing Tick Tack images on their smart phones, express when their parents tell them, "No Mac Do's!"

Even the Chinese appear to be following in American footsteps.[36] Their diet has changed considerably—although they still have a long way to go to match the Americans! I hope I am wrong about the new weight "normal":

BIG IS SO SO BEAUTIFUL!!!

ooo

And so, it was with great trepidation that I entered this country that had made it illegal for members of the Chinese Communist party to live and work—although I had been told it was OK to visit. Then again, I had renounced my Party membership ages ago once I realized that the CCP was not about to reform itself. I had taken that risk even knowing that the Party hates traitors... And now I was no longer Chinese… I had (almost) forgotten…

I handed the Customs Official my French passport and my proof of vaccinations as if I were a tagged beast. Since

I was once again on business for the Foundation, I hoped I would have no problems entering the country. The officer asked how long I intended to stay and where… I showed him my invitation letter to the conference on "The Future of China," and that I would stay two weeks to visit Washington, D.C. My lodging was already paid for by the Foundation for Human Values Forever.

The Customs Official stared a few moments at his computer screen and then looked at me seriously. I was afraid he now knew that I was a political dissident who had escaped China. I was afraid his data told him that my real name was not Jean Valjaur, but a former Communist named Chia Pao-yu. I was convinced the game was up and that the Americans would now force me to confess my story… I saw myself locked up in an over-heated room inside an orange jump suit…

He stamped my passport without muttering a thing.

ooo

We entered a restaurant/ bar with 17 giant TV screens that played 17 different games of men in uniforms hitting balls with sticks and then running fast to the tune of heavy metal rock. I had no idea how the game was played, but the noise was so intense I could not ask anyone. I could not even hear myself think! The (in)famous repetitive drum pounding of the Shaved Eagles of Deadly Metal was being played just as our waiter served us a combo of pulled pork, hamburgers, and chicken breast.

About 20 minutes later the waiter returned to query, "Hope everything is going down OK?"

I tried the pulled pork; in fact, it had no taste at all except for the hot sauce that was spread on top. It seemed imperative to add extra flavoring to almost all kinds of food.

These condiments included taco sauce, soy sauce, pickled relish, tabasco, different flavors of ketchup, aioli, mayonnaise, and others. Some were spicy, extra spicy, or "normal." And too many jalapeno peppers! There was a bright, yellow-colored mustard that did not taste anything like even the most inexpensive French mustard. I guess it tasted "yellow" ("tartrazine" or "E102") plus plenty of excessive salt and sugar, along with other additives, vitamins, minerals, and emulsifiers…

Although I had begun to understand why many French would act so arrogantly when they tasted so-called "American cuisine," I couldn't be too hypocritical: The Chinese were in love with MSG even if were invented by a Japanese biochemist to imitate the flavor of edible seaweed…

ooo

I could almost smell the chlorine on my lily-white chicken sandwich on bleach white pita bread. I was sure it had been sprayed in the "final washing procedure" with antimicrobial rinses made of chlorine dioxide, acidified sodium chlorite, trisodium phosphate and peroxyacids, so as eliminate wonderfully tasty pathogens that can sprout on chicken like salmonella and campylobacter—and that can then eat your guts from the inside out. All this was to avoid the expense of cleanliness from the farm to the plate by raising healthy livestock from the start.

ooo

It was the bucktooth smiling Assistant Conference Organizer who, unlike many of the others, looked as skinny as Olive Oil. She had taken us for lunch outside the university after she had previously met us in front of the large conference room of the Alexander Hamilton School of International Studies. She claimed to be a close friend of LaPlante, or at least tried to present herself like that. With her stringy ear length expresso hair falling around her face and baggy clothes, she looked as if she had been spending her time on the backstage of the cowboy and Indian TV set. She spoke so passionately—to show us her deep concern for the human rights of people whom she never met, could not relate to, nor fully understand.

At least that is how I saw her…

It was she who had suggested I try the sweet potato fries as opposed to traditional "French" fries—yet even the former were saturated in cheap corn or rapeseed or other highly refined cooking oils, high in saturated fat, and coated with both salt and sugar. With grape concentrate added, the glasses of not-so-cheap California wine tasted much too sweet as compared to French wines. Instant headache!

For dessert, there were donuts coated in a glowing pink sugary glue. As it surprised me that they were marked "vegan," I asked, as if I didn't know, what makes these donuts 'vegan' if they are coated in so much sugar?"

The tall young lady with puffy and blotchy pale skin and snarling black Dragon Chimera tattoos on her forearms smartly replied from behind the lunch counter, "oh, Vegan does not mean it's healthy!"

ooo

After such a remark, I chose tasteless green grapes without seeds (that were supposed to be healthy) and a brownie with a scoop of ice cream for dessert that had large chunks of salt inside. That was before I had found out that the ice cream was made with "diary-like" substances, but with no explanation as to what kind of substances and how they were processed and reprocessed…

There was never any explanation as to how and with what any "sustenance" had been washed and cleaned or fast frozen… how the "grub" have been milled, cut, chopped, heated, pasteurized, blanched, cooked, canned, frozen, dried, dehydrated, mixed or packaged… and with what and how much they had been "enriched" with additives such as vitamins, minerals, salt, sugar and other sweeteners, fats and transfats, spices, oils, colors, concentrates and preservatives… both "natural" and "artificial"… "organic" and "not-so-organic," "safe" and not-so- "safe"—in large and even small quantities… It seemed the more I ate and drank, the more I wanted… It seemed as if I was always on edge… tooting like a French horn… yet always hungry…

And who knows how much of this feed was made from genetically modified animals, plants, among other organisms that had been flavored to suit the taste buds of Dragon Chimeras—and thereby would become the "epicurean new normal"?[37] Then again, how many micro-plastics (Made in China) were my guts and prostate now absorbing?

Even as American joggers, bicyclists, and workout freaks ran off to work without breakfast, fanatically trying to make sure that they could still fit in their pants and skirts, the statistics of obesity continued to skyrocket! This meant that the inhabitants of the whole country were like sitting ducks in the slaughter house—literally stuffing their body mass index to death in the name of the greatest "happiness" for the greatest number—in the utilitarian assumption that stuffing oneself with food makes one "happy" even as it induces heart conditions… malignancies… diabetes… as well as susceptibility to the Horseshoe Bat and other diseases…

That is what the French were (in)famous for: The food fed these poor Barbary or Mullard ducks was forcibly stuffed down their throats, wings tied, their healthy livers diseased, their hearts palpitating, all damaging brains cells. Except that it was WE HUMANS who were now willingly and subserviently doing the "gavage" to our own bodies ourselves.

ooo

Remember what Feuerbach said, "Man is what he eats!" But so too are the plants and animals what they themselves feed upon before feeding man…

As a "flexitarian," I am fully supportive of herbivore options and of eating the least meat possible. This is for personal health reasons and to reduce belching and farting methane pollution of cattle that are the world's No. 1 agricultural source of greenhouse gases worldwide. But why make vegan and herbivore imitations of meat products such as hotdogs, sausages, and hamburgers? Why name such products after meat, like *faux gras* that is false liver pâté made of peanuts and cashews, and not of duck or goose liver? Does that not just reinforce stereotypes of meat-eating identities?

Why advertise green eggs and ham that are not made of either ham or eggs? What would Gao/Galvin's *Butter Battle* hero, Dr Seuss, say?

ooo

In this age of post-Álvares globalization, it seems the "feeding" habits of American and Chinese Civilizations are linked in their geo-strategic rivalry: The gavaging of a distended American empire is coming at a time when a lean, hungry, yet overly ambitious China, still subject to under- and not over- nourishment, is attempting to establish its own version of Uncle Sam's Monroe Doctrine—in its voracious desire to achieve the same rank of hegemonic obesity as that obtained by the now truly Balding Eagle.

And as it changes meaning and focus, the ever-shifting American Dream is, at the same time, suffering from grotesque hallucinations of imperial grandeur: There is a significant risk that the gavaging of the domestic and international dimensions of the American body politic—the poisoning of its liver, heart, and brain—is now reaching the point beyond surgical repair.

Future of China Conference

I was proud that the Foundation for Human Values Forever had funded my flight and stay in the country that I had so dreamed about as a youth….

And despite my complaints about the food, as I realized that my tastes had become 'French fried' from living so long in Paris, I was glad to be able to go to the Land of the Free for the first time and participate in a major conference on the "Future of China" in Washington D.C., at the prestigious Alexander Hamilton School of International Studies. As the Balding Eagle was still the predominant country, and certainly not the Gallic Cock (despite its pretentions to be the leading country in Europe, even if Paris and Berlin cannot seem to cooperate), I needed to see and understand the American perspective.

ooo

I could not believe my eyes, but Dr. I.C.N. Jabber, who had spoken at Beijing University on American democracy and the Electoral College on the eve of the November 1988 American presidential elections was on the stage. Wearing a jet black face mask, Jabber was featured as one of the main speakers from the Alexander Hamilton School of International Studies, the graduate school that had become so famous for its brilliant neo-Con, neo-Martian professors, its experts and former officials who had so optimistically advised "Silver Spoon 2" in his decision to intervene in

Afghanistan and then overthrow the regime of Sad-damn "Abu Ghraib" Hussein in 2003. The war would be a "cake-walk" they claimed!

The Land of the Free had opted for that major "cake-walk" in 2003, with the average Ken, Barbie, Handsome Johnny, and John Brown praising the fireworks over Baghdad—despite the fervent opposition of Balding Eagle's major Oceania Allies, the Gallic Cock, and German Golden Eagle. Both Russia's Doubled Headed Eagle and China's Red Dragon, along with the Gallic Cock, would have all vetoed Uncle Sam's war plans in the United Nations—if Silver Spoon 2 had eventually opted for a North Pole Olive Tree Wreath UN Security Council vote.

And to punish the French for opposing the decimation of Iraq by cruise missiles, average Americans dumped French wines into the gutter, trampled the French flag, and dubbed French fries (which were not originally French), "Freedom Fries"—much like the Land of the Free had changed German "sauerkraut" to "liberty cabbage" during World War I. Yet that was at a time when the Imperial German Eagle was perceived to be a real enemy… not at all like contemporary France that is not an enemy, nor even a rival. Since World War I the French have been an ally of the American Colossus, but an ally with an attitude…

At least this time the French were right! France, my adopted country, had correctly tried to argue, but in vain—that diplomacy and international conflict prevention was the best policy! [38] Ironically however, against the French viewpoint, American neo-Conservative neo-Martian Vultures saw the post-September 11 Balding Eagle as following the imperial footsteps of Napoleon or that of Victoria's 19th century British empire.[39]

And what was it all for? What was the result of the near total destruction and occupation of Iraq by G.I. Joe's—in the name of "democracy"?

It would not be too long before "Islamic State" fanatics, waving the black and white flags, buzzed around the collapsed Iraqi state in pick-up trucks mounted with machine guns—ready to behead anyone who did not support their cause—Moslem or not. It would not be too long before ancient Mesopotamia would be infiltrated by the Persian Cheetah that was threatening to develop its own nuclear weaponry—in closer alignment with the Red Dragon and the Russian Double Headed Eagle…

And still, after the failed U.S. military interventions in Afghanistan and Iraq, it seemed impossible for the neo-Martians of the Balding Eagle to get beyond the Napoleonic realm of artificial amoral/immoral Chimera where earthly disputes are resolved only by force and not by diplomacy….

ooo

I had not been there in November 1988 when Dr Jabber, newly minted with his Ph.D., had given a talk at Beijing University invited by the students without official permission—although I did see the ridiculous summary of his speech in the Beijing University student paper. It probably had nothing to do with what he really said. I doubted that he was some form of academic propagandist. I mean it was very dubious that Jabber had said anything about the rise of Japan as a potential threat to China as the *Beida* newspaper article had claimed at the time.

What was true, and what I did hear through the rumor mill, was that Jabber had tried to explain what the U.S. electoral college system was all about, and why "Silver Spoon 1" was going to win the presidency regardless of the popular vote in November 1988. And apparently, no one could understand how that related to "democracy" understood as majority rule! As I am now learning, I am afraid no one in the Land of the Free itself knows how to explain the purpose of the Electoral College either! And since everyone knew "Silver Spoon 1" was going to win the election anyway, what Jabber had said was nothing prophetic—only the obvious. And the Americans still want the whole world to adopt their system of jibber-nance!

It did not matter: Deng Xiaoping and the Chinese leadership were all voting for "Silver Spoon 1" and the Republicans anyway—as Mark King Hayford had joked in one of his many *NewsBlitz!!!* editorials at the time. It was a joke I myself had told him…

ooo

I was dumbfounded by the weight of the personalities at the conference. The experts whose articles and books I had read and whom I had seen on TV and UTube were all standing, right before me, eating gluey French-style croissants and drinking acrid dish water coffee…

Not only was Dr. Jabber there, but so too was Dr. Frank Fukushima, Dr. I. M. Pagan, Dr. Vicky Newconland, plus realist critics such as Drs. Marshammer and Huntforaton, among other well-known personalities from D.C. "think tanks" who have generally had a hard time "thinking" without sufficient cash from (sometimes questionable) Sugar Daddy and Sugar Mommy donors…

ooo

The first speaker surprised me… Dr. A.S. Likker explained that China had constructed hundreds of new "eco-cities" and "eco-districts" particularly after the 18th Congress of the Communist Party of China had stated in 2012 that building an "ecological civilization" was one of the five "objectives of national development."

As I had not lived in my own country for 30 years, I did not know that the Nanning railway station had been completely rebuilt in 2013… It was now the hub for the world's largest high-speed train network… some 35,000 km. In a city that could reach 39 degrees Celsius, it was airconditioned by electronic wind curtains, fueled by photovoltaic panels… Connected by two metro lines, the railway station served a city of 8 million people when it had less than 1 million in my day… He claimed the air was breathable and even the Yong River was free from pollution… It was all part of the new "common prosperity" ... all part of a massive public expenditure project for the Guangxi Zhuang Autonomous Region that, the expert claimed, repeating Party promises, was designed to eliminate rural poverty...

This was a long way away from the heavy coal of my days… What a major accomplishment—if true! The truth, however, as I began to further investigate, was that many cities proclaim themselves to be the showcase of green development—but have unfortunately become mere ghost towns, despite tremendous domestic and foreign funding for "joint ventures."[40]

On the one hand, Beijing had pledged to reach carbon neutrality by 2060 as the world's largest investor in renewable energy, while also pledging to reduce single-use plastics, such as straws and ban non-degradable bags. On the other hand, Beijing has also pushed ahead with nuclear power plants and invested tens of billions of dollars in mega oil refineries.[41] So what were the Red Dragon's true goals?

Once again, in propelling this fifth objective of national development (and always counting in "5's" as Gao/Galvin would exclaim!), China's leadership has forgotten what the "sixth" objective should be: Decentralized Democracy and power sharing...

ooo

By contrast with the opening speakers, who all praised China's tremendous progress, Dr. Jabber made a devastating critique of American global strategy toward a rising China—that he claimed was not living up to all its promises. The Red Dragon remained a menace to its neighbors and American interests. Here are my notes:

Beijing could no longer claim that it is still a "developing country"—in that it possesses 6.2 million millionaires, ranking second in the world in terms of numbers, but not in percentage of population—after the United States.[42]

Jabber excoriated U.S. global leadership—starting with President George Bush, Jr. who had promised to punish Beijing for cracking down on the democracy movement on June 4, 1989, but then did nothing. It was President Clinton who had blown the whole post-Cold War peace when he sold dual use civilian/ military technology to China back in the 1990s, including supercomputers. It was Clinton who additionally brought China prematurely into the World Trade Organization membership that would devastate the industrial and manufacturing base of the American and European economies and impoverish a good section of the U.S. and European working classes—while leaving both the U.S. and Europeans dependent on China for critical strategic raw materials and cheap finished products. All the while the Red Dragon would seek to copy and reverse engineer whatever technologies it could—including AI!

In general, Nixon, Carter, Reagan, Bush, Clinton, Bush had all fostered the myth that global liberalization would lead to the democratization of the Red Dragon. In belatedly realizing Beijing's real game, it was Obama who began to take steps to counter China militarily and economically. Obama's "rebalancing to Asia" policies were then followed Trump's and Biden's even more strict economic protectionism and military containment...

And when President Biden came to office, Congress opted to raise defense spending way above the President's own budget request in November 2021, while concurrently expanding the number of its ICBMs. At that time, the U.S. Congress declared a "Hypersonic moment" and boosted defense spending just after China tested its first hypersonic weapon—much as Washington did in protesting the former Soviet "Sputnik moment"!

Congress had feared that such weaponry in the clutches of Beijing could potentially spoil the American advantage in Missile Defense systems upon which the U.S. had already spent billions... It was thus imperative to beat the Chinese (and Russian) "rattlesnakes" at their games and develop American versions of the same weaponry, and more... and as fast as possible...

At the end of the speech, Jabber made a passionate plea to oppose the Red Dragon's global expansion through U.S. and EU military containment and protectionist measures. He then gave his whole-hearted support for Taiwanese independence backed by the Pentagon's military might to counter Beijing—as the latter boosted its nuclear, conventional, hypersonic, and not-so-conventional AI and robotic defense capabilities.

I could only think, 'So instead of seeking to lower defense spending as much as possible, in response to the Horseshoe Bat pandemic as many citizens had hoped, the Vultures of both the Republican and Democratic parties, significantly augmented the Balding Eagle's military spending, and have kept raising it year after year. In essence, neither the Democrats, nor the Republicans, wanted the Red Dragon to re-brand the 'Balding Eagle' as a 'Paper Tiger' after the Hypersonic moment!

ooo

In the Q and A, Dr. Jabber admitted that he had been a Congressional aide for many of the neo-Martian anti-Red China "Blue Team" of Congress members, Pentagon defense analysts, intelligence officials, and think tanks that had been warning about the China "threat" for years. What Taiwan needed, he said, was much more weaponry…

At that point, there was an angry outburst from the audience…

Q: "I think your rattlesnake analogy is misleading. Russia, China, and the U.S. are not three rattlesnakes hissing at each other in the same cage. Instead, it is Washington hissing at China and Russia from outside the cage!

A: "Yes, Washington is exaggerating the so-called China "threat" to Taiwan to beef up its military spending!" added another from the audience who did not stand up.

Q: "And… there is no…" another started to say…

A/Q: Dr I.C.N. Jabber then froze for a second as if he had been caught off guard, before interrupting, "Yes, I assume you were going to add that the China threat was all made up for the U.S. military industrial complex to boost its profits… to press Congress to give more funds to the Pentagon. If so, then why is Beijing focusing most of its defense spending for the possibility of war with Taiwan while building and securing its defenses on artificial islands?"

A: "Beijing is responding to the U.S. ramping up its military capabilities and strengthening in defense ties with Japan, South Korea, and now Australia!!!" exclaimed the first commentator with big ears and tiny eyes.

A: "And even India is aligning with the Americans!" piped in another.

Q: "So, if there is no threat, then why is China cracking down on dissidents in Hong Kong and throughout China?" replied the Expert.

A: "That is because the U.S. and Taiwan are supporting dissent to overthrow the Communist party…"

A/Q: "If so, then those movements that oppose corruption and dictatorship would need to do much more to overthrow the Party… American support for them is not the real issue… The real issue is that after absorbing Hong Kong, Beijing wants Taipei… There is no way China will respect the 'one country two systems' principle… Beijing has not yet given up the threat to use force! So, you still do not think Taiwan has something to fear???"

A few of the pro-Chinese hardliners walked out… one yelling out, "If you want war, you'll get it!" Those who wanted compromise between China and Taiwan just shook their heads…

ooo

It was time to go. Something struck me as unreal about Jabber's talk. Jabber did not speak Chinese and he rarely visited China itself, only the region. Merely building up defenses was not a solution…. There had to be another, more diplomatic path…

Jabber soon left the podium… His talk represented a perfect illustration that the two sides, the Red Dragon and the Balding Eagle, were still "mental aliens" in Jack London's terms—unable to comprehend one another…

Not-So-Pure China White

Now in D.C., I could finally see for my own eyes everything I had read and could try to determine the truth or falsehood about the city Gao/Galvin had, I presume, sarcastically, called the "Crack Cocaine and Murder Capital of the World." That was back in the 1980s… This was now 20 years into the new millennium. It had to be exaggeration, if not pure propaganda…

I decided to trace Gao/Galvin's old haunts along Columbia Road… and to jog from Malcolm X Park down to Lafayette Park before the White House. All had appeared to have changed so radically since Gao/Galvin had described the scene in the late 1980s in his anti-Marco Polo travel journal… when he confessed that the first drug his young teenage friends would take was not illegal marijuana, but instead, they would sniff legal household and industrial glue… So why wasn't glue made illegal, G/G had asked in his notebook rhetorically???

I had been certain Gao/Galvin had been exaggerating about the varieties of drugs and the depth of drug crisis in American society. There was no way that the drug crisis in the Land of the Free, that had impacted mainly the urban ghettos of Galvin's time, was anything like that of China since the late 19th century/ early 20th century before Mao came to power. I thought it was outrageous that he called Washington D.C.—the "Murder and Crack Cocaine Capital of the World"—and that he had compared D.C. to Shanghai in the 1920s and 1930s… Murder maybe, but Opium like that of China in that era—no way!

Gao/Galvin may have had an acute case of the Stendhal's Syndrome after witnessing such a bewildering amount of the good and bad in ancient Chinese history, art, and civilization. As such, I initially believed that his illness had been compounded by his heightened dope-smoking paranoia that, in turn, must have been laced with pro-Chinese and Soviet propaganda like PCP (that could also be called "Chinese Buffet") in cheap synthetic dope (Made in China) …

What was certain was that the hippie days—when Samuel "Laudanum" Coleridge claimed Opium had influenced the writing of the segments of his poem, *Kublai Khan* until his creative concentration was unfortunately interrupted—were over. There was no way to return to the days when the Tang writer, poet, calligrapher, pharmacologist, and statesman, Su Shi, saw Opium as a medicinal herb, and when the doctors of the Ming era were convinced that opium could preserve *Qi*—or the "vital force"—and that Opium could, accordingly, function much better than Viagra in modern terms—as if a virgin like myself would know!

In short, I believed his views about the drug crisis in the Land of the Free to be a total drug-induced Looney Tune exaggeration—that is, until I saw a beat-up car run up off the roadside and onto the sidewalk as if trying to park. The car doors suddenly opened, and a heavy-set white man and woman jumped out and tried to run toward the George Washington University hospital…

Both seemed drowsy and dazed, tripping over themselves as if unable to stay awake in the middle of the afternoon. Both were huffing and puffing as if running short of breath—until they simultaneously collapsed onto the ground, almost cracking their teeth on a concrete barrier. I looked closer and saw that their skin was clammy, pale, tinted blue… The pupils of their eyes were like the points of darts… They soon began to vomit before the eyes of a startled crowd…

As they groaned in pain, three medics ran from out of the emergency room, telling everyone to stand back. They began to inject the two with what I learned from a bystander was called "naloxone" before carting them off into the hospital…

ooo

Now I saw it! I learned the American drug scene had all started, first with commercial glue, and later with legal "Mother's helpers"—those little blue candies called "valium" that were a favorite of Poncho, MKH's photo assistant. I had avoided him like the plague and never talked to him at any length… His switch-hitting "amphi-erotic" reputation could be read directly in his Stevia-sweet smiling face…

I realized Poncho's drug use was symptomatic of a deeper crisis that was spinning out of control, impacting the entire world, even if it did not yet reach the pre-Mao condition in China…. Almost a million people had died from differing forms of drug overdoses in the United States in the years from 1999 to 2020.[43] Washington, D.C. was listed as the ninth major U.S. city for Opioid deaths. It's located not too far from Baltimore that had the honor of being No. 1… That's where Edgar Allen Poe died drunk in the gutter.

ooo

As I talked in depth with Aiden, I learned how the U.S. and France and other democratic societies had been detaining thousands of people because of largely insignificant criminal offenses that were related to un- and underemployment, homelessness, poverty, and drug use. Ever since the 1994 Violent Crime Control and Law Enforcement Act of the President Bill "Slick Willie" Clitone-era—a law that the Democrats had passed to look "tough" on drugs and crime—American prisons had become overcrowded, unhealthy, unmanageable, in addition to being breeding grounds for the Horseshoe Bat pandemic.[44] The bleak reality was that prison sentences were being increased for minor offences throughout the country—a fact that was merely augmenting the numbers of men and women jailed![45] (A situation that is very similar in France and China as well.)

Those tough laws and prison sentencing—that were supported by both Democrats and Republicans—were simply exacerbating other social problems resulting in criminal behavior. These laws additionally led to the militarization of the police so that participants in protests were often transmuted into "terrorists"—as if peaceful protestors fought like Al Qaeda or the so-called Islamist State.... In their fight against drugs and crime, "the Democrats kept up the pretense of maintaining 'equal rights' for all... when their actual policies were not achieving their stated goals" in Aiden's words.

What is needed, he said, was greater investments in reliable housing and homeless services, community-based treatment resources for substance use and mental health, and investments in better public transportation. And greater Workplace Democracy and Employee Stock Ownership would permit more local decentralized decision-making power in the hands of employees and the community... Words of wisdom. not yet heeded...

ooo

To get back to the drug issue: By the beginning of the 20th century, the problem of addiction in the Yellow Dragon went beyond belief.[46] Once in power, Mao forced some 10 million addicts into compulsory treatment. Dealers were executed and the opium-producing regions were planted with new crops. Mao's repressive tactics appeared to work within China itself, yet his crackdown forced Opium production to shift south to the Golden Triangle…

The Opium crisis was one of the major issues that Maoists used to justify their crackdown on any form of dissent. Could Mao's success in cracking down on drugs really justify his totalitarian rule as the Red Emperor? Or had there been other means to handle addiction forced upon the Chinese by smiling westerners in black suits and red ties?

ooo

By the beginning of the 21st century, it was the American turn to deal with drugs. The U.S. "War on Drugs" did nothing to stop the illicit drug trade since 1971—only divert the paths of drug entry into the Land of the Free. It was not long before Chinese Triads and Mexican Narcos combined to enter the vast American drug market.

Ironically, however, the Opioid phase of the drug crisis had all started with legal Damien Hirst pharmaceutical prescriptions pushed by doctors who, in turn, got kickbacks and freebies from Big Pharma who claimed Opioids were safe and not addictive… The Opioid crisis began with legal, not illegal, drugs. The U.S. Courts ordered Big Pharma, after they lost their trials, to pay billions for destroying the lives of hundreds of thousands of people… *God bless America!!!*… Then again, the question was whether the Big Pharm really would pay out and whether the perpetrators would ever really be punished…[47] This was no conspiracy theory!

As American deaths from both legal commercial and illicit Opioids began to soar, Drumpfists accused Beijing of weaponizing Fentanyl and other drugs by supplying the Mexican Cartels with the components. It was a new triangular trade: American firms sold automatic weapons to the Mexican Drug Lords to fight the Mexican police who were then unable to crush the Drug Lords, so that other Americans (drug slaves) could purchase the Opioids made of Chinese supplied chemicals!

The Chinese Triads, who bribed and threatened Chinese government officials to look the other way, could "legally" sell the chemicals, while the Mexican Drug Lords, who likewise bribed and threatened Mexican and American officials, could make the final product. Yet even cold-hearted Mexican Narcos were beginning to realize that making drugs too potent and dangerous was going to send their clientele to an early grave!!!

Drumpfists in Washington accused Beijing of refusing to crackdown on legal sales of chemicals used to make Opioids to Mexico and of trying to avenge themselves on Perfidious Albion, the East India Co, as well as American drug pushers—who had all schemed to demolish the Chinese body politic during and after the Opium wars.

Yet the contemporary situation was not at all the same as that of China in the mid-19th century! The People's Liberation Navy—by way of supporting Chinese Triads and Mexican Cartels—was not forcing Washington at the point of a cannon to permit the sale of Opiates to American populations—as was the case when the Brits had deployed HMS warships against China during the Opium wars!!!

Nevertheless, as drug chemicals flowed easily into the Land of the Free by air, sea and post, the Drumpfists threatened to attack the Narcos in Mexico with special forces and Reaper drones—whether the Mexican Leadership agreed or not—as if cruise missiles attacks would reduce drug demand inside the schizoid, excessively competitive, money-hungry, women and child-unfriendly, Land of the Free—that was is in desperate need of social counseling and political reforms.

It was crucial for Washington, Beijing, and Mexico City to start talking about how to better deal with the drugs and conventional weapons trade… That is, before the option of targeting China and its Triads would also be proposed and enacted by American Congressional Vultures and the Blue Team who believed Chinese influence would ultimately cross the Rio Grande to corrupt the Land of the Free—when it was the Land of the Free corrupting itself!!!

It Can Happen Here!

The obsessive desire to shoot up, to pop pills, to get high like the Beat Generation writer, William "Naked Lunch" Burroughs, was one thing; the social and political polarization and protests in America were another.

It seemed every day I went to Lafayette Park before the White House there was a protest… I could not believe the array of forces that had been summoned to deal with the demonstrations. I just happened to be there, in D.C., after my "Future of China" conference, in the weeks after George Floyd was killed by police brutality and ineptitude in May 2020…

ooo

It was just after heavily armed police and security forces brutally removed the peaceful protesters, driving them from

Lafayette Square with tear gas, that I saw President Drumpf and his cohorts, some dressed in combat fatigues, standing for a photo op in front of Saint John's Episcopal Church on Lafayette Square, in June 2020. By parading before the Protestant church, with a Bible in his hand, Drumpf wanted to show that all the protest on Lafayette Square had settled down and that law and order had been "restored"—when it had never been upset except by the police themselves. God was on Drumpf's side!

By standing before a Protestant church, Drumpf wanted to signal his alignment with the so-called "Christian Conservatives"—even if many say there is not a Christian bone in Drumpf's entire body. (I would not know, as I am not a Christian.) Moreover, there was no way Drumpf and his *Jee-Zus!!! Freak* America First True Believer buddies could be considered true "conservatives" either... A real conservative may be tough, but still believes in the possibility of compromise...

Not so for these so-called Christian America First *Jesus!!! Freak*s, in their alliance with the anti-Red China "Blue Team," and Rabbi Dr. Geyer's anti-Palestinian, anti-Iranian, messianic movement—groups that all seem to be waiting impatiently for the Apocalypse to come. In no way would these groups admit that their non-compromising diplomacy and support for the use of force have led to disaster—speeding up the Doomsday Clock closer to midnight...

ooo

In his effort to impose "law and order" by force, Drumpf had first demanded that the National Guard "dominate the streets." Otherwise, he declared that he would put the Chair of the Joint Chiefs of Staff "in charge". The Pentagon then began to deploy active-duty G.I. Joe's as a threat to forcefully suppress protests—despite the reasonable dissent of high ranking, yet retired, senior military officials against the use of the American armed forces for domestic "peacekeeping" or really "peacemaking."

Incredibly, this was a replay of Tiananmen Square! The saner voices of the American military sounded much like former senior Chinese military officials who had likewise opposed the violent crackdown on Tiananmen Square as ordered by China's Communist political leadership! And given the President Drumpf's threat to deploy rapid-reaction units from the 82nd Airborne Division to bases just outside Washington, D.C., it looked like the President was actually going to take the same path into violence and repression as did Deng "Little Bottle" Xiaoping on June 4, 1989—almost exactly 31 years after!

ooo

At that point, Mark King Hayford seemed to speak out more vehemently than ever before. And he described the situation much better than I could even though I was there, and he was nowhere to be seen, at least as far as I could tell. After years of polishing American apples, could MKH be becoming more "radical" in his old age? Or was the term more "critical" considered more "politically correct"?

TRUMP 4NEVER!!!

Repression after the Asphyxiation of George Floyd

by Mark King Hayford (May 25, 2020)

"This is a great day for everybody, this is a great, great day in terms of equality," President Trump had proclaimed—as if the national and global protests against brutal asphyxiation of George Floyd by a Minneapolis police officer had suddenly put an end to a long history of *de facto* inequity, segregation, racial discrimination, unemployment, lack of adequate health care, deep poverty, and police brutality and repression that have plagued the Afro-American community in particular since the end of the U.S. Civil War.

It is a grave situation that was never adequately dealt with in the aftermath of the 1960s civil rights movement—and that has largely been aggravated since the 2008 financial and COVID-19 crises.

Trump insincerely claimed that he was an "ally of all peaceful protesters" and yet it is now known that he would have preferred to "dominate the streets" with at least 10,000 active U.S. military troops. Fortunately, somewhat wiser minds prevailed. The Secretary of Defense, the Chairman of the Joint Chiefs of Staff, and major figures in the Republican Party, all opposed Trump's desire to crack down on the protests with more force. Many of the National Guard that had been deployed on the streets of D.C. and in 18 states throughout the country were withdrawn—not so ironically, as Trump's ratings began to drop in the polls.

Nevertheless, after checking out the conditions of his nuclear bunker, the confused man—who cannot figure out whether he is an isolationist Plutocrat or militarist Timocrat[48]—is still waiting for the right moment when he can declare a national emergency. In that way, he hopes to galvanize the American people in his "struggle" against China, Iran, Muslims, and most crucially, immigrants trying to cross the U.S.-Mex border. Trump also has "Fake News" journalists, looters, and other "bad people"—who include "Leftists," "Wokeists," and anti-fascist militants of amorphous group, Antifa—in his gun sights.

After having waved the Holy Book outside St John's Church across from Lafayette Park in Washington on June 1—in a self-righteous form of idolatry—the solipsist President, who sees himself as the center of the universe, is in a desperate search for a bogey man. He is in dire need to portray himself as the one and only Savior against presumed international and domestic threats to American national security.

Trump does not seek to reconcile—but to polarize. In the name of patriotism and national security, he hopes that presumed external "threats" from Russia, China, Iran, North Korea, plus the "threat" of his followers to use force against "Leftists" will help win him the U.S. Presidency in November 2020.

In raising fears of war and domestic revolution, and in manipulating the political intent of peaceful protests, he believes the American people will support his Reaganite "Peace through Strength" doctrine that seeks pressure all U.S. rivals into submission to U.S. demands with the deployment of new "super-duper" weapons—in Trump's own words, while he concurrently seeks to muffle his domestic opposition.

If re-elected, Trump—the man who admires Russian president Vladimir Putin and Chinese autocrat Xi Jinping—hopes to become the first American president-for-life—or at least set the stage for future American presidents to be elected for three or more terms, almost for life... as if one could be resurrected forever!!!

The choice should be Trump 4NEVER!!!

ooo

In March 2018, the Chinese parliament had eliminated two-term limits for the president of the patriarchal Communist politburo, which had been the case under the former oligarchical system of Communist rule for the Chinese President. Mass protests in Hong Kong, in China itself, in Europe, and in America itself, had done nothing to stop the rubber stamped "election" of Xi "Winnie" Jinping as Chinese president in 2013 and again in 2018.

When that happened, President Drumpf did not criticize, but instead praised, "the Great Party helmsman," Xi Jinping—who could technically call himself "president for life" after the new position had been rubber stamped by 99.8% of Chinese parliamentary delegates.[49] The fearless Chinese leader was now backed by a whole Congress of "Yes" men and millions of groupies on Chinese Social Media. That made Don Drumpf 4EVA furiously jealous![50]

In response to Xi's new position in the Chinese Communist Party hierarchy, Drumpf crooned, with cheers from his supporters, "(Xi's) now president for life, president for life" … He's "a great gentleman" … "the most powerful president in years" … "And look, he was able to do that. I think it's great. Maybe we'll have to give that a shot someday!"[51] Drumpf then claimed to be merely joking… but that was not at all evident.

On top of that, Drumpf had shown himself fawning before Russia's Pootin. He had also become Kim "Rocket Man" Jung-un's "new best friend" after a lot of name calling and nuclear threats—yet whose "friendship" he very quickly lost after they met in person—in Drumpf's completely failed effort to negotiate a "deal" that would persuade North Korea to give up its super-duper nuclear weapons program.[52] As I have followed North Korean politics for years, it is clear that Drumpf's use of flattery was totally counterproductive and dangerous. Contrary to his claims that he would "Make America Great Again," his adulation for Kim Jong-un made the Land of the Free look weak, floundering, and ineffectual. And he couldn't make a "deal."

And after praising these dictators, Drumpf and other Republicans proceeded to denounce domestic Antifa (antifascist), Wokeist, feminist and LGBTQIA+ opposition movements as being inspired by Anarchism, Feminism, Gay Rights, the Black Panthers—in addition to "Maoism." And yet, such homespun American "radical" movements—who were also protesting against Drumpf's corrupt, militarist, autocratic, plutocratic, and anti-ecological domestic and foreign policies—were not being supported by the now antidemocratic, anti-egalitarian, and elitist Chinese Red Dragon. Contrary to the accusations of the Drumpfists, Beijing no longer finances western Maoists and radicals—as Mao had once backed the Black Panthers and other leftwing militants during the Cold War. (Mao also supported anti-Soviet right-wingers such as Chile's Fearless Leader, Augusto "September 11" Pinochet...)

On the one hand, the American President denounced those he saw as pursuing Maoist ideology in opposition to outrageous inequities in power and wealth in the U.S. and Europe. On the other, by praising the Benevolent Red Emperor, Drumpf praised one of the totalitarian fruits of Maoist one-party rule—as the Communist Party shifted from oligarchy to autocracy. At the same time, by mandating very tough protectionist measures versus China, Secret Agent Orange *Jee-Zus!!!* also took steps to undermine more than 700 years of Chinese/European/American trade and political-economic cooperation since Marco Polo.[53]

Drumpf's support for Xi as "president for life"—but opposition to China's rise as a major power *for itself* in Sartre's term was an outrageous "contradiction"—but not at all in the Leninist-Maoist sense of the term. His whole approach represented a not-so-friendly effort by Republicans, and by Democrats as well, to sustain American global hegemony against the rising Red Dragon's challenge—ironically proving the Maoist critique of American strategy!

ooo

As a TV "You're fired" buffoon, Drumpf had followed the footsteps of Grade "C" movie star, Ronnie Ray-gun. As both were "Teffylon" presidents, all criticism, even the most strident, bounced right off them. And since it now appears that everyone on the planet has some degree of Teffylon polytetrafluoroethylene molecules of "better living through forever chemistry" in their blood streams, it also appears that only a few Fearless Leaders have been able to adapt to this new bodily chemistry and use it to their personal advantage. Despite engaging in evidently corrupt, repressive, war-mongering, and self-serving policies—nothing sticks to them! Seems "Pootin" and "Winnie" also, like Ray-gun and Drumpf, have Teffylon in their blood as well!

How was it at all possible for an American president to praise the Chinese leader who represents everything the Americans have opposed as "un-American" ever since their 1776 Revolution against Tyranny?! How could Drumpf praise someone who represents everything in China that I have struggled against—in the hope to achieve a better, less corrupt, and more free China?! It was beyond belief!!!

A Confession (Almost)?

In his efforts to seize power 4EVER, Donald Secret Agent Orange *Jee-Zus!!!* Drumpf argued that he had been confronted with a "leftwing" Anarchist and Maoist plot that had been building up since the days of the 2011 Occupy Wall Street movement against political corruption, burgeoning wealth inequities, and the corporate financing of political parties without regulations…

According to the Drumpfists, the plot against them had begun in "parks, rallies, protests, and in radical flea ridden coffee shops". These first took place in Seattle to protest the G-7 meeting before spreading to New York City, Washington, D.C., Los Angeles, Las Vegas, and then to Austin, TX. Groups like Antifa, Anonymous, Black Lives Matter, Malcolm X Islamicists, Led Belly "Woke" movements, and thousands of other "radicals"—who were said to be inspired by Mao, the Black Panthers, as well as revolutionary poets like Amiri "Leroi Jones" Baraka (as was the case for Gao/Galvin)—were all presumably co-conspiring.

As the number of protests augmented, it was the Ferguson, Missouri "No Justice, No Peace" protests that broke out in August 2014 under Barack "Basketball Break" Nobama that helped bring the Black Lives Matter movement to global prominence—while concurrently galvanizing a backlash by the Drumpfist Far Right, White Nationalists, the KKK, Minute Men, and other former G.I. Joe militias.

At that time, several years before the killing of George "I Can't Breathe" Floyd, as Aiden explained, Michael "Hands up, don't shoot!" Brown, an 18-year-old African American, was shot and killed by police officers. The Ferguson Protests, which had begun to peacefully protest Brown's killing, turned rancid when the police purportedly destroyed a make-shift memorial to Brown. Deployed in riot gear, the police used smoke bombs, flash grenades, rubber bullets, and tear gas to counter rioting, looting, and Molotov cocktails—as if they were fighting "terrorists."

The question as to who first provoked whom—the police, the peaceful protesters, or the vandals/spoilers/disrupters—was always the immediate question. Yet from the perspective of the average African American, NOTHING had changed… It was just another in a long line of police beatings and killings: Emmet Till, Medgar Evers, Rodney King, among many others… It was still, "No Justice, No Peace"—a slogan that had been displayed on one of Basquiat's works, "Created Equal," that he had painted back in George Orwell's year of 1984… And way before Ledbelly and Basquiat, there was poetic eulogy of Langston Hughes "for kids who die."

Saner voices argued for retraining the police force and for a reallocation of funding for both the police and social services. Minneapolis city and other cities proposed implementing a "new model of public safety" that spent more on social development and education… That was not "Maoism"—but common sense!

ooo

Yet instead of seeking social and police reforms after the Ferguson protests, the Vultures in Congress granted even greater federal funding to assist state and local law enforcement agencies to obtain surplus military-grade equipment—to enhance their ability to crackdown on protests. Evidently, more armored vehicles, tear gas, rubber bullets, and sound cannons were needed to repress future "Maoist" and Black Lives Matter demonstrations.[54] Militarization led to further militarization… guns for guns… eyes for eyes… the whole Humankind soon to be blind… Was it a natural r/evolution??? Or an artificial paranoid man-made one?

According to the advanced algorithms of the Drumpfists, it would not be long before these extreme "Anarchist" and "Maoist" groups would not only organize rallies and protests around the world—but they would also engage in cyber-sabotage against corporations and states as their computer hacking and AI capabilities improved. Their spontaneous actions and agitprop with no hierarchal organization and directives would be financed by untraceable cryptocurrency.

It would only be a matter of time before radical movements would gain greater and greater popular support….

Much like Robin Hood, they would soon try to take from the Rich to give to the Poor! Drumpf had to strike back!

ooo

Ironically, however, these presumed Robin Hood goals and outcomes were, in reality, the AI-generated mirror images of the very goals that the Drumpfists themselves were already pursuing—but in Drumpf's case, it was the Rich taking from the Poor—and not vice-versa.

Although their ideological goals were not at all the same, Drumpfist tactics were not too dissimilar to the actions of the Anarchist hero, Guy Fawkes. Anarchists often wear the exact same mass-produced face masks of Guy Fawkes, who, as a member of the Gunpowder Plot, had attempted to blow up the House of Lords and then seize power over the English Lion way back in 1605.

Largely ignoring his anti-Protestant, pro-Catholic, pro-Monarchist, ideology, Anarchists often see Fawkes as a hero who had opposed the power of the aristocratic elites of his era—just as they now claim to be in the struggle against autocratic and plutocratic elites today. (Why Anarchists would wear the same identical face mask does not seem very Individualistic/Anarchistic to me!)

Somewhat like the tactics of Fawkes and his co-conspirators that were aimed at overthrowing the House of Lords in 1605, Secret Agent Orange *Jee-Zus!!!* likewise sought to seize control of the U.S. Balding Eagle in January 2021—when Drumpf's supporters violently ransacked the U.S. Capitol Building and allegedly threatened to blow it up with pipe bombs.[55] History almost repeats itself in strange ways!

Unlike Fawkes, however, Drumpf was not captured, tortured, and then convicted to be hanged, drawn, and quartered for high treason. The coup attempt of President Secret Agent Orange *Jee-Zus!!!* that scared Democrats and anti-Drumpf Republicans may have failed; nevertheless, Drumpf vowed he would not give up his efforts to seize power!

ooo

I had left D.C. in late June, a few weeks after the strangling of George Floyd, with fear in my heart. Deep in depression, I began to question why I had risked my neck back in 1989. And although I had initially dismissed the fact that the Balding Eagle had abandoned us on Tiananmen Square, I began to see that we should have never expected American support in the first place. Neither Republicans nor Democrats would strongly support us. Or else they would just pretend to. In retrospect, it was evident that Washington was merely propagandizing in favor of a self-serving "democratization" (however defined) of many countries around the world. We were mere polished stones in a new great Game of Go… between Washington and Beijing.

ooo

Deep in reflection, I began to consider alternative options—what is falsely dubbed as "counterfactual thinking." Instead of supporting hopefully democratic "Color Revolutions" in the abstract—perhaps Uncle Sam should have more quietly and pragmatically urged reconciliation behind the scenes between Chinese authorities and the students during the 1989 Tiananmen Square protests? In such a way, perhaps the Chinese Communist Party would have not thought that the Land of the Free wanted to overthrow its one-Party monopoly over power?

And perhaps the students themselves should have reached out to Chinese leader, Zhao Ziyang—who had claimed he wanted to enter in a dialogue with the leaders of the protest movement? Although Zhao had considered himself a "New Authoritarian," the New Authoritarians also claimed that they would eventually establish a Chinese version of "democracy"—once the stale Communist state bureaucracy was broken up and a more flexible neo-liberal system of capitalism was instituted. Perhaps the student leadership should have worked more closely with Zhao?

And perhaps the student leadership in 1989 could have chosen another, more Chinese-like symbol—as opposed to the pure white "goddess of democracy and freedom"? Perhaps that statue was too much like the Statue of Liberty and thus appeared to be too much like the all-American image—and thus not at all related to the problems of Chinese society and governance? Perhaps a statue that resembled the poet and diplomat, Qu Yuan, or one of the philosophers of peace, Mo Zi—or perhaps Wang Zhenyi, the woman mathematical and astronomical Genius who died too young, could have been the symbol instead? [56]

And perhaps, the student leadership could have vacated Tiananmen Square at an earlier time—as had been originally agreed? Perhaps if all the students had moved away from their camps on Tiananmen Square, we would not have given Deng "Little Bottle" Xiaoping and his cronies the pretext to call in the tanks to smash our protest?

I remembered how militant were those who urged us to stay… those who wanted blood in the streets… Yet we were too naïve. We saw no need for compromise—for we had right, reason and justice behind us. And most of us did not expect such outrageous violence from a paranoid gerontocracy—but perhaps we should have?

ooo

The answers to these alternative "counter-factual" options are not certain. As I told MKH at the time, could we have trusted Zhao if we had reached out in May 1989? Could we have trusted his goals of a New Authoritarian "plutocracy"? And more crucially, would the more powerful Deng "Little Bottle" Xiaoping and Li "butcher of Beijing" Peng have really compromised with us—if the democracy movement offered compromise with them?

By considering the possibility of alternative options involving compromise is, I guess, a kind of confession on my part… at least almost… although I did nothing wrong… What I do know is that if I had been captured, they would have tried to force me to confess my presumed "guilt" … my "disloyalty" … *The Surgeon straps me to the ice-cold operating table in a clean white room alit by flickering of candles, holding his curved scalpel in the air… He insists, are you ready to confess?*

Then again, perhaps I am still dreaming… Was compromise and reconciliation really possible then? Is it possible now?

II.

Reflections:
Year of the Horseshoe Bat

Attestation

When the Year of the Horseshoe Bat began, there was nothing to do but think about the past with little hope for the future—in fear of an invisible enemy.

I remember jogging in the Parc Ranelagh near the Museum Marmottan where the impressionist works of the French painter Claude Monet were on display.

A man with a thick brownish orange beard was staring for at least an hour at the white marble statue *Vision du Poet* by Georges Bareau without moving an inch. The statue had been commissioned for the 100th anniversary of the birth of Victor "*les Miserables*" Hugo—who was depicted like an ancient Greek god sitting beside his Arion lyre. Hugo's section of the *haut relief* appeared to be schizophrenically splitting off like the shifting tectonic plates of an earthquake from the rest of the marble wall that depicts the hopes of struggling and suffering populations.

ooo

I guessed that the man who was standing without moving for so long must have been high on the Project MKULTRA's Looney Tunes—made famous by Ken "psychoactive" Kesey. As I would later learn, in pursuing my thesis on the Beat Generation, Kesey's books (and use of mind-bending drugs) had been denounced by the Society for the Exploration of Cosmic Consciousness (SECC) as distorting that Exploration and not revealing Cosmic Consciousness—as Kesey had claimed. The SECC has thus called for banning Kesey's books and those of others, such as Burroughs and Ginsberg, written during that hippie epoch…

even banning Kesey's *One Flew over the Cuckoo's Nest* that is a classic… That is another issue…

ooo

I saw two blue clad police on horseback ride up to awaken a jogger in black sweat suit who was snoring on a park bench. The half-awake man then searched through his backpack for his *Attestation de Deplacement Derogatoire.* Two other joggers in grey sweat suits then ran past. They were laughing with amusement before staring down at their heart rates ticking away the minutes on their wrist watches. A third unfortunate jogger was soon stopped in mid-run by the same two police officers who looked more like meter maids than like cops or "*flics*" in French slang.... with red arm bands marking their official status…

I could only think as the blue whoops of the sirens of ambulances and police cars buzzed by almost every half an hour: It has been decades since the French police wore flying capes, but they flew nowhere…

While the vast majority of humans now had to pass their time in virtual reality at home during the Year of the Horseshoe Bat, only every-so-often coming to the surface for smoggy air to breathe, pure white swans appeared to be flying in all their glory in the lakes of the *Bassin de la Villette, Lac de Minimes, Lac Daumesnil,* the *Lac Inferieur* in the *Bois du Boulogne.* These were the open-air parks where the Parisians would no longer be permitted to visit.

I/We were soon banned from jogging in the Bois de Boulogne, where there was fresh(er) air! All according to the decree that an overstretched police force would not be able to supervise the parks—only the main streets.

ooo

Before the statue of La Fontaine sat three elderly ladies on separate park benches who were unexpectedly interrupted from their casual *chit-chat* by the two police officers. The women were then "verbalized" by the officers of the law for the crime of sitting outside in the fresh air. They had broken the Horseshoe Bat restrictions simply because they were not standing up and exercising...

To be "verbalized" in French does not mean to merely express ideas and emotions, but to be fined, or really fleeced—when the action words or "verbs" and words for "impounding money" or "fined" become one in the same. The more one infringed the Horseshoe Bat restrictions, the greater the amount in fines one had to pay.[57]

Recidivists who persisted in going outside too often (if caught) would also be liable to six months' imprisonment—where, in overcrowded, and increasingly radicalized, prison conditions, they were certain to be exposed to the omnipresent Horseshoe Bat pandemic—if they were not first converted to jihadist Islam. That, of course, assumed they managed to survive sexual harassment.

ooo

It was not long before the government banned people from walking in the park, forcing them to walk in the streets and back alley ways... where they were pressed even closer together... Going swimming on beaches was banned too... even if it would be somewhat easier to "physically distance" (to be politically correct") on a beach than in a crowded metro or in a bus where those who could not work remotely on *tele-travail* (work by internet) were doomed to travel to their workplace if they did not possess cars… Children accordingly had to play on the street or in parking lots instead of the green park and grassy areas in hopefully cleaner air…

A person could be walking alone, or a couple walking together in the middle of a park, by the ocean, on a mountain top, with no one near them for miles, and yet the police could still ride up on a bicycle, or on a horse, or in a car, to "verbalize" the culprits if they did not possess an "Attestation" that was correctly filled out…

Canines scowled at each other while their masters waltzed with leashes in hand in the park. Revealing the inner fears of their masters, even these dogs seemed suspicious as to who had the plague, and who did not, who was spreading it around without knowing it, and who was spreading it around purposely...

ooo

A devious game of mouse and cat had only just begun—as the French people were already figuring ways to beat the system and evade confinement, particularly whenever the police were on break... A person could, for example, print out multiple copies of the *Attestation de Deplacement Derogatoire* pre-signed with different dates and times if they had access to a printer...

They could also pretend to be going to work with a special attestation... just as I did with "Chinese" ingenuity! That was until the government got somewhat smarter and demanded that people fill out their on-line form on their I-phones or download an app—but only a very few did… Jupiter was always watching!

ooo

This is not to overlook an important literary point about the frog poet, Jean "rob the cradle" de la Fontaine. It was Fontaine who had embellished (to be diplomatic, i.e. did not plagiarize) the fables of the ex-slave Aesop from Latin into French verse by changing both the lines and the textual meaning, here and there.[58] Then again, the difficulties of poetry translation often make the translation, in itself, a creative endeavor—so I guess I should not be too harsh on La Fontaine's appropriation of Aesop's poems.

In the afterlife above, if there is such a thing where our electric-like energy goes after our body runs out of juice, as I learned is the belief of the SECC, La Fontaine must have snickered hysterically to see the three elderly ladies "verbalized" on a park bench for the crime of just sitting near his statue—just where he is overseeing the Fox flattering the Crow in the quest for a chunk of cheese!

To re-phrase his poem, *The Gardener and His Lord*, much as La Fontaine rephrased Aesop, but without rhyming in classic verse in my case: "Even if this disease has been spread by the devil himself… and despite all his/her/its diabolic fits and tricks, I will soon expunge this menace from the face of the planet. I swear I will cure you of this pest—even if that would mean making bets on the value of my very own spirit!"

Why is it that the promises of foxy politicians always seem to go unfulfilled and the people, like crows, still believe in both the promises and those politicians???

ooo

A few joggers in surgical masks passed by as I ran out to the lakes of the Bois de Boulogne. It was like an obstacle course with walkers trying to zig-zag away from runners who paced without ever stopping, with their hot sweaty bodies emanating drops of sweat and whatever germs might be dissolved within that sweat... I saw how their lungs huffed and puffed heavily next to all the people they passed. One problem for foreigners was what the French called "promiscuity"—which meant to be in close contact without "physical distancing"—did not quite translate into English in quite the same sense…

It was all very chaotic... And now, because one could not see a person's whole face behind the surgical mask, one could assume that the enemy who carried the Horseshoe Bat virus could be behind each and every person... And even you yourself could be an unwitting agent of this invisible pathological foe in the eyes of others... Chinese were, of course, among the top suspects…

And as one could only see the eyes behind masks, it was as if the whole country was now wearing *niqāb*s or *burqas*—even if the latter were always confused with *hijabs* by the French who feared the challenge posed by Islamicist propaganda to the pretense of their secular quasi-Atheist/ Catholic post-colonial society that still hoped to dominate its colonies—at a time when the Russian Double Headed Eagle, the Chinese Red Dragon, the Arab Gulf Falcons, the Iranian Cheetah, and even the American Balding Eagle, were all engaging in a new and very violent geo-pornographic "scramble" for African resources and sought to take over French-speaking African countries in particular, among other former colonial holdings. The Frogs feared they were losing everything…

In any case, it was certain the skills of pickpockets and other thieves improved during the Year of the Horseshoe

Bat when everyone was masked—even though home robberies probably went down because more people were working on *teletravail!* And the police were omnipresent!

ooo

As I lived by the Seine near my job at the Foundation, I was already lucky enough not to have to squish into the packed metro mornings and early evenings to be transported to and from work, or else be pick-pocketed in the body sweat and bad breath of the No. 72 bus going up and down the Seine… The French may be famous for exporting their perfumes, but the average person can't afford them….

Then again, that awful "Canal No. 5" stench seemed to be coming back in vogue. It was one the most repulsive of all old lady French perfumes—and one of the oldest known to Americans and the world due to its advertising blitz of the 1960s and later. Ironically enough, No. 5 was a perfume so popular in China that a Chinese company had made an imitation brand, called *No. 9 Flower of Story* that was placed in an almost identical bottle with an iconic white package and gold lining.[59]

Maybe I am being too critical. What if the stench of the France's No. 5 and China's No. 9 were so noxiously lethal that they could both kill COVID No. 19? Maybe both could then be marketed as new forms of zoonotic Corona virus killer—more effective than a vaccine? That could start an excellent conspiracy theory! And expand sales!!!

ooo

Not having to commute was truly a blessing in the Year of the Horseshoe Bat! There was no way I wanted to take part in the daily ritual of what the French sarcastically call in rhyme… *metro… bureau… dodo* (metro… office… baby sleep)… to which I added, due to the protests against extending the retirement age, *en espérant une retraite très tôt* (in hoping for a very early retirement). And hopefully at *taux plein* or the "full" rate—even if the amount was taxable and not even close to "full" salary. It seemed no one in France wanted to work long and hard; while the Chinese themselves were used to working very hard—but didn't want to!

So here is my first effort in rhyming in French:

Metro... Bureau... Dodo...
En espérant une retraite très tôt !!!

ooo

In this paranoid mindset, there were conspiratorial rumors on the social networks that the authorities were spraying some form of anti-Horseshoe Bat disinfectant on the streets early every morning when all were asleep... It was much like the rumors about those puffy streaks of clouds in the sky… those puffs of gas called "chemtrails" … emitted by passenger aircraft… that were supposedly fabricated, according to the daily Social Media conspiracy chit-chat *blah blah blah* spread by bots, to implement at least three nefarious schemes:

1) to spread Horseshoe Bat spittle.
2) to distribute useless and dangerous vaccines to the global population.
3) to poison minds to accept a "new world order" controlled by UN North Pole Olive Tree Wreath techno-rats.

I really could not understand how anyone, including some women and men in the U.S. Congress, could believe these preposterous "Qanon" conspiracy theories—many of which were said to be "weaponized" by Russian, and particularly by Chinese, hackers.[60]

Some of these conspiracy theories, however, propagandized against China in the belief that Beijing was manipulating the Horseshoe Bat pandemic to take over the world! Even if it was true that the Red Dragon has been trying very hard to gain greater influence in the UN North Pole Olive Tree Wreath by stuffing the pockets of UN techno-rats with Chinese Yuan—in its struggle against the still predominant Balding Eagle. Such claims made me want to transform into a raving Chinese pan-nationalist!

ooo

Every 8pm, people would open their apartment windows and applaud those nurses and doctors who were on the frontline helping those in stress, those who were trying to save those whose breath gasped a last desperate gasp—at grave risk to themselves. It gave one faith in humanity once again.

That was… until the moment when people stopped clapping and when many doctors, nurses, medical personnel health care workers, as well as the servicemen, police officers, firefighters, and pilots, were fired from their jobs for refusing to take all three of their vaccines—even if it could be honestly argued those vaccines had questionable effectiveness and had been rushed into the hospitals and doctors' offices and pharmacies without proper and long-term testing…

And then, without warning, after all the absurd and unnecessary lockdowns, the repetitive masking and unmasking of children, along with the closing and unclosing of schools, there was dead silence. Not a single country was enforcing the three-vaccine rule. Was it due to the high costs? Or the questionable efficacy of the vaccines? Were they dangerous? Was the virus dead? Had it mutated? Would it return? It seemed everyone had already forgotten the nurses and health care workers—particularly those who were still ill with the long-term effects of the Horseshoe Bat. Not a single word. Not a single explanation.

As inconsistent as was its policy of minimal repression, France, to its "credit" (yet at the risk of skyrocketing debt) had paid its citizens unemployment compensation if they had lost jobs during the pandemic, or if they were forced to reduce their working hours. By contrast, I could only think that, in China and in other countries, the police had started to deploy Sentinel drones to spy on the population and use oinking dog-like robots for crowd control and to threaten fines, if not imprisonment. After all, in the minds of China's Fearless Leaders, it is better to be safe—even if this means locking everyone up—than to be sorry!

ooo

Perhaps I had been deluding myself, but it seemed that I could breathe much easier during this Horseshoe Bat spittle scare. The grey geese, blue and brown headed mallards, and pure white swans all came to shore to honk at humans with an air of disapprobation—even to the point of braving the toy boats buzzing across the water driven by electric remote control by zealous fathers who risked being fined as they played with toys too advanced for their own children.

Despite the whining of ambulances, and despite the smell of Death in the hospitals, the reports of the Media Fourth Estate had been filled with such glowing optimism. Our lives would be changed in the future! We'd all be more environmentally conscious! Believe it or not, it was said that due to the Horseshoe Bat pandemic, people would now change their habits and consume less, that they would eat healthier, that they would exercise more, and that they would, at long last, recognize the importance of nurses, of sanitary engineers, of firemen, and other strenuous careers.

After the Horseshoe Bat "experience," many believed that all of Humankind would now care more about the general working and environmental conditions and for the workers themselves—so as to prevent the possible spread of such future pandemics. And people would truly care for each other—including their own family members!

At a time when dolphins were believed to be leaping in Venetian canals (I could not verify the rumor!), Humankind would recognize the importance of the natural world and finally understand how WE as a SPECIES had been tearing apart earth's ecosystem, and how, for example, the melting of Arctic tundra would soon cause new pandemics to spread—if such environmental plunder—like the Wild West mass killing of the Indians and the buffalo—did not cease.

The biggest lesson of the Year of the Horseshoe Bat was WE as a SPECIES would find ways to cooperate without war—much as Louis "the sunny King" XIV had named Paris "the City of Lights" because after so many costly foreign wars and civil conflicts, he wanted to show that he truly cared for domestic security and safety. Lanterns were placed on almost every main street and residents were asked to light their windows with candles and oil lamps. This was all to deter criminals from gouging throats in back alleys… Yet the wars never ceased… nor the domestic violence…

There were also positive rumors that fish, but not dolphins, were returning to a much cleaner Seine. It was true that about two years before the Horseshoe Bat pandemic, someone had fished out of that filthy river, a *pacu.* That is a piranha-like "testicle-eater" or "balls-eater" fish—a herbivore with sharp teeth, which must have gotten too big for its owner's aquarium, so it was dumped in the murky waters of the Seine.

And now Paris, at long last, was trying to clean up the Seine for the Summer 2024 Olympics—after having promised to clean it up for more than 30 years![61] As polluted as it was, with a reported 20km stretch of plastic bottles and trash, at least the Seine was still flowing unlike China's Yongding River, the so-called "River of Eternal Stability" that had once flowed through Beijing—but had then dried up. I understand that Beijing authorities have subsequently tried to clean it up… It was just another environmental disaster to plague China—and indirectly the world….

Every day I saw police boats with scuba divers in black suits searching the bottom of that illustrious river. If Paris did have plans to clean up the Seine for the 2024 summer Olympics, the police divers did not seem to be interested in testing the quality of the water. And every time someone approached on the side to ask, the police waved them away… They were in no mood to be talked to....

What were they looking for? For lost keys, telephones, bicycles or other items people or tourists might have dropped by accident? Or perhaps the knives or guns of criminals—or even cadavers of those murdered or drowned by accident, or accidently on purpose, like the Ghanian supermodel activist, Katoucha, who opposed female genital mutilation—and who the Mass Media claimed was once the muse of Yves Saint Laurent?

The Seine was also the river where Inspector Javert—after being so obsessed with the pursuit of a truly blind "justice" in seeking the arrest of Jean Valjean—had drowned himself in Hugo's *Les Miserables*…

ooo

Along with the geese, mallards, swans, herons, and the other beautiful creatures that walked proudly without fear onto the shore during the Horseshoe Bat pandemic, so too did a slimy Coypu slink out of the filthy water and flop its own pestiferous body onto the shore and snarl, displaying its radioactive orange buck teeth…

I stopped jogging to watch the creature frighten those passing by if it were the chimeric Chinese water god, *Gonggong*, whose copper head and torso appear human with an iron forehead, red hair, and the tail of a serpent. In the paranoia of this year, was it true the Horseshoe Bat virus could leap like fleas from such a Coypu/*Gonggong* Chimera and then spread like grease on the hands, face, and clothes?

It had happened with previous plagues in history.

Instead of better social, health and working conditions, as the Mass Media Fourth Estate had promised, the Horseshoe Bat brought with it robotics and AI predictive management and digital surveillance—and much greater social and economic inequities and military spending—that all fed upon each other like twins in the womb who "eat" their brother or sister by osmosis… coupled with freaky unexpected preternatural *Yaoguai* occurrences…

From Pharoah's Rats to Horseshoe Bats

In many ways European and American fears of China and Asia have stemmed from the Mongol invasions that linked war with Black Death….

In his anti-Marco Polo journal, Gao/Galvin had discussed the fact that the "pandemics of globalization" throughout history had revealed how myths about who or what caused pandemics were generated in the geo-history of European-American-Chinese-Mongol relations. The roots of "globalization" did not generate free trade and peace, but war and pestilence—as the Europeans spread guns, drugs, and disease throughout much of the world—while the Mongols counter-attacked, helping to spread the plague that originated in either Central Asia, Mongolia, or in China…

The Mongol Golden Horde breached the Great Wall and sieged Beijing in 1215, before galloping across the Silk Road, raiding Kyiv in 1240—as it had already been too late for the Pope to forge an alliance with the Russians at the time when the Mongols were subjugating Russia, Europe, and China "like devils from the Tartarus." Pope Innocent IV, King Louis IX, and other leaders of Europe clung to the hope that they could somehow convert the Mongols to Christianity and eventually forge an alliance with their Fearless Khan Family Leaders against the Arab Saracens.[62] So, if you can't beat them, join them!

Soon the Golden Horde overran Poland, Hungary, Dalmatia, Serbia, and even parts of Austria, before turning their sights to Baghdad in 1258. Genghis Khan, his sons, family, and companions, all rejoiced in spreading their semen wherever they so desired over the four corners of the Mongol world…[63] That was before Kublai Khan (with the military technical assistance of the Polos in the period from 1271 to 1295) gobbled up the Song empire by 1279—like eating raw guts.

Marco Polo's family was so loyal to the Great Khans!!!

ooo

Much like the Horseshoe Bat sputum has spread globally since 2019, it would be the next century after Marco's visit, in the 1330s, that the blood sucking fleas of the Golden Horde would rejoice in spreading the Black Death, *Yersinia pestis*, through blood and vomit to Genoese traders—the enemies of Marco Polo's Venice. At that time, the Genovese sailed from Constantinople, across the Black Sea and through the Dardanelles, and up into the Mediterranean, before docking in Genoa—thereby permitting the germs to infiltrate Europe as clandestine voyagers. Rats, lice and fleas and human breath were said to be the culprits. But perhaps, as Galvin had queried part in jest, the pandemic originated from the blood of what Marco Polo called "Pharoah's rats"?

The Black Death had devastated the peoples under the yoke of Mongol rule in the four Eurasian Khanates and killed millions in Hebei province—and worked to transform entire societies, economies, and governments from Eurasia to Europe. Its horror provided a ready excuse to blame and persecute minorities, including foreigners, Jews, beggars, lepers, the handicapped.[64]

As fate would have it, those who first spread it, ultimately died from it. After the pandemic wiped out roughly 25 million people in the late Middle Ages (between 1347 and 1351), not to overlook the tens of millions killed by the Mongol democide throughout Eurasia, the Black Death then paradoxically helped to put a sudden end to Mongol rule in China by 1368.

During famine, plagues, and peasant insurrections, the Red Turban movement—led by General Zhu Yuanzhang, who was once a wandering beggar—was able to overthrow the Mongol Yuan Dynasty in 1368 in alliance with the White Lotus Society, which believed in a hybrid of Buddhism and Manichaeism. Zhu then became emperor of the new Ming dynasty, with a mixed record of positive reforms and brutal repression. With *Death to All Mongols!!!* written on slips of paper hidden inside mooncakes, another empire in global history collapsed in a whimper…

ooo

There is so much deep prejudice in this matter—as the Chinese people have once again been blamed as the culprit of the COVID 19 pandemic just as China was once blamed for the Black Plague—*From Pharoah Rats to Horseshoe Bats!!!*

In this regard, many had similarly attempted to blame the "Spanish flu" of 1918 to 1921 on Chinese railway workers who might have brought that devastating influenza to Europe. Yet that pandemic may have more likely originated in the poor farmlands of Kansas before it spread to France by freshly recruited American doughboys—causing more deaths than World War I itself. I mean, maybe China's social and ecological environment is guilty of some things—but it is not guilty for every disease on the planet!

Ironically enough, however, it was not the Chinese who were blamed for the pandemic during the Great War, but the Spanish—even if the so-called "Spanish flu" did not originate in Spain. The Spanish people suffered massively from the flu, yet it just happened that Spain was the only country from which the Global Media of the epoch could report on the devastating impact of that flu because military censorship did not take place in Spain. Spain's freedom of press ironically led what should have been called the "Blue Death" to be called the "Spanish flu." It was the Fake News of its era!

ooo

Such prejudice has returned to haunt us once again. Just as it is wrong to call the "Blue Death" the Spanish flu, it is just as wrong to call the Horseshoe Bat Corona virus the "Chinese flu" or the "Kung Flu" as President "Secret Agent Orange *Jee-Zus!!!*" Drumpf did—in a bigoted innuendo reminiscent of the late 19th century prejudice that Mark Twain had satirized in his not-so-popular writings of that epoch. Then again, perhaps "Blue Death" should be called—the "Kansas Flu"? That is probably more accurate! Yet would that moniker be considered prejudicial against people from Kansas?

ooo

Plagues can revise history in unexpected ways. Galvin had been outraged to learn that the terms of the 1919 Versailles Treaty—that had led to the mass protests that eventually brought Hitler in Germany and Mao in China to power and that had arbitrarily divided the Ottoman Empire and Middle East—could have been indirectly influenced by disease or even the Blue Death!

It turns out that Woody "War to End All Wars" Wilson might have been so disoriented with a case of influenza that he could not argue against the hardline policies of French Prime Minister Georges "*Revanche!*" Clemenceau—who had adamantly urged a vindictive peace against Germany after its defeat in the "Great War".[65] Wilson's influenza might also have been a reason why he had so easily capitulated to the Japanese Red Sun's demand to occupy Shandong province after the Great War—a (non)decision that then led to the May 4, 1919 protests in China and ultimately to Mao's revolution. Mao certainly believed that Wilson was easily manipulated by European liars.[66] But was flu the reason?

Who knows for sure! The real causes for political decisions that lead to wars are not always so clear and rational…

ooo

In the present circumstances, what kind of damage could the Horseshoe Bat pandemic, plus variants, impact the key decisions of today's pathetic leaderships? And what kind of actions could states take as their geo-pornographic tensions rise—unable to resolve their differences?

Conspiracy theories aside, there is a real possibility that many states—including both the Balding Eagle and Great Red Dragon—have already developed such Bio-Chem weaponry in their nationalist penchant for creating weaponized viruses with differing mutating genomes. The writer Jack

London had predicted the possibility of biological warfare between the Balding Eagle and the Chinese Panda to take place in the year 1976 without a shot being fired.

Jack London may have gotten the date wrong, but his futurology was not entirely fantastic: After the so-called "Great War," War Plan Yellow (a not-so-politically correct title) envisioned deploying G.I. Joe's in coalition with troops of other major powers to suppress potential popular discontent in China, much like that of the turn of the 19th century xenophobic "Righteous Fists of Harmony". War Plan Yellow proposed the use of chemical weapons if necessary.[67]

In contemporary circumstances, experimentation with "gain of function" and chimeric viruses by the military-industrial complexes of the Balding Eagle, the Red Dragon, Russian Double-Headed Eagle could provide info for new experiments to develop bio-weaponry. What happened once in history could happen again—as states often take shockingly extreme and immoral measures in the effort to "defend" themselves against actual and feared threats by both preclusive and offensive measures.

ooo

No matter what the Truth of the origins of the pandemic, Gao/Galvin, bless his heart, had gotten one thing right: artists, poets and writers have all been inspired by different forms of plague and pestilence[68]—influenza, cholera, bubonic plague, measles, smallpox, syphilis, delirium, as well as the A-Virus and the Horseshoe Bat/ Racoon Dog! The forces of Creativity are not always pristine and joyful!

These unexpected horrors, much like differing illusory forms of Dragon Chimeras and other artificial amoral/immoral phantoms, have resurrected themselves at unexpected moments in history, particularly during times of war, famine, economic crisis, or unforeseen natural disasters…. What was once referred to as '*magna mortalitas*' (the Great Death) in the words of the ancient Greeks.

Not much has really changed… Much as was rumored in the 17th century, it was evidently witches who brewed the Black Plague from the venom of spiders… And, of course, these witches were secretly encouraged by the French to spread that disease wherever they could… in the fields… in troths of water… in the winds of battle. And just as the French had once been blamed for the Black Plague during the Thirty Years War, it is now the Chinese who are being blamed for the Horseshoe Bat pandemic…

One of my favorite French authors, Albert Camus, was not far from the truth when he had written in his novel, *The Plague*: "A pestilence isn't a thing made to man's measure; therefore, we tell ourselves that pestilence is a mere bogy of the mind, a nightmare that will pass away. But it doesn't always pass away and, from one nightmare to another, it is men who pass away, and the humanists first, because they haven't taken their precautions."

Mary Shelley believed that it would most likely be a pandemic that would eventually obliterate Humankind... And so, as advised by Boccaccio, it was perhaps best to live for the moment... seize the day… *carpe diem…* Then again, as healthy and sound as his counsel appeared, I could simply not follow such advice. A patriot at heart, I was still married to the cause of a more just and less corrupt China!

The year 2020 should no longer be considered the Year of the Metal Rat. Instead, it should be called "Year 1 of the Horseshoe Bat." The world needs a new Zodiac!

More Kung Flu Conspiracies

In 2020, there was a panic over the Horseshoe Bat pandemic, but back then, in the 1980s, there was a panic over HIV (Human Immunodeficiency Virus) and the A-Virus—even though both Horseshoe Bat and A-Virus continue to infiltrate the human body politic… It's a delightful choice between Pest and Cholera, between Scylla and Charybdis, between a Chimp and a Bat!!!

The paranoia of Mark King Hayford and his fellow journalists in the late 1980s about A-Virus was not exaggerated—but Gao/Galvin took that paranoia a preposterous step beyond. He snapped like trout on the Benevolent Big Brother Benefactor KGB propaganda line, hook, line, and sinker. It is a wonder how otherwise intelligent people can believe that AIDS was a result of CIA bio-warfare experimentation on apes in Africa!

ooo

In Gao/Galvin's time, in the 1980s, the A-Virus pandemic in China was being blamed on gays, drug users, shared needles, Uighurs, and other immigrants or foreigners. As illustrated by the December 1988 protests in Nanjing—that had made Poncho's photos famous—students and average Chinese had begun to discriminate against Africans, Uyghurs, and other minorities who were believed to be spreading the A-Virus. In the worldwide paranoia, there were many political and religious and racist manipulators who knew how to score points by framing the "outsider" and the foreigner as a "threat."

It would not be until 2002 that the Chinese government would finally admit that it had a significant A-Virus crisis of its own making on its hands—when the UN North Pole Olive Tree Wreath World Health Organization predicted an "explosive" AIDS pandemic. China's lack of hygiene had begun to catch up with it… The information that Party officials obtained was incomplete… There was no standard public disclosure channel or way to engage in open discussions and transparent dialogue with its citizens.….

There were no way Mao's barefoot doctors—so beloved by Gao/Galvin—could do "! *^$" against the A-Virus (AIDS)! There was no way their outdated methods could protect the population. And only a few had expected the possibility that new forms of pandemics could rain down upon the planet in the future…[69] And now, the Horseshoe Bat—that represents Happiness as the homonym of same word, *fú*—is said to be the culprit behind COVID-19. Its sputum is being sprayed like electric waves across the world… through retirement homes… prisons… bars… restaurants… factories… hospitals... It can attack anyone—particularly those living and working in close quarters...

ooo

Look at how the conspiracy theories and rumors have been buzzing around the planet because of the Horseshoe Bat pandemic and its mutant promiscuous variations! Who knows what to believe?

It is known that chimpanzees could spread the A-Virus. And some people, admittedly primarily Chinese, eat the "wild taste" of the scented anus of an exotic civet or else savor pangolins, mongoose (or maybe even Horseshoe Bats, but I doubt it!)—and allegedly spread COVID 19. Believe it or not, those who eat illegally poached pangolin believe that its head, scales, and bones will somehow provide spiritual protection much like body armor from evil witchcraft and even protection from financial disaster! Incredible! All this is because the ancient superstitions of barefoot doctors affirm that Pangolin meat is helpful for better functioning kidneys, for the treatment of skin, and even for breathing—even if the virus that potentially emanates from such creatures can put an end to your breath altogether!

In some cases, gourmets want these wild animals to be slaughtered directly before their very eyes—so that they know that they are getting the valuable and rare meat they paid for! Such trust! It is a strange kind of super-ego trip to believe that any individual could believe themselves beyond the law for eating an endangered species. Or maybe such people believe themselves to be indestructible supermen/superwomen. I doubt all the terracotta guards of Qin Shi Huang can protect such individuals! Nor can China's Stone Lions, nor European Gargoyles!

As an illegal Triad money-making activity, the poaching of these innocent and rare creatures must be stopped! The destruction of the ecosystem has a major impact on species extinction. Sanitary precautions must be improved! High-tech health care must be made available!

ooo

Back in 2019, Provincial Chinese Party leaders overseeing Wuhan had hushed up eight whistle blowers who had warned of a new virus that could possibly cause a pandemic. The good Party members accused them of spreading rumors: "You're warned and reprimanded for your illegal activity of publishing false information online."

It was not too long before the Fearless Leaders realized their error. At that point, they suddenly feared the Truth of their cover up would leak out—a possibility that seemed to them more dangerous to their status and power than the pandemic itself. For the Truth could spread far and deep within China's body politic. And when the good Doctor Li Wenliang—who had first warned of a possible COVID 19 epidemic in 2019—suddenly became sick and died in February 2020, the Chinese Authorities knew his death would spark public outrage. The local powers told the hospital to make certain that that the good Doctor still appeared to be alive in the eyes of the public![70] The Party believes in resurrection!

Proving that even a totalitarian state is (somewhat) sensitive to the views of the people, Doctor Li has subsequently been lionized as an "eternal hero." Might as well build him a mausoleum!

ooo

While there was considerable doubt that the pandemic truly arose from people eating the Horseshoe Bat at the Huanan Seafood Market in Wuhan, near where Mo Li was born, there was simply no way Beijing could admit that the pandemic might have come from an unsafe lab procedures and experiments—or else could have been a result of its own bio-weapons experimentation at the Wuhan bio-labs run by the Wuhan Centre for Disease Control. Or perhaps the pandemic could have been a result of playful chimeric "gain of function" experimentation—a research project paid for by international donors and American universities and other non-profits—and not just Chinese sources[71]???

The fact was that the information Party officials got about the feared pandemic was incomplete. There was no standard public disclosure channel or means to engage in open discussions… and health standards were just too low. Too embarrassed, the Benevolent Red Emperor's Ministry of Truth could not tell the Truth—only blame it all on foreigners. This is exactly what the Chinese leadership did for the A-Virus in the late 1980s and 1990s.

To counter Uncle Sam and Lady Europa's demands for investigations into scientific activities of the Wuhan Lab, the Red Dragon's editorialists soon demanded investigations into Fort Detrick and "secret experiments in more than 200 biological laboratories around the world." Washington, Beijing demanded, needed "to improve the transparency of its biological weapon development to the international community."[72] (Actually it was a decent proposal—if the Balding Eagle and all other states, including the Red Dragon, would also agree to transparency!)

A Chinese Ministry of Foreign Affairs spokesperson asserted that "It might be the U.S. Army who brought the epidemic to Wuhan" during the World Military Games in October 2019. To counter American accusations, Chinese conspiracy theorists claimed that the virus had been taken from the U.S. Army Medical Research Institute of Infectious Diseases at Fort Detrick, Maryland—to be used a bioweapon against the Chinese people.

It had not been forgotten by Beijing that General MacArthur extradited members Japan's Unit 731 of the Kwantung Army's "Epidemic Prevention and Water Purification Department" that were responsible for crimes against humanity during what has been called "World War II." Unit 731 had experimented with chemical and biological weapons on Chinese citizens and captured G.I. Joe's, including a few Americans. By offering these war criminals a chance to be exempted from trial, Washington obtained data on human experimentation, bacterial warfare, and poison gas experiments. The team was able to continue its brilliant research under American supervision at Fort Detrick—the largest U.S. research center for Bio-Chem weapons.[73]

More propaganda and counterpropaganda! Both sides had bones to pick. Both sides LIE!!! Then again, what if the Horseshoe Bat is not the culprit, but the Racoon Dog, as some scientists have begun to argue??? How would that change the nature of propaganda on both sides?

ooo

The propaganda and counterpropaganda soon became absolutely ludicrous. Yet I never expected such ignorant unscientific statements on the part of an American President. To cure the Horseshoe Bat virus, Drumpf claimed, all you needed to do was zap the body with a "tremendous" ultraviolet light… and then "drink" or "inject" disinfectant![74]

Incredible! Drumpf's proposal sounded like a script from a Sci-fi movie. I am sure both Chinese and American versions of Dr. Victor Frankenstein, under orders from the highest command, have already begun to test such chimeric options at both the Wuhan Institute of Virology and the Fort Detrick Army Futures Command.

Executive Order No. 731:
1) Clean out the blood of "volunteers" with disinfectant.
2) Bombard bodies with ultraviolet light in MRI scanner.
3) Test blood for results.
4) Repeat, if necessary, until blood is "pure."

Such experimentation would not be that much different than when the Land of the Free tested the effects of radiation upon Puerto Rican nationalists and other prisoners in the 1950s and 1960s.[75] Maybe Japanese Unit 731, after it had adopted to American society, proved helpful back then, after all? (An allegation that needs to be investigated...)

Then again, maybe there is a simpler way. Perhaps we should all fly off on our private jets and make a yearly blood change in Villars-sur-Ollon, Switzerland. It's a very simple hemodialysis process: The foul blood is passed through a pump that diffuses any unnatural toxic substances, bacteria, or viruses into the dialysis fluid through a semipermeable membrane.... The mantra is "Let it bleed!"[76]

ooo

Beijing has claimed that it will take strong steps to eradicate the Horseshoe Bat virus. Yet it is still possible for the same, or a mutated version, or a chimeric version combining the DNA of two different organisms, or new diseases to resurface...

There is a real concern that the Red Dragon's cherished Belt and Road Initiative will soon spread new zoonotic plagues.[77] Beijing's global project could inadvertently upset the delicate ecology of the regions impacted and make the viruses of the Horseshoe Bat population and those of other species "go postal" (as Americans say) on the Silk Road and beyond ... The disruption of the natural world could likewise unleash unknown diseases that emerge from the prehistoric depths or from swamps amid vast unexplored forests… So too can the rapid melting Siberian tundra spread new plagues as well…

FIRE AND / OR ICE!

ooo

This is all taking place while Moscow and Beijing both hope to establish new shorter and faster and cheaper trade routes through the Arctic—in the effort to cut the superrich Green and Black Gold Sheikhdoms, among others, out of maritime trade profits. This Eurasian neo-Mongol Axis is almost doing the same as did the Europeans when they circumvented the Ottoman Empire and the bandits along the Silk Road… That was when Columbus had first tried, but failed, to reach Cathay by the oceanic blue water trans-Atlantic route—to be followed by the sailing ships of Dias, Magellan, Álvares, and many others….

The peoples of the shifting sands were cut out of the global deal in 1492 before oil and gas were later discovered there—and could be cut out again in the near future if the China-Russia Arctic route becomes serious business…

Long Lost Acquaintances

I had forgotten to say how the stench of "Canal No. 5" had reminded me of the rancid *patchouli* worn by that asinine American, Mr. Mylex H. Galvin, that Wokeist before his time, otherwise known in Chinese as Gao Mai Li, or Gao/Galvin. Just another one of the Red Emperor's many foolish western "fellow travelers" who claimed to be a "Maoist"—as he worked like a dotted forehead on his never-to-be completed PhD.

I still don't know if it was he who had turned me in—whether accidentally or accidentally on purpose. The ignoramus was being followed everywhere by Public Security and probably did not know it. I could not believe this advocate of free love was stupid enough to ask about my relationship with the journalist Mark King Hayford in front of everyone there including student spies—i.e. his so-called "girlfriend" Mo Li—just after I entered into a debate with Galvin before other students, including the brilliant Tao Baiqing, about the Democracy and Freedom movement.

Then again, maybe Gao/Galvin, knew nothing about Chinese politics—except that the Red Dragon was the "good" Communist state because it permitted western investments. These naïve Americans have no idea how sensitive my knowledge of internal Chinese affairs was to the Authorities—even if I really knew no top secrets or anything of value to the U.S. and Europeans. Just by talking to a foreign journalist, I could be suspected of spying!

One of my friends in the movement had been able to purchase a bootleg photocopy of Gao/Galvin's Anti-Marco Polo. I was then able to read G/G's drivel… his reflections on China, America, and the world. Evidently, I did not think much of it at the time… I mean, what an incredibly bad joke: G/G's comrades in the True Farts of the East Wind (TFEW) had offered him a part-time teaching post at hundred bucks a month, free room and board, plus Chinese language and civilization classes! Who in their right mind would take that offer just to visit a polluted China? And the TFEW itself was nothing but a parrot propagandist…

ooo

It was clear Galvin was influenced heavily by Dr. Woodward-Be-Intellow who had written two volumes on

Western relations with China. The first, *China's Exploitation by the West Since the Era of Marco Polo* (Rotting Shelves Books; 1988) seemed to be Galvin's only source for his Anti-Marco Polo Travel Journal… Now, in his latest academic farce, *China's Struggle with the West: Post-Tiananmen Square* (Global Pillage Press, 2021), Intellow seeks to blame China's June 4, 1989 crackdown on the Democracy Movement on American and western imperialism.

How did he come to that conclusion? The thesis is based on the view that American businessmen, as they were losing hundreds of tons of $$$ due to the length of the student strikes, had complained that the Party needed to crackdown as soon as possible. In Intellow's view, the government of the Land of the Free just pretended to be up in arms when Big Brother finally cracked down. In reality, however, U.S. and transnational corporations were very happy once the students were forced violently back into their classes…

ooo

Contrary to Intellow's views, the Tiananmen crackdown is a perfect replica of the anti-reform repression implemented by the *Ancien Regime* itself at the turn of the 20th century when the Dowager Empress refused to engage in democratic reforms. Later, the Party itself had refused to engage in needed economic reforms once it came to power in 1949, and again when students took to the streets in April to June 1989. The Balding Eagle did not create the democracy movement. Government Corruption did!

In effect, pointing the finger at foreign imperialism is just an excuse *not* to put an end to a vast system of corruption! And the ideology of anti-Imperialism helps to forge a new rationale for a new Imperialism!

ooo

And where do these intellectuals who don't even speak a word of Chinese get their ideas from? How could Dr. "Would-Be-Intellow" write two volumes using mainly western sources and based on a few books poorly translated from Chinese? And how could he win a prestigious award for outstanding scholarship? How could he have even received a PhD?

I wonder: Which is worse? Historians who infiltrate the minds of elites with ideological presumptions and falsely interpreted facts in long tracts that almost no one reads? Or modern "intellectuals" who tweet pithy provocations and meaningless barbs in the effort to egotistically outclass each other that more people do read—but who provide no depth to their arguments?

In the new Social Media, "I tweet, There4 I am" (Or now, "I 'X', therefore I am") has transmogrified into "IShaThere4Iam" And there are even some who consider such manipulable *chit chat* to represent a form of "soft power"—or even "diplomacy"! What a farce!

ooo

Not only did Chinese Red "intellectuals" start to propagandize in support of Mao, but so too did many western revolutionary groups—just like Gao/Galvin's True Farts of the East Wind. But who knows who the TFEW were really working for? … That white-haired Mother Courage, her name purloined from Brecht's masterpiece, was definitely a suspicious individual. And I am sure she had a totally invented background. I really doubt her parents were persecuted by the State Department.

I doubt she moved to the Colombian Cocaine Capital to work "for the Cause." Whose "Cause" would that be? As she seemed so sophisticated, even too worldly, did she really believe in what she had been preaching—that China would be the savior of World Communism and the World itself? And why did the TFEW so quickly dissolve in 1989—just after the collapse of the Warsaw Pact? Whose interests did they serve?

It was also incredible that Gao/Galvin had fallen for Mother Courage's long cycle theories. Her predictions turned out to be all wrong! It is leaderships who make strategic choices—whether to confront, to compromise, to ignore, to capitulate—not economic cycles! Then again, there might be something to these numerological theories.

Did the fact that the "little green men" of Vladaspeare Pootin invade Crimea in 2014—almost exactly 100 years after the start of World War I in 1914—initiate a new cycle of global geo-pornographic rivalry that could once again result in direct major power conflict? Could this conflict be the beginning of a new 21st century version of the 19th century Crimean War—as it has begun to spread from the Ukrainian *rasputitsa* to the Holy Lands and the shifting sands of the "wider" Middle East—and maybe beyond?

And in the next phase, after NATO's White Compass Rose had foolishly provoked the Russian Double Headed Eagle to gobble up the Crimean Dolphin in their games of "encirclement" and "counter-encirclement," could the Balding Eagle similarly provoke the Red Dragon into gobbling up the Taiwanese Black Bear?

ooo

In flashing back to the 1980s in Gao/Galvin's formative years, there was G/G's buddy, Barakee, the eloquent, fast talkin' revolutionary poet, the wanna-be rock star, the true Led Belly Wokeist, the expert on W.E.B. Du Bois, Frantz Fanon, Amiri Baraka, and the Black Power movement. It turns out Barakee had been accepted into an MA program at Princeton. Gao/Galvin was evidently very jealous.... "A Black Maoist—at Princeton?" G/G did not think about it—but Barakee was perhaps not too different than Burne Holiday of Fitzgerald's *This Side of Paradise*—a militant Irish pacifist of his era. Even dissidents went to Princeton—even if they were not always so welcome.

Then again, what would Barakee do with his elite Princeton degree was another matter. Make megabucks as a Marketing Rep. in a corrupt independent Angola for a transnational Jolly "Black Gold" Energy Giant???

ooo

As far as I am concerned, Gao/Galvin—and all his Maoist associates and who are probably now all Wokeists—unless they have transformed into equally obnoxious neo-Con, neo-Martian Vultures—should just stew in the cesspool of those old ladies who wash syringes in plastic buckets behind Chinese hospitals. They should all have their tongues ripped out in the *Diyu* Earth Prison—that possesses even more grotesque forms of torture and punishment than Dante ever dreamed—if they themselves have not yet sold out to the "establishment."

The interesting thing is that Chinese *Diyu* traditions tend to mix Hell together with Purgatory—so there was no clear differentiation. After all, if you are not fully in heaven, then where are you? Can *Jee-Zus!!!* be god and not god or a half-god? (That was a question that has caused and still causes many religious schisms.) Can your spirit be either half full or half empty? Can you only be half tortured through "enhanced interrogation techniques"?

ooo

It was true, Mo Li, became a PLA Captain. She was commended for her excellent spying on student activities. But no, she did not entirely fabricate such horrible experiences about her own life and family. At the same time, she did use those terrible times—which were also experienced by millions of other Chinese—to win G/G's gullible sympathy and affection.

Gao/Galvin should have known that the minds of youth could easily be manipulated—as had been the case with the Hitler "Holocaust" Jüngen who likewise showed no qualms about turning in neighbors and even their own family members. The manipulation of youth for political reasons represents one of the greatest violations of human freedoms and rights—an issue that has rarely obtained significant attention as to how, if possible, to stop it…

Let youth be youth!

ooo

Initially, in 1988-89, during the Year of the Earth Serpent Changing Colors, Gao/Galvin's Chinese friends had toted the "Little Bottle" Party line. Mo Li was no exception. A decade or so after Tiananmen Square, and as some of the Chinese became much richer, however, they and their children would all eventually change tune. It was not too long before they would be able to clink "Thin Neck Bottles" filled to the brim with wine and champagne—while dancing overseas on the sands of Phuket—like many of the "*Wealthy, Wacko Asiatics*" from other countries…

And that would change everything. It was the new China for the sons and daughters of the *nouveau riche Tuhao* and High Communist Party Cadres—who would soon dump their already outdated electric bicycles and vehicles in the junk yard cemetery in exchange for newer models!

ooo

By contrast with Mo Li, who moved up the Party ranks, Gao/Galvin's talentless artsy Beijing acquaintance, Ling Mei Wong, did nothing much but paint by-the-numbers in the new Millennium. He turned out thousands of pathetic copies of works by Van Gogh, Matisse, Picasso, and many others—for internet sales to tourists and foreigners overseas. There is nothing like bad taste to make the whole world go round!

Speaking of Internet, the interpreter and arts middleman, Mr. Zhu Zhiqing, would discover his own gold mountain—but not in Australia. It was Zhu who, in his once upon a time black clothes with the twisted zipper, had tried to sell paintings in hard currency of Chinese artists to Gao/Galvin and other foreigners given his excellent English skills. And now, he had truly struck it rich!

Unable to leave China, Zhu launched his own web site in English. Zhu's project (paid for primarily by Chinese corporate advertising and by some government funding) was to market select Chinese products to Western consumers, while simultaneously broadcasting articles on Chinese culture in an upbeat and hip diatribe. It was all written in a style not too unlike Gao/Galvin's essays on the American arts scene that Zhu must have purloined from G/G's anti-Marco Polo notebook.

I have no idea how he was able to get a hold of it, but it was perhaps the same way he got a picture of Gao/Galvin's ex-girlfriend out of his cluttered wallet. Zhu must have slipped the anti-Marco Polo manuscript out of G/G's room and found a way to copy it and put it back without G/G noticing. Zhu was the type who would sell information to whoever would buy it—assuming it was not something that would get him in trouble.

After all, Maoist or not, Galvin was just another foreigner who could not be trusted. That is how my friends, the Democracy activists, and the Chinese government (as well as the Boys of the Company, I assume) were all able to get a hold of a photocopy of it. And G/G's Anti-Marco Polo diary turned out to be a best seller on the black market once translated into a poor quality of Chinese!

Just after the New Millennium, Mr. Zhu opted to shift into a new field, given "advances" in digital and AI technology. He became a very successful parrot propagandist who programs computer "bots" that write anti-American polemics for Beijing's wolf warrior diplomats!

ooo

The lone Russian spy, Vladim, whom Galvin also met in Beijing, would bungee jump through *nomenklatura* privatization into post-Soviet business as Russia became hyper-capitalistic overnight and when the former Soviet nomenklatura won the lottery by buying up all the employee-owned stock. The average Ivanov, Petrov, Sidorov or Matryoshka had no idea what to do with those scraps of ticker tape.

Vladim then moved up from his meager $20 a month salary as a researcher in Chinese politics to roughly $$$200,000$$$ a year. His game was to buy cranes in

Ukraine, sell them in Russia, before loading them upon the burgeoning European Union market. (This was apparently in addition to engaging in other, not specifically defined, 'illegal' activities that brought tears to his eyes whenever he thought about them.) And after acquiring multiple credit cards, and with a secret Swiss bank accounts at his disposal, he applied for residence in money-laundering Cyprus.

I always wondered if he had become a Pootin fanatic? But then again, while I knew he was in favor of playing a Russian version of the China Card against the Balding Eagle, I am not so sure he wanted Moscow to play second fiddle to a Beijing-led orchestra…

ooo

I don't think either of the two Germans whom Galvin had met was a spy. Yet I did hear a story that the West Berliner was able to make a fortune in East Berlin real estate speculation after what had been nicknamed the "Great Wall of China" fell to the ground in November 1989, not ever to be picked up again by all the Big Brother's men. By contrast, his former "new best friend" (whom he met in Beijing when West and East Germans were not permitted to speak to each over!) Rolf, the East Berliner, soon joined *Alternative für Deutschland*—a far right-wing political party that began to gain strength in the aftermath of the Cold War.

I wonder: Did Rolf ever go out on the streets with the neo-Nazi skin heads to kick some immigrant ass?

ooo

I don't know who that dumpy LA blonde was—the wanna-be Shanghai Lily. I know the Chinese police had interrogated her, thinking she might be one of the few Girls of the Company, but then let her free… She did not act like a real journalist… Strange… She had said absolutely zilch at that luncheon with MKH and the other journalists… Apparently, she never wrote an article about Galvin for some magazine as she had promised. Much later, however, I learned from MKH that Galvin was the only person she had asked him about after both Galvin and I left MKH's party.

One can only question who was able to enter G/G's room and take those smutty photos that Gao/Galvin later found in an unaddressed white envelope in his mailbox just before he was leaving Beijing for good. Was it some form of "black-" mail? From my sources, I learned that the photos were not a Chinese operation… And it appeared certain that the envelope had already been opened and inspected by someone before Gao/Galvin even saw it. But by whom?

ooo

Fortunately, for Tao, the lovely and lonely—and I must admit, one of the most intelligent women I had ever met—was able to escape to study in New Zealand. My colleagues in the Democratic resistance helped her get a plane ticket out of there… without her even knowing that I too had tried to help her.

Unfortunately, I was not able to get to know her as well as I hoped—although I did hear her very perceptive comments at our discussions about the Chinese democracy movement. What an excellent translator and superb interpreter as well! I wonder whether she was finally able to complete her thesis on *The Way and the Great Peace and Equilibrium*? It seemed to be a "mission impossible" subject to study.

It is incredible how the Yellow Dragon, whose elites kept detailed records of everything in its history, could lose, or most likely, destroy, one of its great masterpieces, the *Tai*

Ping Ch'ing Ling Shu by Yu Chi. Of course, that was an era when all books had to be painstakingly copied word for word, and since there were so few copies available, they were very easy for the State to destroy! That was an era when books were rare and really had value—unlike today where no one gives a damn… While some societies seek to burn them or censor them, the deeper problem is that no one reads the truly meaningful and critical ones—even if they are plentiful with advent of the digital age!

And who the hell is making all the $$$ from the advertising that now goes along with all the free articles, poems, artwork, music videos, books and bootlegged pdf's that have been placed on the worldwide web in the egotistical hope that the authors and poets and musicians and artists will one day become famous??? In the meantime, it seems they are all being ripped off for AI generated research and spied upon by corporations, governments, and hackers!!!

ooo

I really can't get her out of my mind. How Tao Baiqing could have fallen for a schizoid Wokeist "free love" Gao/Galvin of all people, I will never understand! Or did she really? That individual, whom I cannot even call "a man," was so obsessed with somehow getting out of his own skin…. so obsessed with women not of his own white, yet swarthy, skin color… It was as if he wanted to transmute into a Chinaman! That was really a form of reverse racism and sexism—truly a reverse Orientalism that romanticized revolutionary China and Chinese people—although he would never admit it…

ooo

I have heard that Tao may have found herself a husband, a Professor of Comparative Religion, in New Zealand. The dilemma was that I could not contact her or anyone else whom I knew in Beijing. Once I went into exile, I could not reveal my new name and identity for fear the Chinese Authorities might be able to track me down or accuse anyone who knew me of being my accomplice… It would be so easy for them to pressure and persecute her…

Even if democracy activists, who have been accused of "radical" anti-government violence, were able to escape the mainland, there was still the danger that they, like the many Uyghurs, Tibetans, Hong Kongers, and other Chinese dissidents, could still be extradited from even major countries, including Belgium, France, and Spain—that still maintain extradition treaties with mainland China. I had to keep quiet; I had to keep undercover.

I hope Tao finds the yellow kiwis far sweeter there, in New Zealand, than the sour green ones exported here, to France. I am afraid I am super jealous… People may think I was gay… but Tao was truly my dream… my pure Daoist Platonic Mo Zi love!!!

ooo

Gao/Galvin may not have understood her, but Tao was right to fear that Beijing's Thought Control Squads might persecute her for studying the history of Daoism and the Yellow Turban movement, among other rebellions and revolutions in China's rich history.

The fact of the matter is that Chinese history is replete with apocalyptic and messianic movements led by Dark Messiahs.[78] Yet instead of praying to the image of Maitreya, the Buddha of the future—whose imminent, luminous, and redemptive coming to a joyous world with no possessions is to be accomplished in a universal cataclysm of the Old World—the Taiping movement had praised the icon of *Jee-*

Zus!!! resurrected once again. A parallel can be seen in the more contemporary alliance between the America First *Jee-Zus!!! Freak* True Believers, the anti-Red China "Blue Team," and the anti-Palestinian, anti-Iranian, messianic movement led by Rabbi Dr. Geyer. All are prophets of the apocalyptic Rough Beast that they believe is now slouching toward Megiddo and/or Taiwan to be born!!!

It is accordingly possible that Beijing might believe that Tao Baiqing was a member of some mystic organization, some form of a new Taiping movement—perhaps most like the contemporary Fallen-Gang sect whose syncretic religious beliefs appear to derive from the beliefs of 19th century leader of the Taiping rebellion, Hong Xiuquan. Hong believed he was going to save China by overthrowing the ancient regime.[79] Incredibly, he claimed to be the brother of *Jee-Zus!!!*

If so, who knows what might happen to those who join the Society for the Exploration of Cosmic Consciousness (SECC)??? And what might happen to Tao—just because she has studied such Daoist movements—if she is believed to be associated with them?

True Believers

Gao/Galvin exemplified what was once called a "fellow traveler" of the Communist "Reds". He was one of the few who remained a die-hard "True Believer" until the late 1980s.... before the Led Belly "Woke" movement picked up in steam, inspired by the 1960s anti-Vietnam War movement and Cultural revolution—of which Gao/Galvin was a militant. What a joke! He couldn't even fire an AK-47!!!

It was incredible how the Maoist craze was able to attract tens of thousands of young and old American and European groupies. With symbols clanging and drums beating, I could just see them chanting the ludicrously strident songs of the Cultural Revolution: "*Sailing the Seas Depends upon the Great Helmsman… Life and growth depends on the sun… Rain and dewdrops nourish the crops… Fish cannot leave the water… Nor melons leave the vines… Mao Zedong Thought is the sun that forever shines!!!*"

What a catchy tune! Everyone should join in and dance! I mean, how could so-called Western "intellectuals" justify such garbage! I mean, their anti-war cause may have been just, and perhaps some of their critiques of capitalism—but why try to justify a so-called "people's war" that was never backed by the "people" with Mao's *Little Red Book*!

ooo

Gao/Galvin believed himself to be a "Maoist" variant of Red—a color that came in many shades: Stalinist, Leninist, Trotskyite, Titoist, Shining Path, Gramscian, Democratic-Socialist, early Anarchist (before the latter transmogrified into Black Cats), Anarcho-Libertarian, Council, armchair intellectual, professor, among many others. There were many such fellow travelers who fell for the Maoist craze in America and Europe, particularly in the 1960s and 1970s.[80] Gao/Galvin lasted as a "true believer" longer than most—inspired by the poet Amiri "Leroi Jones" Baraka's Marxism-Leninism-Stalinism-Maoism.[81]

ooo

And then there was the new form of American pro-Cuban Revolutionary who took on the whole team from the True Farts of the East Wind almost singlehandedly in their battle in Malcolm X Park in 1988 at a demo against Apartheid—that was demanding freedom for Nelson Mandela just a few years before he was released—in a story Gao/Galvin had related in his anti-Marco Polo travel journal. It was in that scrap with that pro-Cuban anti-Maoist Martial Arts weightlifter and his gang on the Malcolm X battlefield in D.C. that Galvin's scalp was split wide open.

As a pro-Cuban African American revolutionary, an Ultimate Fighter as tough as Mohammed Ali, as a macho Metis *café au lait* "new man," he had truly caused Gao/Galvin and his comrades to cower in fear. I realize a shared race or *café au lait* is a not-so-politically correct expression—as people are not coffee drinks… Yet we all have differing skin tones from lily white to xanthic yellow to pitch black. One can't ignore it… that's the issue. Many of us see only the Chimera of the outside before we know the spirit or consciousness of the inside… And more problematically, we all make fun, or even worse, of both each other and of our own kind…

It is much easier to make jokes about one's "own kind" (which can be a shared mix of many "kinds") than it is to make a joke about the color or another human who is not in one's own defined identity group… whatever that is…

An Afro-American can jokingly call another Afro-American the "N word"; someone of Chinese background can jokingly call another Chinese "a Ch-nk" … A white person can jokingly call another, a "whitie" "honkie" or a "cracker" ...

I mean, where is the honesty of Mark Twain?

ooo

It is a very sad world—with so many double and triple standards indeed! I mean what is "correct" or "incorrect" these days in such a world where all is relative? … What is "correct" in a world where everyone has a supposedly "equal" narrative… And where everyone is supposed to be exactly equal to everyone else despite differing intelligence, creativity, skills, interests, visions, loves and hates?

Instead of being proud of our uniqueness and respecting our differences, we are placing everyone in the "same" Procrustean casket which, in practice, only serves those in power—i.e. those who stink of excessive wealth who squeeze the pennies of their employees and the quality of their products so as to boost their profits even more.

The real issue is thus to what degree such differences should justify significant advantages in material well-being and social influence and political power and to what degree should significantly advantages in material well-being, influence and power continue to persist despite those individual differences....

ooo

In speaking of cultural values, who in the hell started that myth that Maoist/Communist China represented a model of Kong Fuzism (Confucianism)?

Even as sophisticated an individual as Henry "Tactical Nuke" Kissinger (at least he is perceived to be sophisticated because of his heavy Germanic accent), thought Communist China represented a model of a "Confucian" society. Contrary to Kissinger, however, there is nothing "Confucian" about Mao's China or even about post-Maoist China. Modern Communism is closer to the ancient Legalism of the Qin Shi Huang era.

It is true that Chinese history has blended differing ideological currents together throughout its historical Red-Yellow clash of opposing forces, as Tao Baiqing argued, resulting in bizarre syncretism of Daoism, Buddhism, Manichaeism, Moism, Confucianism, Legalism, among others. Yet by contrast with Confucianism, Maoism opposed patriarchy, hierarchy, and conservatism. Maoists sought to break up the family, particularly during the Cultural Revolution, and did not seek to sanctify the family under a Barbie-despised patriarchy and phallocracy!

And in seeking to destroy the family, Mao would wreak havoc on the entire society. Ironically, Mo Li, Gao/Galvin's so-called "girlfriend," now works for many of the very same class of individuals who had divided and ruined her own family during the Cultural Revolution and who then ruined her own life… by transforming her into a Dragon/Rat Chimera like them.

It is true, I admit, that to change its syncretic Maoist/Communist, or really, Maoist/Legalist image, Beijing has more recently been subsidizing "Confucian Institutes" in dozens of countries on six continents—as part of its "soft power" propaganda outreach to make its society and governance look more "Confucian"—even if it nevertheless remains Maoist/Legalist…

This might fool poets as intelligent as Ezra Pound and others who believe that Confucian "law and order" would provide salvation for America. For Pound, who admired Mussolini, America should be like metro of people's moving faces conducted by Confucius... a line of "petals on a wet, black bough…." as in a Chinese painting… Very sad indeed…

False Prophecies

The Maoist revolutionaries got their geo-pornography all wrong. Not much would happen the way G/G and his ilk expected or feared. German unification, eastern European liberation, and Soviet break–up were not predicted. How does it feel to be so off the mark!!!!

In the case of the Soviet Bear, Moscow would finally "liberate" Eastern Europe by withdrawing all of its troops—an action that Gao/Galvin and most true-blooded Maoists, including the True Farts of the East Wind, did support to their credit because they despised, with all their hearts, stolid Soviet bureau-rats—in the proclaimed support for permanent revolution although they had no idea where that "revolution" was heading.

In the case of the German Eagle, Bonn/Berlin would not seek out a *Sonderweg*—or a "special way" between capitalism and socialism—as advocated by the tall West German whom Gao/Galvin had met at the Beijing disco. Maoists were not really expecting and wanting German unification to take place under the flag of NATO's White Compass Rose.

And what even Maoists did not expect was that Soviet collapse—that fortunately took place with a hollow whimper and not a Satanic nuclear bang—would make the Russian Double-Headed Eagle and the 15 separate republics look much like a dangerously instable Weimar Germany / Austria Hungary that could soon transmogrify into a revanchist Russian form of fascist dictatorship that differed from the Swastika variety—and was much closer to the Mussolini version.

And Maoists definitely did not expect Soviet disaggregation to threaten a planetary AI military-technological tactical nuclear conflagration—once the Balding Eagle and NATO's White Compass Rose and other Allies aligned forces to counter the resurrected double specter of a Russian-Chinese Double-Headed Eagle- Red Dragon Chimera.

ooo

Contrary to the Maoist view, the struggle in Northern Ireland would not be settled by violent IRA revolution, but, for the most part, by the diplomacy of the 1998 Good Friday Agreement, backed to its credit by the "Slick Willie" Clitone administration—eight years after Gao/Galvin, as a self-proclaimed Irish revolutionary, bit the red dust in January 1990 at the end of the Year of the Earth Serpent.

It took all the way to 1998, after years and years of "troubles," that the Union Jack finally agreed, pressed by the American Stars and Stripes, to negotiate secretly with the Green Starry Plough flag of the Irish Republicans. The Protestant-Catholic power-sharing deal that resulted could take place only once all sides realized that the violence had to stop so that compromises could be reached… The non-violent path wasn't perfect—but it was saner than violence.

ooo

And once again contrary to the views of Maoist and other violent revolutionary theorists—wars of so-called "liberation" in Africa and Asia generally ravaged the very cultures and societies that they were fighting to "liberate." Much like brushfires that could be sparked by a mere match on dry pine needles, these conflicts would be very difficult for the world's post-Cold War peacemaking firefighters to snuff out. Escaping the cycles of violence and counter-violence takes real courage, foresight, and leadership…

As an example of Robert Frost's "semi-revolution," the South African Apartheid system would collapse with a whimper—and not transform into a vampire's blood bath as many of G/G's comrades and other radicals had expected and even hoped for....

In brandishing the proud Union Jack, Maggie "Iron Lady" Thatcher had insisted that she would never "negotiate with terrorists"—whether Irish or South African. Yet pressured to make a deal by Uncle Sam, the British Lioness soon found herself negotiating in back alleys with the Black, Green and Gold flag of the African National Congress (ANC), in addition to the bombers of the Green Starry Plough flag....

At the same time, however, after secret negotiations, the revolutionary Socialist South Africa that had been promised by the imprisoned Nelson "The Fist" Mandela would not be same at that of the freed Nelson "Dalibhunga" Mandela when he was released in February 1990. It was a position that was in opposition to some of Mandela's more hardline associates and more in accord with his nickname meaning "convener of the dialogue".

That was just a month or so after Gao/Galvin's death in January 1990 (not soon enough!)—and just after the Soviet Union had begun to pull its forces out of eastern Europe and withdraw its supports for revolutionary movements around the world.

Once South Africa lifted the ban on the ANC and other Black Liberation parties, Truth and Reconciliation became the word of the day—instead of "necklacing" and "re-education" camps. And unlike Robert "Matabili" Mug-Abe's[82] revolution in Zimbabwe, that resulted in a brutal one-party dictatorship, the Black, Green and Gold South African revolution opened the door to multiple parties. In Pretoria, a neo-liberal capitalism, and not State Socialism, would predominate—even if not everyone would be "reconciled." Apartheid was finally over, yet the financial benefits would not "trickle down" to everyone…

Yet it was not too long before South Africa's ANC revealed the true colors of its Black, Green and Gold flag, when it stated in its "Discussion Document" (2015) that China's "economic development trajectory remains a leading example of the triumph of humanity over adversity. The exemplary role of the collective leadership (of the Chinese Communist Party) … should be a guiding lodestar of our own struggle…"

Yes, the lodestar example of millions imprisoned or killed for good of the CCP! Black for native People, Green for the land, Gold for the Mineral Wealth—and RED for Chinese Yuan! Once the Red Dragon started to pour Yuan into the countries of Eurasia, Eastern Europe, Africa, the Far East, and Latin America in the 21st century—in pursuing the Belt and Silk Road—Beijing had begun to act just like a capitalist neo-imperialist!

ooo

Very few Maoists (or others) foresaw how the demise of the Soviet Bear and resurrection of the Russian Double

Headed Eagle—that began to transmute into a wicked mix of Tsardom and Fascism—would engage in a promiscuous relationship with the Red Dragon.

With Beijing supplying fresh Yuan from its coffers, and the new Tsar providing the military muscle and mercenaries, many countries in Africa and elsewhere started to salute both Great Red Dragon and Russian Double Headed Eagle—suddenly turning their backs on the Balding Eagle and Lady Europa (and France in particular) ... The Yuan, combined with *bai jiu*, mixed with fear and envy, has a way of restoring friendships, while the ruble and vodka, stirred with fear, has a way of making leaderships forget!

Not-so-Beatific Beats

Once I had arrived in Paris years ago, I had gone immediately to the Shakespeare & Co bookstore. Over the years that I lived in Paris the store had changed from a bookstore to a bookstore café. After the first owner Sylvia Beech had published James Joyce's *Ulysses* at a great cost to herself, the original store became a hangout, if not a refuge, in the 1920s and 1930s, for all the great English-speaking writers who visited or lived in Paris—from Joyce to Eliot to Stein to Hemmingway to Pound. It was the place in Paris for all those who craved American literature—like me.

I then learned that, after Beech's death, it was another bookstore, the Mistral, which had changed its name to

Shakespeare & Co—so that it emblazoned itself with a false literary glory that was not truly part of its own the past... In effect, the opportunistic new Shakespeare & Co had nothing to do with the original bookstore. Nevertheless, it then housed many of the up-and-coming American Beat poets—many of whom had been influenced by Chinese and Asian arts and literature. It was they who had initially inspired Gao/Galvin—that Wokeist before his time and the wanna-be Irish American poet version of Amiri Baraka.

There was plenty of material for my not yet completed thesis and for writing literary criticism—if I could only find a magazine to work for that paid a decent salary! As I read through the lines of the Beat novels and poetry, however, I found quite a mixed bag… These critics of America—with their contradictory Anarcho-libertarian-syncretic religious views—were very American—not at all "un-American." Despite their claims, they were not truly critics of American culture—as seen through my French-fried Chinese eyes…

ooo

Allen "Kadesh" Ginsberg was the original pacifist flower child waving a Hong Kong *tongzhi* rainbow flag against the Vietnam war and all other conflicts. He was born of café intellectuals: A schizoid lobotomized Communist mother whose family had escaped a Russian pogrom to be beached in the Land of the Statue of Liberty and a poet Father who thought T.S Eliot had moved poetry toward a too elitist and obscurantist direction… Not entirely wrong...

Ginsberg's line in *America*, "I used to be a communist when I was a kid, I'm not sorry" had angered me, since I quit the Party. Initially, I thought Ginsberg had fallen for the myths created by the Communist parties themselves. I knew that Ginsberg had been welcomed in China, Cuba, and Czechoslovakia because those Communist Parties believed him to be anti-capitalist and anti-Vietnam war.

Then I learned that once he got to those countries, the Fearless Communist Leaders saw him as a troublemaker, a supporter of gay rights, and proponent of the liberalization of certain drugs. And he was a militant opponent of irrational bureaucracy that claimed to be the summit of Socialist rationality—a walking, breathing, hustling, example of truly naked free speech... Naturally, he was booted out…

So while I learned that Ginsberg was not as pro-Commie as he seemed, I also learned that America could be repressive in its own way... as seen in the case of the Black militant Amiri Baraka… Ginsberg had condemned J. Edgar's Bureau (FBI) for its decision to "lay off the Mafia" and "instead bust the alternative media, scapegoating Leroi Jones (Amiri Baraka)… even putting me on a 'Dangerous Subversive' Internal Security list in 1965—the same year I was kicked out of Havana and Prague for talking and chanting back to the Communist police… 'The fox condemns the trap, not himself,' as Blake wrote in Proverbs in Hell."[83]

Ginsberg may have been right to prophesy *The Fall of America*... but the Red Dragon must not take its place!

ooo

Holy Land Judaism was not sufficient for Ginsberg. As a Jewish Buddhist, he truly dedicated himself to the Hairy Kristma movement. Yet it was clear that neither Tibetan Buddhism nor Hinduism could fulfil his deeply ravaged soul or his ever-squawking rooster that, he claimed, "never got laid in Chinatown" … even if he would still desire to "tie (his) head on a block in the Chinatown opium den…"

That was fortunate for him—that is, that he did not get laid in Chinatown. For if he had gotten caught trying to bugger some teenagers there, he would have been taken to a back alley, tied to a wooden chair, and bled slowly to death without losing consciousness, sliced piece by piece, the limbs removed, the heart left intact until the very end… Death by a thousand cuts *(Lingchi)*!!!

ooo

What in the *Diyu* hell did this admitted cruiser for teenagers, this gay "Chickenhawk", this howler of *Howl*, think when the boarding schools of the Hairy Kristma movement—to whose mantras he had dedicated many poems—were accused of beating, denying medical care, sexually abusing, and even raping, its school children?[84] And what would Ginsberg now think about the thousands of priestly pedophile scandals that have been coming out of the Catholic Church in both Europe and the United States—of which Gaspard G. Profita was a victim?

What did these terrible scandals say to those who were sincerely searching for Truth from the priests who had dedicated themselves to the rock of Saint Paul? … What did it say to those who prayed with monks who had dedicated themselves the Bodhi tree of sacred fig enlightenment—when both religions claimed that the Truth lay beyond daily sensual temptations? And what did these scandals say about the balance between body and soul of some of the Beat Generation and others who followed the same path?[85]

ooo

The elder statesmen of the Beats, William "Naked Lunch" Burroughs, was a brilliant gun-toting libertarian drug abusing switch-hitting cowboy—who was born, unlike the other Beats, into an established non-late American immigrant family. Unbelievably, while showing off to his friends, he dropped his pistol, and by accident, shot and killed his second wife. He then got away unpunished in court. At first, he boasted he was playing William Tell. Very funny. Had he been poor, an ethnic minority, or a person of color, would he have been able to evade prison—or escape Old Sparky with its "imprisoned lightning"?

ooo

He called his paintings "shotgun art." What would the gun toting Burroughs think now that there are almost 400 million guns for over 300 million people in the U.S. alone? After all, everyone has the right to self-defense… even school children who don't like their classmates or teachers!

With tens of thousands of mass shootings in the Land of the Free… "No body wants no god damn gun cunt'rols. And if ya' even hint 'bout bannin' guns from public places, then ya cans go to hell… It don't matter if it ain't got nothin' to do wit' huntin'; it's tha god-damn 2nd command-a-ment of da' Bill of Rights 'hat counts... It's free-doom from government cunt-rols!... The Feds 're spyin' on all of us... And like all goddam Liberals, ya mus' be for a femi-nazi dictatorship... It's sure ya' support abort-ion and more taxes too..."

At least that is my stereotyped rendition of Drumpfist language and logic... A depiction that is of absolutely no help for finding a path toward reconciliation in highly polarized American society!

ooo

Another influential member of the Beats was the French-Quebec "Canuck," Jack Kerouac, who had written the famous or infamous, *On the Road,* the spontaneous Bebop hipster Beat classic. As compared to Ginsberg, he saw himself as a Catholic/Buddhist. Yet his book *Dharma Bums,* had nothing to do with pure Buddhism. A rebel like the other Beats, he was not accepted into the mold...

As an immigrant, Poor Jack felt obliged to pretend to live as an "American" with his buddies Burroughs and Ginsberg. At least he dreamed with a French-Canadian maple syrup accent: "*la vie est d' hommage.*" Kerouac may, or may not, have been so pro-Vietnam War as Gao/Galvin and others claimed, but he still appeared to be a stoned fan of the anti-Red, anti-Lavender, Fearless Leader, Senator Joseph "Red Scare" McCarthy... whose legal counsel, Roy "Mafia Defender and Red Baiter" Cohn, subsequently became an Old Testament inspiration for Donald Secret Agent Orange *Jee-Zus!!!*—in the latter's dreams to become President.

Certainly, Kerouac was a French-Canadian ally of the United States, who had adopted a strong skunk scent of American nationalism as do many immigrants. In that way, by reeking patriotism like a Supreme Court Justice candidate reeking fraternity beer,[86] this kind of immigrant would always talk tough, more nationalist than most Americans, to show how much they love the country, sports, and beer—and to prove that they are not Communist. Nevertheless, as a Canadian, Kerouac may have sported a certain empathy for the other side—only because he realized that the Vietnamese Water Buffalo were nationalists rejected by the French before becoming Communist…

In any case, there was no way I wanted to become such an uncritical immigrant nationalist in the Lands of the Free. While Ginsberg howled against both Democrats and the Republicans, both Burroughs and Kerouac, if alive, would probably vote for Drumpf!!!

ooo

Singing "God bless America!!!" was a way to make both Americans and immigrants oblivious as to how the Balding Eagle's gargantuan appetite was not only gobbling up the world's resources but taking over global societies and cultures as well! The WARNING was there. The Americans, the Europeans—and even the Chinese years later in sheer admiration, imitation and envy—were all roaring down Route 666 totally blitzed in CO, NO, PM and VOC emitting, gas-guzzling, combustible engine road trips in wholesome solidarity together into SPECIES EXTINCTION after passing through one RED LIGHT after another…

I must admit, although I strongly disagree with his Wokeist, wanna-be-Amiri Baraka, Irish revolutionary, polemics, I developed some new ideas after reading my bootleg copy of Gao/Galvin's Anti-Marco Polo Travel Journal… I mean I am not… well… guilty of plagiarizing… yet I am simply appreciative of Galvin's acute observations even if his ideology was pure B.S… As Gao/Galvin correctly observed, Ginsberg, whom Kerouac had dubbed "Carlo Marx" in *On the Road*, had been overwhelmed by his own interpretation of Hindu/Buddhist/Jewish metaphysics as revealed in his anti-Napalm anti-Agent Orange poem... Wichita Vortex Sutra #3… *"I lift my voice aloud, make Mantra of American language now, I here declare the end of the War!"*[52]

Here is one of G/G's own more interesting passionate poetic prophetic outbursts…

GINSBERG! WAKE UP FROM YOUR STONED TOMB! YOUR MANTRA HAD TRIED TO STOP THE BLOODSHED IN VIETNAM, BUT MUST NOT FAIL TO PREVENT THE "ARMAGEDDON TO END ALL ARMAGEDDONS" GENERATED IN THE (UN)HOLY LANDS WHERE THAT ROUGH BEAST IS JUST ITCHING TO POUNCE, WITH ITS RAZOR CLAWS NOW SLOUCHING TOWARD THE HILLS OF MEGIDDO, THE EASTERN EUROPEAN BLOODLANDS, THE LOFTY WATERSHED OF THE HINDU KUSH, AND THE YELLOW FROTH OF THE SOUTH AND EAST CHINA SEAS!!!

Western-Chinese Artspiration!!!

I am indebted to France for helping me to make a new life from scratch after I arrived in Paris in 1997 at the tender age of 27. Yet having now lived in France since then, I cannot believe I how paradoxical the country is.

In September 1996, just a year before I arrived, a mainland Chinese artist, in protest over Hong Kong's "dull, colonial culture" had painted Communist crimson over the bronze statue of the Queen "Irish Famine" and "Opium Wars" Victoria—a statue that was already covered with bird droppings, dirt, and atmospheric corrosion. The artist then bent the Queen's nose with a hammer to protest the "100 Years of Humiliation." Her nose job cost $150,000.

For eight days in a Hong Kong prison, the artist was imprisoned for protesting the statue who symbolized the Empire that had once brought China to its knees … His action revealed that the Queen was not the only British imperialist celebrated by statues on Hong Kong Streets. Other streets were named for former British governors, colonial administrators, and military officers—and even for British Opium pushers.[87]

The artist's costly action did not hurt his career… He soon received an award of $60,000 to study in a country of his choice. The French leadership must have suddenly remembered its historical conflict between "La Pucelle" Jeanne d' Arc and British archers and France's loss of North America and India versus Perfidious Albion and its East India Co during the Seven Years War, not to overlook

Napoleon's defeat by the Red Coats—and hence rewarded the artist for his assault on the Queen of England...[88]

Such "artistic" agitprop has been mimicked in the Land of the Free against statues depicting grey uniformed Confederate officers, politicians, and owners of slaves. Yet had any of these artists done the same by smearing Mao's image in China, or that of Kim's in North Korea, or had they replaced supermarket price tags with messages criticizing Russia's "special military operation" in the Ukraine war—that, much like the Vietnam War for the Balding Eagle, has not been considered a "war" at all by Russian Double Headed Eagle—they'd wind up with years in prison[89]—if not worse!

ooo

This is not to criticize such protest art by trying to justify or somehow legitimize what Queen Victoria and John Bull-dog did to China... for it is true that public statues and street names etc. that depict political leaders do tend to legitimize their policies, actions, and beliefs... both the "good" and the "bad"... no matter how ignominious their polices and actions were... The dilemma is whatever horrors those leaders and their followers may have committed was still part of History... they are still part of our confused, and rarely clear, collective Memories... like it or not...

ooo

As if by habit, I must have jogged past the Marmottan museum that displays the impressionist art of Claude Monet many times. At long last I paid the entrance fee. Perhaps it is Monet's work that most truly reveals the influence of the East on the West. It is certain that *The Waterlily Pond* and *Green Harmony* were strongly influenced by Japanese artwork, with its vivid pictorial images, its expression of tranquility and purity. I felt as if I were frozen in time.

Monet, much like van Gogh, was certainly an admirer of the art of *ukiyo-e* or "the floating world." That was the *Japonisme* that Europeans had discovered when the Eastwind had begun to blow back at the West in the 1880s. That was when what has more recently been called "globalization" truly began—when the East (soon to be under the boot of the Japanese *Shuten-douji* Chimera) began to strike back at the West—after West had trampled both the East and the South… As previously argued, the South is only recently beginning to strike back in the 21st century backed by the Red Dragon and Russian Two Headed Eagle…

ooo

For the Japanese *Shuten-douji* who, up to then, had never been fully subdued by foreign powers, that was the era when colorful fans and kimonos, cherry blossoms, woodblock prints and paintings, kabuki actors and sumo wrestlers, historical battles and folk tales, travel scenes and landscapes, 36 views of Mount Fuji, strange flora and fauna, monstrous *Yokai* Chimeras of differing kinds, not to overlook enticingly exotic and erotic women, like the Snow Woman, all began to captivate the Europeans.

Monet had admired the work of Hokusai, the Andy Warhol of his era, who painted one of the most reproduced pictures in the world. Even those who knew nothing about art must have seen the famous drawing of *The Great Wave of Kanagawa.* That famous painting depicts three boats moving through a stormy white foam sea with a massive Prussian-blue wave mounting like a tsunami beneath the venerated Mount Fuji.

Less known, but far more seductively interesting, was Hokusai's erotic *The Dream of the Fisherman's Wife,* also known as *Girl Diver and Octopi.* It was a work that had been threatened with censorship in the newly puritan Communist China and the always hypocritical and pretend puritan America.[90]

ooo

It was Hokusai who inspired *Manga* cartoon stories that have become so popular, particularly in France. *Manga* is about the only thing that teenagers and their elders read nowadays—except for brief tweets on twitter, now called X, and short meaningless scribbles the length of Haiku on other not-so-Social Media with no reflective depth… Almost no one reads short stories, real novels, or deep poetry.

But I must return to my original question. Who influenced the Japanese artists? I don't want to sound too nationalist, but no one seems to mention the Chinese influence on Hokusai! No one mentions how he painted Chinese stone lion chimeras (*shishi*) every morning in ink on paper as a talisman against misfortune—much like the gargoyles are said to scare away evil spirits. Unfortunately, however, his stone lions did nothing to protect him from the fire that destroyed his studio and much of his work in 1839… Just as red-eyed gargoyles had failed to save Notre Dame from the *Diyu* of flames….

ooo

Andy "Campbell Soup" Warhol had claimed to be anti-establishment. Yet to me his work really mimicked a stark colorized celluloid vision of Modern Times Our Ford

Factory mass reproduction for $$$profit$$$: "Making money is art and working is art and good business is the best art," he once exclaimed. It is perhaps not so ironic that both "Campbell Soup" Warhol and Secret Agent Orange *Jee-Zus!!!* have understood that the modern art world is not much more than "marketing." And that this new art marketing, that is in tens of millions, if not billions, of dollars, has helped create a totally unregulated market of fraud and speculation and exploitation… in which the speculators—but not the artists—get a share if the resale value mounts…

ooo

Warhol's portraits of Marilyn with glossy make-up revealed her phony Hollywood image with no connection to the real Norma Jean. Those colorized images, like film rolls, along with other portraits of Hollywood stars, reeked of glamour and the hyped desire to achieve the American Dream—as realized by so few. And they represented an Art in search of greater and greater numbers of fans.

And as Mao had become "chic" among many elites in the Land of the Free, particularly those who hoped to do business with China, and not just among college "radicals" at that time, his portrait represented a very profitable commodity. Warhol's portrait of a pudgy Mao, with bloody revolutionary red lips, thus raised the question as to whether he secretly admired this democidal dictator?

Was it still possible for Art to mean more than mere marketing? Was it possible for art to mean more than what $$$ says it means? Could Art possess real human value?

Perhaps it was Warhol's entry into a dancing drunken, stoned, painting dyad with Jean-Michel Basquiat, with his distorted African mask portraits, the slave mutations of Africans into Americans, which took their work into new and more mind-expanding dimensions. It was Basquiat who began to deconstruct Warhol's square mass production silk-screened girders and panels and cans—and create an Art with a deeper vision.

It was their joint work, *China and Paramount Movies*, that perhaps best revealed their new collaborative vision. That is a painting that foresaw how Ronnie Ray-gun Free Trade agreements with China would soon signal the ability of Beijing to undermine the American economy at the expense of African American and Hispanic jobs, and those of the working classes in general… A future perhaps better understood by Basquiat and perhaps to a certain extent by Warhol. The painting appears to forewarn how Beijing's growing global cultural and economic influence would begin to limit not only the freedoms of American cinema—but the freedom of writing and the arts in general…

ooo

That was something that Gao/Galvin himself had learned back in 1988-89 when he found that he could not even take a picture of anything inside China that would show the country in a bad light. And as China grew more wealthy and more powerful, it would become more and more difficult to say anything critical about China—even outside the country!

Much as the Warhol / Basquiat paintings depicted, it would not be long before the Land of the Free began to kowtow to the Red Dragon—once almost 1 billion Chinese and counting wanted to watch films at all ages… Chinese demand for American cinema was becoming so great that Beijing could begin to dictate what themes Hollywood could and could not portray, what products could be put in to not so subliminally sell to the audience, or else what needed to be taken out …

And as China surpassed Japan in 2012 as the world's second-biggest box office market, it would be Beijing who would begin to determine how the language and images used in each film needed to be related to the Communist Party's interests or else had to be restricted or excised… Hollywood even invited Chinese censors to check over American films. Film producers sometimes showed their eager willingness to alter scripts to fit Communist ideology or else show the "good side" of China—just as Beijing hoped to present itself.[91]

Beijing's Media and Mind Control Bureau, part of the State Administration of Press, Publication, Radio, Film and Television, played a role as a censor and could reject films with excessive sex and violence. It could even reject anything with a supernatural Dragon Chimera content that had so obsessed Gao/Galvin' nightmarish visions—given the Communist Party's goal of combating all forms of "superstition."

One of Xi Jinping's major acts was to ban the subversive Disney film *Winnie the Pooh* in 2018! That was because critics of his regime playfully referred to Xi (or really his false Social Media image, not the person) as "Winnie." It was only when Xi realized that such censorship created deeper resentment and anger, that he ended the ban….

ooo

As I searched through Paris, I learned of the work of Zao Wou-Ki who had moved in 1948 to Paris to study Art just before Mao took over…. Lucky for him! It had been France who discovered his sublime art and it was only in France where I could discover him. I was stunned without words! Zao Wou-Ki's celestial artwork depicted a cosmos… a world beyond… that was dynamic... expanding… scintillating... For some reason, his cosmic vision reminded me of Tao Baiqing's study of the Great Daoist Equilibrium.

Not only that, as I was later told by the Zenzimes, Zao Wou-Ki had been made an honorary member of the *Society for the Exploration of Cosmic Consciousness* (SECC) posthumously—without his knowledge evidently. It was the SECC who would call his work "Artspiration" —in that his work revealed the path toward the self-consciousness of the cosmic consciousness and conscience. "Artspiration" was an invented term, a neologism from the ancient term "spiration"—that meant the action of breathing as a creative, life-giving function of the Cosmic Consciousness.

So too Claude Monet and Mark Rothko were made members of the SECC posthumously. Contrary to the general view, Rothko did not consider the intense spirituality of his own artwork as "serene"—instead he believed himself to be "imprison(ing) the most utter violence in every square inch of their surface"—perhaps much like the "imprisoned lightning" of electricity. In addition to the fact that Rothko refused to associate his work with galleries who sold the chic Pop Art scene, his "Artspiration" also attracted him to membership in the SECC Hall of Fame.

I began to wonder if Monet, Zao and Rothko would really have wanted to become members of such a society that would want them as a member—to paraphrase Gao/Galvin's favorite comedian, Groucho Marx? And what was the purpose of the incorporation of these artists—whose abstract work generally did not reveal a grounding in specific human epochs—into the SECC?

Once again, that is the start of another story…

ooo

And now there is a real danger that Beijing's politics have begun to influence the politics of Art in Europe, as well as in the Land of the Free.

The artwork of several contemporary Chinese artists has been attacked by official Chinese spokespersons as harming the image of "China and Chinese leaders" or as somehow hurting "Chinese people's feelings" and upsetting the "bilateral relationships" between Beijing and other countries. At least, by such statements, Chinese leaders showed that they recognized the importance of Art and how it could potentially impact the society and politics and even global diplomacy. But there is no excuse for censorship!

The Artist may be free in China to express him / herself—but only so long as he / she does not criticize, overtly or covertly, the Party and the Fearless Leadership. There is no way to engage in Art with a political voice—unless the artist kisses the sweet ass of the Party line![92]

ooo

And then, on the opposite side, there is Western kowtowing to Beijing. I heard a story, that I hope is not "fake news," that a diplomat once spoke at an art show in Guangzhou. Monet's "Impression, Sunrise," he affirmed, "represented the universality of the sun rising in the east"—as the painting's depiction of solar rays penetrated the veil of Monet's misty vision.[93] Such diplomatic hyperbole and kowtowing to Beijing are quite astonishing and dangerous too!

ooo

Here lies a deeper issue: The question of who influences whom, and of who holds superiority over whom—is a question that is often raised in artistic and cultural terms. The danger is that such questions transmute into the essential Nikita "Banging Shoe" Khrushchev question, of "who will bury whom"? This issue came to the forefront in the propaganda of Soviet true believers with respect to the intense rivalry between the Balding Eagle and Soviet Bear during the Cold War. A similar contemporary debate as to "who will bury whom" is taking place among American and Chinese elites now.

Such an absurd concern… as if the Arts of differing cultures can even be graded—and by all things, the Chinese Social Credit system!

ooo

Why is it that rising powers since the time of the Nine Five Clawed Dragons of continental Qin dynasty versus the Black Turtle of the coastal Chu kingdom, or Imperial German Eagle and the Nazi German Eagle versus the British Bulldog and French Gallic Cock, or else the Soviet Bear versus the Balding Eagle, always look down on their rivals as cultural "inferiors"? Why are they always labelling their enemies as perverse and decadent?

And why must nationalist Dali "chicken or the egg" questions, as to who controlled this or that territory continue to plague the geo-pornographic relations between states and populations? Why can't states simply agree to share resources and territories and work together to limit pollution and protect the environment?

If debates over such cultural questions did not persist, and if these differences were admitted and discussed, there would be much less chance for war… I know I sound naïve... yet the words "power sharing" rarely enter the vocabulary of rival individuals, corporations, and amoral/immoral Dragon State Chimera—even if power and responsibility sharing does exist in practice…

Take this astonishing example: Even a capitalist egotist like Andy Warhol(a) born in Pittsburgh into a family of Ruthenian immigrants could share a paintbrush with a New Yorker, Jean-Michel Basquiat, of Haitian and Puerto-Rican roots…

My Dissent and the A-Bomb

After the overthrow of several millennia of Monarchist rule, Chinese intellectuals at the time of the May 4, 1919 movement began to contemplate the value of both Western science and its concepts of democracy. Angering Chinese traditionalists, a few European and American intellectuals were invited to speak in China.

At that time, the democratic philosophy of education of John Dewey was respected and influential in China, so too the philosophy of Bertrand Russell, the ethical opponent of all war. And Galvin's heroine, Margaret Sanger, early feminist, founder of planned parenthood, also came to preach birth control to the world's most populous country. Yet, in the long term, it was Mr. Nuclear Science who proved much more valuable, in the Communist Party's eyes, than did Mr. Ethics, Ms. Feminist, or Mr. Democracy.

The more I studied, the more I saw how the Party had distorted history to justify its own crimes. This distortion began with their (mis)interpretation of the monarchist and democratic reformers in the early 20th century—not to overlook their (mis)interpretation of the democratic doctrine of Sun Yat-sen. Influenced in part by Abraham Lincoln's Gettysburg Address and American democratic principles, Sun formulated his doctrine of the Three Principles of the People: Nationalism, Democracy, and People's Livelihood.

Against capitalism, Sun had argued: "Capitalism makes profit its sole aim, while the Principle of Livelihood makes the nurture of the people its aim." Against Marxist concepts of Socialism, Sun argued that progress is achieved not through class struggle, but through the adjustment of major economic interests: "If most of the economic interests of society can be harmonized, the majority of people will benefit, and society will progress." By contrast to American democratic conceptions, Sun had proposed a five-fold separation of powers or "checks and balances", the 'five Yuan' to prevent the rise of absolute power.[94] All branches of the new government were to be held responsible to the People's Congress—and not to the national leader or a single Party.

These additional 'checks and (un)balances' were intended to enhance the qualifications of legislators and make them morally and fiscally more responsible. With these rules, someone without political experience like Drumpf could never be elected!

ooo

There were those, however, who opposed both Sun Yat Sen and Mao. I thought about the fate of the Chinese Anarchist Chen Jiongming. He had supported a multiparty system of governance and wanted a peaceful, more decentralized, unification of China—in opposition to both Mao and Sun Yat-sen. With the support of Northern Warlords (and perhaps secretly assisted by the British, if not by a scheming Chiang Kai-shek), Chen attacked Sun's forces, including his home and office, in 1922. Sun survived unscathed.

Against Chen, Sun had argued that a decentralized federal and multiparty approach would play into the hands of the Northern Warlords who sought to control all of China's provinces. Denounced as a as a traitor by Communists and Nationalists, Chen Jiongming's memory, perhaps much like Trotsky's, has largely been erased from historical memory. How Chinese and world history might have changed had Chen won his battle with Sun Yat-sen to rule China before Mao took over can only be guessed…

ooo

The *Dà Zì Bào* of Wei Jingsheng on the *Xidan* Democracy Wall in Beijing in 1978 was a revelation. This was when Mr. Democracy, banned by Mao, began to influence my thinking. What Wei called the 'fifth modernization' of democracy should, he urged, take place alongside of fearless leader's Deng "Little Bottle" Xiao Ping's four modernizations—that were intended to strengthen the fields of agriculture, industry, defense, and science / technology—in Chinese development planning.

Wei's essay had defined "true democracy" as "the right of the people to choose their own representatives to work according to their will and in their interests" and as "the holding of power by the laboring masses." In that essay, Wei praised the former Yugoslav system of worker's self-management or what is also known as "workplace democracy" or "*autogestion*" in French. This represented an alternative non-racist, decentralized, non-hierarchical, "cooperative" or "mutualist," socio-economic system much like that originally advocated by Theodore Herzl for an "old-new" Israel.

Although unfortunately marred by Yugoslav Communist Party manipulations, the concept of "workplace democracy" was ironically not an ideal that either the Americans or the Europeans supported.[95] Despite the praise Wei received, the Americans and Europeans certainly ignored that dimension of his democratic thinking!

ooo

Americans and Europeans can say what they want and usually get away with it. Yet it remains a crime in China to advocate free speech—where the difference between "freedom to speak" and "freedom to act" (and in what ways?)

became confounded. In China, it has become a crime to advocate a "fifth modernization" of democracy that would give people the right to choose and "replace their representatives anytime so that these representatives cannot go on deceiving them in the name of the people" in Wei's words.

I want to emphasize his words "replace their representative anytime"—as western politicians can often stay in power, reelected, for far too many terms, particularly as prime ministers, but also Senators and Congress people. Even two terms can be too long. One single term should be sufficient! It would change the whole relationship between a President/Prime Minister and the Congress/Parliament.[96]

Wei was accused of passing "secret" information to a foreigner on the war between the two communist "brothers," China and Vietnam. (It was no secret, however, that Beijing and Hanoi weren't really brothers!) Convicted, Wei was forced to serve a prison sentence of fifteen years in solitary confinement in Beijing No. 1 prison.

ooo

Another major influence on my thinking was Fang Li Zhi—the internationally acclaimed astrophysicist who had worked on China's secret nuclear weapons program in the 1950s—a program stimulated by Mr. Nuclear Science, Albert Einstein's E=MC^{TWO} lectures in China in the early twenties.

In 1989, when I was still in China, Fang had been detained by Chinese authorities and prevented from attending a barbecue where he could meet President "Silver Spoon 1" Bush. Fang's "crime": To support the fifth modernization of Democracy and to demand that Wei Jingsheng be released from prison. After considerable harassment, Fang and his wife sought political asylum in the U.S. embassy where couple slept for almost a month—until they were finally permitted to escape into exile—only to be largely ignored in the Land of the Free once they had arrived.

His words in *On Cosmology* had revealed the evidently dangerous link between Cosmology, Nuclear Physics and Democracy: "It is generally believed that structures of the universe evolved from initially small perturbations to collapsed or pre-collapsed massive halos.... A major goal of cosmology is to reconstruct the initial perturbations, and to extract the cosmological parameters from the observed distributions of galaxies, clusters of galaxies, superclusters, quasars, gamma-ray bursts, and absorption clouds and other unseen radiations....."

Cosmology!
Nuclear Physics!
Democracy!
Oh My!!!

ooo

Fang's plight, in comparison with other atomic scientists throughout the world, was not unique to China. One of the founding fathers of the American A- and H-Bombs, J. Robert Oppenheimer, was attacked for being pro-Communist by McCarthy fanatics in 1954. This was primarily because his brother was a Communist, but also because of unproved suspicions that he may have leaked secrets to Uncle Joe "Koba" Stalin[97] ...

Another, perhaps more salient, reason for the political attack on Oppenheimer was because powerful American politicians, with backing of the "U.S. military-industrial-congressional-university complex" did not like the fact that Oppenheimer opposed the "Super," the H-bomb. Instead, he supported the development of warfighting tactical nukes—

a fact not really explored by the movie, *Oppenheimer*, in his name.

Ironically, after Oppenheimer' persecution, it is now the Balding Eagle, to counter superior numbers of tactical nukes on the Double Headed Eagle Russian side, that is deploying new "dial a yield" nukes.[98] In the meantime, the Red Dragon is steaming ahead to develop all kinds of nuclear warheads… strategic and tactical, big and low yield….

After making his fame on reasons why the Balding Eagle might need to fight a nuclear war, the danger is that Henry "tactical nuke" Kissinger may be right in warning that a Balding Eagle-Red Dragon misunderstanding could easily provoke "World War III" … After all, they are still "mental aliens" in Jack London's terms…

ooo

Along with the American nuclear scientist, Ted "MLAD" Hall, John Bull's scientists also spied on Oppenheimer's Manhattan Project for Uncle Joe. These leftwing individuals did not trust the capitalist Uncle Sam with a monopoly on the A-Bomb.

The French too had their leftwing dissidents—who led Uncle Sam to distrust the French nuclear program. The French nuclear scientist and resistance hero, Frédéric Joliot-Curie, was purged from the French Atomic Energy Commission in 1950 after Washington pressured the Gallic Cock to remove all Commies from the government. A decision that did not prevent the French from eventually exploding their own A-bombs over Algerian sands, along with the Polynesian Atolls of Mururoa and Fangataufa—an action that was at first opposed, and then reluctantly accepted, by the Balding Eagle.

ooo

Moscow had its own dissidents as well. The physicist, and vocal human rights advocate, Andrei Sakharov, who had worked on the development of thermonuclear weapons, was forced into internal exile in Gorky in 1980—until released in 1986 by Mikhail "Prohibition" Gorbachev. The latter was an example of Gorbachev's many reforms that did not please Chinese hardliners who believed Gorby's policies would cause the Soviet Communist Party to lose its monopoly of power—which it did. Hardliners feared that similar reforms in China would lead to their downfall as well.

ooo

How ironic it is that top nuclear scientists, who contributed to the making of what was once considered the ultimate weapon—the best and brightest from the Land of the Free, the Gallic Cock, the British Bulldog, the Red Bear, and the Red Dragon—became human rights and political dissidents and were then persecuted by their very different governments!

A few years ago, it was revealed how the French had sunk the *Rainbow Warrior* of the NGO Green Peace in 1985—unintentionally killing one of the crew. The scuttling of the boat was intended to stop Greenpeace from protesting French atomic testing in the Pacific Ocean. When I learned that, I realized that the Atomic interests of all powerful Dragon Chimeras—whether democratic, authoritarian, totalitarian—appear to be sacrosanct.

Dare anyone, Oppenheimer, Sakharov, Juliot-Curie, Fang Li Zhi, or Greenpeace to try to oppose nukes! Every State must possess Weapons of Mass Destruction—or else!

ooo

The ethical dilemma is that any sane man—particularly those who became the creator and destroyer of worlds—

cannot support the often-threatened use of atomic weapons or any other weapon of mass destruction for whatever reason....

This is even more true now that the strategic concept of "mutual assured destruction" or "MAD" or what is really a "balance of terror"—is no longer regarded by the major nuclear powers and anti-state "terrorists" as truly "MAD"—as it presumably was in the Cold War.

MAD had nearly failed in the Cold War as the 1962 Cuban Missile Crisis and NATO's 1983 Able Archer Exercises, among other incidents, came very close to a nuclear holocaust! And now the Balding Eagle's faith in MAD has been undermined by the September 11, 2001 attacks on the World Trade Center and Pentagon that penetrated U.S. nuclear defenses. In what has been called "hybrid warfare," could states and other actors clandestinely imitate those kind of attacks with Weapons of Mass Destruction???

ooo

The contemporary issue is that the deployment of Dr. Strangelove's tactical nukes is no longer determined by principles of MAD—but by the new Gospel of computerized guestimates of Artificial Intelligence.

After the IBM Deep Blue supercomputer defeated Garry "overthrow Pootin" Kasparov in chess, the whole world has been going downhill—while the brains behind Artificial Intelligence have been going uphill! Even more depressing is the fact that DeepMind's AlphaGo program of Google was able to defeat the Game of Go *(Wei qi)* champions, Fang Hui and Lee Sedoli.

Although in appearance less complex, China's ancient *Wei qi* is much more sophisticated and requires more intuition than the games of chess—a game that probably first originated as *chaturanga* in India, ancient China's rival, before moving to Persia, and then to the Arab world... That's a fact that helps to explain why Chinese geo-strategists, I hate to say so myself, appear to be much more clever than Western ones raised on the Zbig "China Card" Brzezinski's clichés of "the grand chessboard."

In geo-pornographic terms, Beijing is like a Monkey who has been watching on the sidelines waiting to pick up the pieces—as the American Balding Eagle and Russian Double Headed Eagle—who every so often threaten to use the "ultimate weapon"—fight it out over the muddy Ukrainian *rasputitsa*. Then again, maybe the Americans are playing nuclear poker or blackjack—and not chess!

The dilemma is that it is no longer the state leaderships themselves who will determine how, where and when nukes and other WMD are to be used—but computer-generated Artificial Intelligence. Much as His AI Holiness Elon "Rocket to Mars" Musk has forewarned, AI's keyboards can guide Dr. Strangelove's A-Bomb's trajectory through the misty grey exhaust of its rocket's red glare with nearly 100% circular T/Error probability! *Oh, say can you see!* ...

At the same time, such Weapons of Mass Destruction will not be only possible tools used in the next global war... In pressing the coded keys of the "Great Automatic Grammatizator," the Targeting Directorates of states and anti-state "terrorists" can not only project Grim Reapers and Grey Eagles and Killer Robots with WMD warheads... but they can also use those coded keys to destroy finance... the political economy... the infrastructure... the food and water supply... the beliefs and even values... of other states and societies… Any of these games of warfare played by the 12 Riders of the Posse Comitatus can be aimed to foster revolutions… coup d'etats…. acts of repression… if not… democide… feminicide… genocide… ecocide…

It is now the 12 Riders of Posse Comitatus who control *the horizontal… the vertical… It is the Posse who changes the deep fake focus to a soft blur or sharpens it to crystal clarity as if playing the keys of an organ or a player piano… in the midst of freaky unexpected preternatural Yaoguai occurrences and the fog of war… And the ultimate outcome of the Earthly/Unearthly struggle between the Balding Eagle's Oceania and the Red Dragon's Eurasia (with other powers deciding who to join), will largely depend upon which side possesses the super-duper versions of the "Great Automatic Grammatizator" … Or else just plain luck with the blessing of the Posse….*

ooo

I could just hear that former Maoist, that Wokeist before his time, Mr. Gao/Galvin, saying, I "told you so" … "Dr. Seuss's *Butter Battle* is returning from the Cold War with a new Itsy- "Bitsy Big-Boy Boomeroo" bomb—but with much more precisely calculated targets…

I hate to admit it, but G/G was not entirely wrong.

Asexual Eroticism

There was no way I could sleep. They could have broken into my apartment at any time day or night… *The surgeon approaches me with his scalpel…*

I knew that I had risked my neck just by talking with the journalist, Mark King Hayford (MKH) or any journalist for that matter. An eccentric, yet charismatic, individual that he was, he seemed more competent and trustworthy than many other western journalists.[99] In their quest for first-hand reporting, junior and even senior reporters would ignorantly cite the names of the individuals whom they had interviewed in their articles or else display hand written, yet unsigned, complaints from prisoners in *laogai* prison camps—as if Beijing's Orwellian police could not figure out who wrote the letter according to its calligraphy and the prison location. What dangerous stupidity!

Those Chinese who had talked or written to journalists, or who had had their pictures taken, could easily be sent to the countryside—that is, if they were lucky. If not so lucky, or if they had no *guanxi*—no connections—it was a long march into the *laogai* "prison" camp—where they would be lucky to survive their torture. The Western journalist would then be given just a slap on the wrist—as if nothing had happened—or banned from the country... After all, the foreigner did the government a favor by helping to identify a "subversive" …

ooo

In my case, I cannot be certain who told the Police Vice Squad about my presumed relationship with MKH. I doubt Hayford himself had leaked something out. I know his apartment had been broken into, and that they may have taken his notes while destroying his all-important U.S. tax records, but MKH swore my name was not written anywhere... Then again, perhaps they found the tapes with my voice...

Apparently, the Vice Squad believed rumors that I was what MKH had dubbed "amphi-erotic." A bicon. A bi-babe. A switch hitter. A Catullus satyr. For this reason, they probably saw me as even more of a threat than were my actual politics and the "inside" stories that I had willingly revealed to the international Press by blabbing to MKH. Yet if Chinese authorities claim they had some evidence of Hayford's "deviant" behavior, it was not with me! Whatever they thought, it was probably guilt by association, that is, with his amphi-erotic colleague, the photographer, Poncho! If I had any longing whatsoever, it was for Tao Baiqing—but as a purely Platonic Mo Zi relationship of unconditional love...

Contrary to rumors, my relationship with Hayford was purely intellectual, spiritual... The Vice Squad may have I assumed that I was something else... but I guess if I must be labeled, I am "unisex" ... a believer in abstinence. Yet I am not to be confounded with Dali's "Great Masturbator," nor with one of Jerzy "Being There" Kosiński's *Cockpit* characters who practice erotic arts of Indian yoga. Nor am I one of the promiscuous characters of Michel "Submission" Houellebecq's masturbating prose! Nor did I have a

Ginsberg-like "Blake Vision" of the Voice of Ancient Days. (As I later learned, the latter was not a path toward Cosmic Consciousness counselled by the SECC!)

No one seems to care that 'whacking the turtle' can become obsessive and take over one's body and soul in night after night in which the soul cries out to rest but simply cannot…The frustration of believing in and struggling to accomplish something that is seemingly impossible to achieve when so needed and desired, something that seems so obvious and rational, but that is not accepted by the powers that be, can lead to a kind of madness and frenzy… almost impossible to halt...

Such an addiction is not as quite dangerous as taking China Girl, Dance Fever, China Town, Dragon's Breath, Chinese Buffet, Murder 8 … or whatever people call Fentanyl often mixed with other not-so-Daoist alchemical concoctions… Nevertheless, it is still an addiction that becomes unbearable… I wanted to figure out a way to go Cold Turkey, without stuffing…

Unable to achieve what I wanted to achieve; I was haunted by recurrent nightmares…. *The Surgeon straps me to the ice-cold operating table. As he approaches, holding his curved blade in the air, in a clean white room lit by flickering candles, he unexpectedly asks, "Are you ready to confess?" And this time, in a split second… I reply without hesitation with a firm "No!"—even if I feared deep in my heart that I might not be able to resist…*

If they ever caught me, I was afraid that nightmare might become my fate… *After surgery, he applies a local anesthetic of hot chili sauce. I see myself dressed in a short, dark blue coat (kua tzu) on top of a long gray garment (p'ao tzu) ...*

ooo

Contrary to the general stereotype, a Eunuch was not always a low-level servant or a slave of the Forbidden City... The great Moslem eunuch admiral Zheng He, who had initiated China's first blue water explorations in the early Ming dynasty, had been forced to take the knife—after Yunnan was conquered and captured by Ming forces. Born into an elite Yunnan family, he became a servant of the Chinese Yongle Emperor. His family name, Ma, was derived from the Chinese rendition of Mohamad.

By gaining the Yellow Emperor's confidence over time in war after war, Zheng's talents permitted him to become Admiral of the great Chinese fleet. A Moslem who ironically prayed to the *Tianfei*, the patron goddess of sailors and seafarers, his nickname was "San Bao" (or three jewels). Like all word plays in Chinese, "San Bao" had three possible meanings. The first was that he was the third son of six. The second referred to the Buddhist "three jewels": the Buddha (the yellow jewel), the Dharma (the blue jewel), and the Sangha (the red jewel). The third (more sarcastic and much more likely), however, was generally not mentioned in polite and hypocritical society. It referred to the castration/ removal of his two testicles and penis—his "three jewels."

Nevertheless, it was, ironically enough, Zheng He, the Moslem Eunuch, who had inspired the whole macho militarist New Authoritarian dream of a "blue water" China with their string of pearls that was first openly dreamed of in the film River Elegy (*Hesang*) during the 1989 protests![100] The New Authoritarians wanted China to compete politically, economically and militarily with the Balding Eagle in their quest for *fu xing* or the "restoration" of China's major power status in the world as a naval power. The New Authoritarian aim is now to re-establish a new Mandate of Heaven—*Tianxia*—for an overseas global imperium.

Much as I admired Qu Yuan—in my own struggle to achieve a better, less corrupt, and more equitable, China—I also admired the truly jihadist self-perfecting Moslem spirit of the Admiral Zheng He—even if I felt in my present situation of powerlessness and impotence that I could never live up to his courage and perseverance.

At the same time, however, I wanted absolutely no part in the anti-democratic and macho-militarism of the New Authoritarians—who were unwittingly using the name of a Moslem and a Eunuch for their own nefarious purposes. Their global blue water imperium would result in permanent conflict—and not peace.

My political goals thus stood in opposition to those who wanted to take control over Hong Kong and Taiwan. I believed that our leadership should improve China first while establishing positive relations with all states and peoples in the world. And despite my feelings of impotence and despair, I truly hoped I could incarnate the vitality of Zheng He and strive for the betterment of China.

Given my strong opposition to their blue water imperial dreams, my New Authoritarian political opponents must have seen me as a hopping *jiāngshī* zombie nightmare—who, if given the chance, would suck the life force (*qi*) from their souls if they could not first condemn me to the *Diyu!!!*

ooo

Having grown up in the no longer most populous country on this miserable planet (as India has superseded China), I saw absolutely no reason to add yet another suffering sad soul to the many millions of humans! I did not want to contribute another human to this overcrowded and polluted empire. Abstinence is for the best!

This is something that no one seems to understand these days—as it seems that everyone wants to put a Freudian or Neo-Freudian interpretation on all behavior and belief—as if sexuality was anything more than a subject for gossip or for spies who think they are going to "black-" or "white-" or "yellow-" mail people.

ooo

I am not nostalgic for Ernest 'Moveable Feast" Hemmingway's Lost Generation macho memoirs.[101] His heavy 'Death in the Afternoon' drinking and largely untreated concussions that left his ears and brain ringing were not the only things tearing him to pieces from the inside out. These are the things that the Boys (now Girls) of the Company, the KGB/FSB Brotherhood, and China's Ministry of State Security, can play with—as they love to drive their critics and dissidents crazy without them knowing it…

Hemmingway claimed he had been hounded to the last days of his life by J. Edgar's Bureau, who he said, was tapping his phone calls… That was after previously serving his country in "World War II," and after being an ambulance driver for the International and the Spanish Republicans. Hemmingway even worked for the Americans in China under the cover of a honeymoon where he was expected to report on the relations between the Communists and the Kuomintang, the Chinese transport system, and the condition of the Burma Road.

In doing his patriotic duty, Ernest had obtained an interview with Chiang Kai-shek and his wife, Sòng Mei-ling, one of the three Sòng sisters who married three of the most important men in China.[102] Not only that, but he secretly spoke to Chinese Communist Party leader Zhou Enlai. And, in the process, partied, gambled, and got himself totally wasted—and perhaps most importantly introduced local drinkers to the Bloody Mary. Or so was claimed!

ooo

Another example: Jersy "Being There" Kosiński, who suffered from heart disease and inability to write, was, much like Hemmingway had claimed about the FBI, harassed by Polish Communist agents who detested his "anti-Polish" writings. His novel, *The Painted Bird,* was banned from Poland during the Cold War. The observations of Kosiński's later character, the clueless Chance the Gardener, who became a presidential advisor in *Being There,* have not entirely been superseded in the 21st century. Media-savvy "experts" may claim to have all the Mediatized solutions to achieve and sustain power, but they still don't get it. Following in the steps of Ronnie "the Gipper" Ray-gun, Drumpf was able to legitimize himself in the eyes of the American public, largely by ignoring advisors, and by playing idiotic 'You're fired" roles on TV… As Chance the Gardener himself put it, "This is just like television, only you can see much further…"

ooo

Critical writers often have their "spy vs spy vs spy" geo-pornographic stories. The secret agents of Dragon Chimera know your illnesses; they know how to destroy you by innuendo and by spreading rumors in public and in the newspapers and now on the internet—any Media possible. They make you sicker than you really are…. They are all porno collectors! And what they leak into the public is not at all the aesthetic quality of the great Chinese novel *Plum in the Golden Vase!*

ooo

In Cold, and post-Cold, War China, Green environmental activists, multiparty democrats, supporters of independence for Taiwan, Hong Kong, Xinjiang, Tibet, among other regions, have all been repressed by the Communist Party. So too, the *tongzhi,* the Hong Kong term for the LGBTQIA+ community, were labelled as possessing a *petit bourgeois* morality after the downfall of the Qing dynasty and the rise of Maoist puritanism and its egalitarian repression of difference… All Animals are, of course, equal, yet some Party Animals are more equal than others, to paraphrase Orwell.

Given the fact that Chinese civilization has had a varied history of tolerating differing lifestyles and forms of sexuality, it seems absurd that China would necessarily repress individuals who manifest such differences. And it should furthermore be pointed out that one's sexuality or lifestyle does not mean that one necessarily shares the same domestic or international politics.

Members of LGBTQIA+ communities can be conservative, moderate, or else radical dissenters… They can be "right" or "center" or "left" depending on the issue. They can include supporters of Nazis,[103] Fascists, Communists, Socialists, Islamicists, Democrats, Republicans, Anarchists, as well as neo-Con neo-Martians, among other "ists," "isms" and "ians."

The real issue is not gender. One's sexuality or non-sexuality does not necessarily determine one's political choices, strategy, or willingness to engage in political action of whatever form—even on issues such as same-sex marriage, adoption, and others. The real issue is not to pressure or somehow force individuals to adopt one lifestyle over another. That includes religion and beliefs as well! Individuals should be made aware of alternative beliefs and lifestyles but should also be free enough to come to their own conclusions as to what is best. Individuals need to forge their own beliefs and lifestyles and not be forced to accept any dogma.

ooo

It can be argued, however, that neither Chinese, nor American, culture has necessarily permitted children to become children. In the land of single Party rule, in China, which pretends to be a Panda Bear, but is more like a Red Dragon, there were many women who had been pressed to abort so as to only have a single child in the period 1979 to

2015. And since the Party had ordered families to stop at one child or face higher taxes, the one child policy led many women to abort females—leaving only "bare sticks" and "little kings" … in an already patriarchal society.

And now, as China's already oversized population has begun to decline for the first time in 60 years, I could even envision China invading Thailand just to balance out the Yin/Yang ratio! Just joking!

ooo

The dilemma for the Land of the Free is different. As Aiden had informed me: "Some 24 'Red' Republican states out of Uncle Sam's 50 states have abolished abortion. And some states do not permit exceptions—even if woman needed surgery as soon as possible for personal health reasons and in cases of rape or fetal health issues—and even at the risk of never having children again…[104] And doctors who assist an abortion can be sued, fined or jailed… even lose their practice…"

Although I wish that no woman should ever need to undergo an abortion, it is nevertheless a woman's ethical right to choose—as difficult as such a decision is. Yet I never imagined that a "free" (that is, if you have $$$) democratic society like the United States would crack down on the right to choose after women were finally granted that right by Roe vs Wade after years of struggle!

If the anti-abortionists claim to be pro-life, pro-children, *then* why don't they fully support free day care, home leave, better education, and very well-paid teaching at all levels of education??? Not to mention more affordable medical care for children—and everyone else?

And now more American men—precisely because abortion has become illegal in many U.S. states—are choosing vasectomies—not really by choice, but by circumstances… True, it is an option that is fairer for women—but it is not entirely fair for the male either…

Incredibly some American men are becoming Eunuchs in China's ancient Yellow Autocratic Monarchical image!

ooo

It was not until 2001 that China would no longer officially depict homosexuality as "deviant". Nevertheless, charges of "hooliganism"—which could include prostitution and homosexual and autoerotic activities—could still bring the death penalty depending upon the whims of the local authorities and whether a person had powerful connections or "*guanxi*."

I stand against the discrimination of those who choose a "smoothy," a "nullo," or who more scientifically change from a "male-to-eunuch" and against all other forms of sexual discrimination. But I may differ on many issues with those individuals and their political beliefs! It does not matter what gender you are. What matters is your moral and ethical behavior! Feminism and Gay rights *without ethics* can become another form of exploitation and manipulation of one *against* or *over* the other—regardless with which community one identifies.

What matters is that all humans should be treated "as ends rather than means." That was what Kant argued. Yet no one in the militarist Prussian Iron Cross caste listened to him then. And very few in the entire world are listening to him now!!!

And although this perspective is not really very Kantian, it is all a question of finding the appropriate balance between yin/yang or yang/yin or yin/yin or yang/yang in the creation of a gylanic power-sharing and profit-sharing domestic national and international society.

I believe this is what Tao Baiqing, bless her heart, had called finding the way of the local, national, regional, global, and cosmic equilibrium—or

Tai Ping Dao!!!

III.

Free at Last???

Free at Last???

It seemed like years, but in the period February 2022 to August 2022, the Horseshoe Bat restrictions were gradually lifted in France—but just as the new 21st century Crimean War broke out over the muddy *rasputitsa* of Napoléonide between the resurrected Russian Double-Headed Eagle and the Ukrainian Lynx…

Homo Geopoliticus et Economica soon found itself confronted with the demands of a new Tsar—one of common blood—whose grandfather just happened to be blessed by being a personal cook of Lenin and Stalin—or so it was claimed—to reconstruct a new Russian empire after the Soviet empire had imploded in a Babel of confusion.

More like the Big Boss of the Bosses, *il capo dei Capi*, than like Stalin or Hitler, the new Tsar, Vladaspeare Pootin, would eliminate any individual who might represent a challenge to his power before he/she gained substantial attention—whether it be a journalist murdered in a back alley of an apartment complex, a dissident secret agent poisoned by polonium-210 in a cup of tea at a Japanese restaurant in London, or a presidential candidate shot near the Kremlin, or another opponent poisoned and put in prison to rot…

And now this new Tsar had massed troops and tanks and missiles to smash the Ukrainian "Comedian" Velocisomyr Freelandsky—whose puppet face Pootin saw as squawking in the interests of the American ventriloquist. From Pootin's mindset, the leadership of Kyiv, backed by the Balding Eagle, was standing in the way of the Russian Double Headed Eagle's determination to gain control of the Crimean Dolphin and eastern Ukraine—in Moscow's vicious battle to counter-act the dual expansion of NATO's White Compass Rose and Lady Europa.

Easily foreseen, yet difficult to prevent, it was the greatest challenge to Europe and the world since the end of the so-called Cold War… Yet I did not care. I was elated, I was free at last! At least, that is, I did not care—then…

ooo

Across the Pont Louis-Philippe bridge over the Seine was my favorite café where I could finally sit for hours in the sun, drink a cappuccino, and nibble the most delicious chocolate truffles that would always smear my pure white jeans. I would then taste the most exquisite sorbet imaginable before the Pont Saint-Louis that crosses over the Seine to the back of Notre Dame—without eating a main course.

If there was anything positive about the Horseshoe Bat pandemic at all, the crises brought more tables, chairs, napkins, forks, and knives onto the streets of Paris… so that one would not be always forced into crowded and smoky restaurant rooms inside… It made "gai Paris" as depicted in Manet's *Un bar aux Folies Bergère*—even more gay!

ooo

As it was close by, I thought I might try to read at Café Floored—one the most famous cafés in Paris. I had always wanted to complete my "Planetary Manifesto" and write articles on western intellectual history, literature and the arts while sipping an overly milky cappuccino.

Upon jogging to that busy Saint-Germain Boulevard, I entered Café Floored and found it much too noisy to hear myself think. I asked the waiter if I could sit outside in the corner by the door where, it was said, that Jean Paul Sartre and Simone de Beauvoir used to sit, that is, when they were not working inside near where the owner had then installed a coal fired stove, and when they were not eating at *Les 3 Magots*. Perhaps it was the meaning of word "Magots" that kept me from going there: "stocky figurine from the Far East." I did not want to be considered such a thing!

Unfortunately, the waiter claimed that the two famous places where Sartre and de Beauvoir sat were reserved, so he pushed me upstairs to the second floor that was not yet crowded. As I attempted to drink my watered-down cappuccino, which I found *imbuvable* (undrinkable and disgusting), I watched as two mice, one brown with white spots and the other white with brown spots, began to dance the *lambada* wildly. I imagined that they must be the tiny doll-like reincarnations of the two famous intellectuals—given the fact that the odd couple had made that café their office and almost their home during the Nazi occupation.

It was evident that their spirits and the spirits of other famous writers and artists continued to haunt this place even if I realized that the restaurant and the whole street were living off their past without any renewed merit. And, if alive, I am not sure that those famous individuals that made their mark in history would want their spirits to continue to haunt these places. Nevertheless, I could envision the Surrealist and pro-Trotskyite poets Guillaume Apollinaire and André Breton clashing with the pro-Stalinist poet Louis Aragon and the pro-Maoist philosopher Jean Paul Sartre—with the pro-American, Albert Camus, snickering in the background.

ooo

I seriously doubted that any brilliant artists, writers, film directors or actors still hung out there anymore. I mean, why imitate what was already past? How could anyone really accomplish anything at all by reading or writing in *Café Floored*—or even in any other noisy French café? No one who was "anyone" was there; and yet their "nothingness" was everywhere, at least according to Sartre…

Then again, I began to realize that the issue went beyond café society and its evanescence. The deeper problem was that real books were no longer "in" anyway. No one really read long and complex works, only pithy sayings, and brief editorials–when one's ears were inundated in pure noise. Books were a lost interest, a lost art. These days everything was put on the fast read, like fast food, multi-media internet and could be ingested for free—so there were no longer any material incentives to write something of interest… There was really "nothing" at all to strive for… That said it all… in their "absence" … it was literally all literary "nothingness" …

ooo

I overheard the existential conversation of a couple I could see in one of the mirror's reflections…

"That was quite an exhibit in Venice, that dialogue between Sartre and de Beauvoir..."

"Very impressive building... beneath the weathervane of Fortuna, with two Atlases upholding the fate of the planet… Very modern…

"Well, she sure ripped right through him..."

"Who… oh… How so...? I don't think so... She seemed to be at his feet… in admiration. I mean it was her farewell, her *Adieux,* to Sartre, published after his death…"

"No… No… Not at his feet! Beauvoir was very subtlety teasing him, trying to show the contradictions in his work. He says he started out writing *Nausea* with some Platonic ideal of what the book was supposed to be about in his head... but by the time he finishes it... He says he no longer believes in what he thought he had started to write. But his argument is not believable…"

"Is that what it was all about? … The segments of the interview between the two?"

"Yeah, she got him... in just a few words… He says that his whole tale was made up of things that were in relation to one another, so that the end cleared up things that were elements of the beginning and the beginning already had a conception of the end… So, everything was almost circular. I mean he contradicts himself!"

"I think I see... You mean his original ideas about what he wanted to write were already shifting course as the book progressed, but that those ideas cannot be considered as totally separate from the final text… Conceptions transform in meeting the realities outside us… but they still shape those realities at the end?"

'You got it… almost… except there's no way the beginning could already possess a conception of the end… as he claimed. The truth is that it all changed in the process of writing… You just can't go back…even if you imagine it is similar… it is not…"

"Almost???… what do you… mean... almost?... What are you really telling me?"

"You know while Sartre was spending his time writing about *ennui* and nausea, Simone was out for years galivanting with an American who could only write books about being drunk and high! She must have written 300 letters to him… A real independent feminist! No marriage. No common life together. No children. She had her own ideas that weren't those of Sartre…"

"So, you are telling me that her ideals about Sartre were already shifting course... that she was seeking her own existential path…"

"Can't remember his name… you ever read his books…"

"Not sure…*ah*…perhaps…"

"Ah…. ah… *Walk on the Wild Side*? You must know the song by Lou Reed. Everyone remembers songs and movies, but not books! Let me think… oh… Nelson… he won a Pulitzer… oh yeah… Algren… He must have been a hell of a lot of fun in real life, always cracking jokes, even bad ones that were definitely funnier than Jean Paul's *Being or Nuddingnessssssss*—or *yyy…ooo…uuu… rrr. sss*!!!

"So, you are telling me in this not-so-subliminal subtext that you want to be just like her! I mean, didn't she also try to introduce notions of mutuality and inter-dependence into Sartre's existential egoism???…"

"No, that's not exactly the message... but I do think it is time to..."

"Time to??? Let me tell you a secret. As boring as he was, Sartre had an American girlfriend when he was writing for Camus's magazine *Combat.* He even told de Beauvoir about her in great detail!"

The woman stared at him. Suddenly she got up as if to leave. Without a moment's hesitation, she poured an almost full cup of hot cappuccino onto the man's lap and rushed out. The man left a few bills and covered his pants with his jacket... *Adieux!!!*

ooo

After hearing that pathetic Socratic dialogue, I had to order a carafe of "the Big Red That Stains" (*le gros rouge qui tache*). I needed something strong, but not too strong, as I rarely drink. It was proof of the existential Truth: With such invisible tensions between the two sexes, being used as an object by the "other" was definitely "hell" in Sartre's terms!!!

Yet it was not long before my own imagination was flushed out of my spirit just as my face flushed beet red. I could only question how anyone as brilliant as Sartre and de Beauvoir could ever call themselves "Maoists". How could they fall for that not only absurd, but murderous, ideology? It was "ism"—not even a philosophy!

Camus and Sartre had fallen out on Maoism in violent disputes. Then again, they never really agreed, at least once their common cause, the resistance against Nazi Germany, was over in the aftermath of the American-backed victory that liberated France. Both thinkers may have smoked like the chimneys of the Camel, Marlboro and Gitane cigarette factories, yet their views differed significantly about the hegemonic wide-winged nature of the Balding Eagle—as it flew over the plutocratic land of the Big Money with its Visions of Sugar Daddies and Sugar Mommies.

For his part, Camus—who refused to call himself an "existentialist" even when he wore his trench coat with the upturned collar—saw the Red, White and Blue Star-

Spangled Banner as an exciting symbol of multiplicity and differentiation. By contrast, for Sartre, Amerika was nothing but a big boring Land of Conformity that produced monotonous commodities and that housed the filthiest, most polluted, city of the planet, NYC.

Sartre outlived Camus who died much too soon. That's the real existential tragedy: being punished, tortured, killed, or dying accidentally like Camus for being right (or maybe, according to conspiracy theories, hit by a car accidentally on purpose)—when all of history and power is against you!

ooo

What did Camus think back then, at the time of the rise of both Fascist and Communist movements after World War I? What did he think about the rise of so many dictators that are almost impossible to count? What would he think today—if he were alive at the end of Cold War, with respect to the renewed rise of self-declared Tsars, Duces, Caudillos, junior Führers, Vozhds, Conducǎtors, Maréchals, Marszałeks, Religious Guides, and Kleptocrats?

And what would Camus think about neo-Liberal New Authoritarian leaders who try to stay many terms in power as Prime Ministers or Presidents or who seek to overthrow democratic "checks and balances"—even the Land of the Free that he thought was so vibrant with variety?

Acupuncture

I found myself drooling in front of the famous *Grand V-4 restaurant.* The *maître d'hôtel* showed me around and let me check out the gilded rooms. I found myself drooling over the menu. Yes, I would have to make a reservation to decide which red velour velvet seat was best—that of Victor Hugo or that of Balzac? I saw a few Chinese inside. There was no way I could afford it…

I went past *The Contremoi* restaurant that seemed more affordable. There too were Chinese inside, who, along with Japanese, Taiwanese, Singaporeans, were all demonically possessed by the disease of conspicuous consumption. They were the *Wealthy, Wacko, Asiatics*[105]—snobby, gossipy, envious, show off, and very class conscious… in one word… they were *nouveau riche Tuhao*…. As one Chinese cliché put it, "with money they could be dragons, with no money, they would be considered worms…"

I could tell by their accents and expressions that some were the Children of High Cadre Communists—the sons and daughters of the same cliques whom I had once known in Beijing. I knew the corrupt ways of these families as my own family and cousins were all well placed in the Party.

Much like Wu Xiaoming in *Death of a Red Heroine*, children of Communist elites believed they were superior to the average individual because they had *guanxi* (connections). They were the ones who hid in their rooms when Tiananmen protests grew risky. And they were the ones who became even richer after the Tiananmen Square crackdown… That was when the Party simply stole the agenda of the pro-market "New Authoritarians" of the 1990s. As another Chinese cliché put it, "With money one may command devils; without it, one cannot even summon a man."

○○○

It is these *Wealthy, Wacko, Asiatics* who want to look Western, act Western, breathe Western, eat Western—and they even make their eyes rounder and more "Western" …

You can see it in many Asian comics… cartoons… artwork… It is not just cosmetics… It's inside the Japanese *manga* whose drawings imitate, or substitute for, real literature… On one hand, they dye their black hair golden, which is no big deal. On the other hand, they seek doctors for real surgical blepharoplasty! I simply could not understand why people would want to imitate others, or even make themselves look like another race… that is, if they could only find a surgeon at a decent price! They mut be under tremendous atmospheric or oceanic pressure!

And ironically, here in Paris, I saw these High Cadre Children and wealthy *Tuhao* eating everything that was not-so-politically correct, not so vegetarian, or even vegan.... I saw them gobbling down duck *fois gras*, the duck throats forced open to be fed. I saw them nibbling on frog legs fried with the frogs still jumping. They loved intestinal foods: *véritable Andouille de Guéménée à l' Ancienne,* plus brain food like *fromage de tête*, *pâté de tête*, and *ris de veau* (sweet breads). They adored *pied de porc*, *langue de bouf*, *viande de cheval*, duck hearts, shots of blood sausage in bearnaise… steak tatare with raw egg… plus Marie Antoinette's favorite, *couilles de mouton.*

It was as if they were all back in China, all searching for that sought-after Wuhan "wild taste" … That was the taste of foods like horseshoe bats or pangolin or mongoose or raccoon dogs, or other creatures—like what Marco Polo called "Pharoah's Rats"—that some scientists believe spread the COVID 19 virus. Perhaps it was a masochistic suicidal thrill to risk the possibility that one might acquire some strange disease after eating a kind of forbidden fruit other than apples? Or perhaps it really represented a hope for immortality after creating a Social Media buzz by eating such forbidden "delicacies"?

ooo

I decided to bus over to the other side of Paris where *Wealthy, Wacko Asiatics* and High Cadre Brats do not go.

Above me, towering on the high rise, inspired by Asian art, perhaps more Japanese than Chinese, was STeW's magnificent painting of a giant blue heron, almost as alive as the one I saw in the lakes of the Bois du Boulogne. In the Chinese language, heron meant good fortune simply because the word for "heron" (*lu*) and "good fortune" (*lu*) were pronounced the same… It is incredible how word games, homophones, and rhymes, so profoundly influence Chinese thinking and culture…

It took me several years to realize that I was fortunate that the French had not put me in this section of Paris called "Chinatown". It is a rathole in the 13th *arrondisement*—what is called the "Triangle de Choisy"—a stale slice of cake between the avenues of Choisy d' Ivry, and the boulevard Masséna, surrounded by cars and trucks spuming and sputtering fine particle exhaust on the *peripherique* that runs directly through Paris—practically cutting the area in two.

On the street, one could hear French-fried versions of Cantonese, Japanese, Khmer, Korean, Laotian, Mandarin, Taiwanese, and Thai, where restaurants serve Viet *pho*, Japanese *ramen*, Korean hotpot, Chinese *hun dun*… All were mixed into a giant stew directly beneath towering high-rise apartments so crammed together that the COVID 19 pandemic ran rampant during the Year of the Horseshoe Bat.

In the 1930s, the area was home to Chinese autoworkers, many of whom remained in Paris after fighting for the Frogs against the Krauts in World War I. Later, in the 1970s and 1980s, arrived the ethnic Chinese refugees who were escaping the horrors of the Vietnam war, the forced labor camps in Communist Laos—and the Khmer Rouge democide in Cambodia.

It's a place where the supermarket in the top of the car park sells fresh items, including the humped back Dorian fruit that had so irritated that self-proclaimed Maoist, the Wokeist before his time, Mr. Gao/Galvin, during his visit to Beijing in the Year of the Earth Serpent. Yet in the bottom levels I learned that one could purchase nearly expired items, both meats and vegetables… for almost nothing…

ooo

I remembered a decade or so ago when there was a media campaign against Chinese restaurants. Nightly on the French news were reports about Chinese restaurants who were selling stewed *rao bao* and other specialty foods made at home in unsanitary conditions in sinks and bathtubs and using nearly expired e. coli burgers, salmonella chicken, trichinella pork. Was it true? Or was it a campaign to drive the Chinese out of the restaurant business?

ooo

The day was sunny, yet cold for April; the wind chill was biting the skin. As I crossed the street, I looked down a back ally. A small gang of Asian youth was hanging out on one of the street corners near the many high rises before the restaurants. I saw what appeared to be red packets of bootleg or fake Marlboros being passed around. The cigarette boxes were also being handed out along with small plastic sacks the size of tea bags. I then saw a large Chinese man grab a North African kid by the shirt and drag him into a back alley.

There was a street urchin of Asian background, in dirty clothes, his shirt unbuttoned, pants unzipped, laughing hysterically on the side; his barefoot grey toes looked as if they were frostbitten. I knew I should not stare at the gang. I ran back to one of the Chinese shopkeepers and asked what it was all about. He replied, in barely understandable French, that the local Chinese Triads were backed by the some of the local community to keep those not Chinese out.

I did not know what to think.

ooo

At first, I had resisted. I had no faith in the practices of ancient barefoot doctors with no scientific proof. There was no way such primitive medicine could handle AIDS and the Horseshoe Bat pandemic. But aspirin and other drugs had failed to relieve me of my trouble sleeping… I had begun to grind my teeth at night, always feeling frazzled, unfocused, and forgetful… My thoughts raced from one place to another… I was not really accomplishing anything, here in France, so far away from home…

I almost wanted to return… Nostalgia, however, is not healthy. Constantly I had to confront the memories of those days back in Beijing at the beginning of the Democracy protests when there was still hope in the air—when hope sailed high in the sky transcending gravity, transcending all rationality, before plummeting like a missile to the ground, its warhead scattering shrapnel in all directions…

As I needed to relieve my constant headaches and back pain, I finally decided to visit an acupuncturist. I waited for at least an hour in her tiny office in Chinatown. I was surprised: she was not Asian, but French. As I was lying there on the white sheet on the hard table, I looked deep into her eyes and asked, "Do you really believe in this ancient hocus pocus… I am sure some of it works, but it can't compete with western medicine…There's no real proof…"

She looked back at me as if she was going to jab me with a Mafia ice pick: "You think so much of modern medicine. You should think again… For years western specialists told me I could never have a child… I began to study fertility and acupuncture… And now I have three children…"

I looked at her with apologetic eyes… "I had no idea!" was all I could say… as she continued to gently place thin spikes into the pores of my face and neck… I could hardly feel them. *I thought about LaPlante… Why didn't she have any children???*

ooo

It must have been hour later… In a moment of euphoria, I looked and felt like a lion on the prowl, calm and confident… It was as if I had returned to my childhood—when I had no fears, no concerns… The craziness of the Chinese revolution had never affected me as it did the families of so many of my compatriots, as with Mo Li.

To celebrate my natural acupuncture high… I decided to stop at a fast-food Chinese diner to eat, for old times' sake, *Kung Pao* duck… Before escaping from the mainland, I had previously vowed not to eat what is called "Chinese" food in the West ever… Nevertheless, I was tempted to try the food at this place called "Chinatown" in Paris…

Upon entering the restaurant, I saw the chef taking the plucked reddish-brown duck from its hanging place in front of the stove. I then watched as he chopped the bird into many haphazard pieces. In just a few minutes, as if in a speed race, the waiter put the overcooked remains before me—

after immersing the duck's fatty body in excessively salty soy sauce, sugar and in palm oil along with what was supposedly Sichuan vinegar, plus dried red-hot chilies, and pepper without corns—and without fresh ginger. I managed to guzzle it all down with a can of *Tsing Dao* beer… and thus try to kill the germs. Fast food, I was fast out of there—never to return… And what an MSG and beer-induced headache I had—just after my hour of acupuncture therapy!

The acupuncturist had just warned me to "fuel up" on plant-based meals and to drink plenty of water. I had not listened! With my head spinning… I felt like I was swimming like a fish out of balance amid the fresco of the Portuguese artist Pantonio—painted in the middle of this Parisian "Chinatown"—the "Tourbillon de sardines" or "Sardine Whirlpool"—that is perhaps more relevant an image for the Portuguese than for the Chinese.

In any case, as the highest fresco in Europe, it was overwhelming. *The more the water spun in circles… the more I envisioned myself to be an enraged Sardine en colère (Sardine in anger) in the process of being broiled alive… along with the rest of the creatures of the planet…*

Before I departed by bus, I froze in meditation before the small monument dedicated to the memory of the Chinese who had died fighting for France during World War I.

The Bridge Man

In October 2022, it was the "Bridge Man" or "Banner Man," called different things by different bloggers, who helped to initiate the protests in response to the brave man's unconventional protests on the Beijing Sitong Bridge. It was a man, standing alone, who dared to oppose China's massive human rights violations, the strengthening of government censorship and mass surveillance, and the implementation of an extreme zero-COVID policy.

Wearing an orange vest and yellow construction helmet, much like French "Yellow Vests", the man placed two of his banners on a bridge and set fire to several tires.[106] Repeatedly he chanted through a loudspeaker, "Go on strike at school and work, remove the dictator and national traitor! We want to eat, we want freedom, we want to vote!"

He then disappeared just as quickly from sight, possibly arrested, possibly not, vanishing into the night…

ooo

The protesters sang:

"We don't want nucleic acid testing, we want food to eat;
We don't want lockdowns, we want freedom;
We don't want lies, we want dignity;
We don't want Cultural Revolution, we want reform;
We don't want dictators, we want elections;
We don't want to be slaves, we want to be citizens."[107]

Another chant:

Life NOT Zero-Covid policy
Freedom NOT Lockdown
Dignity NOT Lies
Reform NOT Regression
Elections NOT Dictatorship
Citizens NOT Slaves

ooo

On Chinese Social Media, the Red Dragon's 1984 Media and Mind Control Bureau tried to completely block users who tried to share information about the "Bridge Man," or "Banner Man." Beijing tried to block any terms that could lead people to read about this one-man demonstration. Censored terms included "Sitong Bridge," "Haidian" and "brave man". Words such as "courage," "bridge" and even "Beijing" were also censored. Such censorship simply got in the way of viable communications that permit a society to function! The government fumbled, shooting itself in the foot…

In Shanghai some cried out, "End CCP rule in Shanghai, where the CCP began!" Some Social Media users attempted to evade the restrictions by referring, as indirectly as possible, to the man's lone protest. Some posted a song dubbed, "The Brave One". Other commentators compared the Bridge Man to the unidentified "Tank Man"—the man who faced down a Chinese tank on Chang'an Boulevard on June 5, 1989. It was said the Tank Man was able to escape to Taiwan. The fate of the Bridge Man was not yet known.

The surveillance power of Beijing's Media and Mind Control Bureau has made it extremely difficult to organize a coordinated protest… This leaves those brave souls who feel they must take a stand to act alone on their own initiative.[108] The dilemma: Was it possible to convince Beijing that these lone wolves were non-violent democratic "freedom fighters"—and not "terrorists" like the fanatic wacko who slit a tourist's throat with a Japanese ceramic knife for absolutely reason on Bir Hakeim bridge in Paris just an hour or so after I had jogged past?

ooo

The 2014 Hong Kong Democracy and Freedom movement had raised hopes—until it too was crushed much like the movement on Tiananmen Square in June 1989—without any real help from the Land of the Free or Lady Europa…

I began to fear that the peaceful struggle for freedom and democracy in Asia was rapidly becoming a lost cause—particularly after Perfidious Albion simply handed the guillotined head of Hong Kong over to the Red Dragon on a silver platter—and even more so, as it appeared the Americans were no longer giving democracy movements any real diplomatic supports…

"It was one of the greatest acts of appeasement that British diplomacy had stumbled into after Neville Chamberlain had capitulated to Hitler at Munich in the hope Nazi Germany would turn against Stalin," argued Prophita, as we discussed the protests in Hong Kong—years after the UK opted to grant China control over Hong Kong in 1997…

"Yes, British policy before World War II was a complete failure on all counts as most of the Czechs in the Sudetenland wanted some form of autonomy, not Nazi controls," replied Russell.

I interjected, "It was evident that the Chinese Communist Party would only recognize British 'administration', not 'sovereignty', over Hong Kong. The Party had been fomenting protest and rioting against British governance when Maoism was an influential global movement in the late 1960s… But people of Hong Kong do not want either British or Chinese 'sovereignty'!"

"Yes, but that is not the nature of power," replied the business associate, "Big states always grab what they can get, and take more too if they can!"

To which Russell replied, "The Hong Kong legislature was not given a role in the secret discussions between Beijing and London… It was totally unfair…unjust!!!"

An angel passed.

Russell persisted, "And as China never really turned against the Soviet Union and then against Russia, as some in the West might have hoped by playing the so-called 'China Card,' it seems even more absurd!"

To which I replied, "Doesn't this all question what democracy really means if those most impacted are not even included in the discussions and decisions that most affect their lives???"

To which Prophita interjected, "I am sorry to inform you, but neither the British Whitehall nor the American White House have ever been concerned with Democracy—except for propaganda purposes and when it serves its own interests… The real question is who controls maritime trade and Black and Green and Grey Gold" … He added, "Grey Gold... That's shale gas/oil… And now the question that follows is, 'What does Beijing's takeover of Hong Kong mean for Taiwan in the coming years? And what will be the American response if Beijing seriously threatens the Beautiful Isle?'"

It was true. As I had hoped for much greater American and European support for the democracy movement during the Tiananmen Square protests, I could not respond.

Sans-Culottes in Rage

It would not take long after the "end" of the Horseshoe Bat pandemic, that the French would once again take to the streets in mocking their President "Jupiter" Macaroon (nicknamed "Jupiter" because of his perceived aloofness). The old/new means of protest was to bang pots and pans in the streets to celebrate all the political promises that were never kept, never acted upon, and that were then promised by their President once again—particularly after he had added two more years to their retirement age, from age 62 to 64.[109]

Retirement before Arthritis!!!

Thousands of people banging casseroles, often at night, was actually an old/new means of protest that perhaps first manifest itself in France in the 1830s—by those who opposed of the rebirth of monarchy under the regime of Louis Philippe I after Napoleon's defeat. That was the French King whose rule was dominated by wealthy industrialists and financiers. It was that Monarchy that had pressed for the colonization of Algeria. And France has suffered the consequences of Algerian popular opposition to the Gallic Cock's imperialism ever since….

The Horseshoe Bat pandemic had well served the global leaderships by isolating and enclosing the population—but it could not hold back protest forever!

ooo

I thought this when I saw a small band of youth, three boys and three girls, perhaps from Saint Denis—the banlieue or suburbs that the French call, pejoratively, the "Neuf Trois" (93) or 93eme *arrondissement*—just outside Paris. They were strutting down a side street as if in a military parade. Their heads held high in pride—as if demanding the respect of G.I. Joe's preparing for battle—they were holding up a portable beat box and blaring French rap music full blast...

The violent revolutionary lyrics forewarned of nationwide protests and riots like those I once witnessed years ago after the accidental death of two teenagers running from police: "*They don't want it to burn again like it did in 2005, yet they are making the same mistakes over and over again...*[110]

ooo

Saint Denis is the place, so the legend says, where, in the 3rd century, the Christian priest, Saint Denis, was buried after having walked with his head in his hands four miles away from the hill of Montmartre where he had been beheaded. The area of Saint Denis, the location of the Abbey that bears his name, is now, ironically, no longer a place for Christian martyrs, but the *banlieue* (suburbs) of many people of immigrant descent—where many Algerians, Moroccans, Tunisians, as well as many west Africans, generally from other former French colonies, presently dwell ...

ooo

That prophetic mini parade took place just a few years before the major July 2023 social protests in France...

It had seemed like a normal day. The people, tourists, and Parisians alike, were all drinking afternoon coffee and wine, smoking perpetual cigarettes. They were staring out of the bistro and at the passing cars and trucks and buses on the street. A few cars were honking obnoxiously, trying to press through the meandering crowds, which surged from side to side, as if anxious to move from nowhere to nowhere. Above, *la Dame de Fer* stared down in steely reflection. No one had any idea in which direction to look for heavenly illumination.

Tilting at an angle like a *bateau mouche* reflected in the Seine, the Eiffel Tower started blinking. Excited and agitated, young teens tossed their *pétards* (firecrackers) onto the street or into the open doors of apartment buildings… The fireworks blasted the ears of those passing by with instant headaches…. At first, it all seemed harmless (except for the blast to the ears). Then, totally unexpectedly, dozens of young men, faces covered in black masks, or wearing black motorcycle helmets, rushed onto the square shooting flames at the department stores across the street—throwing rocks and carrying metal bars…

Multitudes of stars exploded… glowing iridescent hearts and diamonds were sent in a myriad of directions.... Sparklers cascaded like effervescent waterfalls; electric fizzlers radiated in spirals, green and yellow…. The sky transformed from a matt of blue pastels into an irradiated acrylic sunset… The blood rays emanated from severed warheads and streamed in rivulets upon the shattered glass that spread like cluster bombs and shrapnel.

Some of the gangs broke into the shopping center across from the bistro and laundromat. There, they raced to seize I-phones, TV sets, and computers. Others grabbed cornflakes and paper towels and other food and household necessities because that is what they said (after the fact) that their mothers wanted… Even more unexpectedly, a dozen or so women, hair covered in *hijabs*, some with faces masked, broke into another store… And all that was not wanted or distributed or sold later, or that could not be carried out, was heaped onto the dirty floor and set in flames…

It is incredible to think that so many of these young men and women were teenagers...

Red, White and Blue Star-Spangled Banana fireworks purchased for the 14 of July had become bazookas that could shoot rapid pulses of fire... Small gangs set schools, concession stands, apartments, banks, mayor offices, theaters, offices, department stores ablaze... The skeleton frames of cars and buses smoldered for days after, burnt to a crisp... The stench of thick smoke clogged the lungs...

The people on the sidewalk had already scampered in all directions for shelter... Tourists called for the quickest flight home... The stock market faltered, and the hearts of businessmen and women stopped pulsing. The Mass Media reported that it was "burn baby burn!"—despite the pleas of mothers not to destroy the schools, the apartments, the cars of those who live in the same neighborhoods...

Sirens of ambulances wailed in the distance. The police cars arrived along with heavily armored trucks... They wanted to hunt down those whose faces and names had appeared on Social Media and on the internet... those accused of plotting the targets for attack and the places to loot... Only to immediately arrest those who were unlucky enough to be seized on the street... thereby jailing even more chickens inside already over-crowded French chicken coops....

For some, it was burning to purify hate, *la haine*. It was revenge for the *flic's* bullet to Nahel H.'s brain, and for the police killing of George Floyd... They were the two individuals, the first French, the second American, who were murdered within a few months of each other in completely separate worlds, but who nevertheless were experiencing almost the same phenomena… Both were killed in the hands of poorly trained police officers who acted in frustration and anger without any self-control—in the belief that they were doing their "duty."

For others, the burning and looting was a show-off operation, an exercise in style, a way to brag in derision by destroying—to show off whatever crap they were capable of doing in sheer spite… It was the burning of pure rage at always being at the bottom of the social ladder… no matter what… with no respect… always lied to… It was a hollow, and purely emotional, way to protest the hollow promises of foxy politicians that are never fulfilled…

It was yet another nation-wide fireworks even more violent and self-destructive than the nationwide insurrections in the French banlieue in 2005… The "Truth" of the matter is that the French authorities have simply not figured out how to integrate peoples from very different countries, and particularly those with a Moslem world view, into their post-French Revolution Atheist/ Catholic society... where individuals from the banlieue are generally not seen as full members of the larger French community… in a Republic that stands above them—and not always with them…

For their part, the Americans have still not been able to integrate large portions of its former African slaves and later migrants… And the Chinese cannot find ways to treat the Uighurs and Tibetans and others with equal dignity either…

I watched on the sidelines as these new Sans-Culottes and youthful Precariat, the "Neuf Trois" of the Seine-Saint-Denis, set off sonic booms of revolutionary despair. They were now avenging themselves in the storming of the Tuileries that had once pressed the Legislative Assembly to depose the King, "Monsieur Veto" or "Louis the Last" … It was a pillage that more directly hurt those who possessed the least… And like dogs pissing gasoline to mark their spots, the domestic and global fireworks were far from over, spread by self-combustion…

"Off with Jupiter's head!!!" they now cry!

Yearning to Breathe…

The waters were emerald and Prussian blue on the moonlit shore. As I started to walk upon the beach, the winds whipped up the sands, stinging my eyes. I had underestimated the power of the waves and decided to step back and return to the hotel. The next day I learned that a tourist had been standing out on the huge rocks amid the flailing winds. Suddenly Hokusai's Great Wave knocked him into the raging currents. He did not survive the fall.

It was at the end of the summer holidays, but I was still surprised to find that very few foreigners seemed to be here, that is, to say American and European tourists. For in fact, instead of tourists, along the streets and near the market, the river and train station, there were hundreds of migrants, a few women, but mostly men, thin, in blue jeans and imitation black leather jackets, fake designer sunglasses. Some were lounging on benches or sitting in circles on the sand, others were roaming the streets, talking in mobile phones…

In the major towns throughout Italy, and along the French Italian border, so many migrants from foreign lands now suffer from Stendhal's syndrome—as once was the case for Gao/Galvin in China—whether they wanted to be there or not…

ooo

As I walked through the throng, one of the merchants, smoking a cigarette outside his empty store, yelled in poor English at a tourist, "Don't buy from them... They'll fine you at the French border!"

But it is dog eat dog... food. The tourists feign ignorance. No matter what they are told, they go ahead and buy their supply of fake leather wallets, fake designer scarves, box upon box of cheap cigarettes, bottles, and bottle of cheap booze from desperate men who run bags of goods and clothes and jewelry up and down the beach...

Many are Zulu warriors, armed with fake Rolex watches, fake Gucchi sunglasses, fake Prada bags... The world's finest faked goods shimmer and shine... fakes supplied by Italian mobsters and Chinese Triads alike and sold by these desperate men who have no choice... Some had passports... others had lost them... or else they claimed were stolen.... They were young, and not so young, running from poverty, crime, lack of jobs, and in the fear of being either recruited or killed by Mafias, Narcos, militias or mercenaries of the new Golden Hordes....

They are desperate men and women who believed they could escape to freedom... believed that they could cross the border, over the mountainous passages of death, and into France, after having already braved the rough Mediterranean waters to arrive on rickety overcrowded metal boats in Greece or Italy—in the hope to flee to countries where there was more money and more freedom. One they got to Italy, many hoped they could then get through France... and then sail from Calais to the UK...

Or so they hoped...

ooo

I could see them on their Raft of Medusas, in Gericault colors of chiaro di luna… upon the rolling seas… the sky and stars and moon at first clear, radiant… before that moment that vicious clouds suddenly swept down upon them… gushing rain… lightning flashing… all on the boats huddling together… the waves heaving up and down… tipping and twisting… the boats heavily overloaded by Human Traffickers seeking a fast buck from as many desperate souls as possible… as many as could fit on board… children, women, men… from unrelated nationalities, religions, cultures… Syrians, Afghans, Tunisians, Libyans, Kurds, Algerians, Turks, Malians, Ethiopians, Eritreans, Somalis, Egyptians, Pakistanis, Palestinians… peoples who did not even speak the same language… except perhaps for broken English or French…

I could see this microcosm of humanity from the Heart of Darkness holding onto each other in those rickety flat boats heaving up and down through the surging tides… Now arm in arm, body to body… arms flinging seeking balance… Their fates thrown into the same floating basket, all were willing to take the same risk in newfound solidarity… even if it meant plunging deep into the vortex of Death…

ooo

I had flown down from Paris to Nice with Bereft, who had left her three dogs with an intern. We then took a van from airport and crossed the border into Italy where we met our pug-nosed interpreter with short blonde hair who took us to the Director of a Humanitarian Center for Refugees near the train tracks and an olive oil factory.

It was the Director, a woman, with dark brown and determined eyes, who, it seemed, almost singlehandedly, with a skeletal volunteer staff, to be taking care of these courageous migrants in desperation, daily handing out food and clothing to hundreds of men, women, and children with more and more arriving…

At first, the Director told us, through the interpreter, "there was a very kind priest who permitted the migrants to stay in the church. But the townspeople protested. They feared the migrants would scare away tourists. Even the mayor did not want migrants staying inside the church… No one would take responsibility… Not the local authorities, not Rome, not the Vatican, not the European Union… This is why we need your help…"

"And what kind of help?" LaPlante questioned.

"We have set up a camp site high on the border with France. There we hand out more food and supplies… As it rains often, the migrants need waterproof jackets, blankets, and tents… And decent shoes and shoes for climbing on rocks… Right now, we can afford a meal of pasta, bread, and a dessert of fruit or cake…

"You are doing the best you can, I see…

"Yes, but it is only with small gifts of concerned individuals and some businesses… We have no solid funding… Other groups can obtain funding even though we are doing the dirty work without full recognition by the authorities or anyone else for that matter…

"Is that why you have turned to us?" demanded LeBlanc…

"Well, yes… You are known to help…"

ooo

We took the black van a way up the mountain side past the train tracks and highway trestle where there appeared to be thousands of young men all trying to cross the border into France. The Interpreter sat close to LaPlante in the back seat. I sat next to the Director who did not speak. The whole ride was making me car sick as I had to ride backwards, and I could not understand why the Interpreter kept giving me dirty looks. I really didn't understand what her problem was… I came close to vomiting as I once did on that boat escaping China to Hong Kong, but this time, I was able to restrain myself.

We came to an area that was under construction. LaPlante asked the driver to stop. There was an Italian security guard talking to three Africans. He appeared to be pointing for them to go up the road. I was surprised that he was so friendly. We walked up to see what was happening.

The guard explained: "I am not a policeman, so I am not here to arrest them. I am here only to protect this work site. If they are rude to me, I don't speak to them, but if they are polite, I tell them the truth… There is no way to French freedom on this road… It's blocked off by construction… They can only climb over the mountain side…

"Do they really have a chance… to get to France?" asked LaPlante through the interpreter.

"Perhaps so," he responded, "but only if they survive the 'leap of death' that smugglers and those once escaping Mussolini also had to leap…

"Incredible!" LaPlante and I both cried out simultaneously—as if our minds were linked.

"That is the most dangerous, but the least likely to get caught. Otherwise, they can be smuggled in by car if they are lucky enough to pass police surveillance… And if someone is willing to help them at the risk of steep fines and imprisonment."

"Yes, I learned volunteers could be arrested if caught trying to help the refugees… The prison sentence could be five years in prison and a 50,000 euro fine," LaPlante interjected.

The guard continued, "Or they could try to walk at night through the tunnels next to the speeding cars… Or they can try their luck on the trains... both on the inside and or even on the outside…

"Not possible! On the outside?" we said, once again speaking together…

"Yes, they must follow behind a first train and run as fast as possible… If another train enters when they are still inside… they are doomed…

"These people will risk their lives like that just to cross the border to France!!!" Bereft cried out as if she had not understood what the guard had been saying all along—and suddenly had a revelation.

ooo

We drove on further, closer to the French border. There, a couple of dozen protesters were already clashing with the police, halting traffic. People driving to Italy got out of their cars and watched the rainbow warriors try to take on the police in armor.

I did an interview…

"Why did you come here? … Why do you want to go to France…"

The young African from Mali replied in understandable English, but with a heavy French accent, "I risked my neck… in Tunisia… near Sfax … A gang attacked us, all our things were taken… One of my friends was knifed… we had to run… I could do nothing for him…"

Then he added, almost in tears, "Some of our women were kidnapped … I could do nothing for them either…" He lowered his head in shame… "Those of us who escaped had no choice, but to jump onto those rotten boats. I was lucky, but not everyone made it…"

After looking askance for a minute, as if trying not to show any emotion, he continued, "We need to register in the first European country that we can get into… But I don't want to stay in Italy… France is my country… they colonized us… they taught us how to speak French… So, it is *our* country!"

I looked at him with the deepest sympathy, but also with a degree of selfishness: I had been saved by the French and given home and a shelter while he was being rejected sanctuary by that same French government—even though he was more "french-fried" than I. And ironically, while he preferred France over Italy, I had, at least years before, preferred America over France… And although neither of us was European, I was a "political" refugee with working papers and social security; he was an "economic" refugee—despite the horrific wars, terrorist violence and tragedies, that he had experienced firsthand.

“I had no hope back there; I only have hope in France! I won’t give up!!!” the man cried.

ooo

The interview was interrupted by the shouts of protesters:

“Migrants are humans—not ping pong balls!”

“Smash all Borders!!!”

“No borders! No nations! Stop deportation!

“No more racism! Solidarity!”

ooo

On the French side, a sign was chalked on the pavement, REFUGEES WELCOME!!! Yet the dark blue vans of the police blocked the path and would not let the anyone pass… Some had walked on the slimy rocks and jumped into the warm Mediterranean waters in the hope to swim to the French side… impossible… they were soon turned back… by speedboats…

With faces wrapped in scarves, banging make-shift drums, activists and migrants all demanded the freedom to enter France… They blocked the routes for tourists and buses and trucks to cross the border. In the meantime, a few enterprising migrants tried to sell their wares to those tourists who got out of their cars in the hope that they could breathe some pure seaside air….

ooo

Bereft said she had to fly on to her next stop in Lampedusa. I had to return to Paris by train… She said she was going to check out some properties to establish a Humanitarian Aid Distribution Center and would be back in Paris before the annual fundraising evening.

For the first time her pug nose interpreter smiled at me—in such a way that she seemed to be relieved that I was getting out of her/their hair. I could care less!

ooo

Once the van dropped me at the station, I saw hundreds of migrants sitting on the sidewalks or standing on the side by the buildings. Police in bullet proof vests and machine guards stood calmly watching. An elderly street person with heavy makeup and in thick winter clothes like a fashion model ambled about the train station as if amused by the whole scene… In broken English, she asked me for a cigarette, and then a euro, for her "coin collection" … At least that is what I thought she said…

In the station on the way to the tracks, I saw a bright red sign written in eight languages. I recognized only the letters in Italian, English, French, and Arabic…

IT IS FORBIDDEN TO CLING TO THE OUTSIDE OF THE TRAIN...

IT IS FORBIDDEN TO HIDE IN THE NOSE OF THE TRAIN...

IT IS FORBIDDEN TO HIDE IN THE TECHNICAL DEPARTMENT OF THE TRAIN...

IT IS FORBIDDEN TO ENTER INTO THE TRAIN TUNNEL...

ooo

The blue, red and gray train itself was packed like spicy canned mussels, the crowd stunk garlic and olive oil. Everyone was standing. There was absolutely no space near the doors. It was market day, the day when the French, and the even more wealthy *Monégasques,* crossed the border, and arrived by car and train in the thousands. They were all shopping for Italian products that are much cheaper than in France. I saw large cans of olive oil, liquor, bags and bags of fresher fruits and vegetables. There was not even any room by the sliding doors to enter the train, as the people lined up and down the aisles on both floors of the double-decker train cars. I had been very lucky to find a seat after getting to the station and into the train car way before the last-minute rush... And what a Horseshoe Bat health hazard!!!!

Naturally, the train did not start on time. With so many packed-on board, I naturally assumed it was a safety hazard so that some might be kicked off. It seemed evident that many did not even have a ticket. Yet, despite being way overcrowded, the train started to roll out late. In about 20 minutes, it came to a stop at Menton Garavan—the first stop after passing the border. A good number of people left their seats, opening up more space. An African woman in bright royal blue boubou with a matching Gele head turban, who was carrying a baby swaddled in a white cloth, asked if she could sit down next to a white French woman.

A few moments later, a dark blue uniformed border squad, some with rifles, marched onto the train. They went down the aisles of each of the cars, inspecting the toilets and other spaces, pushing people out of the way. They asked everyone who looked foreign, primarily all the dark-skinned passengers—meaning Africans (not me)—for their identification papers or passports. Incredibly, the French woman began to talk to the African woman as if she were a friend.

The police passed by and did not ask the woman for her identification—as they had for all the other Africans... I was sure she had no papers....

ooo

It was evidently the chase for "illegals" ... Those whom I saw sleep curled on cardboard mats, those lying beneath palm trees on the roadside, those whom I saw washing themselves in the Roya River that rafts into the Ligurian Sea with the hundreds of river trout who subsist in foot deep waters. I could see their makeshift cardboard beds where they slept in the mosquito infested brush... if not scared away by the wild boars. Hunted, they hunt for ways to cross over to the French side... Those who speak French generally wanted to go to France; many of the rest want to continue onto the UK if they can get past Calais...

With rosy smiles on their faces, two uniformed French policemen capture two Africans. I could see through the window as four other policemen and policewomen calmly walked six Africans into the station for booking. Most likely, all eight Africans would be sent back to Italy—as there is no way the French want to take care of them. It was all a game of cat and mouse.

Just then a tourist reached for his bag to leave the train. I overheard an Italian man sitting a few seats before me, telling the tourist in English, "Each migrant cost us 900 euros in taxes... My pension is only 620 euros... Figure that one out... You bring in one, and the rest of the 'family' comes, not just the wife or wives and children, but also the aunts, uncles, and cousins... They bring with them only infinite problems..."

It was an exaggeration. Yes, there were problems, yet Italy and France both needed migrants to do the jobs no

Italians wanted to do… They needed migrants to contribute to social security for an aging population… A rational immigration policy, combined with greater European and American assistance to the regions that were generating the most migrants, I thought, could help resolve at least some of the concerns. Those migrants with decent jobs were less likely to cause "infinite problems" …

Then again, as a foreigner, I had no say in the matter…

ooo

We finally entered the Nice station. I looked at the large black sack under the seats across from me that looked just like a large surfboard or ski bag… I thought I had seen it wriggle just before the train had started up, and then again in Monaco, but thought, at that time, that it was just the jerky movements of the train…

Now I saw it moving once again, that sack on the floor… that giant black sack stirring… out of it I saw long black fingers and pale pink tips flexing. The African had been laying still as if slumbering, on the floor tranquil, no threat to anyone—as the train rumbled onto Nice. He had been totally silent despite the evident difficulty of breathing. Certainly, he had been sweating heavily, zipped inside that black cover stuffed with all his affairs in the world. It was inside that sack that… incredibly… he had been lying… absolutely motionless all this time… beneath the stinky bodies and rancid socks of youth who had been speaking about their search for part-time jobs and internships. Everyone in the train car who had passed by must have looked down but didn't see what was there. And when the police and the sniffing German Shepard had trotted by, even the dog had not sniffed him… or if it did, the police had urged the beast to move on… Chance had permitted the man to escape…

As the train suddenly jerked to a halt in Nice, the African arose from the dead and ripped himself out of the bag—like Houdini tearing off his strait jacket. He was wearing a blue sweatshirt marked with the letter "S"? For what? For Sports? Superstar? Sucker? Sneak? Snoop? Savior? Savage? Sycophant? Salafist? Superman? He pushed his way through the jam-packed train car and out into the very crowded station as others filled the space...

Unlike many of his compatriots and comrades in illegal voyage, he had succeeded... But who was he? A normal man willing to risk everything to escape the horrors of famine, floods, joblessness, war? Or another Islamicist fanatic seeking vengeance on the non- "True Moslem" world? Or soon to become one? Or a petty thief willing to do almost anything to survive? Or...

I wondered why Bereft had not wanted to interview any of the migrants herself?

From Barbieland to Boot Camp G.I. Joe???

A Thai-like Tuk-Tuk with bright lights passed me as I was jogging before *la Dame de Fer*. It was being driven by an eastern European, with three Chinese American tourists in the back seat. The speakers were blasting, "*I'm a Barbie girl, in the Barbie world, life in plastic, it's fantastic...*"

There was no way puritanical Chinese Communists, led by Madame Mao, the Red Empress, would permit Barbie to be sold in the Red Empire during the height of the Cold

War. Denounced by Communist puritans as a "sexist" commodity, this molded piece of plastic, transformed into a young girl's idol, only became known to the Chinese masses once Beijing itself opened to the world market in the 1990s.

Since the turn of the 21st century, Barbie has been "Made in China" in Guangzhou—with components such as ethylene (refined oil) from Saudi Arabia, vinyl plastic pellets from Taiwan; nylon hair from Japan, with multi-colored hair pigments and cardboard packaging from the United States—not to forget the magic of Hong Kong management.

The doll was in "Made in China" by union-less Chinese workers—but only after its production had been relocated from Japan, Taiwan, Hong Kong, and the Philippines in part due to high labor costs and friction with labor unions—even after perhaps becoming the most profitable toy in history—sold in at least 140 countries...

More recently, the scantily clad doll, initially inspired by the "Lilli" sex doll, has been banned in countries like Saudi Arabia and Iran… It has been denounced as decadent, perverse, culturally destructive, and even a social danger… This is despite efforts of Matelica Co. to make multicultural Barbies dressed like good Moslems…[111]

And now it symbolizes U.S.-China trade disputes…

ooo

Once the Barbie film was advertised in France, and given Barbie's global social and cultural impact, I wanted to see if the film could be a real work of "art"? Or more likely, whether it was a new, and unadulterated, form of publicizing and marketing… as I suspected?

In any case, although many intellectuals refused to give Matelica Co. and Wartner Bros even more cash, I was sure the film would prove to be a pure classic of American kitsch. The issue was this: How would the film impact the millions who would watch it? It was impossible to criticize it, or understand its cultural influence, without seeing it…

ooo

It is clear the film's sugarcoated critique of capitalism tried to make one "feel good" about the company that produced a variety of multicultural Barbies. This is true even if the film not-so-gently ridicules its all-male board of directors—who made major decisions without employee participation, male or female. And it is also true even if the original blonde in her not-so-feminist pink outfit appears to understand some of the significant problems of the real human world in a "left-feminist" critique of patriarchal Hollywood "neo-liberalism."[112]

As the movie reveals, in lightheaded sarcasm, even Barbie (it/she) gets "emotional" over the fact that there is no free speech and democracy in most corporate fiefdoms. And Barbie is rightly concerned that when corporations assert their rights—as if they were individuals with rights to make profits above anything else, with no concern for the health of people and the environment—that corporate elites were trying "to make our democracy a plutocracy."

And although Barbie (it/she) did not say it, at least directly, there was an even darker theme implied in those two imaginary books—that a pathetic, sour faced, effeminate Ken (it/he) had plucked from the LA public library—in its/his attempt, with Barbie's prodding, to evolve a real personality that could be respected by men and women alike. It was at least an attempt to look intelligent by reading books!

Ken's (its/his) choice of non-fiction, at least in accord with the titles of those two nonexistent books—*Origins of Patriarchy* and *Man Wars*—warns about the future of our patriarchal war-prone reality. There is an imminent danger that a macho *Homo Geopoliticus et Economica* is presently marching Handsome Johnny and John Brown off, plus Ken and Barbie, into yet another old-fashioned war on yet another European, Asian, or other "strange" and "foreign" shore… *I can almost hear its whistle… marching, marching, marching…* to the hoarse and freely clashing UTube voices of Richie Havens and Bob Dylan.

ooo

And now that Barbie has been enlightened, after living like an empty-headed asexual zombie, it/she wants her freedom, it/she wants to become more than a piece of plastic. It/she even wants to become more than a mere "woman" with a vagina… It/she wants to become truly human!

Yet entering the human world presents Barbie with an existential predicament. The dilemma is that if it/she ever did move out of the "plastic fantastic" Barbieland, it/she risks becoming a mere sexless cog in the corporate or state bureaucratic machine—with no power of decision-making… And if "she" did become a real human female, she'd be a mere android with no respect, no say, no rights, no share in the profits of the essentially patriarchal and phallocratic plutocracy… No say in a world of corporate fiefdoms controlled by financial speculations and AI manipulations… No self-expression of whatever or sensuality or sexuality…. And ironically enough, no sex… Or perhaps more accurately…too much sex that did not lead to any sense of fulfillment or meaning… which is perhaps even worse than to have no sex at all… in my mind…

ooo

What's missing in the movie is the danger of reaction against Barbie becoming a real woman, the danger of men believing they are being emasculated by the new feminization of the social and political world. Instead of a marshmallow like Ken, as a boy or girl's "doll," G.I. Joe, the new male model or humanoid "action figure" appears to be coming back—in militant multicultural forms. Asian, African, Latino, and Islamic cultures all had their imitation action figures ready for service and for sale!!!

In the Western case: Trained as a youth by 3-D video games, with his see-in-the-dark spyglasses and his wristwatch tuned into Space XXX satellites, G.I. Joe could now accurately zero in on his target thousands of miles away. Knowing nothing at all about the country, the people, and the "target," his Targeting Directorate could finetune hornet-like drones to strike as few people (become "collateral damage") as possible. Eagerly waiting to enlist, and with the hoped-for blessing of the Posse Comitatus, it would be G.I. Joe who ruled the land—and not the Ken's and Barbie's—even if G.I. Joe had a "smoothie" too…

ooo

Without so intending, the film sparked a real geo-pornographic and media scandal. Incredibly, Hanoi announced to the world that it would ban the Barbie film—ostensibly because it showed a map of China dominating the South and East China seas. Then again, in addition to the misdrawn lines of the map, the government might not have liked the pro-feminist anti-phallocratic marshmallow Ken message either—for it did not depict "real" fighting action figures who drank vodka flavored with snake blood.

Wartner Bros defended the map calling it a "child-like crayon drawing" of the disputed region. For its part, Hanoi accused the map of supporting the Red Dragon's territorial and energy claims to the South China Sea as it drew eight (as opposed to nine) dashes near China. In the Vietnamese Water Buffalo's perspective, the map did not show the presence of the neighbors including Taiwan, Brunei, Malaysia, the Philippines—in addition to Vietnam itself. It seemed that the Red Dragon had already blockaded Taipei's Black Bear into submission without a shot fired!

Should Hanoi's complaint be taken seriously? As already discussed in these pages, Hollywood is already under fire for appeasing Beijing's propaganda machine to obtain the profits of the China market… So, who knows the Truth! In any case, it is clear that both the Balding Eagle and Lady Europa need much greater investment in international cultural education! Peace might depend upon it!

ooo

In sum, with the large number of nasty wars spreading through the planet, and with Narcos, mafias, gangs and militias and mercenaries taking control of illicit traffic street by street, while buying influence in government after government, clashing multicultural Boot Camp G.I. Joes appear to be gaining more and more terrain in the fog of freaky unexpected preternatural *Yaoguai* occurrences and war.

Once, and even if, Barbie (it/she) would ever acquire a vagina and escapes from Matellica's Barbieland, "she" would definitely *not* be living in a truly humanized world—where men and woman truly respected one another in a gylanic society. Instead, the newly endowed woman would discover herself lost in a newfound androcratic world where gang- and fraternity date-rape is the new/old norm….

As the publicity proclaims, Boot Camp G.I. Joe is the new world where the humanoid action figures continue to fight it out since the Korean and Vietnam Wars… where all private militias, clans, tribes, ethnic groups, Narcos, mercenaries, both men and women, are equally bioengineered for combat in unequal test tube conditions—except for the elite few, primarily men (he/him/his)—who own the high-tech military industrial AI future(s).

One does not need an unexpected act of terrorism to provoke these warring factions to engage in brutal combat. It seems that even a seemingly innocuous, even if not entirely "innocent," film like Barbie (it or she)—presumably scripted for children—could launch a very bloody menarcheal war!

Riders of the Posse Comitatus

I had jogged many times on the path near LaPlante's chic *péniche* that was docked on the right bank *Rive Droite* of the Seine. It was just a few hundred meters below the Tsar Alexander III Bridge that linked the right and left banks near the National Assembly.

The dark grey walls underneath that historic bridge that now glittered gold were stained with red and white graffiti and the whole area smelled piss… On the side were the tents where the street people slept without homes (what the French call "SDF" *sans domicile fixe*) … One had a pile of pillows and sheets and two living room chairs for his buddies to sit and shoot the bull… and booze it up… I saw the tents and clothes and equipment provided for free by some of the non-profit groups funded by our Foundation…

In stopping to rest before the Seine, I overheard a fisherman as he explained in poor English to a tourist… "the fish get smarter every year… they now know how to get the bait by eating 'round the hook… And that's not the only thing. We're in com-pet-i-tion with gulls who steal fish from za' line just when we pull them out of the water…"

'Incredible,' I thought… 'The brains of animals seem to be more rapidly evolving than those of humans! Yet how could anyone, human or beast, eat fish from such polluted waters?'

ooo

Every time I passed, I could feel the weight of history. The foundation stone of the bridge had been laid in person by Tsar Nicholas II of Russia in 1896 before it was inaugurated as part of the Paris Universal Exhibition in 1900.

Tsar Alexander III Bridge symbolized the tightening of the Franco-Russian alliance against Imperial Germany and Austria-Hungary since 1891—an alliance signed by Alexander III, the father of Nicholas II, and Sadi Carnot, the President of the French Republic. Carnot was then stabbed by the Italian Anarchist, Jeronimo *"a baker not an informer"* Caserio. Carnot's assassination was seen as an act of "propaganda by deed" and was taken, in part, to revenge the execution of his fellow Anarchist, François "the grave robber for his family" Ravachol—by the National Razor.

In response, the French ratified the *lois scélérates* ("villainous laws") that were aimed at Anarchists and supporters of the Second International.[113] The latter laws were signed just after the French had forged their military alliance with the reactionary Tsarist Russia against Imperial Germany—permitting French and Tsarist police to collaborate… Years after Berlin's annexation of Alsace Lorraine in 1871.

Why is it that I fear something like those same late 19th century "villainous" laws—that place restrictions on the basic freedoms that the West is admired for—are now being resurrected in new forms in France and elsewhere—in the post-September 11, 2001 "Global War on Terrorism"?

ooo

The more I thought about it, the more I thought this so-called "holy jihad" was not only aimed against the colonization of Moslem countries by the Europeans backed by the Americans. Nor were these attacks only in protest against the 1948 Nakba when the newly born Israeli Gazelle expelled Palestinian Gazelles from what Rabbi Dr. Geyer's messianic movement claimed to be their historical homeland—in diametrical opposition to Herzl's original Zionist vision.[114] Nor were these heinous acts only about other acts of imperial conquest of Arab/Islamic countries, by the Russians and Chinese, for example—that conveniently overlooked the Islamization of many peoples in the wider Middle East, whether forced by conquest, or not…

This violent "holy jihad" was more than just an agenda of geo-pornographic *revanche*. It was also a battle against an invisible Chimera: The subconscious fear of the loss of control of those in power over those without power, the loss of power and influence of institutions that were once respected and that were now no longer respected, the loss of control of men over women, and collapse of previous held values… societal fears of Barbie's femininization leading to Ken's emasculation... the fears of LGBTQI+... the fears of the rising social, economic and political influence of other ethnic or religious or cultural minorities... i.e. the fears of those who did not appear to fit the previously established norms and values of the predominant identity groups.

Without any determined purpose to do so, the intangible forces of globalization and liberalization were provoking nationalist, xenophobic and patriarchal backlashes in societies around the world... So many countries and societies seemed to have lost their vision as to who they were and where they were going... Xenophobic Fearless Leaders in both autocratic and presumed democratic countries were then using the general societal crisis accentuated by globalization—as a means to manipulate their followers to their political advantage and control....

And in the general refusal of those in power to incorporate the interests and concerns of all members of society—a refusal that often resulted in a determined effort to repress those who differed—many states were beginning to define specific opposition groups and states as "terrorists" or "enemies"—even if they were not "terrorists" or "enemies" at all—but sought legitimate domestic reforms and international diplomatic compromises.

In searching back into the history of repression and counter-repression, slaughter and counter-slaughter, it was easy to find excuses to repress, or make war, against this or that ethnic or religious group, against this or that nationality or state—against individuals and groups considered to be some form of "Alien." It all depended upon how, and by whom, the "enemy" was defined...

As tensions mounted, nationalities and religions turned against other nationalities and religions, and those of the same belief and nation divided and turned against those who differed even slightly—so that many states of differing denominations and beliefs began to act like "terrorists" themselves... When Silver Spoon 2 had proclaimed, "Either you are for us, or with the terrorists"—it was the signal that *Homo Geopoliticus et Economica* had entered a new polarizing era of self-blinding ignorance and intolerance…

All spun in a full circle… The dreams for global peace of Barbie and Ken were on the way out… Multicultural Boot Camp G.I. Joe's were marching on the way in…

ooo

In 1908, France and Russia aligned with Britain against Imperial Germany. That was six years before the Archduke Franz Ferdinand (a Habsburg of Marie Antoinette of Habsburg-Lorraine vintage) was assassinated by the "terrorist" group Black Hand in "Sarajevo" on July 1914… A month of "Concerted Diplomacy" among the Major Powers could not stop the onslaught of the "War to End All Wars" …

Despite the warnings by the French Socialist Leader, Jean Jaures,[115] the whole horrific confrontation was sparked by a few bullets of an assassin, Gavrilo Princip—who is still a hero in Belgrade. What an unexpected catastrophe resulted from the violent Serb/Yugoslav struggle for national independence and revenge—in a face-off that was supposed to last six months only, to be finished at Christmas—but took four years, with many more people murdered by the "Blue Death" than by inter-state bullets!

The Versailles Treaty finally put an end to the poison gas 'Armageddon to end all Armageddons' from 1914 to 1918—despite the plea of the poet Siegfried Sassoon to end that conflict in 1916—when he protested that the so-called "Great War" had become a war of aggression and not defense.[116] In spite of his well-known valor as an officer in battle, Sassoon, whose family fortune, in part, resulted from the Opium trade in India and China,[117] was almost court-martialed for treason. Sassoon was then forced to suffer in a psychiatric hospital because of his anti-war stance in 1916. He learned the hard way that war always provided an excuse to crack down on even loyal dissent.

Although compromise between London, Paris and Berlin was possible in 1916, the Allies refused to seek a diplomatic resolution until the Imperial German side completely caved in…. no matter how many people died and how much destruction took place in the meantime… and no matter if even more people would die in the future….

The fact of the matter was that the defeat of Germany in 1918 only appeared to have resolved the conflict in the short run. Instead of a durable peace, however, Versailles only achieved an uneasy and temporary truce that eventually destabilized the tectonic plates and set off three R/Evolutionary earthquakes even more traumatic than those of 1914: the Nazi takeover of a defeated Weimar Germany, the Chinese May 1919 Communist movement that gained support in opposition to the pro-Japanese decisions of Versailles, plus the splintering of the Ottoman Empire between the British and the French that has not yet seized to provoke conflicts throughout the wider Middle East.

Much as the poet Sassoon feared, the British Lion and French Gallic Cock refusal to engage in territorial compromise with the Imperial German Eagle in 1916 forewarned an even greater catastrophe after German defeat…

Sassoon's observation appears relevant to today—if *Homo Geopoliticus et Economica* is to eventually to achieve a lasting peace in the aftermath of the "new Crimean War" taking place between Russia and Ukraine since 2014/2020 and between Israel and Hamas in the Holy Lands since October 2023.[118] If states, like people, cannot soon reach real compromises—much as Jaures had warned when it was already too late—I fear that the Vengeance of History will once again overwhelm us with an even greater catastrophe than the "Wars to End All Wars" that took place between 1914 and 1945—and in the not-too-distant future…

ooo

I remembered, back in September 2008, after Ukraine and Georgia were promised NATO membership, and after the subsequent Russia-Georgia War, the lecture of Leon Possy, whom LaPlante, dressed in a stunning canary yellow dress with matching shoes, handbag, fingernails and toes, had introduced as "a brilliant linguist who speaks a dozen languages. In the struggle against the rise of Fascism, he became an active member of the Communist Party in his native Poland. Unexpectedly, he later found himself a victim of Stalin's purges. He was sent to the Gulag for 24 years. Few have survived such horrors…"[119]

"Thank you, Bereft!" Possy replied, "But it is not much of an honor to survive the horrors of the Gulag… I was a fool to let myself fall into the trap"… Taking a sip of water, his aging hands trembled, "It had taken me a few years in the Gulag to realize that I was just one of millions of Stalin's scapegoats… As I was Polish and French, and even though I considered myself a Marxist and an atheist, not Jewish, I finally realized I was nevertheless suspect as a double agent…

"After loyally spying for years abroad, I rushed to Moscow when ordered to do so… I returned even though my Soviet spy team "wife," Georgette, who was part of my cover abroad, had tried to warn me not to return. It was the time of the Great Purge…

"I realized my error much too late—only after I had been sent to the Gulag as a traitor, even if I was not a supporter of Trotsky, or no longer considered myself one… Sometimes it is the wisdom of women who often sense the darker and more sinister realities without even

possessing any absolute facts and certainty… I was naïve, foolish, and head strong. I did not listen… May she rest in peace…"

The crowd applauded his self-deprecating honesty…

Someone asked Possy the question in the Q & A session… "What did you think during the Weimar era? Did you fear the rise of Hitler?

"At the time, it was quite clear to me as early as 1926 that the Nazis were gaining strength, and that the only real alternative was to support the Communist resistance… The liberal bourgeoise were not willing to oppose Hitler and his goons. And even if some of the more liberal elites truly feared the consequences of a Nazi victory, they still saw Hitler as better than the Communist alternative."

His audience spellbound, Possy added, "I was not a victim of Stalin and Stalinism, but a willing accomplice who believed in the world revolution—even if I did not know anything at the time of Stalin's cruel inhumanity… And had I not been imprisoned by the Party, perhaps I would have become just another Soviet true believer—a bureaucratic oppressor just like those who oppressed me…."

He paused for effect…

"Or maybe, had I returned to France, I would have been a smiling member of the French Communist Party (PCF) that for years accepted Soviet funds and ignored Moscow's heinous crimes… Or maybe I would be just like those leftist editors who were afraid the publication of my book Gulag Memories would provide fuel for the French Right to put the French Left on trial."

I had begun to think back to what Possy had said at that conference. I thought about his subservience to the Party and to the Fearless Leader, Uncle "Koby" Joe. I could only think "ditto" for the French and American intellectuals, like that pretend Maoist, Mylex H. Galvin, whom I had met in China in the tragic Year of the Earth Serpent. What I found incredible was how both Stalin and Mao—and now Putin and Xi—could attract followers from outside their countries… Such individuals were not at all forced or pressured to follow or obey either leadership—but believed in the "cause" and acted on their own volition.

I began to realize that a new form of "voluntary servitude" was now arising within country after country. I just could not understand how presumably intelligent people throughout the American and European democratic world could support "populists" or "new authoritarians" on either the Left or the Right—in what had become mere euphemisms for dictators and despots.

Was there any hope for effective democratic reforms that would better represent the people in each country? And economic reforms that would provide a more equitable distribution of income? Why did I think we had moved back to the pre-war years of 1870… or 1894… or 1914… or 1939??? Why did it seem that more and more people were in a quest for a Dark Messiah? …

ooo

I now felt a real, palpitating sense of history almost every day I jogged up and down the Seine. No tourists, particularly Americans, I am afraid to say, seemed to notice or care, nor did many French care either. After all, Our "Model T" Ford, honored and awarded by Holocaust Hitler, had affirmed, "History is more or less Bunk."

It is incredible how Americans, unlike Europeans and Chinese, believed that the dropping of the atomic bombs on Hiroshima and Nagasaki—on the populations of China's mortal "archenemy"—had somehow changed the nature of the global geo-pornographic game. A country with the A-Bomb would never be attacked! The A-Bomb would prevent wars! It was as if all historic complaints and disputes had been swept under the rug and forgotten!

ooo

And how often do I hear Americans adamantly insist that if there is to be "World War III … It will NOT be 'US' who started IT!!!" I mean, if Americans knew anything about history, they would know what is called "World War I" was not the first World War. And even then, we Chinese consider the Sino-Japanese *Jiawu* War of 1894-95—in which Japan smashed China's navy and seized Korea and Taiwan—as the real beginnings of the "Wars to End All Wars." Yet rarely do western scholars acknowledge that fact…

And as we Chinese have much longer memories than even the Europeans, and definitely much longer memories than the Americans, there were many more world wars than what are now called "World Wars I and II." Calling those wars "First" and "Second" is merely a way to divert attention and delude one's conscience and anxieties from having to face up and deal with recurring geohistorical crises of *Homo Geopoliticus et Economica*…

The Seven Years War and the French Revolutionary/ Napoleonic Wars evidently preceded both the so-called

"First" and "Second" World Wars—and even the Crimean War and Franco-Prussian War involved battles that took place outside of Europe—as did the 1688-97 Nine Years War of the French Sunny King Louis XIV against the rest—that is generally considered the first modern global war...

Looking deeper into history, however, one of the first truly world wars was the Byzantine–Sasanian War (602–628) that involved China. And then there was the most obvious global war of all that began in Asia, but that is often overlooked as such: The Mongol/Tatar invasions of Eurasia during the 13th and 14th centuries that, with their tight trade routes helping to spread the Bubonic plague, overran China, India, Iran, Iraq, Russia/Ukraine, eastern Europe, Georgia and Armenia, before raiding Palestine as far as Gaza in period between 1260 and 1300, with the Tatars then colonizing Crimea—after that peninsula had already been trounced by the Scythians, Greeks, Romans, Goths, Huns and Mongols—before being seized by the Russians/Soviets and then more recently by the Soviet-Ukrainian Lynx—and now by the Russian Double-Headed Eagle once again.[120]

ooo

Across the blood red streaks of the horizon, I see the Four Riders of the Apocalypse, Death, Famine, War, and Conquest- Destruction-R/Evolution;[121] *the Four Riders of the Bourse, Profiteering, Speculation, Usury, Exploitation; and the Four Riders of the Black Hole, Weapons of Mass Destruction, Pandemic, Species Extinction, and Artificial Intelligence forging a Posse Comitatus... I see them preparing for combat in the heavens above, jostling for strategic positions to best oversee the coming battle between the Balding Eagle and its Oceania Allies versus the massing forces of the new Eurasian Golden Horde—the warhorses of the Chinese Red Dragon, the Russian Double-Headed Eagle, the Iranian Cheetah, the North Korean Chollima, along with the equines of other Rough Beasts that had begun to trample the bloodlands of Eurasia and abroad…*

Which side, if either—that of the Balding Eagle or that of the Red Dragon and Double Headed eagle—would the 12 Riders choose to support, disrupt, or counter in bloody quagmires throughout the planet? What perverse promiscuous games might these Couriers of Unnatural, Unnecessary, Unprovoked, and Unexpected DEATH play in the effort to influence the ultimate Outcome of forthcoming Earthly-Unearthly Battles?

Péniche Party on the Seine

That week her round face was glowing on the front cover of RAIDER magazine as it poured over the edges of the glossy paper like the white albumen of a poached egg oozing over the crust of a buttered *croque madame* sandwich. Her permed scarlet curls, tinged with copper highlights by a chic French Boardwalk *Avenue des Champs-Élysées* hair designer, hissed with the forked tongues and botoxed lips of a *Fer de Lance*. Only a few saw the white fangs hiding behind the thick red lipstick of her pursed sickly-sweet smile. I certainly did not… at least not then...

ooo

Everything was set up for the big event. The tables were set for drinks, champagne, and mixed drinks, with *hors-d'oeuvres,* but no main course, of course. The *péniche* was sparkling clean after LaPlante's Filipina maid had washed the deck and cleaned up the meeting room. The Filipina had distinctive Chinese features, high cheek bones, with shimmering long black hair that, in the sunlight, appeared tinted with a blue aura…

I assumed her family could have immigrated from China to the Philippine archipelago during the Spanish colonization—at the time when sun never set on the Habsburg empire… But who really knows the "Truth" with so many secrets hidden in the unexplored boneyards of ages past… Nevertheless, as her face seemed to radiate with a sense of pure joy, and as she possessed a surprising beauty, I wondered why she was working in such an undignified menial job…

ooo

In addition to the great number of non-aristocratic moneybags who were present, LaPlante had also invited many *re-de-de* (slang for aristocrat). The Chinese had abolished monarchist rule more than a century ago and I thought the French had done the same in 1789 after the storming of the Bastille. But somehow, Ms. LaPlante seemed to attract almost every member of the European aristocracy, plus some more from non-European countries, whose families had not been executed or abolished by the either the French Revolution, Napoleon's dictatorship, or even the Russian, and perhaps even the Chinese, revolutions…

Most of the males were dressed in tailored suits or double-breasted blazers, mainly navy, charcoal, and black, that were paired with crisp white shirts, starched collars, and silk ties. There were only a few standing clichés who smoked putrescent Havana cigars and who stood next to diamond studded blondes, and who tried to make sure everyone was looking at them, as they smoked their pretentious L-shaped glass Vapes which puffed a lot of steam.

There were other, somewhat more sophisticated, less crass, women who arrived in bright red or pink designer dresses for cocktails or even more elaborate gowns. Their broad-rim hats were adorned with feathers or flowers or woven with intricate designs; they ported designer handbags, statement jewelry, and elegant heels.

All, male, female, yang/yin, seemed to be walking as if on pixie dust, on fine leather oxfords or loafers, made by LTV or by Trucci with matching golden leather belts. The younger, more daring ones, wore no socks, nor ties that were considered hangmen's nooses…

ooo

LaPlante had asked me to serve the champagne… It was an opportunity to become a listening device that could record their conversations in my memory cells…

"I simply adore your handbag! So stylish and unique. Is it a Pierre III?"

"No way, it's a Bulshipiega!!!… Didn't you catch their fashion show? The new collection was truly breathtaking, with its camouflage motif. That's where I found it…"

"Listen, everyone! I'll be hosting a garden party next week at the club.... I discovered a new band that agreed to play the whole night… I hope you all can make it!"

"I'd like to, but not sure… Things aren't great after CBD's stroke… I can't find a decent nurse…"

"I know the perfect candidate… smart, energetic, lively, pretty…"

"No, that won't do… She can't be young, and can't be pretty… And he won't accept a male nurse, he could be… you know… And no Bl…ks…

"Yeah, I think I got it… You heard the CEO of Star-Techs left his Ukrainian nurse a fortune… Must have been a hot babe! Hah! Now his children are trying to sue big time!

"No, but I heard about the alley cat who inherited $$$10 million$$$… And it's the nurse who takes care of it!!!

Overhearing this, I could not believe these people were going to contribute to an organization dedicated to human rights!

ooo

The sick conversation finally got back on track… The desperate quest to find a nurse…

"Not sure how I can help you and CBD… It's sad… but it's best to look on the bright side… At least CBD was already retired and with a golden parachute, I understand… Must be one of the few these days… But my poor friend Sally, her husband just lost his job after getting ill with COVID, they think… I don't know how they are going to pay their dues for the Club… Looks like they can't make it to the party either…

"I'm sure you'll have a good turnout… Maybe you should ask Bereft for some advice… After all, the turnout for this event is exceptional, even though not quite great at her last fundraiser in Geneva…

"Could you believe it! I was just getting into my car after her last bash when this jerk ran up and took my picture with a big fat zoom lens… 'Why the f-ck did you do that,' I yelled as he ran away… The paparazzi called back, 'You're

Richie Marvello, ain't you!' after he had already jumped on his beat-up motorcycle just like the ones who chased Lady Di in the tunnel under Alma… I yelled back at the asshole, 'You got to get your facial recognition right! Sorry to disappoint you, man, but Marvello didn't show up to this blast…'

"Yeah! Jerks like that take pictures of just about anyone in the hope they can freelance the right one that will sell bigtime in the yellow press…"

"Who the hell is Richie Marvello?"

"He's a finance guy… who got a Clitone Presidential pardon… even though he'd been indicted for tax evasion and racketeering… They say he made a fortune by bypassing embargoes and buying and selling oil and arms for states like South Africa, Castro's Cuba, Socialist Angola, the Sandinista's Nicaragua, Gaddafi's Libya, Pinochet's Chile, and both the Shah of Iran and Khomeini's Islamic Republic. That is not to overlook arms for China after Tiananmen Square. For him business was business, a buck was a buck, all sides were good sides…."

"Never heard about him… I don't follow politics… Governments should just get off our backs!"

"They say he had good mafia connections in the Soviet Union, and then in Russia and Ukraine too. And among the Triads in both Beijing and Taiwan. They say he spied for both the Mossad and CIA… Had to be a double or triple or quadruple agent… That's probably why he was pardoned, who knows! He must have been playing a lot of dirty games behind the scenes, just to patch up relations, and profiting on the side!"

"You must be flattered that the paparazzi thought you looked like him! He's Superman!

ooo

The conversation shifted back to the evening event… I could not believe my eyes or ears!

"What a doll is Bereft… I am so honored to know her… Such worthwhile causes… I don't know how she manages to do such great things… I mean French social security kept sending me checks for my children's school expenses… Can you believe that? Send me, of all people, welfare checks! So, I went to the mayor's office and tried to repay them… I thanked them for the thought, but told them I really didn't need the money… I started to write a check… The response, 'Sorry we can't help you!' They would not even let me reimburse them!"

"Yes, the French are so strange…

"True… but there are lots of… ruuuum…ooorrrrs."

"I don't want to hear a thing about them… there is always *blah blah blah* about everything…

"But they say she… she's soooo outspoken… I mean about Palestinians…

"You mean she's anti-Semitic…"

"How can that be, she's definitely Jewish…

"No way, she's not! She's a Celt with Fighting Irish freckles!"

"I hope she's not one of those Peace Now-niks who renounce their heritage!

"Yeah… They're the worse…

"How do you know, she's…???

"Something someone told me… Something she said in an interview on French TV about Israel….'

"What was it?

"I don't remember exactly… I'll ask my friend… I don't speak French, but it's true…"

"That's outrageous! Arabs and Jews are both Semites… They're kissing Abrahamic cousins from the same language group whose tongues don't pronounce the same words the same way![122]

"It's not language. It's not race. It's not religion! It's politics!!! Just because you disagree with Israel's policies does not make you anti-Jewish!"

"That's right… Bereft is for universal human rights… no matter what ethnic, religious or identity, group is oppressed..."

"How can you believe all that liberal crap! If you support the Palestinians… you got to be anti-Israel… They'll try to tear down everything we've done… but they won't succeed!!!"

"That's only if Israel doesn't offer them a decent deal!" interrupted Russell who had started to listen in as the conversation got more heated and as more and more people could hear the nasty debate as well.

ooo

I could not believe it. I thought this was a free society with the right to be critical… but somehow criticism of Israeli policies had become virtually forbidden *verboten* in both France and the United States. I mean it wasn't wartime, even if Israel and the Arabs and Iranians always seemed to be in a constant state of war.[123]

And it seemed that since Pootin's preclusive annexation of Crimea in 2014 and invasion of Ukraine in 2022, no one could talk honestly about the causes and consequences of the horrific clash between the Russian Double-Headed

Eagle and the Ukrainian Lynx under the spell of the American ventriloquist. No one seemed worried that *Homo Geopoliticus et Economica* was entering into a 21st century version of the mid-19th century Crimean war fought in both the Black Sea and the Holy Lands… No one appeared concerned that such a war could expand even further than it already had… and that the Taiwanese Black Bear could be next…

It suddenly dawned on me that Leila Zarwish was one of millions of the Palestinian diaspora—although she now wore a black Abaya characteristic of the wealthy Arab Gulf countries… Inadvertently, by asking Zarwish to speak at the *Cercle Trans-Atlantique*, LaPlante had started a controversy—that should never have been a controversy—without even realizing it…

ooo

And so, the drivel continued… but changed subject once the group realized their conversation had started a scene…

"Ok…ok… that's enough… Who is 'she' anyway?"

"They say she is from a wealthy New England family, the old American aristocracy…

'Hum… I thought,' as I overheard these conversations while hovering like a UFO in the middle of the room, serving champagne, 'Could she have been from a family well-bred on the African slave or Asian drug trade, as Gao/Galvin might joke'?

"Then her father died… the CEO of Robotiks, Inc… Apparently his private jet crashed over the Bermuda triangle!"

"Sounds like the story of Peggy Guggenheim, when her dad sank to the depths with the Titanic!"

"Yeah, they say she is exactly like Peggy—in more ways than one… if you know what I mean, *Hah! Hah!!!…*"

"No way… Peggy spent her inheritance on artsy fartsy stuff, just to hang out in Venice. Bereft is using her money for good causes in Paris! To help humanity!"

The Job Offer

There was a lull in the conservation. No one responded… until one of the women under a wide white brimmed hat that covered her eyes spoke out…

"Her father's end was not the end of it… For some reason, a few months after her father died, her mother took a heavy dose of sleeping pills and gassed herself to death in their suburban Short Hills garage. It was Bereft who stumbled upon her mother's body after waking up for breakfast… She had heard the Mercedes motor still rumbling…

"That is truly tragic!"

"Did you know her?

"Who?

"Suzy?"

"No, I just..."

"Well, sorry, but that's all bunk... I heard another story. They say when LaPlante came to Paris after graduating from Smythe, she hung around the One Season Hotel in the 8th... There she met a Sheikh at the bar who clothed her in Burmese rubies, emeralds, and diamonds...

"Yeah, right... You really believe all those lies about her and Arab Princes? Those stories are just meant to destroy the good things she is doing... No one wants a person of her means to get involved with human rights... Helping people is not good for business..."

"So, what about this Prince Al-Wasta???... I hear he's a strong supporter of Palestinian rights..."

"Yeah, $$$ for the corrupt Palestinian leaders...

'I knew she was anti-Sem...

"Wait a minute... $$$corruption$$$ is on the other side too... the Israeli Attorney General has been investigating Bibi who has been in power as Prime Minister since 2009 and still does not want to give up his position![124]

"Yeah, but we have laws... They don't..."

"*Shhhhhh...*" whispering... "He's right over there!"

"Sorry to disappoint you...." still whispering... "It's all bull... The real story is that Bereft has had two husbands... each wealthier than the previous one... In fact, she came from dirt... and now she has everything!"

"That is almost what I heard…" interjected another woman who collaborated her story… "Yes, Suzy, her mother, died, after her father had been running after every pussy cat in town. But Bereft did not inherit a fortune… Instead, she married into wealth… She would go to a party and say… 'point to the wealthiest man here'… And like a spider, she would spit out her web and entrap her target…"

"Incredible!"

"Even more bizarre was the fact that each of her husbands died unexpectedly… the first by car accident… the second by heart attack…

'You are not saying!!!"

"Of course, not… Yet it is only since she moved more permanently to Paris that she met Prince Al Wasta… but certainly not as a member of his harem…

"Who cares anyway" piped in a third woman with her own diamond necklace glittering around her neck, "She earned it and now she flaunts it!"

"If there is anyone I'd want to be, it's her!" praised a third, "So outspoken… so determined!!!"

"Yeah, she understood the Truth! It's $$$ that paves the way to FREEDOM!!!"

ooo

I could not believe my ears or my eyes… I had no idea what the correct story was—if any of their gossip had any reality at all! And what I found most outrageous was the fact that these "elites" possessed such a nasty disdain for each other. Then again, I realized that they would all stick together when criticized by those whom they did not consider to be one of their class… the Nobodies… at least when it wasn't too personal…

The irony, I suddenly realized, was they wouldn't give a nickel if the person requesting funding did not appear to be of the same class as they—as if anyone of them had any real class, intellect, or individuality at all…

On the one side, it was not certain they really cared that much about the causes they were funding… On the other, I realized that in the days after the $$$multi-billion$$$ rip-offs of Bernie "Ponzi scheme" Madeoff, many of the more glorious moneybags were much more hesitant to hand over their hard earned (or more likely, handed down) earnings to just anyone. Some of those present had fallen for Madeoff's scheme, according to Prophita, and were still looking desperately to make up their losses…

Super wealthy or not, I could not believe that many did not seem to have any respect at all for Bereft and had begun to spread vicious rumors about her family as well.

ooo

It was right out of those trash People magazines…There was the Prince of M and Princess of B whose family owned the glossy RAIDER magazine. RAIDER published the Prince and Princess's daily activities, proudly claiming, for example, how the princess was a university graduate, when she, it was rumored, had never completed her degree… It was high up on the top of the deck, in the twilight, when I was outside breathing the fresher air, that I saw the Princess bent over a chair, with a roll of paper up her nose…

I could, however, understand her… I too would be bored with that crowd… except for the two bizarre individuals and their wives who looked as if they were from Outer Space… They appeared before us like creatures from the Outer Limits or some other Sci-Fi American TV show or movie. Or maybe they just liked sporting the early space suit fashion of Disco stars that I was finally able to see on UTube after all those years of Chinese censorship… I guess for LaPlante's crowd they needed to make themselves look different, if not exotic… since they, unlike most of the others, were *nouveau-riche* and not born into wealth and power…

"Have you met the Zenzimes?" Prophita asked me…

"No, I am afraid I haven't!" The two brothers and their two wives eagerly stuck out their hands to shake mine, which I was reluctant to do, not only because of fear of the Horseshoe Bat, but also because they all looked so bizarre that I did not want to touch them…

The two men were nearly bald and almost hairless, except for their bushy eyebrows… What made them unnatural was the elderly Shaman's large, slanted brow and sharp chin, a slope head that once displayed beauty and status in Mayan eyes. His brother had protruding cheek bones, so too did the cheek bones of their spouses appear to protrude as well… The long silken hair of the two wives was tied up in chic Hermeezy silk head scarves, one red, the other green. Their lips seemed so puffed up with Botox they curled unevenly backward creating an oblong shadow on their chins.

The men did not appear to be Asian, yet their yellowish skin appeared to be patched, as if they were reptiles, such as alligators or crocodiles… At first, I thought it was like the skin disease, vitiligo, that the singer Michael Jackson had, where the skin bleaches white... Then I realized the skin patches were of different colors, as if they had been grafted, somewhat like tattoos of the MS-13 mafia. The two wives had geometrical patterns tattooed on their arms and neck. And there was a third multicolored psychedelic eye on the back of all four of their necks that appeared, like a Rembrandt painting, to stare back at you no matter where you were standing....

Then it hit me: The wives reminded me of the body work of French artist Orlan, the "slow sexual," who was (in)famous for being way ahead of her time with her scandalous 1977 art piece... *Le baiser de l'Artiste*... A beautiful woman, she had transformed herself into a mutated Chimera with horns implanted on her skull. Her grotesque anti-war artwork, *Nouvelle Origine de la Guerre (New Origin of War),* with a phallus grafted in place of a vagina in re-reproducing Corbet's *Origins of the World,* had become her political *fer de lance.*[125] It was pure geo-pornography!

But all that was another issue...

ooo

"You may not know us, but we know you..." they all seemed to speak at once. "We are proud of your efforts to fight for democratic reforms in China at the risk of your life. It was our network in China, with the assistance of funding from Bereft, working with the Buddhists, who set up your escape to Hong Kong. One of our members in China was the first to meet you after Tiananmen Square."

I was dumbfounded.

"Yes, and we are sorry you stayed so long in Hong Kong, but funding shortages, and primarily politics, prevented you from leaving earlier. For some reason, neither the British nor Americans would take you. At long last, we were able to convince the French government to help you and others…

The eldest brother handed me his business card. I looked at it briefly, it was entitled, Society for the Exploration of Cosmic Consciousness (SECC).

"I had no idea. I am eternally indebted!" was all I could reply… as humbly as I could… completely dumbfounded.

"Please stop by next week… We have a proposal that we hope will interest you…

They wanted to say more, yet we were interrupted when some of the most influential people on the planet had suddenly become silent…

The Sales Pitch

At that moment, Bereft LaPlante, in a long green Pratta evening gown and matching Prima shoes, with a dazzling gold necklace strung about her neck, paraded before them microphone in hand, and with a power point projection behind her… but without her three dogs…

"Ladies and gentlemen" she cried out… No one even coughed. "Good evening! Let me say how wonderful it is for you to have taken time to come to Paris during your busy schedules to show your support for this incredibly important cause – the global struggle for human values and democratic rights. It is by respecting the values of freedom of expression, belief, and assembly… the values to be free from torture, slavery, and discrimination… that we can prevent future conflict and war…"

—I thought of the irony that these "values" came out of two violent struggles, the American and French Revolutions…

Today I am going to announce the new approach of the Foundation for Human Values Forever. The struggle for human values must not forget the democratic right to live in a peaceful healthy environment, with sufficient food, water, shelter, and education for all. The fight against climate change is not just an environmental struggle; it is a battle for social justice and human dignity….

Everyone in the crowd applauded! Although she had used the term "democratic right", I could only think in Gao/Galvin's terms—as to how the most vulnerable generally dwell in regions exploited for resources by major corporations that care neither for the environment nor for the people who live in the sludge that remains… In those places, there was not even a pretense of democracy…

"Thank you… thank you!!!… But you must save the applause until we have accomplished our mission… And one of the most profound effects of global warming is the emergence of climate change refugees. Imagine if your family had been uprooted from your home by the mere force of a changing climate, whose devastation is disproportionately borne by the most vulnerable communities… Tonight, my Foundation is raising funds for a number of non-profit organizations that work tirelessly in both democratic and non-democratic countries to address the challenges faced by climate change and to implement a multifaceted approach that combines humanitarian efforts with sustainable development and energy strategies.

By transitioning to cleaner and more sustainable energy, we not only mitigate the root causes of climate change but also democratically empower communities to build resilience against its impacts. By investing in renewable energy infrastructure, we can create jobs, spur innovation, and contribute to the long-term well-being of communities on the front lines of climate change—who must be actively involved in decision-making processes. It is essential to ensure that the benefits of alternative energy projects are shared equitably, and that vulnerable populations are not left behind.

It is our duty to be the voice for the voiceless. Neither the marginalized, the global climate refugees, nor the species that are now facing extinction, possess the basic democratic right to vote. Together, we can build a future where every person can live their life in dignity without poverty, where principles of human equality and justice are respected, and where the natural environment is protected…

I have just returned from a tour of the new locations where Human Values Forever seeks to donate our resources… I witnessed for myself the conditions of refugees and asylum seekers… the French-Italian border, Lampedusa, and the city of Sfax in Tunisia… Tears come to my eyes when I saw such unnecessary suffering…

I know many of you have contributed in the past and I thank you for contributing again in the present! Let us stand united in our commitment to a sustainable future, where no one is left behind, and the beauty of our humanity and our planet is preserved for generations to come! Thank you again!

ooo

There was a long round of applause. The *noblesse de robe* and *noblesse d' épée…* along with all the remaining aristocratic *re-de-de* (in slang) of the *Ancien Régime,* plus a few of *nouveau riche* high-tech barons, came forward to promise support. Some already had checks in hand.

I took note of the commitments. It was only after a two-hour boat ride on the Seine, after cocktails and inspiring conversation, that she had raised an astonishing 10,730,000 Euros, plus promises of more to come.

Could it really be considered "democratic" to be a "voice for the voiceless"? Was it possible to be a voice for those without representation? I could not help but think how she was a true globe trotter… I felt like I was hearing a global alternative energy sales pitch… A speech that was most likely written by the keyboards of "IShaThere4Iam."

ooo

In looking at the guests, I felt I had been visiting the pallid bodies of the morgue on cold slabs. Or looking at the colorized chemicals that leak from the corroded funeral urns of deceased prisoners left unattended for years…

Their names appeared to be right out of the Fortuna 500… Many were children or grandchildren or great grandchildren of the families of the Western and Asian top 1%. There were the seafaring greatgrandchildren of S.N.T. DeLaNose and of S.S. Ruxxell—who were from a family of American east coast seafarers, i.e. former slave traders. There was J.G. Forbex whose family had made a fortune in China, not to overlook the I.M. Cherries, some of whom became politicians, married to Sauce Producers who, once upon a time, imitated Chinese fermented fish sauce with its salt-pickled mushroom and produced a classic American condiment.

There was also the formerly French aristocratic family, the I.M. Delamours, who were beloved for manufacturing an American version of Chinese gunpowder ever since the War of 1812—before expanding their fortune in the modern era by means of "better living through forever chemicals"—and later, in miracle frying pans than never stick. They were the inventors of Teffylon, the substance that toughens the skin of Fearless Leaders. Much like the Polo family working for the Mongols, they became an American version of Merchants of Death.

There was the man from Oklahoma, his ancestors greased with black gold and whose ambulance chasing law firm was run by others much more capable than he, but who soaked up the profits while living in France. A Mastodon victim of the American weight plight, he couldn't walk more than a few feet, practically living out of his limo. He was a self-proclaimed patron of the arts and humanitarian causes who plastered his Dupleix in the 8th with portraits of himself painted as Augustus, as *pontifex maximus*. His role was to ensure that Uncle Sam's pinstriped empire retained the moral support of the gods.

Aidan tried to pun: "With a never finished novel in his drawer, his $$$ draw women to open theirs." My English was not quite good enough to understand the joke.

Among the Americans, who often lived for a few months in France, but not too long to pay heavy burden of French taxes, there was another family of not-so-excellent repute, the Sukkher's, who had given so many $$$millions$$$ to museums, to universities, to foundations… And now they were looking to give to humanitarian causes after giving themselves such huge bonuses during the 2008 financial crisis… and again in the Year of the Horseshoe Bat, like so many other CEOs…

Of the international elites, there a few reps from the wealthy Arab world in white *thawbs* tied at the waste and red checkered *kaffiyeh*, tied with an *ʿiqāl,* a camel hair cord, from the Black and Green Gold *nouveau riche* of the Gulf countries, from what once was once called the Persian Gulf—that is, until the Iranian Cheetah's Shi'a revolution. These included Sheikh Abdul Al-Wasta, with his charcoal black eyebrows, gold rimmed glasses, and Chaplin moustache. They stood apart from each other, revealing their ongoing regional political and religious rivalries—although they were always "Arab brothers" in public…

And then there was one of the *Wealthy, Wacko, Asiatics*, the Macao Heiress, Ms. Wu, who came escorted by three look alike men. Two were Brits who had partially shaved round heads and could pass for Asian, while the third looked Italian, also with a very round skull. The latter was her future husband, while one of the men was her "boyfriend" and the third one was her lover. "That is what Ms. Wu herself had told me," Prophita surprisingly told me. In any case, as a *Wealthy, Wacko Asiatic,* it didn't surprise me. When Money talks, even men walk. More *yin* power to her!

These were all names from the book, "Who's Who,"—with their concise biographies written up and paid for with a certain fee… The irony was that all the names, or at least most of them, seemed to have four things in common: Arms; China/Asia exports; Black, Green and/or Gray Gold; and Drugs of all possible chemical compositions. It could all be boiled down to common denominator of limiting or avoiding taxation.

And finally, there were the very strange family, the Zenzimes, the two brothers and their wives, who had founded the controversial *Society for the Exploration of Cosmic Consciousness*… and who were said to have recently made incredible sums of wealth by playing the stocks of digital currencies… As Prophita told me, "It was they who donated the blockchain technologies that permit refugee camps to obtain interlinked solar and wind energy for 24 hours daily... They are investors in techno-innovations in the areas of advanced AI, alternative energy and sustainable development that can help sustain the lives of refugees and marginalized communities in need..."

He had sounded just like the SECC Marketing Rep.

The Accounts

It was an ultimate high to meet these people, these superrich, decked out in high fashion, with their flashy jewelry, assuming it was not fake, the real stuff kept stuffed in a safety deposit box for fear of theft, particularly in Paris after several high-profile Kardashchien-like robberies… Yes, it was an ultimate high from the trimix gas of helium, nitrogen and oxygen breathed deep in the lungs by deep sea divers...

Nevertheless, I could not suppress my pessimism. The whole situation seemed ultimately bound to implode much like those doomed billionaires who had entered the cramped Titan submersible thrilled to venture near the deep-sea floor in utter darkness to view the Titanic passenger ship, sunk by iceberg more than 100 years before and to witness the necropolis—where Peggy Guggenheim's father and fifteen hundred others went down with the ship.

I could envision those doomed souls as their eyes widened in glorifying the illumination of ocean depths surrounded by strange creatures that never see the light of day. I could envision the coelacanth, related to ancient lungfishes, the R/Evolutionary bridge between sea creatures and land dwellers and the viperfish with their own pretend fishing pole and bioluminescent bait and sharp fangs that curve back close to their eyes.

It was, of course, possible to view such creatures and the wreck much more easily and clearly by undersea camera—but in so doing there would have been no thrill of risk and danger. Although convinced the cylindrical vessel was safe, it was nevertheless unexpectedly crushed by the immense water pressure. The Media Fourth Estate experts claimed that their bodies first burnt to a crisp as the air in the cabin auto-ignited a few milliseconds before the vessel imploded. It all took place too fast to suffer…

ooo

The reaction on earth was immediate. A stunned moment of silence. It was clear that the five doomed billionaires were considered far more news worthy by the omnipresent Media than the 750 Palestinian, Syrian, Egyptian, Pakistani and Afghan refugees, mainly women and children, on their metal Raft of the Medusa that had capsized in the Ionian sea after sailing from Cyrenaica, Libya, in the same week as the Titan imploded…. As many as 500 people perished… the sharks were well fed with the soft flesh of children…

Not only did the Global Media appear indifferent to the plight of the refugees, but whistle blowers revealed that the captains of the rescue ship—who claimed that they had sailed out to sea to "save" those desperate people on floating coffins—had refused to take any major risk or initiative to save the migrants on an already unsafe ship. Why risk their lives and those of their crew if the boat's captain—who, they claimed, was able to leap to another boat knowing well that the rat trap would not stay afloat more than a few more hours—did not request it?

The controversy did not disappear but was diverted and watered down. As the Greek Dolphin leadership was accused by human rights critics of pushing migrants back to the ports from where they had sailed at the risk of the migrants' lives, the pro-government News Media counter-accused critics of being "Agents" of the Turkish Graywolf.

As historical Greek versus Turk propaganda resurrected itself, the tragedy of the billionaire Titan submarine imploding in the depths—with a fluff of Media and Wall Street ticker tape—helped to further divert public attention away from accusations that the Greek Dolphin leadership was not only restricting freedom of the press—but also not protecting and defending the safety and lives of journalists and human rights advocates as well—in the Dolphin's own tradition as the cradle of Western Civ. and Democracy.

It was clear many European governments wanted to blame the refugee issue on the Greeks and Italians—while preferring that it all sink deep into the depths of the Hellenic Trench where it could no longer be seen… not wanting to cope with the future refugee crises to come…

"Crocodile Tears!!! "No!!! to the EU's pact on migration!!!" yelled the Xenophobes…

"No one wants to leave their homes unless threatened by the Fangs of Vipers!!!… All people deserve a right to a safe haven!!!" replied the pro-Refugees…

ooo

Bereft was in heaven. I could see the warm glow in her eyes as she began to shake hands with the few who were already leaving, whether they had donated or not. It was stories like those of refugee boat capsizing that ironically helped to galvanize wealthy people to support her cause…

But the party was not at all over… and could go on for several more hours… So, LaPlante asked me to put the checks downstairs in the business office. I went down to the lower deck…. There I could not believe what I saw! Profita must have been either drunk or in a hurry to go to the party. All the Foundation's financial records and other books were stretched out on the desk before me.

I quickly opened the accounting ledger…

ooo

For a minute, I thought I might be opening the Foundation's secret books that would expose illicit Al Capone-like kickbacks, bribery, payoffs, contract killings—much like the ledgers of Prodnose, Fickelgruber, Slugworth who had tried to destroy the foundations of the chocolate factory of Willy Wonka and Charlie Bucket—a story that depicts not-so-politically correct, slump-backed, Oompa-Loompas, who could be compared with the army of slave labor interns and researchers at the HVF Foundation—who daily sang chain gang songs in the hope of obtaining positive recommendations for real jobs from LaPlante herself.

Yet Al Capone was a false metaphor. The fact of the matter was that everything in her accounts appeared very legal, or at least not too far over the border of legality. After all, HVF was a private Foundation and anyone could donate money to it in the name of human values, refugees, the environment, education, world peace, or whatever.

It was clear the system of philanthropy donations itself was a farce. On the average about 66% of the funds raised by most American non-profits went to the charity itself, while a whopping 33% often went to the personal accounts of the people who did the fundraising. Yet I saw that LaPlante would sometimes take much more—as much as 50% or more—as personal income! I assumed she could get away with it because she claimed her contacts and actual funds raised were superior to those of other non-profits. Outrageous![126]

I then saw the large list of companies that received LaPlante's funding. Many were payments to "for profit" groups who produced sports clothes, shoes, canned foods, and items such tents, stoves, and equipment, which could prove helpful if distributed to refugees and the homeless by non-profits for free. Some of these "for-profit" groups were owned in part by HVF....[127]

That was not all: Many NGOs to which her Foundation for Human Values Forever was providing large sums of money were all serving the interests of her "donors"—or really her investors. Few, as far as I could tell, were local businesses or individuals who needed the cash.

ooo

What next caught my attention was the Foundation's association with an organization founded immediately after the January 2015 Charlie Hebdo attacks. The $$$ were not for the Charlie magazine itself... but for a high-profile Communications group, Babble and Babel Associates, that then engaged in a publicity campaign, *Combat Extremist Propaganda*... Babble and Babel had been founded by the (in)famously wealthy Prince Al-Wasta... who had been able to escape a recent Islamicist coup in his country with most of his billions in foreign bank accounts.

I remember how LaPlante had initially shown no interest in *Charlie Hedbo*, that is, before the January Islamist 2015 attacks that slaughtered its editorial staff.... A month or so before the attacks, I had overheard Prophita talking with LaPlante:

"You know there is a whole big wave of people who want to help out Charlie Hebdo."

La Plante had responded, "What! They want me to support a band of irresponsible Anarchists who have not yet passed through Freud's anal-sadistic psycho-sexual phase?"

"Apparently, they want to organize donations to prevent the magazine from going out of business altogether. Even Prince Al-Wasta is involved..."

"Prince Al-Wasta? Yes, I know him." She had seemed to blush. "But I am very surprised he would support such a group! He is a devout Muslim!" was her reply.

Prophita explained, "Many of the Arab Gulf's Moslem elites support Charlie Hebdo's cause—if only because they hate the militant Islamicists who threaten their own power and privileges even more... The enemy of my enemy is my friend—even if that new friend is an atheist."

I had always wondered, how did the "We are all Charlie" vogue obtain such significant popular and media support so soon after the assassination? And why was I hired just after the "We are All Charlie" protests a month or so after Al-Wasta claimed that he wanted to help the anti-terrorist cause? Incredibly, I saw that my paycheck was coming from Al-Wasta's funding!

ooo

Not only that, but I also saw that the Zenzimes did not "donate" their high-tech AI and blockchain systems as Prophita had claimed. Instead, the Foundation itself had paid for them… and for a very hefty price….

And while I thought (at the time) that I had a decent salary, I noticed LaPlante only paid 600 Euro per month to the part-time house cleaner, the Filipina with the soft brown eyes, thick eyelashes, and very Chinese look.… It was so typical of these liberal elites who talk about saving the world—but who treat their own employees like dirt.

As Aiden had told me, the Filipina, like many others, had migrated to France on someone else's passport and was probably still paying off her human smugglers the 10,000 Euros fee that she owed them. Then he had added snidely, "If LaPlante lived up to her values, she would help her pay off her debts… but, apparently she does not want to admit, or involve herself, in any illegal wrongdoing…"

At that time, I was surprised that Russell would aim his critical consciousness at a domineering LaPlante…

ooo

True, Profita did advise LaPlante to invest in firms that sought sustainable solutions to issues including climate change, food and water scarcity, waste management and recycling—with some emphasis on employee well-being, lifelong learning, and human rights. Yet the reality was that she placed even greater investments in the five big energy multinationals and in the five big arms merchants—not to overlook the top pharmaceuticals that made outrageous profits during the Year of the Horseshoe Bat and at the outset of the February 2020 Russian "special military intervention" that then became stuck in the muddy *rasputitsa* of Ukraine.[128]

In effect, LaPlante diversified her donations to avoid taxes as much as possible while also claiming to support good causes! In the name of humanity, refugees, the environment, education, feminism, LGBTQI+ values, world peace, the money that she raised was actually serving a number of "for-profit" corporations that did (some) human rights work on the side—but whose other purpose was to provide logistics and infrastructure for other more nefarious concerns—including "I Spy" services.

Nor was this to ignore her buying property in the name of the Foundation, then selling it to cronies under value, receiving a huge kickback... I am sure that was perhaps the real reason she had gone to Italy to search for a building that could serve as a "Humanitarian Aid Distribution Center." I found the business card of her Italian "interpreter": The pugged-nose women specialized in high-end real estate…

And now, in following the latest investment fad, LaPlante, advised, I assume, by Prophita, had just placed massive sums in a few virtually unknown (except by the experts) high tech firms that claimed to be on the cutting edge of the AI ragtime player piano rage. She was now playing big time. As her profits during the Year of the Horseshoe Bat pandemic were already phenomenal, it seemed to be a sure thing!

ooo

It seemed that LaPlante's whole non-profit tax deduction scheme was set up as a secular way to absolve the sins of the rich, to mollify and appease the souls of millionaires and billionaires, who all wanted to claim that they were doing *pro-bono* actions for humanity—even if they complained about the risks and incompetence of their employees in the meantime, while generally paying them pittance. In effect,

LaPlante's "help the poor and refugees" scheme helped "make herself and others rich" in the process….[129]

ooo

In opening another book, I felt as I was reliving the nightmare of Tao Baiqing when she saw herself accidentally permitted to enter the secret archives of the Communist Party in *Year of the Earth Serpent Changing Colors*. I learned it was LaPlante's Foundation for Human Values Forever that had saved me by donating to the SECC… What a shock!

It was impossible for LaPlante not to know who had really helped me to escape China—in what was called Operation Yellowbird. The French "*Nous sommes un service unique*" DGSE, the American Boys (plus Girls) of the Company, the James Bond MI6, as well as the secret agents of what was then British-controlled Hong Kong were all participants… Manipulation by non-governmental private entities had permitted the Company to "legally" work with illicit organizations, who operated underground in China and elsewhere—as NGOs served a buffers between the government and enemies of the state. And then there was help from legal groups, such as Chinese Buddhists, who had ties to the SECC.

It was an unexpected alliance of Hong Kong politicians, celebrities, business people, Buddhist priests, secret agents, as well as heavily tattooed Chinese Triad members, who all joined forces to raise funds and help the flight of more than 400 Chinese democracy activists after the Beijing Municipal Public Security Bureau had ordered their arrest on June 13, 1989—including me.

I did not know what to think!

ooo

After having lived in France so many years, I could only think of the irony of how I had been saved from an ideologically puritanical Chinese Communist regime by a French Socialist regime that was strongly anti-Communist—and yet the elites of both countries were plagued by significant, and not too dissimilar, forms of corruption.

The Balding Eagle, the French Gallic Cock, the British Bulldog and Lady Europa, had all strongly supported our movement on Voice of America, the BBC and Radio France International from abroad, knowing full well that WE—and not They—would be the ones sacrificed for the Democratic Cause. Were they really concerned with us? Or were we merely being used as cannon fodder in an ideological Media game that went out of control?

Maybe I was different. Maybe I was the cherry on the cake... To take some of the leaders of the Democracy movement out of China was the proof that the leaderships of the Balding Eagle and the Gallic Cock could do something "good". It was proof that these governments could truly stand by their bold words after having so strongly supported our movement in their propaganda campaign against Beijing at the time—even if that meant working secretly with Chinese Triads who could murder anyone without raising an eyebrow....

ooo

And as I subsequently learned from Russell, who was at first a bit reluctant to explain it to me—I guess because the affair somehow implicated him as well—it was an old man with white hair, and bushy white eyebrows, the French Foreign Minister himself, who had helped orchestrate the exfiltration of many of the dissidents. As had been revealed by the Media, French executives were able to spend millions of francs on political favors, mistresses, jewelry, fine art, villas, and apartments with the help of a slush fund from the Elf energy firm that acted as a "state within a state" for the French elites—a fund that also served the interests of the French elites in Europe, Africa, and Asia.[130]

I wondered if that slush fund had also helped pay for my escape and that of others?

These were questions that my journalist friend, Mark King Hayford, whom I had not seen in years, could perhaps investigate, that is, if I finally took the risk to contact him…

At the same time, I could not believe how the French Media had shamed that white-haired foreign minister—in part because it was discovered that he had bought a pair of very costly hand-stitched Italian shoes with what was said to be his share of the slush fund. From what I could read in the often-contradictory news articles, it appeared that former foreign minister was the "fall guy" for corrupt decisions made at higher levels. He soon fell "defenistered" … figuratively… from the 10th floor open window to the sidewalk below...

I had previously believed such shaming only took place in China! I did not know what to think because this sophisticated man was one of the French leaders who had helped save me from Chinese prison—if not much worse…

ooo

I was also struck by a problematic geo-pornographic *Catch 22.* That is, the ostensible need to work with underground mafias to undermine totalitarian regimes to win "freedom" for a few. Chinese Triads had worked to undermine the Qing empire; these groups later aligned with Chiang Kai-chek against Mao and the Communist Party. Then, the Americans had aligned with Italian mafias to defeat Il Duce during "World War II." When the whole government is controlled by a totalitarian not-so-Benevolent

Big Brother Mafia, are there other ways to destroy it without supporting lesser-sized and less powerful Mafias?

Yes, I was saved, and thankful for it. Yet when one buys the freedom of hostages by paying off "terrorist" groups, drug cartels, or kidnappers, or when one supports Latino Narcos, European and Italian mafias, and Chinese Triads against the states in power… who wins in the long term? And how do these kinds of illicit *Catch 22* underground political affairs impact the affairs of otherwise honest government officials—that is, if there is such a thing as an honest official?

The Chinese Triads are now among the most powerful Mafias in the world. And overtime, those Triads, in working with other Mafias and Cartels, have begun to pressure and buy off politicians and CEOs in China, Taiwan, Mexico, as well as in the Land of the Free, and elsewhere….

ooo

I had closed the book and had been looking out of the port hole for a just few minutes when I felt a pair of soft hands on my neck. I turned to see her pale face with freckles on her nose and scarlet hair and blue eyes staring directly into my eyes. I could smell the heavy stench of champagne mixed with even stronger booze on her breath.

Certainly, I did not think that she would ever approach me like this. Never had I expected her to be so forward. It was not long before she had forcefully pressed her mouth to my mouth, put one hand around my waist, and began to gently draw me toward her bedroom with her hand on my crotch as if she were drawing a magnet…

At first, I could not stop myself and felt compelled by some mysterious force to move with her, to collapse on the bed together. I began to imagine myself with that beautiful Filipina and not this drunken woman with dry sagging breasts and thin lips and bad breath, with skin like that of a scare crow with multiple faces and matching finger and toe-nails, who was now on top of me… Even if it were this woman who had helped me escape from prison—if not from Death itself—I wanted nothing to do with her now that she seemed to want to force me to thank her…

Before I knew what had happened, she had unbuckled my belt and drew my zipper down…. I closed my eyes. I could feel her raspy fingers probing…

ooo

She had become a Wu Zetian, the concubine of the 8th arron-dissement of Paris, who had seized the throne by way of eliminating the Emperor's first wife… And once Wu became "Empress," she began to call herself "Emperor" in adopting the formalities of the male patri-archy and phallocracy… They say she wore male regalia and that she had her male servants and the men in her "harem" dress as women… These perverse stories, perhaps fabricated in resentment against matri-archal rule, were legendary… It was also Wu Zetian who had also encouraged the Tang era of high culture, art, music, and tea…

Or maybe she was a modern Marie Antoinette with coins clink-ing out of her crotch. And in eating from a porcelain plate, it was said that she did not want just to have her cake and eat it too, but that she also desired, as a side dish, one of her favorites, frivolités de la reine or couilles de mouton….

Or perhaps she was the human incarnation of La Dame de Fer who ruled on top of the world… Or else a guppy who eats their off-spring… ditto for mother hamsters, chimpanzees, lions, hippopotami, cats, rabbits, scorpions, and dogs… Or the species of female mantises that do not pray when they devour their mates… Not to overlook some kinds of spiders, scorpions, crickets, grasshoppers, and beetles, which can likewise turn against the male sex…

Or maybe she had become the giant Japanese Tsuchigumo earth dwelling spider youkai who could change shape and, in transforming into a nurse, would inject people with an anti-COVID vaccine that was actually her own venom… And that had now transformed once again into the octopus in Hokusai's Girl Diver and Octopi…

Or more likely, a newly humanized rendition of vengeful Barbie, now with a vagina, an anti-patriarchal anti-phallocratic head of her own non-profit profit corporate fiefdom…

ooo

I, myself, had transformed into a Eunuch of the Forbidden City… Or perhaps an Italian castrato who could not sing soprano for the Sistine chapel… Or else Peggy Guggenheim's Marino Marini's bronze man riding bareback, Angel of the City, permanently unscrewed… Or maybe a plasticized Ken with a marshmallow smoothie… Or else an unfortunate tourist fallen into the Seine, his balls devoured by a pacu testicle cruncher…

With my three jewels pilfered… in no way could I produce that mystical magical chemical life-essential life-sustainable Qi... I had no remaining treasure chest… no San Bao… no three precious jewels… to give in return. Or none that I wanted to give her….

My pants now unzipped… I turned toward her, my eyes now glaring with desire that I did not expect and could not control… Having abstained for almost 30 years, my life force *Qi!!!* burst forth like a celestial flower unfurling its pollen into the heavens, a ballet of shimmering seeds that floated in an unholy aerial insemination throughout the room like the confetti fluff of poplar catkins, planted by Mao, in the Beijing spring… Spontaneously these pure and not pure white seeds were set aflame—*yang* versus *yin, yin* against *yang,* within a cosmic *Dao* of unreconciled unbalanced unproportionate agonisms—all flickering like a blinding kaleidoscope of spectral light…

I don't believe her desire had anything to with some form of vengeance or retaliation against me personally, but perhaps against what she considered an inferior 'Menkind' in the abstract who did not respect or flatter her… Her eyes at first glowed demon red but faded rapidly like a gargoyle that had lost its apotropaic power. She then screamed as if seized by allergic reaction to the blast of my non-pollenating gunpowder and ran in utter shock, shame, and in pure disgust with herself… or with me… or perhaps even in fear… before she hurtled herself weeping out of the room… As soon as I could, I jumped to the door while trying to pull up my pants… I almost tripped on my face racing up the stairs and speeding onto the ramp onto the shore.

ooo

A perverse thought crossed my mind in thinking about that submarine crushed in search of the lost treasures of the Titanic… The apparently chill and indifferent attitude of those Coast Guards toward that ill-fated sea voyage of 750 refugees from Libya to Greece did not appear any worse than LaPlante's own attitude… LaPlante was raising funds to "save" humanity… but somewhat similarly without taking much risk at all… Her culpability, however, was even worse than those Captains and their Fearless Leaders…

The irony was that those who sounded the most alarm, who made the most righteous pleas in shaming others for human rights abuses, were often the first to profit from the misery of others or else the first to look in the opposite direction when real help was needed… Few could truly care about sunken Rafts of the Medusa… except for some of the families and friends concerned…

The deeper concern that the tragic shipwreck death of those millionaires/billionaires had raised was an issue of another order—a wicked issue that raised something no one wanted to talk about… $$$ ...

What would have happened if Peggy Guggenheim's millionaire father had not gone down with the Titanic as gentlemen should? Would Peggy still have become Peggy "the art addict"? Or more likely Peggy, "the drug addict"? Would anyone else besides Peggy have protected and promoted the abstract work of the controversial artists like Marcel Duchamp… or Max Ernst… or Yves Tanguy… or Man Ray… or Hans Hoffman… or Jackson Pollock… or Wassily Kandinsky… or Mark Rothko… among many others??? After all, some of their art did not look any more creative than children's drawings…

One could likewise wonder what might have happened if LaPlante had never "inherited" or somehow never "acquired" her fortune—that is, if at least one of the stories about her life possessed a semblance of truth? Would the Foundation for Human Values Forever even exist? Was there something better that could take its place?

ooo

And then I wondered… Could LaPlante herself have planted those contradictory rumors about herself… so no one would know the Truth, *so help me God*? After all, it does not matter what people say about you—as long as they keep talking. And the Social Media buzz can now keep you alive forever—depending on how it is manipulated!

I saw her trying to flag down a taxi… She dropped a tissue wet with bathetic tears onto the pavement…

Bicycling Bois de Boulogne

True, I felt indebted to her for helping to organize my exfiltration from China and for helping others to flee. And yes, her human value cause seemed to be somewhat just and may have helped a good number of people throughout the world—while concurrently helping a lesser number of her wealthy donors and best buddies… and a few governments as well.

Yet there was no way I could become one of her "minions" "bellboys" "subalterns" "lackeys" "valets" "flunkeys" "midnight cowboys" or "gigolos." I could not flagellate myself before her tyrannical success in using the misery of others for her personal profit. I had to get out of there as fast as possible to sustain my integrity and independence… to protect my self-esteem and self-respect.

I was not certain if she knew that I had looked into her accounts, but she could have guessed since nothing was locked in the safe… In any case, she realized she could not buy me off with sexless sex… And she had certainly not expected me to fight back with lust in my own eyes…

ooo

A few weeks after I had begun to work for the Society for the Exploration of Cosmic Consciousness—which is the beginning of another story—I decided to rent a bicycle for the first time ever. I wanted to glide through the Bois de Boulogne on a Sunday—instead of jogging. It had been years since I even rode a bicycle in Beijing in the era when black one speed bikes, the only color available, with balloon tires, clanging and clattering, ruled the street and cars were only driven by High Communist Cadres. I was not at used to riding a bike and hated going onto the street—if I could not be on the sidewalk… And I wished I had not.

Once in the *Bois*, I found myself, sometimes out of control, on a beaten green path on a beaten light blue rental bike traveling the bumpy dirt paths where there were old men playing *bocce* ball, where women were sunning themselves with reflective sun cones… where the sons and daughters of the French elites were lounging, chit-chatting in the grass… and where African, Filipino, Spanish and Portuguese housekeepers were supervising the young children—now chattering in the native dialects of the servants…

I sped past where the sons and daughters of migrants would sell their hashish and helium shots and other forms of dope that were just beginning to be peppered with Opioids from Chinese-supplied ingredients… just like a French African grounds caretaker once told me—as if some of the older children of French elites did not sell drugs as well…

ooo

There was an old lady standing in the middle of the sidewalk shaking her finger like a witch as I squeaked by her. She stood there, frozen, a wax statue, cursing me for having upset her balance… The old people were cursing, "*Incroyable!* You do not own the sidewalk!" or "There are, after all, bicycle paths next to the road; no need to take the sidewalk!" Not only the elderly, but the young suits alike cursed, "The sidewalks are for feet, not wheels!!!" As cars still ruled on the still perilous road, and with pedestrians asserting their rights, there was really no hope for the bicyclist… Some with helmets, most without…

ooo

Upon the crystalline lake, husbands strained muscles to paddle their families through water lilies upon heavy row boats with thick wooden oars wrapped with water weeds. A barefoot funambulist tried to balance himself in walking upon a bright green line tied between two tree trunks, before suddenly turning in the opposite direction; his slender arms swayed up and down before he leaped to the ground. Beneath giant pines, children learned to bicycle next to adults on sleek electric scooters. Happy dogs with long tongues hanging chased birds running in-between humans playing volleyball…

Huge pure white swans spanked the water with their webbed orange feet as they lifted off into the skies showing their offspring how to fly. While the birds of Alfred "Psycho" Hitchcock screeched from the treetops, the ravens of the artist Bernard "the Miserabilist" Buffet pecked through the paper garbage bags of overturned garbage, while those of Edgar Allen Poe cried out, "Nevermore!!!" Mocking birds cawed out in ridicule.

An arrogant blue heron stared frozen, icy-eyed, into the lake without moving an inch for hours. He appeared to be looking for big carp (La Fontaine) or for big perch (Aesop)—yet, unfortunately, he only found a small tench/goldfish (La Fontaine) or a snail (Aesop). In some versions of the story, the bragging heron finds nothing at all to eat. One wonders for how long such wildlife will remain wild—if they will soon exist at all?

ooo

I was riding faster than normal; it looked like a storm was coming up from countryside… Teams of professional Dutch and French cyclists spun around on the paved roads signaling to each other while seeking to frighten pedestrians out of the way. Americans by contrast buzzed on sidewalks on green electric scooters passing Roma women begging the drivers of cars stopped at the stoplight for $$$…

Hundreds of Filipinos were packing up in the park. They were the maids, the cooks, the nannies of La Muette's Golden Triangle. Most were probably unauthorized or illegal… The Filipino's seemed to be the only social group I found in "multicultural" France with any real sense of solidarity… Every weekend I saw them in the park playing games, grilling satay on the barbecue… organizing dance lessons… even setting up a yearly amusement park… I thought I saw the radiant Filipina who cleaned LaPlante's *péniche*—the one woman who could possibly make me break my secular vows of chastity… Yet the yard was too crowded to approach her, and I did not want to interrupt the barbeque party, the dancing… the singing…

Their community interaction was all so un-French!

ooo

The hour was much later than when I usually did my jog around the Bois de Boulogne and the surrounding lakes. The light was now transforming from early twilight evening into that moment *entre chien et loup*… the moment between dog and wolf… when all howls in suspense…

That elderly lady, with the baggy hippy dress and beads around her neck, with a living red parrot on her shoulder, was once again sitting behind the fountain of youth as I bicycled by. Besides her, dozens of black and grey rabbits hopped helter-skelter, without an apparent care in the world. It had been several weeks since I had seen her when I was jogging and had wondered if she was still alive. The first time I had seen her, she was sauntering nonchalantly down the dirt path. I had noticed that her once long grey hair had been chopped straight…

She seemed to have started a fad; over the years I had begun to see more and more men and women with parrots on their shoulders. I had even seen green and red parrots flying wild in the trees… I assumed I was not hallucinating… A boon companion in loneliness—even if the bird could only imitate the few words it had heard… I would hate to think what such birds would say after hearing the perverse conversations on LaPlante's *péniche*…

ooo

I then spun around the lake with Parisian sunbathers leaving the grounds, children throwing breadcrumbs to the geese and a few giant swans, who roared over the waters on take-off, flapping their webbed feet on the surface, and then sailed over the dirty alleys of the circus camp. There were many people, hand in hand, women and men, men and men, women and women, walking along the lake and admiring Monet water lilies that were beginning to bloom… Under huge pines a few Chinese women, not knowing a word of French, picked through the brush for prickly hazelnuts and other herbs… for their restaurant recipes…

Up from the sublime green gilded *art nouveau* restaurant next to the Grand Cascade, I huffed up the hill past the *Monument des Fusilles* where members of the Free French Resistance were shot in August 1944—just before the defeat of the Nazis… The names of the dead had been engraved upon a monument sculpted with the Cross of Lorraine. The bark of trees surrounding the massacre, ribboned off with *blue blanc rouge*, still bore the traces of bullets…

At least their sacrifice was not entirely in vain…

ooo

In the back woods, by the space of disheveled buildings that once upon a time must have been a farm, had become a restaurant, *Le Relais de Bois du Boulogne*. That was where I had once, for the first time, tasted ostrich and mashed potatoes with truffle with Bereft. That was when I realized that LaPlante had begun to make eyes at me, or so I believed, at a fundraiser for the Foundation. That was long before the building had become a wooden ghost restaurant, like a broken-down Hollywood stage set, in the middle of the *Bois*—an abandoned building now rotting, the owner and chef having moved away, or having died years ago, like so many decent restaurants that are not fat fast-food chains.[131]

I remember how wonderful it was when we had eaten outside under the pines, even if a yellow jacket had stung me on the wrist. It was still fresher air… And I remember that marvelous dinner near the top of the *La Dame de Fer* at another fundraiser with the pianist playing Chopin overlooking Paris in all its glory… That too was another era… when there still seemed to be hope…

ooo

On the side of the main road that cuts through the park, I could see the phallus of the Hôtel Concorde La Fayette at Porte Maillot that overlords all Paris. In the midst of the great trees of the *Bois du Boulogne* and the grey-white stream, Parisians let their dogs splash in the filthy waters. It is there, men, women, and other individuals, he/she/it, tall or short, dark or blonde (fake color or not), usually sporting black high heels, speak strange languages—perhaps Romanian, Ukrainian, Russian, Brazilian, Spanish, or some other. They jumped in and out of beat-up white vans with cracked windows. With one hand, they powdered their faces, while smearing thick red lipstick on botoxed lips with the other…

An almost naked African Queen… the tips of his/her/its curly black hair flaming yellow, with her/his/its yellow brown panties covering a Brazilian Butt Lift with hips stuffed with fat injected after liposuction from its/his/hers stomach and sides, with matching bra projecting boobs like headlights made of silicone implants… was strutting in matching yellow high heels behind a much shorter and younger woman, with thick painted eyebrows, her dirty blonde hair covered by a green *hijab*, who was wearing bright white sneakers under a brown potato sack—as she strolled with her infant on a small tricycle upon the park sidewalk…

How is it that very superficial, not even close, resemblances and attributes, can unexpectedly, and for no real reason, remind one of others???

ooo

Having worked for the Foundation for Human Values Forever, I had never asked the million-dollar question, 'What is the true value of an individual?" How is it determined? What gives the body its value? Is it its look? Its strength? Its brain power? Its creativity? Its health? Its gender? Its ethnicity and race? Its class or status? Its use? Its geostrategic position in the geo-porno nexus of the local, national, regional, or global market? Its luck? Its very being and existence? Yes, what was the body worth? And what is the value of the Soul? And which was of greater value: the Soul or the Body?

In 2022, the body's mineral content, which was not so rich in phosphorus and calcium, was worth roughly $585—without the Spirit.[132] And yet the human flesh by itself—while ignoring the spirit still linked to it—could magically be worth much more than that amount if used for multiple pleasures. The "whores of the Republic" who work in the 8th arrondissement primarily, or those who belong to private sex services, could earn $$$thousands$$$ of times more than those in the Bois de Boulogne or in Pigalle, whose pimps were illegal in France—but nonetheless managed "affairs" behind the scenes…

So why do some individuals possess and obtain much more material value than others? And what was I worth, what value would my body have—if I had nowhere to go, become a refugee without a job, a street person crammed into a make-shift tents handed down from the HVF Foundation besides the noxious fumes of turnpikes? What I am worth with skills, but without opportunities? Would a Fearless Leader's Boot Camp G.I. Joe even recruit me? These were sick thoughts. I had not yet reached rock bottom… at least not yet…

ooo

A beat-up black van pulled over by the stop light. A man who seemed to be a Brit called me over to look at a map… He asked me for directions to Calais… Calais from Paris? I could not see who or what was in the back. I thought for a second. Why in the hell in the middle of the *Bois de Boulogne* would someone be asking for the route to Calais—the city from where migrants hoped to reach the paradise in Perfidious Albion? It seemed absurd.

I thought a bit more. I was in the *Bois*. Strange things could happen. Here, the police would bust men suspected to be pimps or clients; there were wars among the pimps who were illegally profiting from harems… There were refugees who sold themselves, but were still desperately looking for ways to prevent themselves from being forced to return to their homelands… There were other passers-by who were drugged, beat up, if not killed, simply in the hope to get a wallet…

Who knows! It could be a *guet-apens*, a trap designed to grab me, with a knife to my throat, even if I had nothing worth taking… Instead of moving closer to the van, I yelled "*Desolé!* Sorry!" and sped off on my bike… I was about to turn the corner, when out of the blue, another black van sped by and cut me off.

Without warning, without a sound, the second van forced me to swerve off the street and onto the sidewalk and into the brush… It was as if the driver had never mastered the French driving code—unable to understand the Napoleonic rule of *priorité à droit* which does not exist in the USA or the UK, where people drive on the left side. There were many in France who had argued for a reform of the regulation—but it was too late in this case…

At first, I had tried to make it all a joke, yet I began to believe my paranoia was for real… There were probably more people inside those vans whom I not could see… Were they refugees seeking to flee to the UK? Or captured slaves? Or more goons trying to capture me?

ooo

I began to see myself chased by men with no hair but bubble heads and raised cheek bones and bulges at the tip of their scalps. They were all wearing dark red orange robes—but were not monks at all. They appeared to be communicating with each other by some form of electronic telepathy… I sped into the crowd at the amusement park, the yearly La Fête à NeuNeu, initiated by Napoleonic decree in 1815. It was powered first by horses, and then by "imprisoned lightning" by 1900. As the park was too crowded to pass through, I dumped my bike and entered a strange space, the Sanson's Home of Horrors. I hoped those people whom I assumed to be chasing me did not see me enter…

Projected by silent videos, each room presented various techniques of execution, from the ecological and sustainable… from stoning, crucifixion, hanging, death by a thousand slices (Lingchi)… to the ultimate advancement of death by the National Razor… and then toward the modern un-sustainable techniques of capital punishment… the firing squad, lethal injection, Bulgarian umbrella guns, polonium poisoning, nitrate oxide, and perhaps the most absurd and anti-ecological… death by the "imprisoned lightning" of Old Sparky…

On the screen were honored Kings and Queens, Presidents, and CEOs of Big Conglomerates, past and present, awaiting their sentences, guilty of sex crimes and crimes against humanity. They were being judged by the hunchback Quasimodo dressed as the Pope while Notre Dame burned unprotected by red-eyed Gargoyles and Stone Lions. It was a group portrait of the modern royalty mixed with energy barons and the new Knights of AI high-tech companies side by side plutocratic "Our Ford" entrepreneurs—much like the aristocracy once depicted by Francisco Goya's etchings and deep aquatint contrasts…

They were the VIP "Los Caprichos," the High Communist Cadres, and the "Tuhaos" who had no idea that they were the subject of their own deep satire. Their clothes may appear to have changed since the revolutions of the 18th, 19th, and 20th centuries, but nothing else. The '60s cultural revolution, sex drugs and rock 'n roll certainly had no impact… These elites had adapted to the "new" ways, even if they still wore coats and ties in some settings. They had learned a simple lesson: Not to call for a popular draft, but to urge valiant and needy G.I. Joe volunteers to risk their lives in endless "blank check" wars…

Encircled by the faces of Wangliang demons, and with half-human Jiāngshī Dragon Chimera guffawing above me, the atmosphere of Sanson's House of Horrors was haunted by a shimmering aureole borealis of absurd superstitions, scams, and deep fake narratives, and by not-so-subtle prejudice and bigotry… by selfishness and self-flattery… by cowardly servility in which the Fearless Leaders and wealthy and not-so-powerful and not-so-wealthy engage in mutual manipulation. For the sake of their consciences, to perpetrate their own social position and survival… all point their fingers at whomever are seen as the heretics of the moment…

I could see their grotesque inbred faces distorted... I could see living stereotypes dedicated to corruption, debauchery, infidelity... "The sleep of reason does truly produce Chimeras..." in the words of Goya...

In this gargantuan clash between giant safes and cloth bags stuffed full of coins protected in armored vans in the midst perpetual wars, I could see populist bullies, tinpot dictators, Narcos, tattooed Chinese Triads and MS-13 mafias, as well as sidekick "terrorist" groups, with their religious pretentions... And near them, I could see the opposite: Good souls turned bitter after engaging with full hearts in the struggle for a better and more just and peaceful world...

I then saw those defenders of human rights and values who were accused of wrongdoing, but who had done nothing wrong except not support those Benevolent Big Brothers in power. Once their confessions had been dutifully detailed and recorded, they were held in a global open-air refugee camp like free ranging bio-chicken ready for slaughter... after forcibly losing their lands, stores, industries, and livelihoods...

Some sported triangles of differing colors in accord with their "anti-social" qualifications, their nationalities, their ethnicities, their social and religious backgrounds... Others were marked with a unique category that was shaped in the form of a circle with a palette of all colors... It was a full circle that represented those individuals and peoples who had once struggled for freedom from persecution—only to become violent oppressors themselves...

With the unofficial fireworks of the July 14, 1789, I could see the Sans-Culottes and street urchins of the Neuf Trois (93) storming the Bastille celebrated two weeks early in protesting the need to struggle daily for bread... for a paycheck that could buy something of worth... that could bring something of real "value" to their miserable lives... In response, the generals and their camp followers claim that they were all ready to do battle in pretended support for the daily suffering of the people—as they kowtowed before the newly enthroned cuckolding and castrating Dowager Empress, scented heavily with No. 5...

After the French coffers had been drained in support of the ungrateful American Struggle for Liberty, by 1792 all of France was ready to march to the militarist tune of the Marseillaise—the Chant de Guerre pour l' Armée du Rhin… It had taken only a mere extra three years for the fireworks initially invented by the Chinese to explode into world-wide gunpowder blasts… In the battles against the Monarchist alliance and the Roast Beef of King George, the French Frog-eating Man-eating cannibals set off a regional and global fireworks that did not fizzle out entirely until 1815… scorching the Ukrainian rasputitsa in combat with the Russian Double-Headed Eagle—although much differently then than now…

At first marching in the heels of Barbie, then in the boots of G.I. Joe, *the new march toward a global Butter Battle had begun… I needed to find a way to escape… If not careful, I could see myself dancing in step with the Satan Salsa and driving in circles upon the Roue de la Mort… I could be eaten alive by Jurassic Earth Serpents and the Gonggong Chimera that roamed the fields looking for edible suckers to cross their paths…*

Like every youth who dreams of landing on Mars, I stared at the ride that shot its voyageurs spinning some 80 meters in the air and as fast as 120 km per hour and thought of propelling myself to Mars on the Rocket Booster MADMAXXX—in a space race between the Balding Eagle, Lady Europa, the Russian Double-Headed Eagle, the Indian King Cobra, and Chinese Red Dragon… His AI High-Tech Holiness had said that Mars was the one place that appeared to promise the liberation of all of humanity from the threat of asteroids—even if that planet had many more asteroid attacks than did the Earth. Yet I could only escape if I would sign on the dotted line to be drafted as one of the Red Planet's first Colonists….

Unexpectedly kicked in the gut by those chasing me, I puked like those youth dizzily getting off their voyage into inner space….

ooo

I awoke from my running nightmare… Without looking around for those thugs whom I feared could still be following me, I ran in and out of the crowd of parents with their children licking giant spiraling lollipops or phosphorescent red or blue cotton candy, or of other sickening flavors… Soon I raced through the brush into an area of the park thick with brush that I knew very well and where I hoped they could not follow me… There I could quickly run a long way without coming close to the roadside.

I could only wonder: What might be my fate if I had been captured by these goons? … Were they working for the Red Dragon? If so, would I be sent to a "re-education" camp? Would I be put to death by a thousand slices? Or would they make me take the knife if I would not confess? And confess to what—as I had nothing to confess? I had done nothing wrong… *The surgeon, with the robe of a priest, held his curved scalpel in the air, demanded, "Are you ready…?"*

The only thing I could be certain was that Beijing—unlike certain states in the Land of the Free—would in no way go to the expense of plugging in the excessively high energy usage Old Sparky just to sizzle my flesh into carbon dust with "imprisoned lightning." There were many other means… *And in a split second… the curved knife flashed again…*

Then again, what if those goons were not working for the Red Dragon???

ooo

In the grey cloud islets floating above, I could once again see the 12 Horsemen/Women of the Posse Comitatus—the Four Riders of the Apocalypse, Death, Famine, War, and Conquest- Destruction-R/Evolution; the Four Riders of the Bourse, Profiteering, Speculation, Usury, and Exploitation; and the Four Riders of the Black Hole,

Weapons of Mass Destruction, Pandemic, Species Extinction, and Artificial Intelligence.

They were all riding roughshod above me—looking down in judgment from the heavens above upon the new Eurasian Golden Horde as it roared zigzag like a thunderbolt exploding… I saw as they sought ways to confuse, disorient, and then force, the Balding Eagle and its Oceania Allies, to tumble, without parachutes, down to earth…

Would some members of this Posse Comitatus, if not all, seek to intervene in the coming panoramic combat between the Balding Eagle and its Oceanic Allies vs. the Golden Horde—as they fought at a distance and through proxies over the muddy plains of Ukraine and the Holy Lands... and then throughout much the planet?… If so, what perverse games might they play in assisting or opposing the two clashing sides? And what would be the ultimate Earthly- Unearthly Outcome?

Post-Mortem

by Mark King Hayford

It must have been just a few days after those goons had attempted to kidnap Chia Pao-yu in the *Bois du Boulogne*, that he unexpectedly disappeared despite his pleas to me for protection…

This is the email Chia sent to me just after what he believed was an attempted kidnapping. Unfortunately, I only replied several days later. I simply did not recognize Chia's adopted cover name, Jean Valjaur or JV. He had not put his real name in the title or on his email address. As I received so many emails from supportive fans, and even more from those who strongly detested my political viewpoint (if not my very person!!!), I rarely opened the emails of those people I did know or recognize the name. I guess it stemmed from the fact that I had become famous… perhaps too famous…

It was much too late to act!!! I wish he had written to me sooner. I can understand why he did not. I will never forgive myself… for I loved him dearly as a friend… a real friend… a brave man… one of the bravest on the planet!

August 15, 2023

Dear Mark,

I know this email will come to you as a surprise—if not a shock. I know it has been more than 30 years, but I was not captured after Tiananmen Square as many believed. I guess you believed that as well. I probably should have written to you earlier, but I feared it would be at the risk of exposing my new identity. I think you will see that it is truly me from my attached commentary about those incredible times we had together—when the whole world must have thought that there was something between us. And maybe there was! In any case, I hold no regrets…

The good news was that after I was hidden somewhere in Hong Kong, France kindly offered me political asylum after a desperate 8 year wait! Once in France, I began to work for The Foundation for Human Values Forever. At first, I thought it was a worthy cause. A few years later, I learned otherwise as you will see when you read my memoir. I was then offered a job with the Society for the Exploration of Cosmic Consciousness (SECC). They said they had helped me to escape from China by working with Buddhists and with the French and American governments. I then learned the Chinese Triads and other questionable organizations were also involved. That was a real eye opener…

I am only just beginning to understand what kind of organization SECC is. When they first hired me, they said they greatly appreciated my arguments in favor of democratic reforms in China. They told me that they would translate my "Planetary Manifesto," and other articles, into as many languages as possible and then distribute my work to their multiple Centers around the world. At first, I thought it was a new beginning. After my outrage in learning how the Foundation for Human Values for Forever was being managed for personal profit, I now believe what is happening in the SECC concerns the entire planet…

I believe you should investigate both organizations. I would gladly serve as a whistle blower with your assistance as I had done in Beijing! How I remember those days when it looked like the whole world was changing—and all of China as well!

In the meantime, I fear that my cover may have had been blown. After a hallucinating incident in the Bois de Boulogne, I believe they may go after me again… Who "they" are is not entirely clear—most likely agents of Beijing—but even that cannot be taken for granted… If I had died by a mere traffic accident in the Bois, at the very least it could be said that I had died existentially like Camus, the greatest of my

French literary heroes… I now, however, see myself drugged, neutered like a Eunuch, after being tortured in a cell like the *Man in the Iron Mask*… All this for dreaming of, and demanding, a peaceful (rêve)volution in China and the rest of the world… Please call me ASAP on your personal cell number, so that we can talk directly… I hope we can meet again—and soon!

—Chia Pao-yu Tel: +33 7 22………

ooo

The fact that Chia's kidnapping or "disappearance" took place just a couple of weeks after the publication, by this strange Society for the Exploration of Cosmic Consciousness, of his brilliant Manifesto in multiple languages, in addition to Chinese and English, appeared to raise several questions. Was there someone who might have wanted him "out of the picture"?

What also raised questions was the fact that Chia had "disappeared" just after LaPlante had suddenly passed away months after the Horseshoe Bat pandemic was said to be over—but was, it was said, making a comeback when no one was "physically distancing". At least one can assume it was the Horseshoe Bat, or some variant that killed her—that is, if the coroner's certification was correct. Up until then, LaPlante had seemed to have been in perfect health—although she was known to hit the Crystalline bubbly, and few other delights, a bit too often…

The problem was that the amount of money involved reeked the possibility of foul play. It all had the making of a coup although I did not have enough proof. No, the 100 million euros or so in her Foundation's bank account—although hardly anything as compared to the new billionaires/trillionaires—did not suddenly disappear. And it would continue to be donated to "noble" causes. The Catch, I soon learned, was that it was all now controlled by her Business Associate, Gaspard G. Prophita, in association with the Zenzimes of the SECC. Once LaPlante was no longer in the picture, the SECC moved in as a partner. And Prophita immediately told the Human Rights lawyer, Aiden Russell, that his services were no longer needed… *"You're fired!"*

What was definitely fortuitous was that LaPlante's passing and Chia's kidnapping took place just a few weeks after the movie Barbie had announced its first $$$billion$$$ in box office receipts and after an unknown individual won a billion dollars in the California lottery—at about the same time that stocks in "IShaThere4Iam" and other AI firms were said to be worth $$$trillions$$$.

And it appears that the Zenzimes were ready to cash in… They had already played the digital currency financial markets and had luckily avoided the Ponzi bitcoin and cryptocurrency schemes. They were truly financial Wall Street Yellow Brick Road High Tech Wiz Kids.

As I continued to investigate, I learned that there were fairly credible rumors that the SECC had also been into what is called "pig-butchering" in which individuals are sweet-talked into investing into crypto currencies… by claiming insider tips… only to find that they have lost all of their investment… It was a new scheme that made millions in Southeast Asia, one of the favorite regions for the religious entrepreneurs of the SECC to win newly impoverished converts just after those same speculators had lost their money unwittingly to the SECC itself… After earning enough cash through such nefarious ways, it appears the SECC opted to go straight before they got caught.

To be investigated…

ooo

RAIDER magazine wrote a glowing obituary about this world-famous Socialite who had raised millions for human rights and other noble causes…

In Loving Memory: Bereft LaPlante

With heavy hearts, we bid farewell to a beloved socialite and philanthropist, Bereft LaPlante. With an innate sense of empathy and a magnetic personality, Bereft tirelessly organized and hosted numerous charity events, galas, and fundraisers, each of which became a resounding success under her visionary leadership... At the service to celebrate her extraordinary life, held at Pere Lachaise, the extraordinary Archbishop, Leo X. Spraynote, stated, as if speaking to her spirit directly: "Rest in eternal peace, dear Bereft. The impact of your philanthropic endeavors will continue to reverberate through time and live on through the transformative work you inspired... In lieu of flowers, donations should be made to the *Foundation for Human Values Forever*, your most cherished cause. With a heart full of love, you, Bereft, have embraced humanity and left an indelible mark on the world."

ooo

At roughly the same time, *NewsBlitz!!!* published a brief notice about Chia Pao-yu stating the concern, not yet proven, that the Chinese authorities may have seized him at the airport in Hong Kong just before he was able to fly safely to the French utopian haven… I found out through my contacts that it was the HVF Foundation that had provided that information to *NewsBlitz!!!*—an allegation, of course, denied by Beijing.

The more I investigated, however, the more I began to realize that there was a very different story… As I wrote on my blog site, the truth of the matter was that Chia Pao-yu may have been seized in Paris—just before he was able to get back to his artsy apartment complex—after one of his many jogs throughout Paris… I cannot cite my anonymous "inside" sources, but based on Chia's own words that he had emailed me just before he unexpectedly disappeared, it is highly credible that three black suit goons, much like those three Keystone Cops who had once escorted me to the Beijing airport and expelled me from China for publishing allegedly "top secret" info, had forced Chia into a filthy van…

The real issue was a secret exchange—an exchange of a real western spy, European, or perhaps, American—for Chia, a poor and helpless Chinese dissident… And the kidnapping allegedly could only take place after Chia Pao-yu's patron/ benefactor, Bereft LaPlante, had unexpectedly died, whether due to a Horseshoe Bat lung infection or not. The fact that Chia's name had been put by the Red Dragon on the Red List of the Europot Security Agency placed the French government under some obligation to turn Chia Pao-yu over… but probably not without some form of *quid pro quo.*

ooo

The disappearance of Chi'a Pao Yu (or JV) brought great grief and sorrow among the few who knew him personally. His legacy brought with it the beginnings of a universal recognition of his struggle for democracy, justice, human rights, and peace in China and throughout the world—which, as he himself had begun to recognize, were all not always the same thing, as there could be peace without justice… There could be democracy without human rights…

Nevertheless, the more people learned about him, the more his writing and speeches became well known, the more the world's population began to adore him. It was not long before he appeared to reach the status of the Moslem and Eunuch Admiral Zheng He… Or even the cult-like status of the great poet and diplomat, Qu Yuan… Or even… the Jean Jaures of China…

Truly, if his life had been a novel… the outcome of his life experience could have never been anticipated from some preconceived Platonic concepts of a Cosmic Ghost-writer… Or by some "Great Automatic Grammatizator." In his life narrative, there was no way "that the end cleared up things that were elements of the beginning" and that "the beginning already had a conception of the end" as Sartre put it in describing his own nauseating text. No one could have predicted Chia's ending, starting as a "good boy" from a not-so-good Chinese Communist family to a twice disappeared "bad boy" … and now a virtual Superstar…

ooo

I admit, one could question: Was my "inside" informant telling me the truth? Was LaPlante's death really the moment when Chia lost his social protection from whoever wanted to make him "disappear"? Or perhaps Chia's name had been exposed to hackers the instant he sent me his first email? Perhaps Beijing (who denied everything) did seize him on its own initiative and not as a trade-off for a European or American spy? Or… perhaps, much as was the case for Galvin's death, was I looking in the wrong direction?[133]

No matter what the Truth, what appeared correct was that Chia had "disappeared" once again. At the same time, there was something odd about the fact that his apartment was rapidly cleaned out by a group of individuals in Horseshoe Bat proof white suits and black face masks almost as soon as his disappearance was reported. They stripped the place, and bagged everything of Chia's, most importantly, his original "Planetary Manifesto." Whoever they were, they had not been asked to do so by the Concierge of Chia's apartment complex—at least that is what he told me…

ooo

And that is what I have uncovered so far… Chia had told me by phone that he would explain in more detail what was happening at the SECC… That was already suspicious… And it led me to think that there was something much more troubling going on. What was this bizarre Society of the Exploration of Cosmic Consciousness that he mentions haphazardly throughout his memoirs—but never fully explains—really all about?

It was the SECC who had published—yet on different websites and under different organizational rubrics—a condensed and radically redacted version of Chia's *Planetary Manifesto* just a couple of weeks after his death, plus selections from his "Reflections: Year of the Horse Shoebat," including "From Pharoah's Rats to Horseshoe Bats" and "Not-So Beatific Beats," but not, for example, "From Barbieland to Boot Camp G.I. Joe???". And since that time, some of Chia's "writings" have not only been updated on the SECC's own website, *Non-Alienated Intelligence*, but also on other sites as well, yet in differing variations.

What one may read floating on different websites on the Internet and in podcast form is thus not necessarily the original version. Some of the passages of his acclaimed "Planetary Manifesto"—that are critical of all sides and that I publish here—appear to have been censured on both the web and in paper form. Many of Chia's critical "Truths" have been garbled in a mishmash of computer-generated verbiage and (dis-)interpreted and generated in such a way that it is nearly impossible to tell what he himself argued and what has been added or altered…

Much of "his" work has already been generated on a podcast in a voice, in both Chinese and English, which sounds exactly like his... And likewise, several tracts were distributed in book form and on the internet and on the not-always-so-Social Media—yet "re-written" in his name, Jean Valjaur. All this, I have learned, can be accomplished by the advanced AI "Automatic Grammatizator" that culls bits and pieces of data from a person's writings, speeches, conversations, and then constructs rational arguments that sound almost like the views of the individual—yet are nothing but "Deep Fakes"—as are the computer generations of his voice and image that speak to the planet from the so-called "underground"...

ooo

As a final *Adieux* to a person whom I considered a true friend, I have thus decided to annotate /anecdote his seminal "Planetary Manifesto"—or at least what I understand to be the original version. I have added footnotes to his memoirs that he had sent me—just before he vanished without a trace in very strange circumstances.

In this excerpt, he ridicules the impact of alcohol on the decisions of political leaders...

The Chinese "Sleeping Giant" has suddenly awakened—even if the moniker was probably falsely attributed to Napoleon.[134] Beijing has begun to spray its flames of flying cash and credit (along with the spittle of the Horseshoe Bat pandemic) throughout the planet—while seeking to hook its Red Dragon claws into the nooks and crannies of the United Nations and every government and society possible...

Beijing is no longer ruled by Party mandarins who drink Red Star *bai jiu* from Deng Xiaoping "little bottles." The government is now overlorded by Red Party elites who savor real French wine from Chinese investments in Bordeaux or Chinese-made Dynasty Cabernet Sauvignon aged on oak barrels from Ningxia for over $1500 in Xi Jinping "narrow neck bottles". For some, however, the new rage is Dreamy Blues *bai jiu,* fermented for 6 months in century-old liquor pits, and stored for 15 years in an underground cellar… It's a 52% pure alcohol dream for individuals, for nations, for countries—embodying tranquility, tolerance, and gentleness! …

One could make the case that the character and actions of different societies are influenced by the kind of alcohol they drink. Wine certainly makes the French melancholy and unwilling to act. Beer makes the Germans rowdy and belligerent. Vodka makes the Russians wild and daredevil. And Dreamy Blues *Baijiu* makes the Chinese hallucinate. For the Americans, whiskey makes them stir crazy with heavy hangovers!

Then again, Adolfo "Holocaust" Hitler, unlike Winstoned Churchstill, rarely drunk more than a shot. ~~And apparently, neither does "Agent Orange *Jee-Zus*!!!"—at least not since his wild NYC SoHo nights *at Spy Bar, Kit Kat Club, Wax, and Chaos.*~~[135]

So, whether the Chinese leaders are heavy drinkers of Dreamy Blues, we can't blame the new Chinese version of totalitarianism and imperialism on Drugs and Alcohol!! ~~Nor will we be able to blame the new homespun American version of McCarthy Fearless Leader-like fascism on Drugs and Alcohol either!~~

+++

The following excerpt is a bold and powerful critique of the dangers that AI poses for Humankind that was heavily censored when published in written and oral form…

~~It is crucial to emphasize that Beijing was not at the origin of these new mass surveillance technologies. Instead, the Transnational Corporations of the Balding Eagle and Lady Europa blazed the path for the Red Dragon to follow.~~

~~It is in following the dreams of Marco's Millions that the major high-tech firms of the Lands of the Free have assisted China to develop such technological capabilities with extensive operations. Just like~~

Marco Polo and the Mongols, and like Henry Ford and the Nazi's, U.S. and European firms and the U.S. military industrial congressional-university complex have all provided good old U.S. know-how to help Beijing boost its military, high tech, digital, and dual use-capabilities.

This assistance to China includes Supercomputers, AI research centers, data centers, manufacturing capabilities, not to overlook biotech and viral Wuhan research labs. The Balding Eagle has even provided Cloud service and made entire computer operating systems for the Chinese government—which only belatedly complained about American implanted computer viruses—just as the Americans have complained about Chinese and Russian bugs!

Many major firms, whether knowingly or unknowingly, have been working with Chinese "businesses" who are really "intermediaries" between the foreign countries and the *lao gai* prison system, so that it is millions of prisoners who could actually be making many products exported abroad—from pregnancy tests to barbed wire in extremely poor working conditions, with workers in danger of torture if they fall behind in production. Given the outrageously low costs, despite the mark up for the profits of the prison and the intermediary, even U.S. and European firms should suspect there is a something wrong going on.

Techniques of social control were accordingly refashioned by the Chinese after they observed American counterinsurgency techniques that were used in the futile multi-trillion-dollar wars in Afghanistan and Iraq. Use the Body, Control the Mind!!!

Learning from American GWOT military interventions, Beijing has been able to magnify its own mass surveillance and confinement capabilities in addition to ironically utilizing techniques involving Maoist style-thought reform to "re-educate" and "deradicalize" Islamicists and other opponents of the regime. Blood is on their hands!

+++

After adopting American, European, Japanese, and Taiwanese technologies (the latter produces the best), Beijing is now taking the global lead in expanding mass surveillance and AI capabilities. In advance of most other countries, including ~~the U.S. and~~ Russia—that had already initiated experiments with such technologies in riot control, social protests, and surveilling pan-Islamist militias and radicalized individuals—multi-billion dollar Chinese corporations are now fully developing the new technologies of facial recognition with 90% accuracy, coupled with data from bio-genetic testing… Video and internet surveillance, phone taps, supercomputers, 5-G and 6-G technology, and other AI capabilities, plus HUMINT (human intelligence such spies and informants) can be combined to inquire into all possible state, military, corporate and personal secrets from undersea to Outer Space…

Not only that, but China's algorithms and AI, ~~and those other governments,~~ will be able to profile, case by case, the nature of an individual's attributes and to determine how he/she/it thinks and predict how they might act—no matter where they are. Hours of taped conversations, thousands of emails and other data can be condensed for easy assessment without the need of many human spies. If individuals possess knowledge of key information, Beijing can find a way to acquire it.

In effect, Beijing ~~(and other states)~~ can calculate how individuals will act based on ethnic, social or religious identity; type of work, salary, use of credit cards and finances; home life, friends, acquaintances and sexual behavior; medical history, health and insurance records; email and phone messages; preferred books and newspapers, all obtained through surveillance into both "private" and "open" info that the individual may have (foolishly) put on their Social Media sites. ~~And even though China was able to further develop computer capabilities that U.S. firms had developed through the skills of its own experts, i~~(I)t is now claimed by U.S. intelligence agencies that China has a bigger hacking program than every other major nation combined, ~~although, for its part, Beijing claims that it is Washington who has more advanced AI!~~[136]

~~The danger is that AI can cull info from hundreds of thousands, if not millions, of images and written texts, and then try to assess facts, half-truths, lies, and biases. These items include those that have been published in illegal "shadow libraries" and those that could be~~

~~imaginary, or fake, or Deep Fake. This stealing of Info, Theories and Conclusions from researchers, investigative reporters, scientists, and others, is supposed to be in accord with "fair use"—yet the system borrows and repeats many basic concepts and facts—here, there, and everywhere—without citation and by plagiarizing without payment… And the AI system (it?) does so without necessarily revealing to those who considered themselves to be its "masters" the data that it used to obtain its observations/ conclusions—or the process by which it reached those observations / conclusions.~~

~~Without greater personal, local, national, and international controls over the data that American, European, Chinese, Russian firms and governments can collect, and strong controls over how that data can be used, AI can easily be manipulated, by the Fearless Leaders of any country or organization or group of hackers, to steal funds and other illicit acts. And governments can use AI in the effort to make themselves shine for their domestic populations and their followers throughout the world. And with so much Fake and Stolen Info, is it even possible for true "Democracy" to continue to exist?~~

~~Given the fact that it is always more difficult to explain and demonstrate what is always a more complex reality, and that it could take forever to determine when the Fearless Leaders are "faking" and when they are not, AI's phenomenal ability to both use and generate false info will make AI more likely to be misused for purposes that are more nefarious than positive… And by giving this high-tech computerized advantage to Fearless Leaders, it will prove much too late to prove its Artificial Prognostications False!!!~~

~~It will not be long before "IShatThere4Iam" and more advanced AI systems—with their false claims of superior intelligence and knowledge—will infect the consciousness, creativity, and conscience of the entire global body politic as AI takes control over one center of power, finance, and social influence~~

after another—spreading unevenly as rapidly as the Horseshoe Bat virus had contaminated the planet...

+++

As Chia develops themes from dystopian futuristic novels whose predictions are already coming true, this excerpt, also heavily censored, warns of a future era in which the Lands of the Free become increasingly unfree—in part due to their global rivalry with the totalitarian Red Dragon and its lesser partner, the Russian Double-Headed Eagle... but also due to disputing messianic political factions within the Lands of the Free themselves...

The predictions of George Orwell's *1984* (Orwell forgot the Indian subcontinent in the battle between Oceania and Eurasia and Eastasia) in a syncretic mix with those of Aldous Huxley's *Brave New World* and Sinclair Lewis's *It Can't Happen Here*, plus Yevgeny Zamyatin's *We* and Kurt Vonnegut's *Player Piano,* not to overlook one of my favorites, Roald Dahl's "Great Automatic Grammatizator"—are becoming reality. And those who think that it can't happen in the Lands of the Free should think again. It can. And already is beginning...

Already in the Land Becoming Un-Free,[137] CEO's have threatened not to hire those individuals engaged in constitutionally protected protests dealing with conflicts in the Holy Land. The surveillance of individuals involved in the protests will impact them both during their lives, and in their afterlives, given the messianic beliefs of Christian America First *Jee-Zus!!! Freaks,* the anti-Red China "Blue Team," plus the anti-Palestinian, anti-Iranian movement of Rabbi Dr. Geyer.

It is the McCarthy era in full circle all over again, but with new actors and targets! Once one's name is on the secret digital "blacklist," it will prove nearly impossible to remove it! And nothing matters because the Apocalypse is imminent no matter how many innocents are slaughtered by all sides in the name of the "right of self-defense" against Islamic revanche in the so-called "Global War on Terrorism"!!!

Given its rule-less and aggressive nature, the Red Dragon's totalitarian norms will be able to permeate the Stars and Stripes of America and the Blue & Gold Flag of Europa by means of threats and osmosis. As time passes, all countries and societies will begin to transmogrify into Beijing's Red-Brown-Black image in the effort to survive.

Those Transnational Corps., including the Film industry, who want to stay and do business in China must follow the rules of total censorship in the country. And they must not speak badly about China abroad or they will lose their share of the China market. As China rises, its totalitarian panopticon influence will expand to all corners of the globe. If China has 5-G or 6-G, then everyone must have 5-G or 6-G!

The coming danger is that U.S., European and Japanese firms already need to compete with major Chinese companies whose work rules permit long hours, and who attempt to keep wages, health care and social security benefits as low as possible, while also reducing or eliminating regulations dealing with food safety and environmental protection. And if Beijing could pressure Taiwan in such a way that it could control its shipping and trade, China could possess the world's most advanced semi-conductors and AI capabilities..

This next selection warns of the possible failure of nuclear deterrence to prevent major power war…

After much permutations—as hypersonic missiles flash in the proxy war between the Double Headed and Balding Eagles over the Ukrainian *Napoléonide*—as the Red Dragon and Balding Eagle grimace at each other across the Taiwan straits and in the South and East China seas—as the Indian King Cobra, the Pakistani Markhor, and Chinese Red Dragon all envy the Hindu Kush and Indian Ocean—as the Israeli and Palestinian Gazelles and Iranian Cheetah eyeball each other with irradiated pupils—and as the rest of the world drowns on Rafts of the Medusas upon an overheated planet—two interstate Hydra- and Virgo-sized alliance constellations have begun to face off into opposing factions ready to shoot down space satellites and cut undersea cables… So far, the Red Dragon is just sitting on the sidelines and laughing like a monkey watching tigers fight… at least for now…

A new Eurasian Axis of the Chinese Red Dragon, the Russian Double-Headed Eagle, Iran's Cheetah, Pakistan's Markhor, and North Korea's Chollima, among other Chimera, is being forged to counter the Oceania Alliance of the American Balding Eagle, NATO's White Compass Rose, Lady Europa, the Ukrainian Lynx, Israel's Gazelle, Japan's Macaque, South Korea's Siberian Tiger, and Australia's Kangaroo, Taiwan's Black Bear, among other Species… In the meantime, the Turkish Wolf, the Saudi Camel, the Brazilian Jaguar, the South African Springbok, the Indian King Cobra, the Indonesian Komodo Dragon, among others, cannot decide which side they will take… unless and until they are pressed to do so… And if they choose the "wrong" side… then major power war could break out…[138]

~~These Chimeric Alliances have begun to polarize domestic societies and the interstate system into rival factions—thereby forcing states and populations to choose sides, whether they like it or not… If you are not with us, evidently you are against us. Each side points to the repressive acts of their rivals and respective martyrs. The imprisoned and deceased anti-Pootin activist Alexeï Navalny becomes a martyr for critics of the Russian Double Headed Eagle; the repression and CIA threat to assassinate Julian Assange becomes a cause célèbre for the critics of the Balding Eagle. Both the Kremlin and the White House (with the Western Media overlooking the much less hyped assassinations / imprisonments by the Chinese *Zhongnanhai)* appear equally guilty—even if their crimes are very different and not entirely comparable.~~

~~The outbreak of a new 21st century Crimean War is just the beginning… In the tragic Hegelian battle versus Kant, and between "Right" vs. "Right", the questions remain: How much territory will each side control? And does a "total victory", if even possible, overweigh the price in lives and destruction? Does anti-war geo-pornographic compromise necessarily mean "appeasement" or "capitulation"?[139]~~

It is believed that flashing the threat to use nuclear weaponry in accord with the theory of Mutual Assured Destruction (MAD) will deter conflict—but that is only assuming the leadership on one side or on the other—or really their AI calculations—will not take the risk that they can strike first and get away with it… Already no system of Mutual Assured Destruction has prevented cyber-attacks from taking place between all major powers, nuclear or not… The whole US nuclear arsenal did not even cause the 4 Riders of the Apocalypse to blink and reconsider their September 11, 2001 attacks. So, are nukes and WMD really the salvation? Will they prevent or cause even more destructive wars???

On the one hand, Pootin has declared his hope for a Russian Double Headed Eagle "victory" over his enemies after the titanic historical battles against Napoleonic France, Wilhelm's and Hitler's Germany—even if a contemporary Russian "victory" over the Ukrainian Lynx might mean the use of so-called "tactical" nuclear weaponry.

On the other hand, the Balding Eagle and Lady Europa have hoped for a victory over the Russian Double Headed Eagle more like of the mid-19th century Crimean War. Or perhaps they are hoping for a victory similar to that which led to Tsarist collapse during World War I—that would morph the former Soviet Bear into "a giant without arms, without eyes, with no other recourse than trying to crush her opponents under the weight of her clumsy torso, thrown here and there at random, wherever a hostile battle cry was heard" in the words of Karl Marx…

In reality, the only "victor" will be the Red Dragon… Can we learn anything at all from global history? Or are historical analogies as to the causes of wars of worlds past always doomed to misinterpretation?

+++

Below, Chia Pao-yu predicts the years in which China could try to seize, or more likely, pressure Taiwan into submission—if a peace accord cannot be reached soon:

Given its claims to Taiwan, the Chinese Mainland has been engaging in what some call "wolf warrior diplomacy" named after a bombastic Chinese version of a Hollywood Rambo film. It is a tough no-compromise form of diplomacy (so it is not diplomacy at all!) that asserts what it claims to be China's "national interests," but that are really the chimerical interests of the Red Dragon….

For those into numerology, there are key dates for CCP's hope to force unification with Taiwan, perhaps using Taiwanese Triads as a fifth column. One date for seizing Taiwan has already passed—2021—the 100th anniversary of the CCP's founding. A second date is 2049—exactly 100 years after China's "liberation" by Mao. Yet as "Winnie" may not be alive then, a third date appears more plausible—2035—the year that China is expected to become a "modern socialist nation."

A more meaningful date to seize Taiwan might be in the Year of the Water Pig, in 2033… about 350 years (7x5x10) after Shi Lang attacked Zheng Cheng-gong (Koxinga) in July 1683 in a battle of "mighty swords" (*tian ye*) between *yá zì* hybrids of wolves and dragons over what was then called "Formosa," the beautiful isle, in Portuguese. It was a battle in which Shi Lang, Commander in Chief of the Manchu Qing Navy, defeated the Formosan Admiral Koxinga…

Perhaps Beijing will not wait that long. One former U.S. Admiral has warned that Beijing could decide to seize control of Taiwan by force by 2027. One active U.S. Airforce General predicted a future war with China by 2025—although still hoping he was wrong. Some analysts are predicting war even sooner… ~~(Then again, some of these predictions may be a scare tactic to boost U.S. military spending in a presumed effort to better pressure China from a position of strength!!!)~~

~~The real option might be for Beijing to blockade the island and seek to control the shipping of Taiwan's advanced semiconductors and AI capabilities. Such a scenario would make it even more difficult for the Pentagon to supply Taiwan with food and resources than had been the case for the Berlin crisis in 1949….~~

~~The longer the U.S. and Taiwan wait to engage in real diplomacy the more likely chance that the boots of G.I. Joe will trounce over the~~

~~hopes for the establishment of a cooperative Barbie- and- Ken-land—on the way to yet another war on Asia's and/or other "foreign" shores.[140]~~-

+++

This final excerpt urges peace, urging the establishment of what Chia Pao-yu calls *Tai Ping Dao*, a Daoist concept (that he borrowed from his fellow PhD student Tao Bai-qing) that seeks the establishment of a local, national, regional, global, and cosmic equilibrium. It is heavily censored:

~~Let us hope these predictions of war are all wrong! And a Grand Compromise can be implemented!~~ We must make Beijing see that war with Taiwan is not in the interests of the Chinese people as a whole—nor in the interests the world either! ~~… If there is a war over Taiwan—a war which is also being quietly pressed by Moscow in order to push China into a confrontation with the Balding Eagle—Beijing will try to blame it on the democratic movements that are trying to reform the country… The question becomes: What realistic actions and goals should be prioritized to achieve a modicum of global peace and domestic social justice? To prevent the 'Armageddon to end all Armageddons,' the Balding Eagle and the Red Dragon must soon come to terms and agree to engage in mutual domestic and foreign policy reforms…That will not be an easy prospect and our struggle for greater social equity, power sharing, and democracy could be ignored or suppressed in the so-called interests of "national security."~~

No matter what happens, *Homo Geopoliticus et Economica* must not succumb to the thick smog of China's toxic clouds as it tran-smog-ri-fies from a Bright Red illuminated by Golden Shooting Stars to a much darker Red-Brown-Black night sky that blots out the telescopic orbiting satellite panorama of the entire Cosmos….

~~There is still hope for *Tai Ping Dao*!!!~~

+++

As you can see, I have left the sections of this text that were ~~crossed out~~ without Chia Pao-Yu's permission and that appear to have been censured by those who have published his work, primarily, but not only, by the Society for the Exploration of Cosmic Consciousness (SECC). For it also appears that the SECC sold some of his writings (or those created in Chia's name) for profit when possible. It is in this way, that the SECC, or other organizations, perhaps including a number of "I Spy" agencies, have co-opted his writings—using what seems to be his own voice and words—in the effort to spread their own propaganda in Chinese, Russian, English, French and multiple languages and dialects…in the name of JV…

What is for certain is that as long as there is electricity, as long as there is "imprisoned lightning"—whether it is generated by coal, oil, gas, nuclear fission, or preferably by solar, wind, ocean current, hydrogen, and maybe fusion power in the near future, and as long as the AI "Automatic Grammatizator" and the digital connection is maintained and updated—and does not cancel itself out in rival AI wars of mutual non-assured destruction—then the Planetary Manifesto and the words of the martyr Chia Pao-yu (or JV) will live on for eternity.

Yet instead of serving to tell what remains of "Truth" to Power, Chia Pao-yu's words may well live on in ways he never intended… serving to foster one-sided, yet convincing, half-truths, Deep Fakes, and outright LIES… To put it coldly and bluntly, that could be the "real" Legend of JV…

ENDNOTES
Annotated / Anecdoted by Mark King Hayford

[1] See "Coda: When It Really All Began" in Hall Gardner, *Year of the Earth Serpent Changing Colors*
[2] The number of deaths is hotly debated. A UK diplomat reported that, according to secret high-level Chinese sources, there were at least 10,000 civilian deaths on Tiananmen Square. Hundreds of additional executions in the provinces were carried out in secret or disguised to look like normal executions for criminal activity. See Mark Kramer, ed., *The Black Book of Communism* (Harvard University Press, 1999).
[3] Donald Trump repeatedly used the term, claiming he did not know its fascist origins—or its roots in Queen Isabel's Spain. https://www.nbcnews.com/politics/donald-trump/trump-poisoning-blood-remarks-never-knew-hitler-said-rcna130958
[4] By 2012, the U.S. Social Security Administration had accumulated roughly $1.2 trillion in what is called the Earning Suspense File from the social security taxes from wage reports that are largely from unauthorized migrants without appropriate working papers. This amount could be used to help legalize illegals in carefully overseen circumstances! This, of course needs more up-to-date data! https://digitalcommons.law.udc.edu/cgi/viewcontent.cgi?article=1107&context=fac_journal_articles
[5] Charlie was meant to be the namesake of another comic character, with a more wholesome, more politically correct, sense of humor, Charlie Brown, and who had somehow been amalgamated in the minds of the Charlie Hebdo editors with their rightwing political nemesis, Charles de Gaulle.
[6] French anti-terrorist laws, like the U.S. PATRIOT act, can be used against any group or individual who makes too much noise! https://www.france24.com/en/20151129-france-climate-activists-house-arrest-cop21-summit-state-emergency. It seems no criticism was allowed even if the yearly Climate Change Conference—become a "world's fair" dominated by Big Energy lobbyists—has not yet reduced greenhouse gases to the amount

required to prevent global warming from increasing above a minimum of 1.5 degree centigrade.

[7] This character appears to be based on the ex-Soviet dissident Victor Balashov. See the Manifesto that Balashov helped to write that parallels the demands of the Chinese Democracy movement in the fight to "overthrow the political hegemony of the Soviet Communist Party" https://www.americanpushkinsociety.com/about-us/liac/soviet-dissidents/

[8] The "Epstein affair" had filled the Media with conspiracy theories… and even more profits…. Some stories claimed Epstein escaped prison… Others claimed he had been murdered… Others accepted the suicide verdict… Who knows the Truth? Epstein claimed that he was only wanted to raise millions for a "charitable" fund, while concurrently seeking to blackmail those powerful men he had already seduced with young women…. Once dead, the charges were inexplicably dropped against him… His victims thereby "denied proper recourse"—unless they could eventually win an appeal…

[9] These words sound very similar to those of Yemeni Nobel Laureate, Tawakkol Karman: "Peace within one country is no less important than peace between countries. War is not just a conflict between states. There is another type of war, which is far more bitter, that is the war of despotic leaders who oppress their own people. It is a war of those to whom people have entrusted their lives and destinies, but who have betrayed that trust. It is a war of those to whom people have entrusted their security, but who directed their weapons against their own people." https://www.nobelprize.org/prizes/peace/2011/karman/lecture/ I trust that Darwish, or more likely, *IShat-There4Iam* was not plagiarizing.

[10] See: Chinese Artist Ai Weiwei Describes His 81 Days in Prison—And the Extreme Surveillance, Censorship, and "Soft Detention" He's Endured Since | Art for Sale | Artspace

[11] I saw the Dario Fo play in London in 2023. What Chia says is true. If he had been given a chance, Chia could have been an excellent theatre, movie or literature critic!

[12] The "Arab Spring" movement started when an allegedly crazy Tunisian fruit vender set himself on fire—sparking what seemed to be unending revolutions/wars/repressions throughout the Arab/Islamic world. There were also the Israeli Social Justice and National Tents movement; the Iranian Green and women's freedom movements; the massive Tahir Square protests in Cairo; the Taksim Gezi Park environmental protests in Istanbul. For a while there was hope in Sudan, but not for long. There were also the "three fingered" Hunger Games salute of the Red Shirts who opposed the 2006 Thai military coup…

[13] The Three Gorges Dam is now key to clean and renewable electricity generation for 400 million people in the region. It is said that even nuclear power plants cannot compete with its power capabilities. Shipping on the Chang Jiang river has been enhanced as the dam can also lift giant ships. At the same time, Chia Pao-yu was not entirely wrong: The dam needs continual maintenance to prevent it from cracking, it puts tremendous water pressure on two major seismic faults—a potential cause for earthquakes. It is claimed the dam has prevented as many as 63 major floods but has not altogether prevented the monsoon flooding of the Chang Jiang. Another danger: the Dam could be a prime target in case of war between China and Taiwan.

[14] The attack on the Chinese embassy was a major mapping blunder (or so Washington claimed!). One "conspiracy" theory argued the CIA wanted to destroy Stealth technology kept for safekeeping in the Chinese Embassy after the Serbs had shot down a Stealth aircraft and sold it Beijing. Beijing has not forgotten what it considers to be Washington's lies in a war that brought China and Russia into closer ties and helped bring Vladaspeare Pootin to power in Moscow….

[15] Hall "Cassandra" Gardner accused me of plagiarizing sections of his editorial, "Stealthy Missile of Appeasement—For Naught" that appeared in the *LA Times* (December 20,1989) just a few days before mine. It's pure BS. I never read his editorial!

[16] Gao/Galvin was infatuated by MAD magazine and his belated discovery of Dr Suess' *Butter Battle*; Chia Pao-yu seems to

have taken a fancy to the cynicism/lyricism of the children's writer, Roald Dahl's "Great Automatic Grammatizator" that satirized AI at its beginnings.

[17] The yellow vests had called for a national citizens' referendum (*référendum d'initiative citoyenne RIC*), that is somewhat similar to California's referendum system. In France, the referendum was initiated by Napoleon III, and can be a tool that can be used or mis-used to push through new legislation—in that it usually only presents two options or a "yes or no" option instead of providing a choice of several real possibilities… A multiple option referendum or a "preferendum" might be a better option.

[18] See Hall "Cassandra" Gardner, "Far from Beijing, the Students Stand Up" LA Times (May 18, 1989)

[19] Chia Pao-yu did not follow the issue, but the *gilets jaunes* obtained some economic concessions, but not many political ones. https://www.rfi.fr/en/france/20190114-macron-appeals-yellow-vests-open-letter. Yet nothing came of the political proposals for a more progressive income tax with more tranches (the French only have 5!). No steps were taken to tax the big companies (Mac Do, Google, Amazon, Carrefour...) and to better protect French industry to prohibit relocations, as demanded. No indexing the salaries of all French people as well as pensions and allowances to inflation, while limiting the number of fixed-term contracts for large companies and providing the same rights for all employees.

[20] I have to agree: a more unified Lady Europa is needed to deal with the environmental and migrant crises as well as defense and security issues. Yet that does not appear to be happening!

[21] COVID regulations: https://www.france.fr/fr/avant-de-partir/info-coronavirus-la-situation-en-france

[22] There are numerous studies. Yet it is clear a number of billionaires made outrageous profits during the COVID pandemic, leading conspiracy theorists to question their role in the management of the crisis. The toll for the global economy could range between an "optimistic loss" of $3.3 trillion in case of rapid recovery, and $82 trillion in case of economic depression.

[23] Jacque de Molay purportedly damned Pope Clement, Knight William, and King Philip "until their thirteenth generation…" according to the novels, *The Accursed Kings* or *Les Rois maudits* by Maurice Druon that have been said to be the predecessors to the *Game of Thrones*. The reality is that de Molay probably said something like "God will avenge our Death". Nevertheless, the Pope died in 1314, so too did Philippe le Bel, just six months later, and so too Le Bel's the descendants. What is certain is that the French monarchs appeared doomed to the fifteenth generation of Louis XVI of the Capetian branch. It took the French Revolution to finally put an end to the farce of corrupt absolute monarchist rule—only to be replaced with new political instabilities and not-so-democratic lunacies.

[24] Quite a horror story: Sanson, the father, performed 2,918 executions, including that of Louis XVI; his son Henri had the honor of executing Marie-Antoinette.

[25] During the Reign of Terror, Jean-Paul "Seborrhea" Marat, a member of the Committee of General Security, had argued that "Five or six hundred [aristocratic] heads lopped off would have assured you repose and happiness; a false humanity has restrained your arm and suspended your blows; it will cost the lives of millions of your brothers." The brutal reality, however, was that the Reign of Terror executed many more commoners than aristocrats. Millions of civilians and soldiers became the cannon fodder for the French Revolutionary / Napoleonic Wars versus the Monarchies of the epoch…

[26] On the terror of the Chinese Revolution: https://www.sciencespo.fr/mass-violence-war-massacre-resistance/en/document/chronology-mass-killings-during-chinese-cultural-revolution-1966-1976.html

[27] The Protestants were slaughtered by the fervent Catholic leadership of the House of Valois, King Charles IX—on St. Bartholomew's Day, way back in 1592—in part a result of Catholic failure to appease the Protestants by means of marrying Charles's sister Margaret to the Protestant King Henry III of Navarre, soon to become King Henry IV of France.

[28] In July 1997, Hong Kong had been returned by perfidious Albion—who had "annexed" it in 1842 at the end of the First Opium War and then "leased" even more of the surrounding territory for 99 years in the 1898 Convention for the Extension of Hong Kong Territory to Imperial China. Ironically, John Bull never really expected to give it all up!
[29] Hall "Cassandra" Gardner was correct to warn of the rise of the New Authoritarians: "A Troubled China Needs Democracy" The LA Times (April 23, 1989.) Chia had been very upset, however, as Gardner appeared to have stolen his prediction.
[30] It is revealing how many states, both democratic and authoritarian, oppose any form of autonomy arrangements in the fear of actual secession, such as France and Corsica, Spain and Catalan, the U.S. and Texas. In the case of China, the National Security Law depicts four crimes of supporting secession, subversion, terrorism, and collusion. The latter particularly concerns the backing of foreign organizations linked to Taiwan or the U.S. Any open advocation of the secession of Hong Kong, Tibet or Xinjiang Province from China is also considered a crime. The law permits authorities to surveil, detain, and search any persons suspected of such behavior and to requires publishers, hosting services, and internet service providers to block, remove, or restrict content the authorities determine to be in violation of the dictate.
[31] In the Chinese context, the wall's name is a reminder that John Lennon's song "Revolution" had denounced anti-Vietnam War protesters who carried pictures of Chairman Mao and advocated violence—even if Lennon later wore a pro-Mao pin and tried to distance himself from the previous anti-Maoist song…
[32] The five demands to negotiate an end to the conflict: 1) the complete withdrawal the extradition bill; 2) that the Hong Kong Chief Executive, who is not chosen by popular vote, step down; 3) an inquiry into police brutality; 4) the release of those who have been arrested; 5) institutionalization of democratic freedoms and human rights.

[33] The real problem was not the structure of the spy agencies—but the poor quality of US strategy and diplomacy.

[34] As exposed by whistleblower, Edgar "Escape to Moscow" Snowden, the PATRIOT Act permitted NSA government analysts to search emails, online chats and browsing history, but also telephone services, mobile phone audios, financial transactions and global air transport communications—while also "enhancing surveillance-based logic of accumulation" that permitted Google to collect consumer data. See Shoshana Zuboff, *The Age of Surveillance Capitalism* (Profile Books, 2019).

[35] A loose translation of Celine's *Journey to the End of Night*... "Soldats gratuits, héros pour tout le monde et singes parlants, mots qui souffrent, on est nous les mignons du Roi Misère. C'est lui qui nous possède! "

[36] While the U.S. in 2021 had the 12th highest obesity rate in the world at 36.2%, China is ranked much lower, at about 6.2% of its population, and roughly 169th place in the world.

[37] For a critique of Genetically Modified Organisms, https://www.nongmoproject.org/gmo-facts/what-is-gmo/

[38] Chia is referring to the French government's opposition to military intervention in Iraq in the UN Security Council during the presidency of Jacques Chirac.

[39] Chia appears to be referring to Napoleon's influence on Francis Fukuyama's fallacious neo-Conservative (neo-Con) / neo-liberal *End of History* argument. See Hall Gardner, *Crimea, Historical Analogy and the Vengeance of History* (Palgrave 2015).

[40]https://www.forbes.com/sites/wadeshepard/2016/01/19/one-way-that-china-populates-its-ghost-cities/?sh=388cc1986e53

[41] See contradictions in China's energy policy: https://earth.org/why-is-china-building-oil-refineries-when-fuel-demand-is-stalling/

[42] Statistics can be tricked, but this one seems valid. But what is a "developing" country? https://www.statista.com/topics/5788/millionaires-in-china/#topicOverview

[43] From 1999-20, some 932,364 Americans died from overdoses. In 2021, more than 106,000 persons died illicit drugs and prescription opioids, among other substances.
[44] The Violent Crime Control and Law Enforcement Act of 1994 had been strongly supported by President Clinton and then Senator Joe Biden—and was enacted when liberal democrats were seen as "soft" on crime. Over time, the 1994 Act augmented the number of prison cells by 125,000, hired 100,000 new police officers, increased mandatory minimum sentences and applied the death penalty to 60 kinds of crimes. The number of people under correctional control was 7 times greater than at the beginning of the Johnson administration, and the black-to-white ratio for incarceration rates had risen from 3-to-1 to 6-to-1. https://www.meer.com/en/62522-it-can-happen-here
[45] Drug convictions have doped up the U.S. federal prison system itself—with over 350,000 people incarcerated as a result of some form of drug offense. An estimated 2 million people are held in 1,566 state prisons, 98 federal prisons, 3,116 local jails, 1,323 juvenile correctional facilities, 181 immigration detention facilities, and 80 Indian country jails, as well as in military prisons, civil commitment centers, state psychiatric hospitals, and prisons in the U.S. territories. https://www.prisonpolicy.org/reports/pie2023.html
[46] I have to admit the former Maoist, Gao/Galvin, has a point: Both the U.S. and Chinese Revolutions were provoked by the profit seeking mischief of the British East India Co… tea in the case of the United States… Opium in the case of China… See Hall Gardner, *Year of the Earth Serpent Changing Colors*.
[47] By contrast with natural opium and marijuana, these more potent chemical concoctions were more profitable as they were easier for Chinese Triads and Mexican Narcos to transport and mix. There was no longer any need for large scale opium production manned by hundreds of peasants—as had been the case in the 1930s in the Maple Village in China of Su Yong's *Opium Family*. That is, before Mao's loyal supporters took control of

the Opium farms by force… Now, a patch of hidden land high in the hills or deep an underground cave or even a basement or garage would do fine…

[48] Hall "Cassandra" Gardner accused MKH of stealing his Platonic "Plutocrat vs Timocrat" ideas!
https://www.meer.com/en/authors/701-hall-gardner
https://www.taylorfrancis.com/books/mono/10.4324/9781315262871/american-global-strategy-war-terrorism-hall-gardner

[49] Xi Jinping declared himself "President for Life" in March 2018. Previously, the Chinese oligarchical leadership believed that a two-term, 10-year presidential limit would lead to stability and orderly transfers of power. But by 2018, Xi had enough influence to abolish term limits. Xi was then named in December 2019, *renmin lingxiu,* or "people's leader" with the full accord of the Party hierarchy and its "yes men" parliament. Xi is thus considered by some neo-Maoists to be the "Party Helmsman" almost as powerful as Mao Zedong, the "Great Helmsman." Maoism probably killed a lot more than did the Red Emperor's hero, Qin Shi Huang-di (221-210 B.C.). Yet that's known as historical "progress" in Stalinist-Maoist terms!

[50] Friends of Drumpf in Europe, Israel, and America are jealous of Winnie, Pootin and Little Rocket Man, but so too are the more "liberal" democrats. The "old boys," and a few of the "old girls," want to revive authoritarian modes of "democratic" governance so as to continue their rule for as many presidential terms or prime ministerial mandates as possible. And wars serve as good excuses to extend one's reign as long as possible—as if other leaderships are not possible!

[51]https://www.reuters.com/article/us-trump-china-idUSKCN1GG015 Trump still hopes to seize the opportunity to win the November 2024 presidential election—by trying to use charges of the January 6, 2021 treason by Democrats to boost his popularity and become president with absolute powers, and let U.S. presidents, like Putin and Xi, "serve" more than 2 terms.

[52] Trump apparently had to explain to Kim Jong-Un why he called him "Little Rocket Man" and what it meant. That must have been an interesting exercise in diplomatic language from someone who is not skilled in diplomacy at all!
[53] Protectionist measures on China were generally strengthened by Drumpf's rival, Joe "Lost in Space" Bidung—once the latter became president.
[54] The slogan, "Defund the Police" that became popular in both the U.S. and France during the George Floyd protests—fell into the trap of Drumpfist and rightwing propaganda—making the protesters appear "weak" on crime and migration.
[55] On U.S. court punishment for the Capitol protests. https://apnews.com/article/capitol-riot-jan-6-criminal-cases-anniversary-bf436efe760751b1356f937e55bedaa5 The key question is whether the Supreme Court will make the fateful decision as to whether Donald Trump violated the 14th amendment during his "March on the Capitol". Not to decide, or to decide in Trump's favor, will make the U.S. Constitution and its checks and balances look like a farce, undermining its legitimacy. Yet to give Trump the chance to run for president is to court dictatorship. No matter what happens, Trump and his former G.I. Joe Militiamen will cause turmoil—whether he wins or loses. See Trump's speech: https://apnews.com/article/election-2020-joe-biden-donald-trump-capitol-siege-media-e79eb5164613d6718e9f4502eb471f27. On the Constitutional debate, see US Historians Sign Brief to Support Colorado's Removal of Trump From Ballot (rsn.org)
[56] The Chinese woman warrior, Hua Mulan, a crossdresser like Jeanne d' Arc, could have possibly been chosen in 1989 as the Goddess of Democracy. Years later, Mulan became a Disney heroine. The leading actress of the film publicly supported the crackdown on Hong Kong. As Pao-yu might joke, it would have been much better to depict the former hooker/pirate Ching Shih as the Goddess of Democracy instead! The credits of the Disney film referred to groups linked to the Uighur "reeducation" camps in Xinjiang.

https://www.cnbc.com/2020/09/08/disney-thanked-groups-linked-to-china-detention-camps-in-mulan-credits.html

[57] Depending upon how many times an individual was caught by not-so-ever watchful authorities, the fines could increase from €35 Euros to €38 to €135 up to €1500 Euros, and then to €3750 for each person.

[58] In the Aesop version of the "Fox and the Crow," the Fox states the Crow has a cracked voice, but then insinuates the Crow has no wits at all, before fleecing the Crow of his cheese through flattery... Not so for the La Fontaine version... In that version, the Crow promises not to be fooled by flattery again. All depends upon the species of interpretation…

[59] The French firm, Chanel, sued and actually won an unfair competition lawsuit under article 6 of the Anti-Unfair Competition Law of the People's Republic of China. How well the lawsuit has been enforced is another issue. I have not been able to engage in any further research. https://www.fashionlawbusiness.com/flbstories/chanel-prevails-in-unfair-competition-case-over-its-perfume-bottles-in-china

[60] Certainly, the purpose of spreading such theories is to cause confusion and dissent. Yet if a conspiracy theory originates in the USA itself, can Russia and China rightfully be accused of "weaponizing" such theories if they themselves were not the origins of such garbage? See https://edition.cnn.com/2021/04/19/politics/qanon-russia-china-amplification/index.html

[61] It is called the "Swimming Plan"! I predict public transport will go to hell when millions of people swarm into the City of Lights! Inflation will mount. No sports stars will swim in the Seine! And let us hope no acts of terror like the Munich Olympics of 1972!

[62] In 1245, Pope Innocent IV sent Friar del Carpini on a mission to the lands of Gog and Magog in the hope that the grandson of Genghis Khan, Guyak, might align with the Church against the evil Saracens in Holy Lands. Upon his return empty handed, he realized he had escaped the clutches of

demons… In 1253, King Louis IX tried again by sending William of Rubruck on his pony for a similarly failed mission.

[63] According to Woodword B. Intellow in *China's Exploitation by the West Since the Era of Marco Polo* (Rotting Shelves Books 1988), 869, as referenced in *Year of the Earth Serpent Changing Colors*, about 16 million men appear to be related to the Khan family in an area from Central Asia to the Pacific, as observed in a scientific study of star cluster chromosomes. Then again, the scientific study was done in 2003… after Vol I had been published… sic!!! See criticism of the star cluster theory and the Khans: https://www.iflscience.com/fact-check-are-one-in-200-people-descended-from-genghis-khan-65357

[64] I refer to Wikipedia for expediency even if Hall "Cassandra" Gardner claims he forbids his students to cite it. This is because the details of the Wiki references often change in accord with the bias of the contributor, even if many references may be accurate. On the spread of the Black Death, see https://en.wikipedia.org/wiki/Black_Death

[65] Cited in John Barry, "The Great Influenza: The Story of the Deadliest Pandemic in History" October 4, 2005.

[66] Mao had described Wilson in Versailles as ignorant, manipulated, but not a liar: "like an ant on a hot skillet. He didn't know what to do. He was surrounded by thieves like Clemenceau, Lloyd George, Makino and Orlando. He heard nothing except accounts of receiving certain amounts of territory and of reparations worth so much in gold. He did nothing except to attend various kinds of meetings where he could not speak his mind." Perhaps because he had the flu??? (I can't find the reference to Mao's statement, but it exists.)

[67] See Jack London, "The Unparalleled Invasion" in *The Strength of the Strong* (Macmillan, 1914). London's story envisioned biowarfare by the U.S. against China in 1976. Hopefully he didn't just mix up the predicted dates.

[68] Artists inspired by pandemics: Hieronymus Bosch and Albrecht Durer. Poets: Giovanni Boccacio (The Decameron) and Geoffrey Chaucer (The Canterbury Tales); Writers: Daniel

Defoe (Journal of a Plague Year), Alessandro Manzoni (The Betrothed), Mary Shelley (The Last Man), Jack London (The Scarlet Plague), Albert Camus (The Plague), Curzio Malaparte (The Skin) Thomas Mann (Death in Venice), Margaret Atwood (Oryx and Crake) ….

[69] As many as 40 million people died globally from A-Virus—but incredibly, that number did not cause quite the same panic as has the Horseshoe Bat pandemic! The Horseshoe Bat has thus far killed more than 5 million people world-wide. Perhaps that was because of the "profile" of the people who the A-Virus tends to target???

[70] On Dr. Li Wenliang https://www.nytimes.com/2022/02/07/world/asia/chinese-doctor-li-wenliang-covid-warning.html

[71] As DARPA, part of the Pentagon's military-industrial-congressional-university complex, decided not to fund a proposed "gain of function" project called DEFUSE using bat genes, China, along with American universities and other governments and institutions, may have opted to have funded some of "gain of function" research themselves. See articles on origins of Covid-19, gain-of-function research (usrtk.org)

[72] This is an apparent Chinese counter propaganda effort: https://news.cgtn.com/news/2021-06-18/From-Unit-731-to-Fort-Detrick-What-is-the-U-S-hiding-from-the-world--11bPpnpvfr2/index.html

[73] This is not conspiracy theory: 'Surgeon General' Shirō Ishii, who commanded Unit 731 of the Kwantung Army's "Epidemic Prevention and Water Purification Department" was invited to serve as a [bioweapons] advisor at Fort Detrick. Others in Unit 731 entered the Japanese medical community. By contrast, many Nazi war criminals who did similar experiments in Europe were prosecuted by the Nuremberg war crimes tribunal. https://news.cgtn.com/news/2021-06-18/From-Unit-731-to-Fort-Detrick-What-is-the-U-S-hiding-from-the-world--11bPpnpvfr2/index.html See also, https://www.archives.gov/files/iwg/japanese-war-crimes/select-documents.pdf

[74] After Trump suggested that disinfectants be considered a possible treatment for COVID 19, a number of people poisoned themselves—even if Trump had later claimed his comment was sarcastic. This narcissistic individual has no idea how dangerous his irreflective words can be! https://www.poison.med.wayne.edu/updates-content/kstytapp2qfstf0pkacdxmz943u1hshttps://www.politico.com/news/2021/04/23/trump-bleach-one-year-484399
[75] On radiation experiments on Puerto Rican nationalist Pedro Albizu Campos: https://voiceofthelily.water.blog/2022/02/05/don-pedro-albizu-campos-a-genius-revolutionary-revised-version-with-podcast/ In 1994 President Clinton apologized about U.S. human radiation experiments: https://ehss.energy.gov/ohre/roadmap/achre/summary.html
[76] Perhaps Trump heard something about the *Let It Bleed* life of the rock group once called *Little Boy Blue and the Blue Boys* before becoming the *Rolling Stones*? Given his life in the poppy fields, it is said that one of the Blue Boys was able to purify the China White from his blood in yearly dialysis. Fact or Myth?
[77] China's Belt and Road could prove to be a real disaster. Pandemics have continued to break out periodically in China, Kazakhstan and elsewhere in Eurasia... Beijing has planned to build a massive highway and highspeed rails along the ancient Silk Road into Uzbekistan, Pakistan and Iran, into Turkey and southern Russia and Belarus on through to Poland, Germany and down into France—so as to sell industrial goods as well as silk, spices and porcelain… This is in addition to building roads through the Balkans… and from Greece… Is this progress??? Even if so… it is scaring the Americans!
[78] These include the Yellow Turbans in 184, the Maitreyist revolt of Faqing in 515, the Manichean rebellion of Fang La in 1120, the White Lotus movement in 1351, and the Eight Trigrams of 1813, and perhaps the most destructive of all… The Taiping Revolution and its repression—that was indirectly responsible for between 20 million and 100 million deaths, thereby causing the population of China to fall from 410 million in 1850 to 350

million in 1873. That insurrection, like previous ones, sought to synthesize Christianity, Daoism and Buddhism.

[79] The fearless leader of the "Fallen-Gang" (really *Falun Gong*) is said to live in the USA, and purportedly believes himself to be an extraterrestrial creature who has come to save the planet from war, immorality, and high-tech perversion and other noble causes! As Chinese authorities appear to fear a new form of Taiping revolution, seen by Beijing as potentially backed by the Balding Eagle, members of the *Falun Gong* claim to have been persecuted as revealed by the controversial dissident Harry Wu—who had spent at least 19 years in 12 different *laogai* prison camps. Wu had dared to speak out during the Red Emperor's Hundred Flowers Campaign… https://www.martinennalsaward.org/hrd/harry-wu/

[80] See discussion, Woodward B. Intellow, *China's Struggle with the West: Post-Tiananmen Square,* Vol II (Global Village Press, 2021), 397. Cited in Gardner, *Year of the Earth Serpent Changing Colors* https://globalvillagepress.org/Intellow%20B. https://history-itm.files.wordpress.com/2013/08/peck.pdf

[81] Allen "Kaddish" Ginsberg explained that Leroi Lones (Amiri Baraka) "was the victim of much more attack than people understand, and, in that context, his anger is understandable… The waste remains, the waste remains and kills!" http://afilreis.blogspot.com/2010/06/allen-ginsbergs-fbi-file.html

[82] On Mugabe: https://www.greatzimbabweguide.com/death-robert-mugabe-names/

[83] Ginsberg was outspoken on just about everything! http://afilreis.blogspot.com/2010/06/allen-ginsbergs-fbi-file.html

[84] What did Ginsberg and other pro-Hare Krishna freaks think?https://www.maryellenmark.com/bibliography/magazines/article/my-generation/testimony/M

[85] Then again, what happens if a schoolteacher meets the teen of her life who is destined to become the President of one of the major countries in Europe? (i.e. France)

[86] An apparent reference to Brett Kavanaugh, who Trump chose as Supreme Court Justice. During testimony to the Senate Judiciary Committee in 2018, when he was accused of multiple counts of "sexual harassment," he stated… Yes, we drank beer. My friends and I. Boys and girls. Yes, we drank beer. I liked beer. Still like beer. We drank beer." Kavanaugh was a principal author of the (1998) *Starr Report* on the Bill Clinton–Monica Lewinsky sex scandal that argued for Clinton's impeachment. Clinton likes "Snakebite beer"—a mix of beer and hard cider. Beer Boys of differing feathers don't necessarily stick together!

[87] British drug pushers are immortalized at Jardine Terrace and Matheson Street named for a company that trafficked opium, tea and anything that would make a buck.

[88] See Chinese Artist Pun Sing-lui https://www.scmp.com/article/174630/promising-artist-accolade-red-paint-vandal

[89] Artist Alexandra Skochilenko was jailed for 7 years. https://www.aljazeera.com/news/2023/11/17/russian-artist-jailed-for-seven-years-over-anti-war-price-tag-protest. Artists in the Land of the Free, such as Nan Goldin, have been arrested for protests against the lack of state legal action in response to the role of Purdue Pharma in pushing Opioid addiction. https://hyperallergic.com/515015/artist-nan-goldin-arrested-in-protest-outside-governor-cuomos-office-in-nyc/

[90] Pao-yu has a point: Perhaps it is these kinds of issues and the puritanical Salem Witch trials of the American Pilgrims (social conflicts that had also been fueled by war, immigrants and plague at that time) that American and Chinese societies possess a common psychology and understanding?

[91] Films like "Mission: Impossible – Fallout," "Transformers IV," "X-Men: Days of Future Past," "Looper," "Gravity," "Iron Man 3" "Venom," "The Meg," and "Pacific Rim: Uprising." "Venom," "The Meg," and "Pacific Rim: Uprising" and many others appear to have adapted their plots to placate Chinese censors and audiences. Sony decided to cut scenes of aliens blasting a hole in the Great Wall of China from the movie "Pixels" to improve the chance that the film would be shown in China.

Leaked Sony e-mails show similar concerns for "RoboCop." Brad Pitt was banned from entering China from 1997 to 2016 for starring in the film "Seven Years in Tibet" (1997).

[92] In opposing his political art, Beijing tried to block a number of Badiucao's art shows in Italy, Czech Republic and Poland. Badiucao's work examines topics like the repression in Hong Kong and Xinjiang, the Communist Party's response to the COVID 19 pandemic, and the June 1989 Tiananmen Square crackdown. https://edition.cnn.com/style/article/badiucao-italian-exhibition-chinese-embassy/index.html

[93] Chia must be referring to a story that was reported in the *Financial Times*. Evidently, just as the bustling port city of La Hague blossomed, so too "the most famous sun in the world rises today" over the ports of Guongzhou... to bring the light of hope" to the world! https://www.ft.com/content/d2d8107d-e198-4c7a-8dbe-5c6d2d0755ad

[94] A variant of Sun Yat-sen's five-fold system of checks and balances has been established in Taiwan.

[95] See *Black Book of Communism,* 256

[96] By contrast with "Ronnie Ray-gun" who wanted Presidents to run for as many terms as possible, Jimmy "Born Again" Carter was right when he argued that no matter what he did, people would question whether it was a selfish "campaign ploy" or "genuinely done in the best interest of our country." After all these years of supporting the American system of democratic governance, I confess—I was wrong! And I now agree that a single presidential term of five to six years is sufficient. Congresspeople, in both the House and Senate, should both serve one six-year term. Also, the Supreme Court term should be limited to 12 years. Moreover, the military industrial complex needs to be converted to non-defense industries dedicated to sustainable development; the personal income of CEOs of major transnational corporations, bankers, and venture capitalists need to be taxed at higher rates... while most enterprises need to implement new forms of employee participation in decision making and stock ownership... Those reforms seem possible to achieve

without constitutional amendments, as Hall Gardner argued in *World War Trump* (Prometheus Books, 2018). Yet to implement other proposed reforms, such as merging the Senate and the House into a unicameral system, appears impossible.

[97] Stalin's nickname referred to Persian King Kobades, who conquered Eastern Georgia in late 5th century; Stalin, as a Georgian, was thus seen as a traitor to his own people.

[98] The film, Oppenheimer was an excellent portrait, well-acted, but the issue of tactical nukes could have been addressed more directly to show the complexity of the issues involved. The tactical nukes of Oppenheimer's era are coming back into vogue. Washington may point its fingers at Russian tactical nukes, but the Pentagon has been deploying war-fighting tactical nukes like the new B61-12, that possess "dial-a-yield" upgrades.

[99] I guess this was flattery, so I left it as is—although I hope people do not think I am too eccentric!

[100] See Gardner, *Year of the Earth Serpent Changing Colors*

[101] That work was based on his notes, locked in an LV suitcase at the Ritz, that the macho Bullfighter Hemmingway almost lost, but were then published after his suicide…

[102] The three Sòng sisters married the greatest men of their times: a wealthy businessman; Chiang Kai-shek; Sun Yat-Sen. This led to the expression: "One loved money; one loved power; one loved her country."

[103] Heinrick "the good father" Himmler had complained about gay encounters in the SS—yet there were many more "deviants" than he apparently realized. And who knows, maybe the real reason Hitler killed SA *Sturmabteilung* leader Ernst Röhm and massacred his Brown Shirt paramilitaries was because Röhm's overt hyper-masculine homosexuality represented a challenge to Hitler's own ambivalent ego?

[104] In an outrageous travesty of justice in the name of the laws against abortion, one woman was forced to escape the state of Texas to the North—as if she had to follow Harriet "Moses" Tubman on the underground railway of the pre-bellum South!

105 This appears to be an oblique reference to *Crazy Rich Asians* by Kevin Kwan. Just another example where Chia and/or Gardner probably saw the movie but didn't read the book!
106 I hate it when tires are set aflame. I am sure Chia Pao-yu and Gardner agree! There is already enough corporate and official pollution. No need for revolutionary pollution as well!
107 For the full text: https://languagelog.ldc.upenn.edu/nll/?p=56731
108 See Teng Biao, https://www.scholarsatrisk.org/spotlight/teng-biao-on-human-rights-in-china-i-cannot-be-silent-and-i-cannot-give-up/
109 Once I studied the question, I learned 62 was the early retirement age for almost half of European countries—but that 64 was the age that most French actually retire anyway. Still, who wants to retire that old?
110 The actual words of *Prêt à partir*, written by the rappers SCH et Ninho, *Ils veulent pas que ça brûle comme en 2005, pourtant ils refont les mêmes erreurs »* were written in 2018 before the nationwide riots of 2023. https://www.youtube.com/ watch?v=ieH1pPktlgg
111 See "How about Barbie in a "Burqini" swimsuit?" https://www.csmonitor.com/World/Global-News/2009/1122/burka-barbie-to-raise-funds-for-save-the-children. French authorities acted to fine, if not ban, both the bikini and the burqini in their very different cultural epochs!
112 Does Barbie's critique include fair compensation for writers, greater contributions to health plans—and the growing need to regulate the use of scripts, photos, films and other materials that are being produced using AI or similar technologies—which in turn can steal original ideas without naming or compensating sources—given the new tendency to use AI confabulations? https://variety.com/2023/tv/news/wga-pattern-of-demands-1235537514/
113 Chia had begun to dive into French history: After a number of bombings and assassination attempts, the latter "villainous laws" restricted the 1881 freedom of the press laws and could punish anyone who had "encouraged one or several persons in

committing either theft, or the crimes of murder, plunder, fire...; 2. Or (who) has addressed a provocation to military from the Army or the Navy, in the aim of diverting them from their military duties and the obedience due to their chiefs."

[114] Rabbi Dr. Geyer (meaning vulture in German) was the anti-Arab leader of a messianic political party in the novel, *Old-New Land*, by Theodore Herzl, the founder of Zionism. Herzl did not expect the formation of Palestinian political parties against the State of Israel—but that was largely in response to the Nakba—the expulsion of Palestinians from their lands in 1948—whose impact on Palestinians parallels the contemporary war in Gaza and the West Bank since October 2023. One character describes Geyer: "He's a cursed pope, a provocateur, a blasphemer who rolls up his eyes. He wants to bring intolerance into our country, the scamp! I am certainly a peaceful person, but I could cheerfully murder an intolerant fellow like that!"

[115] You saw the war in the Balkans… An army of 300,000 men departed for battle, and now 200,000 men rest in the fields and in trenches, while the last 100,000 are in hospital beds, infected with typhus. Think of what a disaster war would be for Europe. It would not be, like in the Balkans, one army of 300,000 men, but instead four, five or six armies of two million men. What a massacre! What ruin! What barbarity! And this is why, when the storm clouds are above us, I still hope that this crime will not be committed. —Jean Jaures, July 31, 1914. Ukraine today?

[116] The poet Siegfried Sassoon should be considered as a true hero for demanding an early end to the so-called 'Great War' in 1916. Sassoon had written his superiors, "that the war is being deliberately prolonged by those who have the power to end it… I believe that the war upon which I entered as a war of defense and liberation has now become a war of aggression and conquest…. I am not protesting against the conduct of the war, but against the political errors and insincerities for which the fighting men are being sacrificed."

[117] The Sassoon's global business, which extended as far as major Japanese cities, sold yarn and opium to China, and then sold

silk, tea and silver to Britain. https://www.timesofisrael.com/the-rise-and-fall-of-the-opium-fueled-sassoon-dynasty-the-rothschilds-of-the-east/ The poet Siegfried Sassoon just happened to be a cousin of Sir Victor Sassoon—who was the owner of the Cathay Hotel in Sin City (Shanghai) during the Roaring Twenties and Thirties—with its reputation for wild *a-go-go* parties among ocean cruising elites. That was before the hotel was renamed into a more politically correct "Peace Hotel" just after Mao's Revolution in 1949.

[118] See Hall Gardner, https://www.other-news.info/the-new-crimean-war-and-global-geopolitical-unrest/

[119] This character appears to be based on Jacques Rossi who spent 24 years in the Soviet Gulag. https://www.radiofrance.fr/franceculture/jacques-rossi-le-francais-qui-a-fait-24-ans-de-goulag-4900912

[120] It was in the 13th century when Pope Innocent IV had reached out to the Golden Horde for a *cum non solum* alliance against the Khwarazmian Turkic-Persian Empire—in the failed effort to liberate the Holy Lands after the Sixth Crusade…

[121] There are differing interpretations as to who the Fourth Rider is, but all represent different dimensions of conflict!

[122] Israelis and Palestinians are distant cousins sharing the same Y chromosome clusters despite the fact that both believe themselves to be distinct. Ann Gibons, "Jews and Arabs Share Recent Ancestry" *Science.Org* (30 Oct 2000) https://www.science.org/content/article/jews-and-arabs-share-recent-ancestry

[123] The conversation took place before the horrific October 7, 2023 Hamas attack on Israel. It is evident these unnamed characters had forgotten—or more likely had not read—the political philosopher and prophet, Hannah Arendt, who critiqued the nature of "antisemitism" and Zionism, and who warned that the Zionist project was doomed if the Israelis could not live with the Palestinians and the Arab world side-by-side in accord with Herzl's original vision. Arendt drafted a letter, co-signed by Albert Einstein, that denounced the so-called "Freedom Party," a Zionist party led by a future Prime Minister of Israel, Menachem

Begin, that was "closely akin in its organization, methods, political philosophy, and social appeal to the Nazi and fascist parties," and that was "formed out of the membership and following the former Irgun Zvai Leumi, a terrorist, right-wing, chauvinist organization in Palestine." See Hannah Arendt, *The Jewish Writings* (Penguin Random House, 2008).

124 In 2019, Israeli Prime Minister Bibi "Dr. Geyer" Netanyahu was indicted in cases involving breach of trust, accepting bribes, and fraud… The trial continued even after the October 7, 2023 war. Netanyahu has used his Iron Dome and "Teffylon" blood to stay in power for as long as possible… See Hall Gardner https://www.other-news.info/resolving-the-gaza-crisis/

125 The situation in the artworld had grown so far out of hand that it seems only pornographic obscenity could shock the public into an understanding that could (possibly) force politicians to act. The Arts could represent something meaningful… not all was marketing. Then again, the artist has to survive too…

126 As a charitable donation, the donors would get an immediate tax deduction. By law, LaPlante only needed to give 5 percent of her Foundation's assets out each year to her favorite causes. The rest of the money could just earn interest or be invested. Another option was to put tax-deductible funds into "DAFs" or donor-advised funds that work like charitable bank accounts. For a critique of philanthropy, see Bella DeVaan, Chuck Collins, Dan Petegorsky, Helen Flannery, "Until the River Runs Dry" Institute for Policy Studies (June 6, 2023).

127 LaPlante had a number of "for profit" businesses registered in the U.S. Virgin Islands. This meant she could reduce her U.S. federal income taxes by 90 percent. Her 501(c)(3) non-profit was located in Nevada, with no taxes on estates, inheritance, capital gains, corporate income, or individual incomes.

128 The major ten arms firms made record profits in the Year of the Horseshoe Bat—and following the outbreak of the war in Ukraine in February 2022. Rising energy costs likewise served the multinational energy firms as well, but no one else. The top 10 pharmaceuticals additionally made fortunes before the

Opioid craze went sour; and the pharma market later picked up tremendously as the pandemic spread globally. Investing in the military-industrial-congressional-university complex these days was very easy. As Prophita knew, all one needed to do was see what weapons systems Washington was going to "sell" to Kyiv, Tel Aviv, Saudi Arabia (and other Gulf countries), South Korea, and Taipei—and then place huge bets in the stocks of the American firms that made those weapons.

[129] I too saw the light: It was time to overhaul the rules governing philanthropy. There were better ways to more directly help people and environment. To reduce outrageous gaps between rich and poor, significant reforms were needed to discourage the sheltering of charitable wealth. See https://inequality.org/great-divide/charity-reform-video/?emci=c0ff5389-3f05-ee11-907c-00224832eb73&emdi=ea000000-0000-0000-0000-000000000001&ceid=7927801 Chia also seems to alluding to the "Patriotic Millionaires" who want to augment taxes on the rich. Taxes on the wealthy should be raised but the question remains: If the political system remains the same, and employees have no say on corporate boards, where will the taxes be invested?

[130] In 1991, a French arms firm wanted to sell 6 Stealth frigates to Taiwan that Foreign Minister Roland "Elf Affair" Dumas said would harm French relations with China. And yet Dumas allegedly obtained megabucks in "embezzled funds" from Elf's slush fund once President Mitterrand permitted the sale.

[131] At least 15 major fast-food chains became highly indebted during the Year of the Horseshoe Bat—after crushing so many mom-and-pop restaurants. Maybe people no longer want to eat dog food!

[132] This is sick! I can't believe it wasn't censured. https://socratic.org/questions/what-is-the-cost-of-a-human-body-in-terms-of-the-different-elements-that-make-it

[133] As I knew both, I must make a final observation. The life of China Pao-yu dramatically contrasted that of Mylex H. Galvin, who died by suicide, accidental or not, or else was murdered on

purpose whether because of a drug deal gone bad, a case of mistaken identity, or some sort of political revenge by anti-Maoists who hated him, or else by Maoists themselves who saw him as a turncoat. And while the memory of Chi'a lives on through the eyes of SECC, there has been a major effort by Drumpfists to snuff out the memory of Gao/Galvin and all of his "Maoist" fellow travelers, whether they called themselves Antifa, Wokeists, or Black Lives Matter. Once can wonder what might have happened if Chia and/or Galvin had obtained their respective goals with regard to Red Dragon and the Land of the Free? Would those apparently contradictory dreams be implemented in the ways that each hoped? Or would they be perverted? Or would some of their respective dreams begin to merge so that they would begin to share a common viewpoint as to how the "liberate" Humankind from wars and political and social repression through greater forms of participatory democracy and power sharing in more careful interaction with agriculture and the natural environment?

Notes on Chia Pao-yu's *Planetary Manifesto*

~~[134] Gardner blew it on the much-quoted Napoleon prediction of China as a "sleeping giant." Napoleon had apparently never said it. See Hall Gardner, *NATO Expansion and U.S. Strategy in* Asia (Palgrave, 2013)~~

~~[135] On Trump's alleged wild past life. https://www.vice.com/en/article/zmp7qe/does-donald-trump-drink-alcohol~~

~~[136] NSA analyst Edward Snowden exposed the international range of U.S. spying, including on American allies, Germany, France, in addition to Russia and China. See "Edward Snowden in Hong Kong" *South China Morning Post Chronicles* http://multimedia.scmp.com/snowden/~~

[137] ~~U.S government efforts—under the Espionage Act against leaking classified information that had never before been used to target journalists—to persecute Julian "Wikileaks" Assange~~

for publishing "national secrets" with respect to U.S. military interventions in Iraq and Afghanistan (as discussed in U.S. diplomatic cables leaked by former U.S. intelligence officer, Chelsea Manning) is a test case for the rights of freedom of the press, speech and expression—similar to the Pentagon Papers on the U.S. military intervention in Vietnam leaked by Daniel Ellsberg. In 2021, Ellsberg released a secret 1958 Pentagon contingency plan for a nuclear first strike against China if Beijing attempted to take Taiwan to show its contemporary relevance.

138 Chia has adopted Gardner's thesis that the threat of key "pivot states" to shift alliances—at the time when alliance systems are beginning to "polarize" against each other—can alter the global geo-strategic equilibrium and provoke major power war—as argued in Gardner's first book, *Surviving the Millennium* (1994).

139 It is worth examining whether Beijing's efforts to seek peace between Ukraine and Russia, particularly after it was alleged the U.S. and UK had derailed UN and Turkish peace talks with Moscow and Ukraine in 2022, possessed some elements of reason. At least Kyiv listened to Xi—even if no peace deal had been reached. Then again, Beijing wants to extend its influence into both Russia and Ukraine! See Michael von der Schulenburg, "How The Chance Was Lost For A Peace Settlement Of The Ukraine War" (michael-von-der-schulenburg.com)

140 War is not inevitable. See Hall "Not Always a Cassandra" Gardner, "It is Time to Rethink U.S.-China Relations," MEER, 18 April 2023, (https://www.meer.com/en/73198-its-tie-to-rethink-us-china-relations

Edition Noëma
info@edition-noema.de

www.edition-noema.de
www.autorenbetreuung.de